them have become superb weather forecasters, climatologists, professors, and teachers. Perhaps Cleveland Abbe, the master editor of *Monthly Weather Review* said it best back in 1902, "It is thru a professor's scholars, by giving them his best ideas and guiding them as they work, that a teacher may hope to accomplish for his special branch of science far more than he could do single-handed." Indeed, without question, my students have transformed that hope into reality.

Randy Cerveny
President's Professor
Arizona State University
June 2005

others) has spurred me into undertaking this seemingly unending task of compiling worldwide oddities in weather.

My tremendous chance to communicate that excitement and joy of weather can be directly attributed to the encouragement of the great people at the magazine *Weatherwise*. In particular, I still remember fondly the incredible support and enthusiasm that Pat Hughes, legendary weather historian and editor of *Weatherwise*, showed me when I first asked him whether he would be interested in publishing an article on the weather associated with prison escapes. Since that time, the succeeding editors of that magazine, the multitalented Jeff Rosenfeld, the energetic Doyle Rice, and innovative Lynn Elsey, have always been incredibly kind, enthusiastic, and supportive to my sometimes "unusual" way of looking at things.

Also, I offer my sincere appreciation to the incredibly diligent and innovative librarians at the ASU library system (particularly the staff of the ASU Interlibrary Loan) as well as the owners and operators of numerous used and rare bookstores around the country (especially the many members of Abebooks, a bookseller's Web site). Many of the stories contained in this book originate from very old manuscripts that simply would not have easily been obtained without their incredible assistance. Captain Skip Theberge's superb online Photo Library for the National Oceanic and Atmospheric Administration has been a fantastic resource. Also, the many wonderful people at numerous small towns mentioned in this book have been absolutely wonderful.

But, first and foremost, I must acknowledge my unparalleled undergraduate and graduate students—they undoubtedly are the ones to whom I owe the greatest debt for this book. Their conversations, their questions, and their enthusiasm for meteorology and climatology have been my primary motivations over the six-year course of this book's writing. I am proud that so many of

ACKNOWLEDGMENTS

A S I GREW UP IN THE SMALL TOWN OF FAIRBURY, NEBRASKA, WITH its sporadic blizzards, thunderstorms, tornadoes, and heat waves, I quickly learned that weather—for better or for worse— is an integral part of everybody's life. That realization has spurred my avid passion for collecting stories of weather oddities and led to the wonderful interactions I have enjoyed as a professor of geography and meteorology at Arizona State University. The many fascinating talks and discussions with my colleagues at ASU (Bob Balling, Ron Dorn, Tony Brazel, Drew Ellis, Pat Gober, Libby Wentz, and Mel Marcus particularly come to mind), in the local community (with NWS personnel such as Tony Haffer, Doug Green, Dave Runyon, as well as others such as John Moore, Royal Norman, Ed Phillips, Dave Munsey, and Ron and Penny Jube), and colleagues around the world (especially Ron Holle, Joe Schaefer, Mary Ann Cooper, Charlie and Nancy Knight, Merlin Lawson, John Harrington, Russ Mather, Bob Maddox, Captain Skip Theberge, Chris Landsea, and many

W9-BAR-573

The Petticoat
Doctor

Paige Winship Dooly

Heartsong Presents

In memory of my precious grandma, Mary Ellen. You will be missed, Gram! I love you.

A note from the Author:
I love to hear from my readers! You may correspond with me by writing:

Paige Winship Dooly
Author Relations
PO Box 721
Uhrichsville, OH 44683

ISBN 978-1-60260-304-2

THE PETTICOAT DOCTOR

Our mission is to publish and distribute inspirational products offering exceptional value and biblical encouragement to the masses.

PRINTED IN THE U.S.A.

one

Train travel wasn't at all what Abigail had hoped it to be. After years of continuous study, the twenty-four-year-old was ready for a change, ready to explore the world outside the walls of her school and even ready, perhaps, to have an adventure. Instead she sat in an overly warm, crowded train car where her nose stung with the disagreeable odor of coal smoke. Soot clung to the windows, walls, her hair, and even her wrinkled traveling dress. Nothing seemed immune to the sticky substance. Though the maroon seats were sufficiently comfortable, her muscles screamed for a chance to stretch for a longer period of time than their rapid stops allowed.

The stench of unwashed bodies, sweaty from travel and too-close quarters, filled the air around her. Abigail glanced out the window. Even the birds had it better. They were able to settle on the roof during stops where they could feel the wind upon their faces instead of sitting in a smelly, confined car like her. Granted, the smoke and soot would be even worse up there, but the birds could always take flight on a whim for some uninterrupted fresh air as the train sped up.

But she had to admit, the view outside more than made up for her discomfort. Though the window was dirty, it didn't hide the beauty that surrounded them. Tall, majestic mountains stretched high above, bumping up against a brilliant blue sky, some of them even taller than her eyes could

5

see. Vivid green pine trees climbed the sides of the mountain, and once in a while their glorious scent wafted through the air around her. She savored the moment, knowing from her research that the view in central Utah Territory, while beautiful in its own rugged way, would be nothing like that of the Rocky Mountains that momentarily surrounded her.

The train careened around a curve, and even after several days of travel, Abigail found herself clutching her jacket in fear.

"Are you all right?"

Abigail glanced at her most current seatmate. Thin and regal, the white-haired woman had settled in beside her at the last stop, and though they had sat next to each other for the better part of an hour, the dignified woman hadn't spoken more than a few obligatory words until now.

"I am all right. Thank you." Abigail forced herself to relax. "I can't seem to get used to these ridiculously fast speeds. I've heard at times the train can go up to forty miles per hour! And some can even go sixty. Why, if the train jumps the track, I can only imagine what will happen to us!"

The woman patted Abigail's hand, her maternal touch reassuring. "I know how you feel. But I've ridden the rails many, many times, and I have never run into a problem. Ever since my husband passed away, I've traveled back and forth between my two daughters' homes. And as for speed, with all these twists and turns, I doubt we'll top fifteen miles per hour. By the way, I'm Hattie McPherson."

"I'm Abigail Hayes. And you simply cannot imagine how relieved I am to hear that you've never had a problem." Abigail took a deep breath and pointed at the newspaper beside her reticule. "I've been reading about the area since my last stop. The articles are unnerving to say the least. One mentioned the

most recent train derailment, and the story covered the entire front page. The inner pages weren't any better. There are stories of outlaws and villains. Stagecoach and bank robberies. One article even talked about travelers who were cut off from their journey by a wall of rocks. And I'm traveling to that very area! Well, actually, slightly north of the area. . .as a matter of fact, central Utah Territory but still. . ." She stopped, embarrassed. "I'm sorry. I'm rambling. I tend to do that when I'm nervous."

Her new friend laughed. "I have nowhere to go. Do continue. How ever did the travelers get through? Or did they turn back?"

Abigail suspected the older woman only encouraged her as a distraction, a gesture she very much appreciated. "They had to blast their way through the mountainside. They dubbed the area Hole-in-the-Rock. It was a very interesting article. But the thought of the train derailing is what really unnerves me. I guess these articles aren't the best choice of reading material when traveling by the very same mode of transportation into the very same area."

"Never fear, nothing like that should happen to us. As I said, in all my travels, I've not once run into any of those situations."

"Good, because the thought alone has made me quite jumpy."

As soon as the words left her lips, the brakes squealed, and the train suddenly slowed to a stop. Abigail's hand returned to her chest, this time to clutch at the cross she wore on a thin chain around her neck. Her parents passed away soon after she began medical school, and she'd sold most of their belongings to pay her tuition. The small gold ornament was all she had left from her mother.

Hattie again patted her hand and gave her a kind smile.

"I'm sure it's another routine stop, dear. I've not traveled this direction often enough to be sure—I'm on my way to visit my sister this trip—but most likely we'll join the masses in trying to get a quick bite to eat before the train takes off again, and that will be the most exciting aspect of our stop."

Abigail shook her head. "I've managed to evade that particular experience other than buying a boxed lunch here and there. It's pure chaos at the stations. I brought along enough provisions to last for the journey and then some. As a matter of fact, I have extra if you'd like to join me for lunch. Here, let me show you what I have." She opened her bag and began to dig around inside.

When her new friend didn't immediately answer, Abigail glanced at her. She noticed Hattie's thin face had gone pale as she stared past Abigail and out the dusty window.

"Ma'am?"

Still Hattie didn't speak; she just lifted a shaky hand and pointed outside.

Abigail shifted in her seat, lifting her heavy skirts as she moved around for a better view. She searched through the murky glass for a moment before her eyes lit on the subject of the other woman's focus.

"Oh my." Abigail's voice came out as a whisper, but in the sudden silence of the car it sounded to her like she'd bellowed. She pushed back the curls that escaped her fancy hat, but the view remained the same. "We're in the middle of a train robbery? But you just told me. . ."

"There's a first time for everything, I suppose."

Fear mingled with dismay in Abigail's chest as she glanced down at the newspaper beside her. Would this potentially harrowing adventure make the next front page? She couldn't even imagine such horrible things happening, let alone ever

desire to read about them in the future. Yet here she sat, on a train entering Utah, to live with her older brother, while a band of train robbers held them up.

Because the track ahead curved gently to the right, Abbie could see the entire scene as it played out before her eyes. The front gunman moved forward. He spoke to the conductors and motioned toward the cars. Their conductor stepped inside. Abbie watched people begin filing out of the train, and several minutes later the conductor arrived in their car.

His voice wavered as he spoke, and he leaned against the wall for support. "I need to request that all passengers calmly leave the car and line up outside in a row."

A large man in the front seat loudly refused. "You can't make me go out there. We're safer if we stay put."

"He's right. I'm not going out, either. My children are dependent on me for their safety." The speaker, a plump woman, hugged her children—a boy and a girl—close.

"If we don't do as they say, the outlaws will enter the cars and escort you out," the conductor explained.

Panicked wails erupted from the children.

The conductor's face paled, and drops of sweat beaded on his forehead. "They made it clear that anyone who refuses to obey their commands will be singled out as examples."

His words had the passengers shoving for the doorway. Abigail watched as mixed emotions ranging from anger to fear moved across the faces of people sitting nearby. The conductor, his expression now sympathetic, aided each passenger as they stepped to the ground. She and Hattie, whose seats were in the middle of the car, slipped into line and moved slowly down the aisle.

They exited into the suffocating midmorning air and lined up with the others as the gunmen had requested. A

pile of dynamite blocked the track. Irrationally, Abigail registered the slight breeze that blew past—the only good so far to come of this experience—which momentarily cooled her overheated skin. She found her legs were shaking and stiffened them. Anger gradually replaced her initial shock. Hattie wavered beside her, and Abigail took hold of her arm.

"We're going to be fine, Mrs. McPherson. We'll do exactly as asked, and I'm sure they'll send us safely on our way. They won't want to stay around too long and risk capture." Even as she said the words, she took hold of her necklace and slipped it beneath her collar. Though she had money and valuables in her reticule, which she'd tucked under the seat as she exited, the necklace would be far more painful to lose.

The outlaws rode closer, guiding their horses as they slowly moved along the line of dozens of travelers. A couple of them jumped down to leer into the passengers' faces.

Abigail's breath hitched as they neared. Hattie's shaking grew stronger. Inhaling deeply, Abigail forced herself to remain calm. She'd learned to keep her wits about her during medical school back in Philadelphia and would keep her wits about her now. Though fainting would be a welcome respite from the ordeal, it would also single her out and render her helpless.

The leader neared, and Abigail stared him fully in the face. His beady eyes met hers, and she released the full venom of her anger into her glower.

He pointed in her direction. "You. The lady in the fancy hat. Step forward."

Abigail glanced around her at all the women in fancy hats, and they all stared back at her. Realization set in as she slowly returned her attention to the vile man.

"Me?" Her voice squeaked, hardly depicting the ferocious

image she'd meant to portray only moments earlier.

"Yes, you. Step forward." The despicable man leaned forward on his horse, his gums pulling back into a leering grin to reveal yellowed teeth. His other men fanned out along the line of people, their rifles held at the ready. Hattie gasped audibly and grabbed for Abigail's arm, frantic to hold her back, but Abigail gently pulled from her grasp. Somehow their brief friendship had gone from Hattie being the encourager to Abigail being the protector.

"What do you have for me, little lady?" The man's raspy voice caused a shiver of repulsion to run down her back.

Abigail noted with distaste that his stringy red beard was caked with what looked to be dried tobacco juice.

"I have nothing." At least her voice had grown stronger. She squared her shoulders and looked directly at him, trying not to retch at the putrid odor emanating from his unwashed body.

"Oh, I'm *sure* you have *somethin'* you can offer. Is your life worth nothin'?"

"Only when it comes to you." The words came from deep inside her, but why her lips let them escape she didn't know.

"Is that so?" The man's eyes hardened, and he motioned for one of his men to move forward. "We'll be taking you along with us. You'll regret your insolent words." He motioned to the others. "Search the passengers."

The second man, just as disgusting as the first, grabbed Abigail roughly by the arm and dragged her toward his horse. Abigail heard Hattie's panicked voice call out for someone to do something. A moment later, looking over her shoulder, Abigail saw that the woman had dropped to her knees and bowed her head in petition to God for Abigail's life. Hattie prayed loudly for God to intervene.

Just as the leader stalked forward to silence her, a shout from the far end of the line distracted him. The man holding Abigail loosened his grip as he tried to see what the commotion was about. A moment later he shoved Abigail roughly to the ground and ran for his horse. The leader and the other bandits did the same, then turned their mounts and headed for the nearby hills.

As the men scurried away, shouts of relief rang forth from the crowd as the passengers worked their way back toward their various cars. Abigail pushed to her knees, and a handsome older man with a black mustache and derby hat held out his hand to assist her. Dust swirled around them from the hasty dismount from his horse.

"Are you all right, ma'am?"

The man steadied her, but it was his quiet, gentle voice that soothed her rapidly beating heart.

"I think so. Thank you." Though he was older than she by at least a few years, if she had dreamt up a hero, this kind and thoughtful man would define him.

"You get on back to your seat then. I'm sure my friends have chased the bandits far away by now. You won't have to give them another moment's thought."

She couldn't prevent the slight quake in her words. "Perhaps I'll not give further thought to those men, but how many others like them are out there?"

"Are you traveling far?"

"Not far from here, I don't think. I'm heading for Salt Lake City, then on to Nephi."

His mouth quirked up into a brief smile. "In that case, I can pretty well assure you that no other outlaw will prevent you from reaching your destination."

"I surely hope not." She steadied her hat on her head with

all the dignity she could muster. Her breath caught as she choked back the sob that threatened to escape now that the danger was past. "Are you after those men?"

"No. I chased my share of their sort in the past, though. For now I'm just a writer passing through. We saw them holding up the train and stopped to help. I hope the rest of your journey is uneventful." He tipped his hat and swung up onto his ride.

Abigail shakily returned to the train's steps where an awestruck conductor helped her aboard.

As she glanced back, the rider had already slipped into the trees at the base of the hill. She hurried to her seat, and Hattie, frantic, pulled her into a firm hug.

"Do you realize who just assisted you?"

"He only said that he's a writer."

"That, my dear, was the infamous Bat Masterson."

"Really?" Abigail raised an eyebrow and glanced back through the window. "I had no idea."

Obviously she'd had no idea about anything this dreadful trip would entail. She appreciated that the former lawman had intervened and saved her life. But at this point, she simply wanted this frightful excursion to be over. With her parents deceased and her estranged brother, Caleb, as her only family, she suddenly wanted nothing more than to reach the end of her journey and settle in at his ranch in central Utah. She'd decidedly had enough surprises and ordeals to last her a lifetime.

two

"Hank feels 'slightly irregular'?" Jake jumped down from the cumbersome wagon and jerked his worn gloves from his hands. He didn't have time for this. He'd purposely left early to tend to business in town. At the rate they were going, they'd barely meet her train, business notwithstanding. They'd already lost valuable time leaving the ranch due to Hank's sour stomach several days earlier. Now he felt "slightly irregular"?

"What on earth does 'slightly irregular' mean?" Jake glared at his men who cowered in light of his rage. He should have left the newcomer behind.

"He's sick, boss. He ate something bad, and it's doing terrible things to his stomach. He needs to make pretty frequent runs for the bushes, as you've noticed."

"For the love of—" Jake bit off the rest of the words. He'd made a conscious effort not to swear, and he wouldn't mess that up in a moment of frustration.

"God?" Scrappy, the youngest member of his group, his watery blue eyes huge, interjected the word with reverence. Tall and thin, the young man had a propensity for getting into skirmishes, hence his nickname. Jake had peeled him off the ground in an alleyway a few months earlier, where he'd been abandoned after losing a fight.

Somewhere along the line, Jake had begun the practice of collecting strays as his ranch hands.

"Jake wouldn't use the Lord's name in vain, Scrap. It's

Pete, right, boss?" Grub pulled his worn hat from his large balding head, slapped Scrappy across his shoulder with it, and slammed it back in place. The cook's huge jowls jiggled as he chewed a piece of hardtack.

"Pete?" Jake echoed, confused. As usual, he had no clue what the men were talking about with their wandering conversation.

"No, a good woman." Red nudged Jake suggestively in the ribs. "You were about to say, 'for the love of a good woman.' Right?"

"Sorry to disappoint you, Red. I wasn't going to say anything of the sort. I just...," Jake shook his head. "Never mind. The point is we need to get back on the trail. Caleb trusted me to get Miss Hayes safely back to the ranch. Scrappy, go over and see what we can do to nudge Hank along."

Scrappy paled and gulped air like a dying fish. "Go over... there?" He looked toward Hank's horse with pronounced dread. All traces of humor disappeared. "I can't, boss. Sick people make me..." He gagged dramatically without finishing the thought.

"You can't be serious."

Scrappy gagged again.

"All right." Jake sighed, looked around, and focused on his cook. The man made a living by killing animals with his bare hands and then turning them into delectable meals. Surely he wasn't squeamish. "Grub?"

Grub froze where he leaned against the wagon, biscuit halfway to his mouth, and gulped convulsively. He stared at Jake in horror. "Me?"

"Yes, you."

"Can't. It ain't good for my digestion. I've only just eaten and wouldn't want to mess up my constitution."

When *wasn't* the man eating?

Jake shook off the irritating thought and turned to the third man in their group, Red. Red's name defied him. Yellow-bellied would have been a more apt description, but since Jake wouldn't call a man such a thing to his face, the name Red blurted out and stuck. The man was small and wiry, but women appeared to consider him handsome with his dark auburn hair and roving blue eyes. More than once his nature had gotten him into trouble when he was caught flirting with the wrong woman. Off he'd go, full speed out of town when a husband caught wind of his behavior, leaving Jake and the others to clear up the mess. Red considered himself to be the ultimate ladies' man, and he was—if a person overlooked the fact that his natural tendency made him run from all stressful situations.

"Huh-uh." Red raised his hands up in front of him and backed away. "I'm not goin' over there. From the sounds of things, he's half dead anyway. Maybe we should just leave him."

"We aren't going to leave him. I'll check on him myself. Scrappy, take care of the horses." Jake stalked off in the direction Hank had taken after pulling away from the group. His horse waited near a stand of scrubs, and from the sounds on the other side of the bush, Hank wasn't going to feel better any time soon.

Jake had a gut of lead, and the noises from behind that bush weren't welcoming no matter how tough a person might be. He froze in his tracks, spun on his heels, and hurried back to his motley band of misfits.

"Problems, boss?" Scrappy snickered.

Jake silenced him with a look. Somehow his men had it in their heads that if they provoked Jake too thoroughly,

his temper would boil over. He came from mixed Irish and Mexican roots, and while his father had lived up to his Irish heritage in temper, Jake liked to think he favored his Mexican mother, who had the sweetest nature Jake had ever seen. He let the men believe their illusion. The Maverick men of the past had a history of temper, and apparently it was his father's Irish blood that the men feared.

He began to pace. He didn't have many options and made a quick decision. "If we don't pick up our pace, Miss Hayes will be waiting at the station before we can make it into town. I'll take the wagon along with Scrappy and Grub and head on in to collect her. Red, you stick around and wait for Hank to feel better, and then you both can join us."

"We'll be dead before we get there. You've heard the rumors of Injun attacks in this area."

"They're only rumors, Red. You can't put stock in such a thing. You know the Indians have moved to reservations."

"Well, there are always the stragglers—the way I heard, not all of 'em wanted to go. And what about renegades? There's something behind the stories. I've heard of several attacks."

Scrappy scratched his head, and his face contorted—a sure sign that he was deeply contemplating their dilemma. "I say we dump Hank in the wagon and tie his horse to the side."

"Very thoughtful, Scrap. I'm sure Hank will appreciate your sentiment when he feels better."

Scrappy's eyes widened briefly, and he clamped his mouth shut. One run-in with the mouthy greenhorn had apparently been enough for him.

"The boy's got a point, boss." Grub popped in the final morsel and spoke with his mouth full. Crumbs spewed out with his next words. "Maybe we don't dump him in, but we could make him a pallet and move on even if he has to

balance over the side of the wagon to do his deed."

Jake tried to get his mind past that image and contemplated the rest of the idea. He didn't have a better one, and they did need to move on. "Prepare to pull out then. I'll go tell Hank the plan and secure his mount." He started in that direction.

"Boss?"

"What is it, Red?"

"How we gonna know what Miss Hayes looks like?"

Jake hesitated. "Caleb said she has long blond hair; a lively, inquisitive personality; a ready smile; and a gentle, soft-spoken nature."

"She sounds like a true angel." Red's awe was palpable.

"She sounds like nothing but trouble." Jake narrowed his eyes in warning. "And you'll do well to keep that in mind." The last thing he needed was Red—or any of the other hands—flirting with the woman. He hurried off to round up Hank.

❧

Abigail sat on her trunk at the train depot waiting for her brother and wondered why it was such a surprise that he wasn't there to meet her. After the eventful trip she'd just experienced, nothing should shock her.

The station had bustled with activity when she'd first descended the stairs of the train, but now only a few stragglers remained. A man and child eagerly embraced a well-dressed woman who had traveled in Abigail's car, and Abigail felt a wistful smile twist her mouth as she watched them. The lines at the ticket window had long ago disappeared, and only a wagon here and there passed by on the nearby road. Abigail suddenly felt very alone.

She carefully studied the face of each passerby, but no one remotely resembled her older brother. Thinking of the years

that had passed since she'd last seen him, Abigail's heart thumped in eagerness for their reunion. Thankfully, she'd been able to clean up from the trip before greeting him. She tried to smooth the wrinkles from her dress, but when that proved fruitless, she settled with splashing some water on her smudged face from the nearby hand pump.

She found herself missing Hattie and wished her new friend had continued to Salt Lake City. Instead the woman departed the train a few stops earlier, and now Abigail waited alone while tamping down a growing panic that stemmed from not knowing a single person in town.

A well-dressed man approached. After looking about the now-empty platform, he politely inquired about her escort. When she mentioned she was expecting one momentarily, his face wrinkled into a frown. "Might I accompany you over to the hotel and help you secure a room? It isn't safe for a woman to wait alone."

Though not nearly as handsome as her rescuer during the train robbery and not nearly as muscular or tall, this man had kind eyes and his own type of charm. He wore a crisp white shirt and neatly creased gray pants—so perfect that they looked ready-made and straight off the store shelf. His hair lay meticulously pressed into place under his pristine black hat. His apparent care in choosing his attire showed an attention to detail, which Abigail could appreciate. And which made her feel dowdy in comparison.

"I appreciate the offer, but my brother will be along shortly." She frowned. The fact that she'd missed a connecting train due to the attempted train robbery unnerved her. Then several other delays had put her into town way behind schedule, causing her to miss her connecting train into Nephi. And while she could take another train down to

Nephi, she wouldn't be able to get one until the next day. She didn't want to leave and miss her brother in passing. Even after that wretched experience with the train robbers, safety concerns about sitting here alone hadn't entered her mind until now. She'd felt perfectly secure waiting for her brother, but what if she had a false security? Her stomach clenched in fear, and she sat up straighter in an effort to hide the tremble that rolled through her body.

What if Caleb had arrived earlier and, not finding her, had headed back home? Earlier in the day, when she'd first realized she was behind schedule, she'd sent a telegram to Nephi, informing Caleb about the delay. When she arrived at Salt Lake City, she found a return telegram telling her to stay put because Caleb would meet her there. Why hadn't she thought to have him leave more specific word so she'd know more clearly what to do? She had no idea when Caleb would arrive or how long she should wait before heading over to the hotel.

Surely he'd wait and check several trains first. But if so, wouldn't he already be at the station? Again she fought back her panic. She'd made it through school at the Women's Medical College back in Philadelphia—a difficult but satisfying achievement—and she would make it through this final leg of her journey. It wouldn't do to fall apart now. Most likely Caleb had stepped across the street for a late noon meal and would return shortly to collect her.

"Is there anything I can assist you with? You look most unhappy. I hope it wasn't something I said."

She started to shake her head, but was distracted when she saw movement out of the corner of her eye. Eagerly, she peered around the friendly man as another male hurried along the rough-hewn sidewall of the station. She looked up

at him with hope. Her heart plummeted, though, when he glanced her way. The handsome but dangerous-looking man most assuredly wasn't her brother. Though she hadn't seen Caleb since she was fourteen, his fair coloring and playful nature wouldn't have changed into this scowling, brooding man even in the decade that had passed. Nor would this be the type of man that the Caleb she remembered would ever associate with.

Though she knew it wasn't polite, she couldn't help but study him with errant fascination. For the first time since disembarking the train, she felt she'd really arrived in the Wild West. A low-slung belt around his waist held two pistols, one on either side of his slim hips, and a lethally sharp knife lay sheathed next to one of the pistols. His form-fitting tan pants outlined sturdy leg muscles as he stalked along the walkway, and he wore his shirtsleeves rolled up far above his elbow, which highlighted his sun-kissed arms and accentuated strong biceps. As an avid student of anatomy, Abigail couldn't help but appreciate the years necessary to hone the man's muscles into such an enticing package. The men she'd known back in the city were all pale and thin with no muscle tone to speak of.

She forced herself to move her perusal on to his face and froze in mortification.

His dark brown eyes bore into hers, and for a long moment she forgot to breathe. He'd stopped walking sometime in the last minute and now stared back at her with raised eyebrows. Long black hair dusted against his collar and framed his strikingly handsome features, perfectly balanced by high cheekbones. He deepened his scowl, which marred his classic features into a most unapproachable and disgruntled grimace. Abigail shivered. Thank goodness for her innate ability

to judge character. She'd do well to avoid the likes of him and to warmly embrace the protection offered by the kind gentleman at her side.

The well-dressed man beside her turned his back on the newcomer and stepped protectively close. Abigail sent him her most charming, grateful smile. At this moment, more than ever, Abigail welcomed his reassuring presence.

⁂

Jake bit his lower lip in frustration. He knew he should have been on time, but situations happened and he couldn't change that now. He'd arrived in Nephi, only to find a telegram stating that Abigail wouldn't make the connecting train from Salt Lake City. They'd left the wagon there, sent a return telegram telling her to stay put, arranged passage for the men and their horses on the train, and had just arrived in Salt Lake City.

His men were still unhappy with the decision.

"I still don't see why we had to ride in, boss, instead of waiting for her to arrive in Nephi in the morning," Red had grumbled.

"After Bert beat up Caleb and left him for dead, he told Caleb his final revenge would be to kidnap Caleb's sister."

"But how would he know she was in Salt Lake City, especially if her train's late?" Scrappy's confusion had shown on his face.

"He might not know, but if he's here waiting, hoping to intercept her, this would give him the perfect opportunity. We can't afford to risk it. I have a bad feeling about the whole situation. If Bert gets to her first, I'll need each of you and our horses to go after them."

But the only woman in sight rested on a large trunk and didn't begin to match Caleb's description. Her dress, though tousled, spoke of money and class, and she wore her hair

pulled back severely and tucked beneath a huge frilly hat. The woman's cool green eyes studied Jake with blatant interest, much longer than propriety allowed, before suddenly dismissing him with disdain. She obviously belonged with the man who stood intimately close to her side. Jake didn't envy him. He certainly wouldn't want to be saddled with such a disloyal woman. She returned her attention to her oblivious companion, and Jake backtracked to his waiting men.

"Just as I expected, she isn't here." He sighed, wondering if the day could possibly get any worse. A rumble of thunder in the distance proved that it could. "Scrappy, Grub, go check the restaurant across the street. She might have decided to eat dinner while she waits." He hesitated. If Grub stepped into an eating establishment he'd surely want to taste all that was offered. "On second thought, Red, you go with Scrappy. Grub, you'll come with me, and we'll check the nearest hotel and boardinghouse."

Hank, who had made a miraculous recovery once they resumed their trip, offered to go and talk to the stationmaster. "I'll see if he remembers anyone with her unique description."

Jake nodded and stalked away, Grub's heavy legs double-stepping to keep up.

three

"I simply cannot let you sit here alone a moment longer. Allow me to escort you to lunch, and then we'll set about finding you a decent place to stay while waiting for your...," he paused, "brother, did you say?"

"Yes. My brother Caleb. And how very kind of you to look out for my best interests in this way." She hesitated. Back home she'd never have spoken to a strange man, let alone let him escort her anywhere. But maybe things were different out West. And what choice did she really have? Besides, a restaurant sat just across the road. How much trouble could she get into on such a short walk? After seeing the arrogant man who had rounded the corner last, she had no idea what the next scoundrel's arrival might bring.

The dapper man held out his hand, and she allowed him to assist her to her feet. Her legs were tired from the long wait, and despair coursed through her. How would Caleb find her if she left? And how would she transport her trunk?

"What is it?" The man dipped his knees to peer directly into her eyes. "If you'd feel better, I can find some people to vouch for my character."

"It's not that. If I leave, I don't know how my brother will find me. And what about my trunk? I can't just leave it here."

"Sure you can. Stationmasters look after people's belongings all the time. And we'll leave a message for your brother. He'll ask about your arrival at the window, will he not?"

"I suppose. If you're sure." Thoroughly disconcerted, Abigail

suddenly felt as if this man were her lifeline. If he were to leave, she'd be terrified. All her brave aspirations that had brought her thus far now deserted her. The enthusiasm that accompanied her from Philadelphia had seeped from her bones with her energy. She hadn't had a solid meal in days. And she didn't know where to go even if she had the courage to do such a thing alone.

A sudden realization hit her. "Wait!"

He stopped and spun on his heels, anxiety creeping across his features. "Is there a problem?"

"Only in that I've agreed to accompany you to dinner, and I don't even know your name."

A strange mix of relief and annoyance battled across his face before he smiled and hurried back to her side. "Please forgive my complete lack of manners. I was so distraught to see you here alone that I forgot the most basic rule of etiquette." He pulled his hat from his head and gave her a slight bow. "Allow me to introduce myself. I'm Robert Sanchez. At your service."

"Abigail Hayes. And all is forgiven. I'm so tired I'm not thinking clearly myself. I'm sure that once I have a nice meal and locate a safe hotel room, I'll feel much better. I can have my trunk brought over as soon as I have a place to stay."

"Sounds like a good plan."

His eyes surveyed her oddly, almost in question, and Abigail felt a peculiar anxiety form in the pit of her stomach as he sauntered over to the stationmaster.

She glanced across the street and saw a large family enter the eating establishment. No harm could come from one meal with a stranger—a kind stranger at that—could it?

Robert hurried back to her side, led her along the boardwalk to the front of the station, and gestured for her

to move ahead of him toward the steps that led down to the road. She carried her valise along. Surprisingly, he didn't offer to carry the large bag for her. So much for chivalry. As she paused at the edge of the road to check for errant wagons before she began to cross the street, he put his hand to her back and guided her instead toward a cluster of horses.

"Oh." She stopped on the spot. "I thought we'd eat over there, somewhere close where I can see my brother if he arrives."

Robert leaned closer than propriety allowed. "Change of plans. If and when you eat, it will be far away from here. I can assure you that your brother won't be showing up to surprise you."

Abigail stared at him in stunned silence before looking around for someone who might offer her aid. Though the street bustled with activity, no one was near enough to do her any good. Maybe if she screamed. . .

"Don't even think about it."

She felt a small cylindrical object press against her side. She glanced down. He had a *gun*? Her pulse raced, and she struggled to breathe, her breaths coming in rapid gasps. "But why?"

"Let's just say you're the payment for a little debt your brother had to settle with me."

"My brother? Why would he ever associate with the likes of you?" Her own inability to trust her instincts rested heavy upon her heart. She'd fallen for the deceitful man's trap. Why wouldn't her brother? Gullibility apparently ran in the family. From this side of the situation, even the rough-looking man at the station might have been a better choice of company.

Robert pushed the gun harder into her side. "Get up on

the horse and don't bother trying to make a scene. I've shot more than one man dead in the street and rode away to tell about it. It won't bother me a bit to try the same with you." He smirked at her, his eyes suddenly cold.

She did as he asked, but stepped hard on his foot with her pointy heel as she stalked by him.

He grunted in response and shoved her.

The horse loomed above, and she struggled to mount him. The horse danced in irritation, and Abigail clutched at the saddle horn.

"Leave the bag behind."

"I will not. It contains things I need."

"Fine. It's your choice, but don't expect any of us to carry it for you."

He grabbed her waist and shoved her up and almost over the other side of the huge beast. She clasped the saddle horn with one hand and her large bag with the other and dangled precariously toward the far side before righting herself. She sent him her most haughty glare as his words sank in.

"Us?"

"My men or myself."

He had men? What on earth had she gotten herself into? All her life she'd been sheltered and pampered. Not until her parents died had she ever been alone. And by then she'd been deeply enmeshed in her education, and her school responsibilities carried her through the grief. Only now, for the first time, did she have an inkling of how utterly alone in the world she'd become. "What have you done to my brother?"

He made a hard sound. "You don't have to worry about him. Your brother turned me in on gambling charges. He agreed for me to take you as my bride in exchange for the debt."

"He'd never agree to such a thing."

The man had the audacity to laugh. "Well, maybe he didn't exactly agree, but he wasn't in any shape to disagree when I left him. I figure if I have you along, I'll have a little leverage in the event the law catches up with me. Suffice it to say, you won't have to fret about him coming after you. He's been taken care of."

"Taken care of?" As a physician she'd promised to do everything in her means to protect the life of her fellow man. This man made her want to betray that promise. "Did you hurt him? Because if you did. . ."

He leaned close. "If I did. . .then what?"

He trailed a dirty finger along her cheek, and she fought off a shudder. How had she missed the obvious signs of the disreputable man who now blocked her path? She refused to let him know how much he disgusted her.

"You'll be sorry."

He looked at the man who had watched the horses and grinned, sarcasm dripping from his raised eyebrows. "Did you hear that? I'll be sorry."

He suddenly swung back around and grabbed her by the arm, almost yanking her from her mount. "You listen to me. If you don't do as I say, *you'll* be the one who's sorry. Your brother is dead. Now shut up and move along." He squeezed her arm hard before releasing her, and she grappled with balance once again. Tears formed, but she furiously blinked them back.

Terrified, she did as he said. Abigail remained silent as she rode up the street alongside her captor. If it was true and her brother was dead. . .she had nowhere to go. But if he was dead, who had sent the telegram from Nephi? At least someone out there knew of her arrival. She could only hope

they'd come after her. She'd worry about her future when she was safe.

Part of her felt it would be better to make a scene and let the dust settle as it may. But another part of her insisted upon staying safely in the saddle. She somehow knew she'd get away. Even if her intuition had failed her, surely her intellect would prevail. It had to.

They met up with his gang outside of town, and he didn't even bother to introduce her. She felt grateful for that fact. As far as she was concerned, the less contact she had with the ruffians the better. The dirty, unkempt men brandished a variety of sidearms and looked as dangerous as the men who'd held up the train.

Abigail hadn't been in a saddle for years, and it took all her concentration not to bounce off while juggling her large bag. According to the sun's location, they were heading south at a fast pace.

Robert moved ahead as they neared a small cabin and called back over his shoulder. "Stay with her, Boggs. We'll check things out."

"Sure, Bert. I got her covered." Boggs, a burly looking man, dropped back to ride beside her.

"I don't need to be 'covered.' I'm not going anywhere." Abigail wasn't foolish enough to try to escape. At least not yet. But *Bert's* intentions at the farmhouse had her more than a little concerned. Though the last thing she wanted in the world was to speak to the vile man beside her, she couldn't help asking. "What are they going to do?"

He leaned forward in the saddle. "Do you want the graphic version or the watered-down one?"

Abigail gulped. "Watered-down, please."

"They're going to get supplies."

"Will they hurt the people who live there?"

"I thought you wanted it watered down."

She shuddered. "Never mind."

Against her will, tears began to course down her cheeks. Though she wasn't familiar with prayer, she tried to recall Hattie's prayer back at the train robbery. Maybe if she could find the right words, God would watch out for the people inside.

Dear God, I don't know You real well. Actually, I don't know You at all. But I saw how Hattie's prayers were answered at the train, and I'm wondering if You could consider doing the same for me. I'm willing to read up on how all this works in that book of Yours, but I can only do that if I survive long enough to get away from these awful men. And please, if I can put in a special request for the people who live at this cabin, could You somehow keep them safe?

"What're you muttering about over there?" Boggs pulled his horse closer.

Abigail sighed. "Nothing." Most likely it *was* nothing. She didn't feel any different or better, and the sky didn't split open and release a lightning bolt to strike down the miscreants. As a matter of fact, the storm that had brewed on the horizon all afternoon still lingered there.

Bert kicked through the front door, and the men filed inside the homestead. A few moments later they exited, looking disgruntled. Abigail's heart picked up speed. Bert motioned for Boggs and Abigail to move forward.

"What's the problem?"

"No one's here. Ruins all the fun."

Sick, despicable man. Abigail felt a scowl pass over her face even as she felt a jolt of excitement that her prayer had been answered. Or had it? The people hadn't been here in the first place, so did that really count as an answer to prayer?

She didn't begin to know. She did know she felt happy that a family wouldn't be hurt. At least, not if the gang resumed their journey before the occupants returned.

"So, how far behind us do you think anyone chasing us might be?" Her innocently phrased question had the desired effect.

"Let's get a move on." Bert directed a couple of guys to ransack the house, and he headed toward the barn. Abigail tried to relax in the saddle, but the sound of gunfire and a panicked squeal from the barn had her swinging down and running to the open door.

She raced through the opening, anger making her careless. Bert whirled and turned the gun on her. At this point, she didn't care. Dying by his bullet was preferable to whatever else he might have planned for her.

"What have you done?" She glanced around and tried to identify the victim. She saw a large pink shape in the dusky interior and stepped closer for a better view.

Apparently Bert decided to let her have a look because he lowered his weapon and motioned her forward.

"You shot a pig?" she asked in disbelief. She surveyed the animal before them. A tiny piglet squealed and clambered around Abigail's skirt, tripping over her boots. The rest of the litter huddled in a far corner. She bent down and scooped the panicky baby up into her arms. "Why?"

"Why not? There's nothing else here to shoot."

Abigail heard snickers behind her at the door and glanced back to see the other men gathered there.

" 'Sides. We gotta eat, don't we?"

The piglet had calmed in her arms. Abigail stalked past the vile men and headed for the barn door. No way would she eat the piglet's mother in front of him. She'd starve first.

"I'll take you along with me, but you have to behave." Abigail had a feeling if she left the piglet, Bert would shoot it, too. Most likely he'd still shoot it, but she had to try to protect the innocent creature. Her own inability to protect herself drove her to it. If she had something to care for, she wouldn't feel so vulnerable. "I'll call you Hamm, but we'll work hard to make sure you don't become one."

Abigail realized the men were focused at the moment on planning the best way to remove the larger pig to a place where they could cook a meal. She quickly headed for her horse. Wrapping the piglet in a soft cloth, she secured him on top of her open valise. With newly practiced ease, she balanced her bag on the saddle and swung up to sit behind it.

Tufts of dust rose up from the north, and she prayed it was a rescue team sent to retrieve her, not the owners returning home. She lost valuable moments debating her next move. If she rode toward the dust and ran into the homesteaders, she'd lead the gang straight to them. She couldn't live with that thought so turned the horse around to head the other way. She could always double back.

"Where do you think you're going?" Bert had exited the barn and walked her way.

Abigail couldn't resist one more glance toward the north.

Bert followed her motion with his eyes.

"Come on out here," he bellowed to the others while climbing on his mount. "We gotta get going."

Disappointed, Abigail consoled herself with the knowledge that at least no one else would be hurt because of her poor decision-making skills.

A loud squeal burst forth from her bag. Well, no one would be hurt unless Hamm met his demise due to her rescue attempt.

"What was that?" Bert rode closer.

"What was what?"

The squeal resumed as the piglet head-butted the interior. The bag shifted, and Abigail had to grab for it so it didn't fall to the ground. "Lay still, Hamm."

She held her head high and continued forward.

"You brought the piglet along?"

Abigail shrugged. "I'll make sure I give restitution to the owners as soon as I'm able."

"He's the runt. He's already been ostracized by the rest of the litter. The owners will likely shoot him." He stared hard at her. "You know he's not going to make it."

"I know I'm not likely to make it, either." Abigail turned to look him fully in the eyes. "But I'll do my best for us both in the meantime."

Bert momentarily stared at her in shock and then let loose a sinister laugh. "Yes, you do that. You'll each fill a specific appetite when you fail."

four

Jake looked around. His chest tightened with anxiety, and he felt each passing moment weigh heavily upon him. They'd lost a lot of time looking for Miss Hayes. Though he'd peeked into the boardinghouse's dining room earlier, he thought he'd check one more time in case he'd missed her. This was the most likely place for her to wait if she'd indeed arrived. The commerce area was mostly silent, with townsfolk likely home preparing for their evening meal, but a few couples strolled along the boardwalk here and there.

Jake stepped into the rough-hewn building, and his mouth watered as the pungent aroma of baked chicken teased his nose. He glanced around, taking note of each diner that lined either side of the sturdy wood table, but none of them fit Abigail's description. A woman bustled through a doorway on the far side of the kitchen and waved him to a seat.

"Just pick a place and make yourself comfortable. I'll bring you a plate in a moment."

Jake waved her away. "I won't be staying. I'm looking for a friend. A female friend."

The woman hesitated, wiping her hands on her apron. "Tell me what she looks like, and I'll tell you if she's been through here today."

"She came in on the train, or at least she was supposed to." He described Abigail to the best of his ability, but the friendly woman shook her head before he finished.

"No one matching that description dined with us today."

34

She hesitated a moment, and her expression turned thoughtful. "There was a lady across the street. . . ."

"Did she match the description?" Jake hoped he'd found a clue to Abigail's whereabouts.

"Well, she was far away, and it was hectic, but I glanced out and saw a couple across the way a couple of hours back." She frowned again, contemplating her words. "I was able to see her clearly enough to see her confident smile as she started across the street toward our establishment. She appeared to be escorted by the man, but when she moved in this direction, he stepped close and said something to her. Suddenly her entire countenance changed. She glanced around, and her expression turned to panic." The woman twisted her apron in her hands. "I figured perhaps she'd taken ill because she glanced down and the man took hold of her and guided her the other way. I lost track after that because things became hectic again. I'm afraid from there I don't know what happened to her. I'm really sorry I can't be of more help."

Jake asked for a description of the woman's attire, and his heart sank. She matched the description of the woman at the train depot. Surely she hadn't been Caleb's sister! If so, who was the gentleman with her? *Please, Lord, don't let it be Bert.* Caleb hadn't mentioned Abigail having a travel companion. "You said she looked distraught?"

"Yes, she did. I'm so sorry. I got busy and didn't give it another thought until now. I do hope she didn't fall in with the wrong person. It's generally safe around this area, but you never know."

"No, you never do." Jake thanked her and headed out the door. He saw Scrappy and Red heading his way and met them in front of the train station. "Any news?"

"No, boss. We didn't find out a thing. No one saw hide nor hair of anyone matching Miss Hayes' description." Red rubbed his chin. "What about you?"

Jake shared his information, and both men's faces reflected his own concern. "Where's Hank? Maybe he found out something new."

As if his words called forth the man, Hank rounded the corner of the train station and jogged down the steps to join them. "I hate to tell you this, but a woman matching Miss Hayes' description arrived on the last train and left with a man awhile back."

"How long ago?" Jake bit out the words, now more sure than ever that the woman on the trunk must have been Abigail.

"Not more than two hours. He said she waited alone for a bit before a man came up and made conversation with her. The only reason he remembered her was because she left a trunk with him."

"Has she returned to fetch it?"

Hank shrugged. "I didn't think to ask."

Jake bit back his retort and instead took the steps two at a time and hurried to the ticket window. The man checked a pocket watch, stuck it in the pocket of his pin-striped vest, and stepped Jake's way. "May I help you, sir?"

Jake didn't waste words. "I need to see the trunk the woman passenger left behind."

"I'm afraid I can't do that, sir. I can only release the trunk to her or her escort upon her return."

"That's just the thing. I *am* her escort. And I think she's fallen into the wrong hands. I need to verify that the trunk belongs to the woman I'm here to pick up."

"I can read you her name." He ruffled through some papers

and picked up a note. "Abigail Hayes."

"Send the trunk on to Nephi."

A frown of concern furrowed the man's forehead. "Has she met up with foul play?"

"I sure hope not, but it appears that way. I'll head over to alert the sheriff before I start out of town."

❧

Abigail watched with horrified fascination as the drunken men who held her captive staggered around their makeshift camp and waved their loaded weapons brazenly in the air. They'd traveled hard for two days, and Abigail had lost hope that anyone would come to rescue her. If she were to get away, it would be at her own hand.

She jumped as gunfire went off nearby. The acrid stench of gunpowder drifted through the air and made her sneeze. The low fire offered little light, and she stayed in the shadows, hoping the despicable men would leave her alone. Boggs, who had apparently assigned himself her temporary protector, was the only man not drinking. Bert, her husband-to-be, drank slower than the others, but still he'd had more than his share.

No sooner had she thought his name when he dropped to sit beside her in a fluff of dust. "Well, bride. I see that you're staying awake to watch the festivities?"

"If you consider the suicidal acts of imbeciles festive, then yes, I guess I am. Though it's a tad hard to sleep when wondering if a stray bullet will cause my demise at any moment."

He reached out and ran a calloused finger up the sleeve of her blouse. "Well, after tomorrow you'll worry no more."

A prickle of fear coursed up Abigail's back. She asked the question she knew she didn't want answered. "Why is that?"

"Because tomorrow night you'll become my bride." His

sinister laugh repulsed her. Everything about him repulsed her.

"I can't. I won't." She scrambled backward, tufts of dust encircling her boots. "I won't become your wife tomorrow or ever." She waved the dust away from her face, but the force of her words was weakened by the dust-induced sneeze that followed.

Bert clutched her skirt and yanked her forward in the dirt, her backside dragging through the dusty soil, and pulled her hard against him. He grasped her hair, wound his fingers into her curls, and pulled her face up against his. "You can marry me, and you will. Do you understand?"

Her eyes blurred at the pain his tight grasp caused her tender scalp. More than once during the past two days, he'd reacted in the same violent way. Most of her hairpins had come loose and were lost due to his rough handling. She knew she'd die before she ever became his wife. His terse words and hard eyes dared her to defy him. Before her lips could form the sharp retort in rebuttal, another loud crack filled the air, and this time a scream of pain quickly followed.

"You *shot* me, you idiot!"

"Only 'cause you jumped in front of my grun. . .gurn. . .um. . . gun, you imbecile."

Bert released his tight hold, and Abigail sank back from him. She watched as the two men staggered dangerously close to the fire before the shooting victim fell to the ground. Though she'd still not been introduced to the men, she knew from hearing them talk that the gunman, Walter, had shot the meeker man, Bill.

She didn't want to get involved, but she'd taken an oath and felt compelled to honor it. "I can help him." She spat the words through clenched teeth.

"Oh yeah? What are you going to do. . .shoot him again?"

Bert glanced at Boggs and laughed. Boggs didn't respond. Instead he nodded and directed Abigail to move forward.

"Boggs, could you bring me my bag?" Abigail hurried to the fallen man's side and tried to see the severity of his wound in the dim firelight. Boggs arrived at her side with the bag and took hold of Bill's healthy arm and dragged him closer to the fire. He then hurried off to grab some kindling to throw on the blaze, allowing Abigail more light to work with.

The bullet had entered the front of his upper arm, but hadn't come out the back. "I'll need to remove the bullet before packing his wound."

"You ain't touchin' his arm." Bert had moved close behind her, and she jumped at his nearness.

"If I don't he'll get an infection and die." She dug through her bag and lined the necessary items alongside her on a clean towel. "Boggs, I'll need some water boiled over the fire."

Boggs hurried off to do as she directed.

"Wait a minute." Bert's words were slurred as he watched her movements. "How do you know how to do this?"

"I'm a physician." For the first time, she stared him hard in the eyes. "I'm trained to do this."

"A fish-ish-ion? Like, a doctor?"

She nodded and registered the look of respect that momentarily passed over his features.

"Well how d'ya like that? I'm marrying a lady doctor."

"No, you're not."

"Yesh, I am." His eyes rolled up, and he fell backward.

Boggs returned with the water and set it to boil. He grasped Bert by the heels and slid him from the area. Again the dust tickled her nose and made her sneeze. A coarse laugh behind her made her glance away from her ministrations to Bill's arm.

Boggs squatted nearby, ready to help if needed. "You'd best get ahold of yourself with those sneezes. If you're sensitive to the conditions now, you'll be miserable as summer progresses."

A small smile shaped Abigail's mouth. "I can't stop myself from sneezing, now can I? Apparently there are a lot of unknowns on this trip I hadn't expected." She tore Bill's sleeve off, and he moaned.

"And I'm right sorry, Doc, that things are working out this way for you."

Abigail stilled her hands and looked over at him. "Then why are you going along with it? Why don't you stand up to Bert or help me get away?"

Boggs sent her a sympathetic frown. "I would if I could. But Bert has a way of finding folks' weak spots. With you, it's your brother. With me, it's my wife and child. He knows where they are, and he's threatened that if I don't do his bidding, he'll make them pay for my foolishness in getting involved with him."

"So you'll let him control you forever? When does it end? Your wife and child are alone while you're out here with him, miserable. I can see it in your eyes."

"Aye, I am miserable, but at least they're safe."

Abigail placed a hand on his arm. "Boggs, you need to get away. If you go now, he'll let you leave. He's too focused on me to change plans. You go get your wife and child and take them away from here to safety."

He sighed. "And leave you behind? I can't do that when you've been so thoughtful. Look. I deserve to be with the gang. You don't. I voluntarily rode with them before I realized just how corrupt they were. We'd fallen on hard times, and I thought some easy money would be nice. But you came along and suddenly I'm thinking of my wife and her spunk and I'm

missing her. She'd want me to help you. You leave, and I'll hold them off. I'll figure out a way to lose them later."

Abigail glanced down at Bill's silent form. "If I leave, he'll die. I need to remove the bullet and stop the bleeding. He'll need watching for the next couple of days." She remembered Hattie's prayer and her immediate answer. Though Abigail's own later prayer had gone largely unanswered, she felt in her heart that if she did the right thing—if she stayed to save the rotten life of the big oaf before her—she'd somehow be all right.

&

Jake pulled back on the reins and slowed his mount. "I don't understand. Why haven't we caught up with them? We know the direction they headed. We talked to the people whose homestead was ransacked. We've followed their tracks this far."

"They have to be running their horses hard." Hank rode up alongside him. "We can't keep up the same pace. The mounts are tired, and the men need to rest."

"We'll continue on as long as the moon is bright enough to travel by. I won't lose any more time. I have no idea what the man's intentions are, and I won't have Caleb's sister terrorized when I'm supposed to be watching out for her."

They rode in silence. The moon shone down to highlight the landscape into eerie shapes. Jake's neck prickled in response. He sent up a prayer for protection. Something evil was afoot, and he wasn't sure what.

Hank broke the silence. "Jake?"

"What?"

"The stationmaster told me Miss Hayes apparently went willingly with the gentleman. He said they appeared to be friendly."

"And what do you make of that? She didn't come in on the

train with the man. She never wrote to tell her brother of a chaperone or male companion who would meet her when she arrived. What is it you're getting at?"

"I don't know exactly, other than those are the facts as I know them. Something isn't right, and I just figured you'd want to know. She might not be the sweet little sister Caleb remembers her to be."

"Did the stationmaster mention the man's name? The one that she left with?"

"Robert. Robert Sanchez."

Jake's stomach did a slow dive. "Robert Sanchez? Are you sure?"

"Positive." Hank looked at him from under his hat. "Why, do you know him?"

"He's the man who intended to send Caleb to his deathbed. Caleb helped the sheriff capture Bert for gambling charges. Bert got away, and Caleb paid a price. If I hadn't found him when I did, he'd be dead right now. The fact that Bert left his real name at the station means he intended to send a message to me. . .or more likely to Caleb. I'm sure Bert figured Caleb would pick her up if he survived the attack."

"But where does his sister fit in?" Hank persisted. "If she knew Bert, do you suppose she had something to do with Caleb's attack?"

"I have no idea, but for now I think we should keep quiet about our connection to Caleb when we meet up with her. I need to find out more about this Abigail Hayes before taking her to see Caleb. I won't have him hurt again."

❧

Morning dawned with the beautiful sky painted in hues of pink, orange, and lavender. The day—her *wedding day*—so perfectly bright and sunny, mocked her panic over the passing

of time. She needed a miracle. She could feel her hair arc out in a halo of wild curls after the restless night she'd spent caring for Bill. He'd pulled through and didn't show any sign of fever, much to Abigail's relief.

She sat up and stretched, taking in the location of each of the men around her. They'd passed out in various sections of the camp. She smiled when she realized Boggs had disappeared at some point during the night. Perhaps he'd heeded her suggestion and had left to take his wife and child to safety. She hoped so. If that were the case, at least one good thing would have come out of this sorry mess.

Abigail checked Bill's wound and leaned back on her heels. Today would be a turning point; she could feel it. She wouldn't "marry" Bert tonight as he planned. With no reverend around, there'd be no proper wedding, and she refused to act and accept anything less when her time came.

Since she'd stabilized Bill, she had the perfect opportunity to slip away while the others slept. God willing, she'd escape and find help before the gang caught up with her. The thought gave her pause. She had no experience with the rugged landscape and from what she saw, nothing but mountains and scrub bushes and dry landscape surrounded them. She had no idea how to get food, or how to find water, once she left the men. After securing Hamm in her bag, she snuck over and quietly worked to loosen her mount's ropes as her mind raced through her options. She could backtrack and try to follow their previous trail and the landmarks she'd noted as they rode by on the previous days, which would allow her to find water and possibly even food. Or she could continue south and hope to find another ranch or homestead, though the area appeared to be pretty barren.

Lord, I tried this before and it didn't go so well. I don't feel like

You heard my prayer. But if possible, I need a miracle. I need out of this situation. Please don't make me marry Bert. I don't have many options, but maybe You could help me find the best one.

As she contemplated her choices, a chilling scream filled the air. Her horse reared and pulled from her grasp and took off at a frantic run. The hair on the back of Abigail's neck stood up, and she watched as the men stumbled to their feet, disoriented.

The horrendous scream sounded again, and the men jumped into action. Bert snatched up his rifle and jumped onto his mount in one fluid motion. He never once looked around for Abigail or anyone else. Walter's horse left him behind, so he began to run on foot, carrying his boots. Bill lurched sideways, stumbling weakly away from the commotion. Abigail stood rooted to the spot, not knowing what was happening. After a moment she followed the men's lead and grabbed her bag and, without her mount to escape on, ran toward a large boulder. She ducked behind it as the men fled the area.

More screams filled the air and, petrified, she watched between cracks of the large piece of stone as a band of fierce Indians surrounded her captors and struck them down with their weapons. Bert never made it to the trees. Walter lay face-down, his boots still clutched in his hand. Bill lay a few yards away from him. Abigail gulped for air, trying to quiet the terror that tried to force a scream from her own throat. She knew her life depended upon her silence. She rocked back and forth on her knees, hugging Hamm close against her chest, willing him to stay quiet.

The chaos died down along with the men who'd captured her. The savages stood and surveyed their handiwork. Abigail began to shake. Though the gang of men was despicable,

no one deserved to die at the Indians' hands as these men just had. The dust settled over the area, and Abigail's panic increased as she felt a tickle in her nose. If she sneezed, they'd know she was there. She dropped her head and prayed as she'd seen Hattie do during the train robbery. She threw herself forward, facedown, and muffled her face in the folds of her skirt. But try as she might, she couldn't contain the sneeze that burst forth. She peeked through the crack between the rocks and watched in horror as a tall Indian, dressed in black leggings and a black shirt and who wore his long hair in beaded braids, began to walk in her direction. She felt faint, but instead of giving in to her fear, she gave in to her anger.

"That's *it*!" Abigail screeched. She jumped to her feet in a complete rage. At the same time, she held Hamm close and cuddled him protectively against her breast.

The approaching Indian stopped in his tracks. His face registered a look of complete shock.

Abigail felt the fury seethe out from her eyes as she surveyed the sickening massacre before her. Never in her life had she felt such a pure, unbridled wrath. She stomped her foot, hard, and shrieked again—the sound foreign to her ears—before stepping methodically forward. As she walked with slow, steady steps, she flipped back the mass of blond hair that had tumbled loose the day before when she'd lost her hat.

The Indian looked over his shoulder, but the other braves had retreated at her first scream. With a look of trepidation, sprinkled with confusion, he also took a step backward.

Abigail's chest heaved with each deep breath of air she forced into her lungs.

"In the past seventy-two hours," she hissed through clenched teeth, "I've been held up in a train robbery, kidnapped by an

outlaw and his gang, and attacked by Indians—*you.*" She spat the word and poked the surprised man in the chest with her finger. "I've watched my friends *die.* Well, maybe they weren't my friends and maybe they were more like enemies, but still, they *didn't* deserve to die!"

She continued to punch her finger into his chest as she enunciated to underscore each of her words. She paused, panting and trying to catch her breath as the anger coursed through her. "So, if you have it in your minds to do something awful to me and Hamm, then by all means," she spat at the man's chest and released the last of her rage in a scream that defied definition, "get it over with *now!*"

Hamm's reaction to her pitch was immediate. With a loud squeal, he poked his head from the blanket and stared into the native's face. The man, after seeing the pig's head pop out from beneath the blanket, backed up so quickly that he tripped and went head over heels. Without missing a beat, he flew to his feet and retreated, motioning for the others to flee, while repeating the same foreign word over and over.

Abigail tipped her head back and let out an anguished cry as she dropped to her knees. She knew without checking that all the men were dead. Her inexperienced prayer had caused their deaths. She hugged Hamm close and curled up into a ball. She hoped the Indians came back. She didn't deserve to live.

She crawled back behind the boulder to shut out the gruesome sight before her. The terror of the moment caught up with her, and in shock she fell into a deep sleep.

five

"Whoa." Jake pulled back on Steadfast's reins and motioned for his men to stop. He remained in the saddle, surveying the landscape in front of them. They had headed south toward Provo, and he was sure this would be the day they caught up with Abigail and her companion.

"What's up, boss?" Red rode up beside him.

"I'm not sure." Jake hid the anxiety he felt and tried to appear nonchalant as he settled back in the saddle. "See the smoke over there? It's midmorning. If the smoke is from Miss Hayes' campfire, why would they still be here at this late hour after running so hard the past few days? Seems to me they'd have packed up and left at dawn's first light if that were the case."

"Maybe one of 'em's sick. Or maybe we took a wrong turn and we've been trailing someone else."

The other men pulled up to join them.

"I guess it's possible one of them can be under the weather. Miss Hayes isn't used to traveling in these conditions or the climate. But I know we're following the right trail. We didn't divert off to follow the wrong group."

"So we gonna sit here all day or are we gonna go check things out?"

Hank's words grated on Jake's last nerve. Something about him rubbed Jake wrong. As soon as they returned to the ranch, Jake planned to settle up what he owed the man and send him on his way.

Jake chewed a piece of grass and took his time answering. "I suppose we might as well check things out." He spat the stalk to the ground, wishing he could rid himself of the troublesome ranch hand as easily.

He led the other men and followed the valley as it wound along the base of the hills. The smoke grew clearer in the distance, and they could smell the acrid scent of burning wood. The aroma made Jake long for the ranch. He wished he were sitting in front of a roaring fire at home instead of chasing after his friend's errant sister. The spring air was crisp and hadn't yet reached the full intensity of midday. The setting felt contradictory to the chill that ran up Jake's back as they neared the camp.

The men remained quiet as they entered the area. Not a person or creature moved, yet they could see at least one horse huddled up against a stand of trees.

"Somethin's not right for sure." Scrappy pulled his horse close to Jake's. "What do you make of this, boss?"

Jake didn't answer. Instead he chose to continue forward. As he rounded a cluster of rocks, his heart sank as he took in the scene before him. The kidnappers from the train station, as far as he could tell, Bert and his men, lay scattered about on the ground before them. Reluctantly, while fighting his churning stomach, he rode Steadfast closer, checking each man for a sign of life. Their wounds proved without question that no one had survived the attack.

Scrappy took in big gulps of air from his place behind Jake, while Grub rode to a nearby bush and lost his breakfast. Red sat motionless on his mount, while Hank suddenly moved faster than Jake had ever seen him. He rode until he reached Bert's crumpled form and dropped to his knees.

His anguished cry took Jake by surprise. He exchanged

startled glances with the other men and rode closer, trying to make out the man's words.

"It wasn't supposed to be like this. It wasn't."

"What wasn't?" Jake dropped down beside Hank, keeping a tight hold on his horse. The horse, skittish, fought at the reins.

Hank didn't answer.

Jake placed his hand on Hank's shoulder. "Hank?"

Hank reacted violently, jerking backward and splaying his arms around in the air. "Leave me alone!" He shoved Jake backward, hopped on his horse, and rode out of sight.

The rest of the men remained rooted in place.

"Hank, get back here. It's not safe!" Jake called after him, but Hank continued on as if death itself were on his heels.

"What was that all about?" Grub seemed to have semi-recovered, though he remained pale, as did all the hands.

"I have no idea." Jake glanced back at the emptiness where Hank had disappeared from sight and stared, trying to decipher the man's actions. "I mean, this isn't easy for any of us. But that seemed to be a strange reaction no matter how you look at it. And the last thing he should do is ride out of here alone."

"Something's up." Though Red's words stated the obvious, the men nodded in agreement.

Scrappy kept his eyes on the hills, refusing to look around. "I thought the Indians had left this area. Didn't they sign a treaty a few years back?"

Jake nodded. "They did. But a band of Utes tried to kill their chief after the signing. They weren't all happy with his actions. As we said the other day, I suppose it makes sense that not all of them rode willingly onto the reservation with him. And there have been rumors of other bands of Indians

getting permits to go off the reservations to find deer. In the process, they've also shot cattle and had altercations with the ranchers. But the attackers could be from anywhere, possibly just passing through."

Grub's voice, much quieter than his usual robust exuberance, echoed from behind them. "And that doesn't mean other tribes don't have rogue bands in the area."

Jake forced his attention back to the grisly scene that surrounded them. He didn't relish the thought of informing Caleb that his sister had been involved in an Indian attack. But now that he forced his thoughts in that direction, he realized he hadn't seen any sign of Caleb's sister.

"Where's Miss Hayes?"

"Where's Miss Hayes, indeed," Grub repeated. "Maybe they took her with them?"

"I don't think so. She'd be a liability to them. From the violence here I think they'd—," he cleared his throat, "—do the same to her."

"Oh no. Not Caleb's sister." Scrappy shook his head. "He won't take that very well. We need to locate her."

"Sorry, boys, but there's no way she survived an attack of this magnitude. Look around. They didn't have a chance. That one over there was half dressed, still putting on his boots. Bert was hit from behind." His throat constricted as he fought off the urge to follow Grub's lead and run for the bushes.

"Then where is she?" Red rode forward, suddenly the brave one as he searched out Caleb's sister's remains.

"Fan out and look for her." Jake heard the hard edge in his voice, but he couldn't help it. This wasn't how the trip was supposed to go. Abigail was his responsibility. He'd let her, and Caleb, down.

God, why would You allow something like this to happen? I just got Caleb on his feet. He's still weak. Bert wasn't much of a loss, and I can't mourn him completely because of what he did to Caleb and to Abigail. But even he didn't deserve an attack like this.

He swung up onto Steadfast's back and rode with purpose away from the others. The least he could do would be to gather Abigail's belongings for her brother and to give her a decent burial, which wouldn't be easy in the hard-packed dirt at his feet.

A thorough investigation of the area turned up no sign of Abigail.

"She isn't here. Are you sure they wouldn't have taken her?"

Jake wasn't sure of anything anymore. "It doesn't make sense, but maybe they took her somewhere else to. . ." He refused to voice the thoughts that passed through his head. "Maybe they had other plans for her."

Before the others could register what that meant, Scrappy leaped from his mount. "Over here!"

He lifted up a lone piece of paper.

"What is it?" Jake joined him.

"I dunno. It looks to be some type of scientific paper."

Jake reached out to take it from him. The paper was smudged with dirt. "It's handwritten notes from a medical journal."

"A medical journal?" Grub scratched his head. "Why would they have something like that?"

"According to Caleb, his sister had some type of medical training. She's here. Look harder."

They spread out and began to search behind brush and rocks and scrub.

Jake heard a moan from behind a pile of rocks and hurried over to check the area. Abigail lay on the ground, her blond

hair fanned around her. She looked nothing like she had in town. Her face lay hidden under the long locks of hair. Hesitantly, he moved forward and lifted a soft strand, afraid of what he might find beneath.

With a shriek of terror, she bolted backward. Jake tumbled the opposite direction, startled by the transformation.

"You're alive!" Though she'd just taken ten years off his life, he couldn't hold back his laugh of relief. "You survived the attack!"

He could hear his words echo behind him as his men spread the word that she'd been found alive.

He watched as she buried her face in her hands. He slowly moved forward. "Abigail. Miss Hayes?"

She didn't respond.

Again he pushed back some strands of hair that hid her face. She reacted violently, her hands scratching at him like a wildcat. "Noooo!"

"Miss Hayes!" He grabbed her arms. He felt blood run down his cheek from her attack. "My name is Jake. We're here to help. Listen to me." He gently shook her, and her eyes vacantly sought his.

When they met, the cloudiness evaporated.

"You." She whispered the words. "The ruffian from the train station."

"I don't think I turned out to be the ruffian you expected. I'm here to help you, remember?"

"But you looked so threatening."

"Looks can be deceiving, as I'm sure you figured out by now. Obviously your kind friend Bert wasn't quite what he appeared." The moment the words left his mouth he regretted them. The cloud returned to her eyes, and they filled with tears.

"I killed him."

"You killed him?" Jake looked around. "I don't see how you could be capable of something like this."

"I prayed him dead."

Before he could further question her, the others surrounded them.

"Is she hurt?" Scrappy knelt gingerly down beside them. "Miss Hayes, I'm so sorry for what you've endured. Are you all right?"

Scrappy talked to her as if she were royalty. Though Jake had to admit the man probably hadn't ever been so close to such a lady in all his years.

Jake hadn't even thought to ask. "Are you hurt?"

Abigail shook her head and frowned, her forehead crinkling with confusion. "I don't think so."

She sent Jake, then Scrappy, a small smile. "Thanks for asking."

Scrappy sat inches taller at her words.

Jake watched as she put a shaky hand to her forehead. "I'm so sorry. I think I have a touch of shock." She glanced at the ground around her. "Hamm? Where are you? Hamm!"

The men exchanged bewildered looks.

Red leaned close to Jake's ear. "Who do you reckon Hamm is? One of Bert's men?"

"Not that I've ever heard. The only one I can see who's unaccounted for is Boggs."

"Do you think he has the capability to do this?"

"No way. I've only run into him a couple of times, and each time I came away wondering why a man like him would run with a gang like Bert's."

Abigail pushed to her feet and swooned. Jake jumped up to stabilize her. "Ma'am, it's probably best if you sit for a

moment and get your bearings."

"I have to find Hamm." Her voice rose in pitch. Jake knew she was at the edge of hysteria.

"Can you describe him for us? We'll help you look."

She looked at Jake like he'd grown a second head. "He's small and pink, with a snout."

"A snout? As in a pig snout?"

"Yes."

"Boss, do you think she's hallucinatin'?" Grub watched her in fascination.

"I don't know."

Jake supported her full weight, and when she made note of that fact she pushed him gently away. She slowly spun in a circle, surveying the rocks. "There you are." Relief softened her words.

A small pink pig nestled securely in the rocks beside them, sound asleep. Abigail moved forward on shaky legs and gathered him into her arms. The piglet nuzzled the soft skin of Abigail's neck, and she gave a short laugh as tears flowed from her eyes. "You survived." A sob replaced the smile. "You survived and I survived, and no one else did."

"Miss Hayes." Jake kept his voice quiet, not wanting to send her further into her grief. "Please." He took her arm, not sure of how she'd react, but instead of fighting him this time she turned and burrowed her face against his chest.

After a moment's hesitation, he wrapped his arms around her quivering body. He looked over her shoulder at his men for help, but they all scattered in the other direction.

"We'll get to work digging a grave, boss."

It shouldn't surprise him that they deserted him in his time of need. After all, since he'd found them all in various forms of avoidance, why would they suddenly grow backbones now?

Her sobs turned to convulsive, heartrending cries of pain.

Words escaped him, but he tightened his hold and let her cry. She felt so right in his arms. Her soft form molded to his, and he pushed her hair back from her face, this time savoring the feel of the silky strands. After several minutes, he found his tongue. "There, there, Miss Hayes. It's going to be all right. We're here with you now. We'll get you safely far away from here."

She pulled away, her green eyes searching his as if seeing him for the first time. "And how can you guarantee me that?" She motioned around them. "They seemed to think we were safe, too. But look how that turned out."

"It turned out with my standing here, that's how. They didn't get us in the attack. They didn't get you. Perhaps you had a Divine intervention on your part. I have no clue how you survived, but you did." Jake was surprised to see a look of guilt flash across her face. Now that he really looked at her, he had no idea how he could ever think of her as severe as he had at the station. She had beautiful, delicate features.

After resting her head against his chest for a moment more, she stepped back. "Thank you. I'm sorry I fell apart like that."

"I think you had good reason."

Her body trembled with a shaky sigh. "I've seen as much and worse in hospitals during my training. But I guess the difference is back home I'd have been in charge of the situation. I didn't expect. . .this. Not out here."

"Your training?"

"I'm a physician. I trained in medicine."

That surprised Jake. Caleb had said she trained in medicine, but Jake thought he'd referred to nurse training or something of that sort. He thought it best not to show his surprise. He

didn't think she'd take too kindly to that type of reaction. "It's the West, Abigail. You can't predict anything. You can't let down your guard, ever." Nothing like a few words of comfort to make a person feel better, but she needed to know what she was up against. He tucked his thumbs in the waistband of his pants. "It's not civilized out here like it is back East. And the farther we head south, the more risky the terrain becomes. Outlaws hide in the rugged land out this way."

"Thanks for the encouragement." Her sharp retort inspired him. At least she wasn't the simpering female type he'd pegged her to be at first glance. "But I beg to differ on your assessment of the East. I treated stab wounds, gunshot wounds, and wounds from broken bottles used during bar fights. Human depravity exists everywhere, not just here."

"I stand corrected."

They stood and assessed each other silently.

"I'm a horrible judge of character." She sighed.

"Is that so? Why would you ever think that?" He tried to keep the sarcasm at bay, but it crept in anyway.

"You saw Bert at the station. He looked kind and showed concern. How was I to know it was a farce?"

He didn't respond.

"And you." She looked him up and down. "You came barreling up the walkway looking dangerous with your dark scowl and all those weapons fastened around your waist."

"Weapons that would have prevented this attack had I been here." He crossed his arms in challenge. The woman had transformed from needy to annoying.

"So you say." She tightened her grip on Hamm. "You didn't see it happen. One minute things were quiet. And the next, things went crazy. The men were all running, and I didn't know what was happening. By the time I saw the Indians. . ."

Her throat convulsed. "Before anyone could react. . ." Again her words drifted away. She cleared her throat. "Before anyone could react, the men were all dead."

"I'm so sorry you had to experience that. I'm sorry we weren't here sooner."

Suspicion laced her features. "Why are you here?"

"Excuse me?"

"Why should I trust you?" She backed away. "I saw you at the station and now here you are, out in the middle of nowhere, playing Knight in Shining Armor. How do I know you don't have ulterior motives? Or maybe you even knew about the attack or planned it."

"Ouch." Jake accentuated his wince. "Or maybe I was sent to help you."

"How would you know I needed help?"

"Because you left town with Robert, and nothing he ever does is on the up-and-up."

"For all I know, my brother also owed you a debt and you called it in, same as Bert."

"Same as Bert? What'd he tell you?"

He studied her as she turned a shoulder his way and looked far off into the distance. She bit the corner of her lip before uttering carefully calculated words that were laced with pain. "Apparently, my brother traded me in marriage to pay off a debt to Bert. Bert blackmailed him because Caleb turned him in for gambling. Tonight was to be our wedding night." She shuddered.

Her words and obvious repulsion brought a whole new wave of anger to Jake. Somehow the attack didn't seem as vicious after she spoke. The man deserved his fate. He felt immediate guilt at his reaction but brushed it away.

"Your brother would never have traded you off for

anything. Bert lied. He took you to get even."

How typical of Bert to add to her trauma by making her dread the passing days, knowing what awaited her.

"Abigail, there's something you should know. Caleb didn't—"

"Boss, Hank's back."

Jake scowled at Red's interruption, but sure enough, Hank lurked just outside the clearing, hovering suspiciously behind the trees.

six

Distracted, Abbie looked over at the edge of the trees where the men were all staring. A man rode from the shadows and headed their way.

Jake stood tall, hands fisted on his hips, and waited for the man to come closer. A slight breeze stirred and blew his dark hair around his face. Absently, he pushed it away. "You doin' all right, Hank?"

"I'm fine." Hank bit off each word, his response anything but friendly.

In fluid movements, Jake stepped over and caught hold of Hank's horse's bridle. Though his actions appeared to be casual, Abbie had the feeling they were anything but. "What did you mean by 'it wasn't supposed to be this way'?"

Hank scowled, looked away, and answered vaguely. "What do you think? We were supposed to pick up Miss Hayes and return to the ranch. Seeing the aftereffect of a massacre wasn't in the plans. Not that I was aware of anyway."

"You sure?" Jake stared him down for a long moment. "You seemed to take an extra interest in Bert."

"What interest would I have in the man?" Hank ran his hand through his messy hair, and his eyes darted to the man's still form.

"I don't know. That's what I'm trying to figure out."

Abigail ran her fingers through her own tangled tresses and watched the men with interest. She'd been trained to watch for signs and signals when treating her patients, and

it was more than obvious there were undercurrents here she didn't understand.

Hank glanced her way. "Miss Hayes?" Ignoring Jake, he headed toward her. "How interesting that you alone survived." He took her wrist and pulled her around, forcing her to look over at the massacred men.

She pulled from his tight grasp. His forwardness and cold tone unnerved her.

She noticed that Jake was watching their interaction with interest. He scowled when he met her gaze. His brown eyes bore into hers. Her chin raised a notch, and she refused to look away. Her reaction spurred him into action.

"We need to finish up here and move on. It's not safe to linger." He grabbed a small shovel from his saddle and joined the others in digging a shallow pit.

Abigail turned her head, not needing to see the rest. She peeked a few times and saw them move the bodies and then place stones they'd gathered from the area over the mound. Scrappy checked her wayward horse after leading him from the trees and readied the saddle before heading her way.

"Do you have everything you need?" Jake's voice, coming from behind her, made her jump.

Her fingers stuck on a tangled strand of hair. "I have all my things gathered up if that's what you mean. I only had the one valise. They made me leave my trunk at the station."

"I know. We checked there first. They're sending the trunk on to Nephi where we'll retrieve it."

He assisted her to her feet and up onto her mount.

"Thank you." She caressed the horse's mane. Other than Hamm, he was the only thing familiar to her. She didn't know what else to say.

Jake stood below her, staring. He, too, raised his hand to

pet the stallion. "What's his name?"

"I'm not sure. They," she glanced at the mound of earth and winced, "had him waiting at the station and weren't much for small talk."

"Better pick out a name then. He's yours now."

Before she could say anything else, Jake stalked off and swung onto his own horse.

&

Hank stayed near her side the entire afternoon. Though he didn't say a lot, his angry glances made her increasingly uneasy as the day passed. Jake took the lead most of the time, which kept him to himself.

As the shock of the day wore off, Abigail began to wonder about their destination.

"Excuse me. I need to speak with Jake." Hank looked at her in surprise, but made no move to stop her as she rode forward and came alongside the man in charge. Jake's eyebrows rose as he surveyed her, then narrowed into a scowl. She had no idea what she'd done to turn him from rescuer to disgruntled guide.

"I have some questions." She noticed he made no effort to slow their pace in response, which was fine. Though a tad sore, she'd become a pretty adept horsewoman during the past few days.

"I don't guarantee I'll answer them."

Surprised at his tart response, she could only stare. They rode on in silence while Abigail formulated her words. "If you're trying to intimidate me, it won't work."

Her comment brought a slight smile to his lips. "It won't?"

"No, it won't." The trail narrowed, and she let her horse drop back as they diverted around shrubs and strange-looking brush. Large mountains loomed in the distance.

"What is this?" She rode back up beside him and pointed to the plant in question.

"Sagebrush."

"Really? I read about it! The Indians use it for medicinal purposes."

"Is that right?"

His comment, somewhat sarcastic, caught her off guard.

"I've somehow offended you." She pulled her attention from the landscape and focused back on him.

"No."

"You talk even less than Bert and his men."

"I'm not here to talk. I'm here to keep you safe and to take you to the ranch."

"But I told you, I have questions."

His chest heaved in exasperation. "What are they?"

"Where are we going?"

"To the ranch. It's south of Provo, near Mount Pleasant."

"Why you?"

"Your brother sent me. He was in bad shape and in no condition to travel. I said I'd fetch you and bring you back."

Her heart lurched as she recalled Bert's words. She couldn't even begin to think about what her future held without Caleb. She didn't want to discuss it with this distant stranger. She'd sort everything out after they arrived at the ranch.

"But is he...?"

"Boss, someone's trailing us." Red rode up to the front of the line and edged Abbie out of the way. "Want me to ride back and check it out?"

Jake worried his bottom lip with his teeth. "No, let's pick up the pace and see what happens. We'll skirt Provo and make camp on Utah Lake."

He dismissed Abbie with a nod and spurred his own mount

to a faster pace. Abbie mimicked his actions and kept her place at his heels. She studied him as he sat in his saddle. Though he'd originally looked menacing from her city-girl point of view, she'd quickly learned the value of traveling fully loaded with weapons. She'd seen him use his knife earlier as they journeyed, and now he reached down and grasped the handle of his gun, checked it for bullets, and slipped it securely back into its holster.

They didn't speak for the larger part of an hour. Abigail noted a town to the west, but they stayed clear of it. Finally, Red moved back in place alongside Jake and stated that their followers had either disappeared or had dropped far enough back that they weren't leaving any dust by which to track them.

"Let's continue the pace for another hour or so, and then we'll pull off and make camp. Red, you and Hank drop back and see if you can find any sign of our pursuers. Most likely it was someone bound for Provo, and they turned off at the road into town."

Red tipped his hat at Abigail, and she found herself responding to his warm smile. A glare from Jake sent him scurrying down the line. After he and Hank turned the other way, Grub fell into place behind Abbie, and Scrappy brought up the tail.

Abigail sneezed as Jake's horse kicked up a pouf of dust, but not nearly as bad as she'd sneezed while riding with Bert.

Jake turned his sour expression on her. "Are you ill? Do we need to seek medical care in Provo?"

"No. *Achoo!*" Abbie dug a handkerchief out from her valise. Her movements disturbed Hamm, and he began to squeal. Another sneeze followed.

"Why do you keep sneezing? I heard you awhile back and

thought you'd sneeze yourself off your mount. And by the way, have you named him yet?"

"The dust affects me, as do many of the plants in the area. This is why I keep sneezing. And if I were to need medical care, I'm more than capable to treat myself. I'm trained as a physician, remember?"

"Ah yes, Doc, I do seem to remember a conversation about medical school."

"And I've not yet had a chance to think up a name for the horse. I'll make sure that's a top priority in the near future."

"See that you do. It isn't right for a creature as magnificent as yours to go nameless."

"He's not mine."

"I told you, he is now. His owner is gone. Consider it your pay for the trauma you endured at Bert's hands."

Her voice dropped to a whisper. "I'd rather not have endured the trauma at all."

His eyes hardened as he stared at her. "I know."

So that was it. He somehow knew she was to blame for the men's deaths. She'd prayed to God for a way out, and their demise was His answer.

❧

Jake winced as she paled and speared him with pain-filled eyes. He turned to hide his reaction.

She blamed him for the whole Bert disaster, he could tell. Once he brought it up, her eyes had widened and then narrowed, and now she rode in silence. He could kick himself for leaving her at the station. He knew the thought wasn't rational; she hadn't matched Caleb's description and Bert had thrown him off, but Jake was the one sent to collect her, and he'd messed up. She had every reason to be upset with him.

He cut west and headed for the lake. They'd make camp

and set out early in the morning for the ranch. Another few days, barring any more problems, and they'd be there.

"Where are we going?"

"I thought we'd stop at Utah Lake for the night. You can clean up and relax, and the men can fish and catch us some dinner."

Her features tightened with apprehension.

"You don't like the idea?"

"I don't like much of anything since getting here, to be honest."

"I'm sorry."

"It isn't exactly your fault."

So maybe she didn't hold him responsible. But it didn't matter. He held himself responsible. "But it is. If I'd collected you from the train station at the beginning, you'd not have suffered at Bert's hand."

She surprised him when her mouth widened into a grin and her green eyes twinkled in amusement. "And what about the train robbery on the way out? Do you want to take responsibility for that, too?"

He pulled his horse to a stop, momentarily stunned. "You were involved in a train robbery?"

She grimaced and nodded. " 'Fraid so. It's not been the relaxing journey I'd hoped for."

They prodded their horses to move on.

"I guess not. And then you arrived at the station only to find out that Caleb—"

"Yes." She interrupted him, not allowing him to finish.

She looked away but not before he saw the tears that filled her eyes. The fact that Caleb had been laid up and couldn't meet the train must have really upset her. If that were the case, he'd do well to avoid the subject until they got to the ranch

and she and Caleb settled up their relationship. He'd do well to change the subject right now as a matter of fact.

"And the horse's name is. . .?"

She tucked a strand of hair behind her delicate ear. "No name. Not yet."

"No Name. That suits him."

"I didn't mean. . ." Her voice drifted off, and she looked contemplative. She reached out and ruffled the stallion's mane. "You know. . .I think it does suit him. His new name is No Name."

Jake reined in Steadfast and jumped down to the ground, ready to stretch his legs. "Whoa, No Name." He reached up to assist Abbie. "Let me help you down, Doc. We'll set up over there."

❧

Abigail followed the direction of his finger and saw a beautiful lake just ahead. She released Hamm from her valise and set him loose on the hard-packed dirt. He rutted around and snorted as he began to chew on strands of plants at their feet.

Scrappy and Grub came up behind them, and in the distance she could see Hank and Red turn their way.

Abbie felt at odds while they set up camp. She didn't know how to help, so she tried to stay out of the way. She called for Hamm and walked to the water's edge. It looked shallow enough, and she hoped there'd be a way for her to bathe. Her hair was a mass of tangled strands. Though they'd passed several streams and creeks while she was with Bert, she hadn't dared ask to bathe with them around. For some strange reason, she felt she could trust Jake and his men.

The sun sat low on the horizon when Jake headed her way. "Okay, Doc, why don't you head on over and relax in the water, and I'll watch over our things. I can make sure you're

safe from here, and the men are heading down around the bend to another area to fish."

Abbie hesitated. *Could* she trust him? She reached up and touched her hair. She had no choice. She couldn't leave it in such a condition a moment longer. And she refused to arrive at her brother's ranch in such a state. The hands and staff would think her a mess.

She gathered a bar of lye soap from her bag. She'd wash her outfit as best she could while in the water. Hamm trailed her to the water's edge and hesitantly dipped his front leg into the surface. When he made contact with the water, he squealed and backed away. Two more tries assured him that water wasn't something he wanted to mess with, and he curled up on the ground a short distance from shore.

Abigail looked around and couldn't see anyone other than Jake, and even he was only a tiny figure near the campfire. She waded into the water, relieved to find it a pleasant temperature. Tiny fish darted around her ankles, and she swished them away before they could nibble on her skin. Once she'd reached waist depth, she lowered herself to the surface and, holding her breath, submerged herself. She slipped out of her outer garments and used friction to clean them as well as possible. The lye soap clouded the water, but she didn't care. It would feel delightful to be clean once again. She waded out and after wringing her dress as well as she could, she draped it over some stones at the water's edge.

She returned to the water and lathered up her hair. She scrubbed it, running her fingers through the tangled tresses. She wouldn't be able to do much without her brush. She wished she'd brought it to the water's edge, but she was too lazy to get out of the lake and retrieve it. She floated on her back and swam underwater, and before she knew it, the sky

had darkened further and she knew it was time to head to the campfire.

The water smelled fresh and stars studded the sky. She kicked and moved toward shore, but when she stood, her dress wasn't where she'd left it. A shiver coursed through her. Perhaps she had been wrong to trust the men after all. Her underclothes weren't proper attire to wear while sitting around a fire with a bunch of men.

"I took your clothes." Jake's voice broke through the silence, and she lowered herself into the water. "I put them near the fire so they'd dry."

"And what am I to do—sit here in the water until they do?"

"Of course not. I brought you a blanket to wrap in. It will be completely proper until your clothes are dry."

"But the men. . ."

"Have been instructed to sit tight at the other campfire until dinner is ready and we head over their way." He motioned to a fire in the distance. "I'll join them as soon as I know you're safely sitting in front of this fire."

"Drop the blanket and move away."

"As you say, Doc."

He did as she asked and moved into the shadows, keeping his back to her. She stepped out of the water and hurried over to grab the wool coverlet. It felt heavenly as it warded off the shivers that had enveloped her as soon as she stepped from the water.

"I'm all set."

He returned to her side and picked up her valise.

"Would you mind getting Hamm for me, too?" She motioned to his huddled form on the hard-packed beach. "It's awkward to try to carry him and hold the blanket together."

"I can imagine."

She hurried forward, not wanting to know what else he might be imagining. She stepped into the circle of light from the fire and quickly settled down on a boulder near the warmth. Her thin underclothes would dry quickly in the heat of the fire.

Jake stepped beside her, looking dangerous in a new way. She hadn't realized exactly how handsome he was until now. His presence filled the area until she felt she couldn't breathe. His dark brown eyes sought hers, but she avoided them, looking toward the fire instead.

"Do you need anything else?" His warm chuckle surrounded her, making her feel even warmer.

"No, I'll be fine." She reached forward and pulled her brush from her bag and began to pull it through the tangles. They were in such a mess that she couldn't make any progress.

"Here, let me."

"No!" She hugged her brush against the blanket covering her chest.

"Doc, I have three younger sisters. I'm not a stranger to brushing tangles out of snarled hair."

"It wouldn't be proper. And thank you so much for painting me in such an attractive way with your words. Every woman dreams of being referred to as having snarled tangles."

He chuckled again, this time his breath warm on her cheek as he settled down behind her on the boulder. "Give me the brush."

"I won't."

"You're a physician, correct?"

She huffed out her exasperation. "You know I am."

"And aren't there times when you cross the boundaries of propriety when dealing with patients?"

"Well, of course. But that's different."

She felt gooseflesh prickle her skin at his nearness. Her heart began to beat faster, and she wondered if she'd have some type of episode if it continued at such a pace.

"It's not different. This is a unique situation. I promise to behave as a complete gentleman. But I'm a starving gentleman, and if we all have to wait for you to get this brush through that hair before we can settle down for dinner, it won't be pretty."

"No one's asking you to hold off your meal. By all means, go join the others and eat your fill."

Her traitorous stomach growled loudly at the thought of food.

This time Jake laughed out loud. "Your stomach seems to have a difference of opinion from the words that escape through your mouth. Now stop being so stubborn and let me have your brush."

Before she could refuse him again, he reached around and snatched the brush from her hands. His arm bumped against hers, and her skin tingled at his nearness. She clenched her teeth in consternation, but if they didn't want to die of hunger while battling the issue, she needed to give in and let him help her.

As she expected, her clothes dried quickly in the heat. And she had to admit, it felt wonderful to relax beside the fire while its warmth spread through her. The scent of burning wood enveloped them into their own private world, and she let her eyes drift closed. She hadn't slept well since her arrival days earlier, worried to let down her guard.

With Jake she felt safe and protected. She didn't realize she'd fallen asleep until Jake cleared his throat and said in a tight voice, "There you go. I'll let you finish up, but I think I got the worst of the tangles out."

Abbie's eyes popped open, and she found that she rested against Jake's firm chest. She didn't want to move. She glanced upward and found Jake's face inches away from her own. His dark eyes bore into hers. The fire reflected in their depths. Her mouth opened, but no words came out. They studied each other silently for a moment before Jake pushed her gently upright and moved several feet away.

"Thank you." Heat filled Abbie's face, and she lowered her chin to her chest. She pulled the blanket more securely around her. "I'm sorry. I guess I drifted off. I'll dress and be over at the other fire shortly."

"Doc." Jake squatted at her side and pushed a few errant strands of hair from her face. She regretted it. The curtain of hair shielded her from his gaze, and now she felt exposed. She refused to meet his eyes.

He reached out a finger and lifted her chin, forcing her to look up at him. His solemn face transformed into a delightful smile. "You didn't do anything wrong. I'm honored that you felt safe enough in my presence to sleep. Wouldn't you want the same for any of your patients?"

"Yes. But. . ."

"But nothing. I doubt you've slept at all the past few nights. You're safe with us. You're safe with me. Now, I want you to get dressed and join us at the other fire. We'll have your dinner ready. As soon as we've eaten, I want you to go to sleep. We'll take turns with the watch, but we've chosen a safe place for a reason. No one can move in on us from the water, and we can see well in advance if anyone comes the other way. Tonight you'll sleep soundly."

Abbie doubted it. She doubted she'd sleep a wink with the handsome, enigmatic man anywhere nearby.

seven

Abbie dressed quickly, not wanting to keep the men waiting, and hurried over to the other campfire. Jake stood at the outskirts of the little group, looking out toward the mountains in the east. Red, Scrappy, and Grub saw her coming and yanked their hats from their heads as they hurried to their feet. Hank remained seated, reclining on a couple of large boulders with legs crossed at the ankles. Jake moved their way and scowled at him. With a look of impudence toward his boss and a grimace at Abbie, he leisurely stood to his feet.

"Don't bother with formalities." Abbie waved them back toward their various rocks. "From everything I've seen we're far from the civility of town."

Jake stepped into the circle of firelight. "I disagree, Doc. I expect the men to continue to show respect for each lady they come across, whether they are in town or at a dusty, remote campfire. It doesn't do to let down on the manners."

"I stand corrected." Abbie walked to the boulder near Scrappy and sat primly on the edge. Whatever good mood Jake had when he left her, he'd lost on his way over here.

Grub neared the pot over the fire and began to plate up servings of fish. He seemed to favor his right hand. Abbie looked closer and noticed fiery red skin on his right appendage.

"Grub? What happened to you? Let me see your hand."

Abbie moved closer to him, and he backed away. His eyes moved from Abigail to Jake and back.

"No offense, ma'am, but I ain't lettin' no petticoat doctor do any medical tinkering with me or my hand."

Jake fisted his hands on his hips and glared. "Oh Grub, c'mon. I thought we discussed this before she headed our way. You agreed to let her take a look at the irritated skin and at least give her professional opinion."

"I didn't agree to any such thing. Did I agree to let her look at my hand?" His eyes moved over each of his friends' faces, who respectively shrugged their shoulders in response. "I ain't never had a lady doc messin' with me in the past, and I don't aim to start that nonsense now. As a matter of fact, I'm not real big on any kind of doctor messin' with me."

He reached for the spatula and moved another piece of fish on the nearest tin plate.

"Grub." Jake's jaw set in a firm line, and he glared down at his cook. "I didn't suggest you let Doc look at your hand. I ordered you to do so."

"The fish are gonna burn if'n you make me leave the fire right now."

"I'll take over." Scrappy hurried to Grub's side and pulled the utensil from the heavier man's hand. Grub looked as if he'd like to slam it into the side of Scrappy's face.

Abbie intervened before they could come to blows. "My bag's over at the other fire. Grub, why don't we head over that way, and I'll look at the hand while the men here finish cooking dinner. If we hurry, we'll be back before they can eat the first bite."

"I ain't happy about this."

"Guess what?" She lowered her voice, tucked her hand reassuringly around his arm, and leaned close. Her mouth formed into a conspiratorial smile. "I can tell."

He muttered under his breath, but allowed her to lead him

to the other camp. The fire, not having been replenished, burned a deep red. Abbie stoked it with some more brush, and it flared. She motioned Grub to sit on a nearby rock and went to collect her bag.

"This is all a lot of nonsense. I've burned my hand many times before."

Though he blustered at her ministrations, Abbie didn't miss the fact that sweat beaded upon his forehead. He was in more pain than he admitted. The night air was brisk, and he'd been away from the cook fire long enough to cool down.

She gingerly opened his fingers, and he paled.

"How'd you do this?" Abbie kept her voice low and her tonality gentle, a method she'd perfected to set her patients' minds at ease.

"I always keep a cloth close by when I'm workin', in case I need to lift a pan from the fire. Tonight I got distracted watchin'. . ." His eyes darted to her and away. "Um. . .I mean, I wasn't payin' attention, and the pan slipped. I reached out and grabbed for it without havin' time to grab my cloth." He stopped talking as she gently wiped his palm. His breath came faster. "I couldn't afford to lose our dinner to the fire."

"I see." She opened a tin of salve and began to dab it on the inflamed skin. "Though I imagine we'd all have given up a night's meal in order for your hand to be unscathed."

"Maybe you would have, but I'd have never heard the end of it from the others. Especially Hank."

She glanced up at him and smiled. "Hank gets your dander up, does he?"

He seemed to be warming up to her and smiled back. "Hank seems to get all our danders up."

"So I've noticed." She kept him talking as she wrapped the wound in clean white fabric.

Grub looked down at his hand in surprise. "You're finished already? That wasn't so bad after all."

"So my doctoring skills pass muster with you?"

"I suppose you'll do." He gazed off over the top of the fire and then back at her. "I didn't mean nothin' by my reluctance. You seem like a nice enough lady. . .but. . ."

"I know. But therein lies the problem. I'm a lady. A woman doctor. Believe it or not, I've done enough doctoring of men to understand how you all think."

Grub wrung his hat in his hands. If he twisted it any harder, he'd tear it in two. "I've offended you. That wasn't my intent, either."

Abbie raised her eyebrows and gave him a moment.

He shuffled his feet, sighed, and looked up at the starlit sky. His lips moved as he talked to himself. He looked back down at her, his large face flushing, this time in embarrassment, not pain. "What I meant to say is, you done did a fine job of fixin' my hand, and I sure do appreciate your ministrations."

She laughed and settled her hand back into his arm. "Well then, if I meet your approval, what do you say we head back over to dinner? I heard the chef is masterful with his creations."

Grub puffed out his large chest in pride and, beaming, escorted her to the other men.

Jake surveyed them both with a scowl. His disposition had soured further in the short time it had taken Grub's to sweeten. "From the look on Grub's face, I can assume everything's all right with his hand?"

"Of course everything's all right," Grub chided, interrupting. "Miss Hayes is a wonderful doctor, Jake."

Red snickered from the far side of the fire, and Jake sent him a warning look. Scrappy looked at both in confusion, but

when Abbie looked at Hank, he sent her a look of challenge.

He stood and sauntered over. "Well, Doc, if that's the case, I have this skin irritation I'd like you to look at."

Scrappy elbowed him out of the way. "I have an infected toe. It's all scaly and sore, looks right awful."

Not to be left out, Red hurried over. "And I have a cut that's not looking so good. I tore my side on a thorn a few days back, and it's festering."

Hank shouldered through the men. "Wait your turns. I got to her first."

"Well, maybe Doc would like to see who she'll treat first." Scrappy looked at her expectantly.

Abbie stood rooted in place. Earlier her apparent new nickname had been uttered with distaste. Now they stated the title almost reverently.

"How about *I* tell you what is going to happen?" Jake's frustrated tone didn't brook any arguments. "We're all gonna sit down and eat a good supper here around the fire. After we eat, if any of you have any life-threatening injuries, I'm sure Doc will be glad to look them over. In the meantime, you're all gonna step away from her and let her sit down a spell."

He took Abbie by the arm and led her none too gently to the nearest boulder. "Sit."

Abbie sat, looking up at him in surprise. He scowled at her, picked up a plate, and shoved it into her hands. "Eat."

She didn't move. The hands stood around on the far side of the fire, as if afraid to come near Jake, Abbie, or the food. She glanced back up at her rescuer. "Is it all right if my patients sit, too?"

"They aren't your patients," Jake snapped. "They're vying for your attention. I've never seen such a needy gaggle of men in my entire life."

He snatched his plate and sat beside her. Abbie didn't know what to say. He was thoroughly disgruntled, and she had no idea why.

"If they all have various ailments, it isn't a bad thing to have me look them over. Perhaps they've held back because you seem. . .well. . .rather overbearing when it comes to this topic." His hand rested on the boulder between them, and she gently placed her hand on top of his. "Jake? Did you have a bad experience with a physician sometime in your past?"

He jerked his hand free as if she'd burned him. "A bad experience? No!" He glanced over at his men and snarled, "Why are you all just standing there? Don't you have something better to do than stare at us? Eat!"

The men scrambled to oblige. All except Hank, who narrowed his eyes and folded his arms over his chest. Jake engaged in a silent stare out with him for a few moments and then dismissed him by turning his back.

"Doc, these are my ranch hands. The whole lot of them." He sighed and maneuvered himself to face her. "Since we found you, they've turned into a blathering group of idiots. It's annoying to say the least."

Abbie fought back a grin and lost. She lowered her voice. "Jake, I hate to say it, but I'm not sure these men have changed all that much since my arrival. I know I'm new to the area, but I was sort of under the impression that most cowboy types are rough and ready—mean, focused, and independent. These men don't quite seem to fit that description."

She glanced at his crew. Scrappy lifted his plate from the edge of the fire where it had been set to stay warm. He carried it by the hot end, which caused him to quickly shift it to his other hand, and he lost his piece of fish in the process. He picked it up from the ground, dusted it on his pant leg, and

placed it back on the piece of tin in his hand. Red winked at her as he sat down—missing the boulder completely in the process—and sprawled awkwardly onto the hard-packed dirt. Grub just stared at her with a silly grin on his face and waved his bandaged hand. Hank paced around the perimeter, sending venom-filled glares at Jake.

She felt like a specimen on display at one of the local museums back home.

Jake laughed quietly from beside her. "I kind of see what you mean."

Abbie settled back. "May I ask how you collected them?"

Jake chewed a bite of food and then dipped his head to look at her. His hair had pulled loose from its band during the long afternoon and now curled enticingly at his neck. Humor danced in his dark eyes as he explained how each man had come to be in his service, and Abbie felt her heart soften toward the gruff man. He might prefer to put on a brusque exterior, but deep inside he had a heart that cared about people.

"That's really sweet."

He winced. "Sweet. Just the way a rancher wants to be described."

"It isn't a bad thing, you know."

"It is if any of the hands get wind of it. I'd never get anything done around the land."

She raised an eyebrow and skimmed the men with her eyes again before looking his way. "I'm not sure it will make much of a difference either way." She giggled.

He fought a laugh, but it followed hers anyway. "Well you can't blame a fellow for trying."

"True enough."

They ate in silence for a few minutes, Abbie constantly

aware that she had a continuous audience from across the campfire. She held up her fork. "You all caught some good fish here. I've not eaten this well since I left Philadelphia."

"Aw, it weren't nothin'." Scrappy's face glowed in the firelight.

"I used my special spices," Grub inserted. "I bring 'em in 'specially for trips like this."

Red leaned around with disbelief written on his face. "You grow 'em on the ranch. They're basic herbs. Why are you tellin' her things like that?"

"I still bring 'em in 'specially for the trips. Not everyone can grow something like that."

"You're right, Grub, and I really appreciate the fine cooking." Abbie tried to diffuse the situation.

Scrappy appeared at her side. "Miss Hayes? Doc? Would you allow me to escort you back to the other site? I'm sure you're ready to retire by now."

Jake answered for her. "I'm sure she's more ready to finish her meal, Scrappy. Why don't you stop fussing over Doc and settle down to your own plate? We'll all walk over together after we finish our meal."

Abbie wondered how much longer it would be until they reached their destination. Never one to enjoy being the center of attention, she didn't like the feeling any better out here in the wilderness. "I'm sure I can find my own way over after I finish eating, but thank you for offering, Scrappy. It's very sweet of you."

"I had no doubt you'd find your way, Doc, but I was more worried about your running up against a coyote or such in the dark."

A chill passed through Abbie. "Coyote prowl out here?"

"Yes'm. They're all over the place at night. I thought you

might sleep better if you avoided a run-in with one or more."

"I'm sure I would. I'll take you up on the offer as soon as we've finished eating."

She glanced at Jake, but he'd bent his head over his plate and didn't respond further. The man was a puzzle for sure. But Abbie didn't mind. She enjoyed a good mystery and the challenge to solve it. She'd find out in time what made Jake act the way he did.

So far she knew only that he kept his distance with his men—and apparently with her—yet he was gentle and caring under that harsh exterior. He looked up and caught her studying him. Her heart sped up, her hands went clammy, and her bones turned to liquid. She pressed her hand firmly against the rock for balance. The physician in her tallied her unfamiliar symptoms as his brown eyes pierced hers with a questioning stare she didn't understand.

Abruptly, she stood on shaky legs and hurried over to Scrappy. "I believe I am ready to head back after all. I'm not feeling so well and a good night's sleep will surely put things back in order."

Scrappy offered his arm, and Abbie dared one more glance Jake's way. He hadn't moved. He leaned casually against the rock, fork relaxed in his hand, and continued to study her as she quickly hurried away.

eight

Jake stayed at the fire's side long after the others bedded down for the night. Doc Hayes was a source of constant frustration to him. Since her arrival—or should he say rescue—the men had become like toddlers vying for a mother's loving attention. Though he didn't expect much out of them—other than hard work when they were on the ranch, which they did with a passion—he didn't understand their obsession with the doctor.

He kicked at a rock with his dusty boot. Who was he kidding? He completely understood their reaction. He had the same instinct; he just kept tamping it down. The woman wasn't just smart, having her doctoring degree and all, but she was beautiful, too. When she stared at him with her guileless green eyes, she truly had no clue what she did to his insides. She didn't fawn all over the men, waiting for their adoration. She naturally brought out that reaction in them. And didn't seem to notice when she did.

Assisting with her hair had been a bad idea. Necessary because it was such a mess she'd never have been able to brush through it on her own, but a bad idea all the same. As usual he saw something that needed to be done and barged right in to handle the task. He'd helped his little sisters many a time and didn't even think of the act as an intimate one. But the moment he'd touched Abigail's silky tresses, something akin to a lightning bolt had passed through his fingers and straight into his hardened heart. The act

shattered something deep inside that had kept him frozen and away from kindness for years. The only other time he'd even briefly allowed himself to care for someone was when he'd ministered to Caleb and perhaps when he salvaged each of the men from their various predicaments.

The thought disturbed him, and he hurried to his feet and stalked off into the darkness. "She's nothing but a botheration anyway." The moon lit his path, and he walked toward the water's edge. Moonlight rippled where it reflected on the surface, mimicking the ripples Abigail Hayes sent through his body.

And the worst thing was that he didn't feel he could trust her. She'd escaped an Indian massacre. A massacre that was unusual—although not unheard of—in this area. Hank had been sure she'd left willingly with Bert from the train station, yet what purpose would she have to leave with him and then lose them all at the attack with hardly a backward glance? Granted, the massacre had affected her. She'd been pale, and the look of devastation on her face couldn't have been faked. But was the devastation over losing Bert? Or over the attack itself? Yet Hank was the one who caused his distrust.

Jake had a lot more questions than answers at this point, and first thing in the morning he intended to ask those questions and demand some answers.

"Just as I thought, nothing but trouble," he muttered.

"What's nothing but trouble?" Abigail's voice came out of nowhere and made him jump. "Maybe I can help."

"Maybe you can." Jake turned to her. She stood a few feet behind him, silhouetted by the moonlight. The glow made her look like an angel. For a moment he couldn't find his words.

She hugged her arms around herself. "I couldn't sleep."

"I'm sure this is different than anything you've ever experienced. It has to be unnerving."

Abbie laughed. "That's an understatement." She looked over her shoulder toward the fire. "Actually, it's more the men's snoring that's disturbing me. Each time I drift off I have a nightmare about being back on the train, which startles me right back awake. I didn't sleep much on the train, afraid I'd sleep through my next stop."

Jake found himself smiling at her words. "I hardly think you'd sleep through the squealing of brakes and loss of speed."

"You'd think as much. But during my medical training we'd be woken up at all hours. There weren't many nights where we'd sleep straight through. We became accustomed to sleeping when and where we could, and when we did we slept hard. Now that I've finished my training, I still experience the same problem."

The breeze tossed Abbie's hair, and the scent of lye drifted to him. He'd never thought lye a pleasant aroma—until now.

"Can I ask you a question?" Jake folded his arms and pinned her with his gaze. He hoped she wouldn't bolt. "Make that several questions."

She turned candid eyes on him. "Of course. What would you like to know?"

He searched for the right words. He didn't want to offend her or scare her off. "Can you tell me how you alone survived a brutal Indian attack when more experienced men didn't have a chance?" He closed his eyes and chastised himself. That wasn't quite the gentle approach he'd planned.

Silence greeted his question. He opened his eyes and looked at her, half expecting her to have disappeared into the darkness. Instead she stood nearby with soundless tears

coursing down her face. Tears that he'd put there as surely as if he'd captured water droplets from the lake and dropped them onto her cheeks. But genuine pain lay behind the tears.

"I'm sorry. I didn't mean to make you cry."

She shook her head, still hugging her arms around her chest. "It's not your fault. It's me. You see, I did a terrible thing."

Jake's heart sank. Just as he'd suspected. And if she'd set up an attack on the outlaws, what fate did Jake and his men have at her hands? This was a side Caleb hadn't had time to warn him about. Or more than likely, a side Caleb hadn't even known about. The band of Indians still roamed the hills nearby. They wouldn't have had time to go far. "I see. Please continue." He could hear the coldness in his own voice.

Apparently she did, too, because her eyes hardened as she continued. "Coming out on the train, we were held up by train robbers. They singled me out to go with them as a hostage—or something—and my new friend, Hattie, sank down onto her knees and prayed for my deliverance. Almost immediately help arrived in the form of Bat Masterson." She glanced at him. "Of course, at the time I didn't know who he was. I just appreciated that he was kind and he intervened and got me safely back on that train." Her voice lowered. "He was very kind and handsome, much like you."

Jake had to lean forward to hear her words. She thought him kind and handsome? Another piece of ice thawed inside his heart. But she'd just admitted it was her fault that Bert and his men were brutally murdered. Perhaps he should keep his mind on the matter at hand and not allow himself to be swayed by her charismatic charm. He realized they were only inches apart. He quickly stepped away, wishing instead that he could step closer and pull her into his arms. He cleared his throat. "Please continue."

Her voice shook. "Last night we were making plans for this morning, and Bert reminded me that today would be our wedding day. One of the men, Bill, had been injured. This morning after I woke up, I checked his injuries and realized that moment might be my only chance to get away. I quietly packed my valise and grabbed Hamm. I prayed that God would intervene and save me from my fate as Bert's wife. I had my horse, ready to lead him out of the area, but suddenly a horrible yell pierced the air. I wasn't sure what was happening." The tears turned to sobs, but she continued. "I hid behind a boulder and dropped to my knees. I remembered what Hattie had done for me, and I followed her lead. I bowed down to the ground. I prayed. I prayed God would help me."

"You said you killed Bert and his men."

"I did. I killed them as surely as if I'd done it with my own hands."

"How do you figure?"

Her voice became a whisper. "I prayed them dead."

Now, as she stated the comment in a flat tone, he recalled her earlier comment at the scene of the massacre. She'd uttered the same words then.

"You prayed them dead?"

"Yes."

He softened toward her. "Doc, you can't pray a person dead."

"But I did. The result was almost instantaneous. I prayed, and they died. As simple as that. And I alone survived."

"You were behind a boulder?"

"Yes."

"And the Indians never saw you?"

"They did."

Jake hesitated. They'd seen her and didn't kill or capture her? Perplexed, he pushed her. "Are you sure?"

"Positive. We had words."

Stupefied, he stared at her. "You had words. With a ferocious Indian."

"Yes."

Surely she was in shock. She had been at the time and now she was from the memory.

"What words did you exchange?"

"Oh, we didn't exchange words. I was the only one who spoke."

"Perhaps you should try to explain what happened word for word."

Abbie took a deep breath, and her mouth formed the words several times in silence before she actually voiced them. Again they came out in a whisper. She shivered as she relayed them. "The dust of the area seems to annoy my senses. With all the dust stirred up at the savages' arrival, I sneezed. They'd already done their damage, and I was hoping they'd go away."

Jake winced at the images in his mind. Her terror. The screams of the men. The scent of blood that would have floated around her. And her nose tickling with a sneeze that surely would mean her immediate death.

"But they didn't, and you sneezed."

"Right." She paced a few feet away and turned her back on him. "Silence greeted my sneeze. Suddenly my fear turned to blind fury. I've never been so angry in my entire life. I'm a strong, independent woman. I looked forward to this trip to see my brother. Then the train was held up, Bert stole me away from the station, he told me I'd been promised as his wife, and I spent the longest days of my life with a band of outlaws and watched as they shot at each other, each time

wondering if a stray bullet would find its way to me. I lost all my confidence. And in the end, I prayed up an Indian attack."

Jake tried to keep up with her thoughts and explanations. "What did you do after you sneezed?"

"I froze. I couldn't breathe. I heard soft footsteps on the ground, coming my way. I knew it was all over and I was about to face the same fate of the brutal killings I'd heard. It made me angry. I grabbed Hamm and jumped to my feet." Her arms gathered around an invisible Hamm as she spoke. She hissed her words through clenched teeth, as if reliving the experience too clearly in her mind. "I jumped to my feet and screamed all my rage at the Indian who approached. He fell backward and did a complete flip before returning to his feet, staring at *me* as if I were an apparition. I rushed forward and poked him in the chest with my finger. I told him about my trip out here and about everything that had gone wrong. I told him if he was going to kill me, to do it and be done. He continued to stare, along with his men. We stood that way for what seemed forever until suddenly Hamm poked his face out from the blanket."

"You'd wrapped Hamm as you would an infant?"

"I suppose so. I never really thought about it. But yes, that's how I carried him."

"What happened when Hamm poked his head out from the blanket?"

Abbie considered his words. "Hamm squealed, and a look of pure panic passed over the warrior's face. He screamed something to the others, and they retreated. I sank to my knees behind the boulder and remember falling into a deep sleep. Next thing I know, you and your men were there."

Jake felt a huge peace descend upon him. She hadn't set up

the attack, nor had she had anything to do with it. Indeed, it was quite the opposite. He still didn't understand why the attack had taken place, but perhaps it was simply a random situation that would never be fully explained. He did know one thing. With Abbie's wild blond hair and her total lack of fear as she clutched a "baby" to her chest during the warriors' arrival and then a pig's snout and squeal emerging from the wraps, the Indians must have thought her a spirit for sure. As superstitious as they were, she must have terrified them. The image had his mouth twitching with a desire to smile.

He took one look at the genuine devastation on Abbie's face and fought off the urge.

"Doc. Listen to me." He stepped close and took her by the arms. "Look at me."

As the moonlight shone down, she raised her eyes to him and pain reflected from their depths. The breeze stirred again, this time from the west, carrying the scent of the lake their way. It teased the silky strands of hair that lay beside her cheek. The dust swirled at their feet, and Abbie sneezed.

Her half laugh turned into a sob. Jake pulled her against him.

"You didn't pray them dead. You sent up a prayer for intervention, and coincidentally, the intervention came on the heels of your prayer. Their fate was already sealed. I do believe you were divinely protected. Are you a believer?"

"Not really. Though after all I've been through, I'd like to learn more."

"I can help you out with that." He pushed the hair from her face with a tender finger, more tender then he'd ever thought he could be. "But I want you to understand and know that you didn't cause their deaths. Do you understand? The circumstances are unusual, but their fate was sealed without your help." He moved away from her and paced

beside the water's edge. "Did any of the men get away?"

"Only Boggs."

The hairs raised on the back of Jake's neck. "Someone did survive?"

"I think he left during the night, long before the attack."

"So he could have been involved. He could have planned the attack. Why else would he leave that particular night?"

"It wasn't like that."

"How so?"

"I actually encouraged him to go. I knew with my pending marriage as a distraction, Boggs could get safely to his family and take them away. Bert had used them as a threat to keep Boggs at his side all this time."

Jake nodded. After what Bert had done to Caleb, he could see him doing the same to others.

"But what kind of man would leave without you? He doesn't sound like much of a man to me."

"Jake, he was a perfect gentleman. He begged me to go with him, but Bill, one of the other men, had been shot during one of their bouts of drunken shooting and I needed to care for him. Otherwise he would have died."

"He died anyway."

"Yes, but I didn't know he would at the time."

Her response solidified his trust that she was telling the truth. Otherwise, what was to keep her from escaping during the night with the other man?

They heard the snap of a branch nearby, and both looked in the direction of the sound. Jake held out a hand to stay Abbie while he checked it out. He couldn't see anything in the moonlight, but the lighting had dimmed and he couldn't guarantee what—or who—had made the sound. "Doc, I want you to return to the campfire and try to get some sleep. We'll

have a long day tomorrow, and I want you well rested."

The crackle of brush sounded again, a bit farther away. Whoever—or whatever—had been there had left. Jake couldn't tamp down the feeling that someone had listened to their conversation. He escorted Abbie back to her bedroll and stood nearby as she settled in. The others lay about, snoring as she'd said. Only Hank was unaccounted for. He'd been on watch duty and appeared promptly from the other direction. He'd had time to circle back around, but Jake couldn't be sure. Hank entered the cleared area, and firelight reflected off his face. He sent Jake a look of challenge, and Jake motioned him to rest. Jake would remain on watch for the rest of the night. He'd do everything in his power to prevent Abbie from experiencing any more fear on this journey. If someone lurked in the shadows, Jake would roust them out and deal with them without her knowing.

nine

Jake stepped quietly through the brush surrounding their site. The wind blew over the lake's surface, bringing along a chill breeze. Though the moon was bright, he didn't see any signs of an intruder. Small night animals scurried through the brush, but other than that no other sound broke the silence.

He circled around to the far side of camp and stood just outside the clearing. Everything appeared to be as he'd left it. Their gear, neatly piled near the horses, stood ready for morning's first light. One of the horses snorted and shuffled around on the hard-packed dirt. The fire burned low, emitting just enough heat to keep the area warm. On the far side, Abbie slept, her angelic features framed by her mass of hair. Her face wore an expression of peace, something he hadn't seen during her waking hours. Red coughed and shifted to his back, but Scrappy and Grub didn't budge.

Jake sat down and relaxed against a large boulder, just out of sight of the fire, and laid his rifle across his lap. He leaned his head back so he could rest but didn't let down his guard. He stayed in that position until the sky began to brighten in the east. The mountains were silhouetted as he stood to rouse the others.

Grub stretched and emitted an incoherent grumble as he slowly started over to prepare their morning meal. Scrappy rubbed at his eyes, tried to focus on Jake's face, stiffly worked his way to an upright position, and headed over to look after the horses. Red jumped to his feet, always ready to move on,

and began to sort through the things that needed repacked onto the horses.

"Hey, Doc. Time to wake up. I want to make an early start." Jake held back his smile as she groaned quietly and pushed to a sitting position. Her hair, though cleaner, looked almost as rough as it had the morning before when they'd found her. She smoothed it with her hands and surprisingly, for the most part, it pressed into place. She squinted her eyes and blinked at him. From her actions, it was clear she wasn't an early riser by nature. "We need to keep moving so we can get to the safety of the ranch."

"It's still dark. You aren't kidding about an early start." She stretched, glancing around at the others. Jake did the same.

Hank still lazed on his back, his hat pulled over his face, as the others worked to move out. Jake toed him with his boot. "Hank. Up and at 'em. We need to get moving."

Before Hank could respond, Scrappy let out a yelp of pain. One of the horses reared. Abbie was on her feet and at Scrappy's side before Jake realized anything had happened. He hurried forward as Abbie led Scrappy to a rock to sit down. Red spoke quietly to the stallion, calming him.

"You have to relax, Scrappy. I just need to take a look."

Jake bit back a grin as Scrappy batted at Abbie's hands. "Scrappy, take it like a man. Doc needs to look at your leg. Last night you were tripping over each other to get her attention."

Scrappy shook his head and ignored him. "I like you and all, Doc, but you ain't gonna be touchin' me on my leg or anywhere else."

"Don't be silly, Scrap." As she talked, she continued to roll up his pant leg, appearing oblivious to his oppositional hands.

"What does a petticoat doctor know about doctorin' men?" Scrappy succeeded in rolling the coarse fabric of his pants

down a notch. "Just because Grub fell under your charm doesn't mean I'm gonna. I ain't gonna be your guinea pig."

"Goodness gracious, Scrappy. I've doctored plenty of men during my training. I trained with all women doctors, but we had plenty of male patients. And I'm not going to do surgery out here. I just need to see what stung you. Red, could you please bring me my bag?"

"I bet it was a scorpion. Did you see it, Scrap? Those things can be deadly. First you have trouble breathing and you can swell all up. I hear it's an excruciating way to die."

"Red!"

Jake and Abbie's voices melded in unison as they both chastised Red for his untimely comment. Scrappy's face froze in a mask of fear. His blue eyes watered more than normal, and Jake had the uneasy feeling that the grown man was about to cry.

"I think my chest feels tight. Am I swelling? My pant leg feels tight." He sucked in panicked breaths of air.

"You're making yourself breathe too hard, Scrappy. Try to breathe slow and deep. You're going to be fine." Abbie glared over her shoulder at Red. "I really need my bag." She turned to her patient. "It's not a scorpion bite, okay, Scrap? You're going to be fine. Unless—" She glanced up at Jake and bit her lip, worry creasing her pretty features.

"Unless?" Scrappy's voice raised an octave. "Unless what?"

"Are you sensitive to bees?"

"Not that I know of. But I've never been stung before, either."

"Isn't it a bit early for a bee to be about?" Jake pulled his hat off and ran his fingers through his hair. Couldn't any aspect of this journey be easy? They should be pulling out, and instead they were all gathered around Scrappy, with no

food on the fire, and the horses still unpacked.

"Apparently this one doesn't know that and is an early riser." She looked across the camp. "Unlike Hank over there."

Jake looked over at his newest hand and stalked across the ground. He should let him go on the spot. But for now, the more hands they had the better. There was safety in numbers. And until they escorted Abbie safely onto the ranch, he wanted all the numbers they had.

"Hank, I told you already to get up and prepare to pull out. We need to get out of the area." He paused. "You saw what the Indians did to Bert and his gang. Do you really want the rest of us to end up that way?"

The man went pale at the thought, and he hurried to stand.

"Scrappy was stung by a bee. Doc's taking care of him. I need you to prepare the horses while Grub gets our food ready. Can you do that for me?"

Hank nodded and headed in the direction of the horses, but he kept his gaze on Abbie the entire time. Red returned to his assigned area and sorted through their gear. Jake hurried back to Scrappy's side. "How's the patient, Doc?"

"Doin' just fine, boss."

Jake laughed at her attempt at a drawl. "I'm not your boss."

"More or less you are." She grinned up at him. "Until we reach the ranch, I'm at your mercy and need to do my part. I don't mind getting my hands dirty."

"Well, you seem to be doing fine earning your keep just by using your doctoring skills. We're mighty blessed to have you along with us."

"I'm glad to hear that." Without looking up at him, she settled on her knees and dug through her bag. She pulled out a scalpel.

Scrappy slapped at her hand. "What are ya doin' with that thing? Doctor or not, you ain't cuttin' nothin'."

Red and Grub hurried over and crowded in close to watch.

"Will you relax?" Abbie's voice dropped to a soothing tone. "I only plan to use it to scrape the stinger from your leg. If we pull it out with tweezers, more venom will seep in. The more venom in your body, the sicker the sting can make you. And if you aren't sure about sensitivities to a sting, we need to be very careful. If you have a reaction to the sting, we could be in trouble. You need to tell me if you have any difficulty breathing or feel anything out of the ordinary."

"I feel pain."

Abbie laughed. "That's to be expected."

"You ain't cuttin' nothin'?"

"No." She glanced at the other men. "Don't you both have better things to do?"

Amused at her authoritative side and his men's rush to oblige her, Jake continued to watch from nearby.

Abbie scraped the stinger out, applied salve to the irritated area, and dusted her hands on her skirt as she stood. "There you go. That should do it."

"It's hurtin' somethin' awful. Are you sure you got it all? And are you sure it was a bee sting?"

Abbie placed a comforting hand on his shoulder. "I'm afraid it will hurt for the better part of the day. And yes, I'm sure it's a bee sting. Bees die after they sting, and your little fella is right over here." She pointed to a spot near Scrappy's foot.

He raised a boot and stomped on the insect.

"Oh." Abbie's hand flew to her mouth. "I guess he deserved that after the pain he inflicted on you, though he was already dead to start with." She looked over at Jake, laughter dancing in her eyes.

So the good doctor had a sense of humor.

"Well, now that the crisis has been dealt with, what do you all say we hit the trail? Grub, pull us something together that we can eat as we go. We've lost too much time."

Grub pulled out some cold biscuits and passed them around. Red and Hank had the gear stowed and their mounts ready to go.

They rode steadily through the morning and early afternoon, and several times Jake felt the same sensation that they were being watched. Though he stopped to look around, he never saw a sign of anyone trailing them.

Jake reined in Steadfast and motioned for the others to join him. "Let's head down toward Nephi, and then we'll cut from there over toward Mount Pleasant."

Hank leaned forward in the saddle. "So we're looking at a few more days on the trail?"

"More or less. We've made good time today. We'll set up camp just ahead, this time near the base of the mountains."

He pushed them until sunset. He wanted to double back around and see if he could flush out their pursuer.

"You seem worried."

Obviously Abbie's skills as a physician didn't stop at treating ailments, but she also had a knack for assessing a person's mental state with apt precision.

"You did well today, keeping up and all."

"Don't change the subject."

"I didn't." He grinned and crossed his arms as he leaned back against a large tree trunk. "I merely started one of my own. And wouldn't you say I have reason to worry? I need to get you back to the ranch. We need to get your trunk and our wagon and secure your passage through the mountains. There could possibly be a band of Indians following us, anxious to

do the same thing to us as they did to Bert and his gang."

Her face crinkled into a frown. "You think someone's chasing us."

How she could hone in on that one item from his comments, he didn't know. But she was a mite too close to the truth, and he didn't want to worry her.

"I've kept watch all day and haven't seen any physical sign to prove that we're being followed."

"That was a good attempt at a nonanswer. But still, you think someone's following us."

She was tenacious. Her raised eyebrows dared him to deny what she felt she knew. The top of her head didn't even reach his chin; yet she stood straight, waiting for him to respond.

"I'd like to double back and check to be sure."

Now her expression became troubled. "Do you think that's wise? What if the Indians have tracked us? You saw what they did to a whole group of men. Do you think they'll hesitate when it comes to one lone man?"

"I'll be careful. You don't have to worry."

"Why doesn't that make me feel any better?" She huffed out a breath and narrowed her moss-colored eyes. "I've had plenty of doctoring experience on the trail without your adding to it."

"Then I'll take one of the men with me. Would that make you feel better?"

"I suppose. But of course, that leaves only three of us here."

"You're right. Doc, I need to go alone. The more of us that go, the more noise we'll make, which in turn will jeopardize my security. There's no reason for all of us to go. Grub needs to start dinner, Scrappy needs to rest his leg, and Red needs to reorganize our gear. Hank can care for the horses."

"I can help with some of that. Just tell me what to do."

"You, Doc, need to check Grub's hand and look at Scrappy's leg, then you need to relax. Tomorrow will be another hard day of riding, and after that we'll cut through the mountains. I want you rested for that leg of the journey. It won't be easy."

She measured him with a look and turned away. "Grub? Could you use an extra hand with dinner?"

"Yes, ma'am. My hand is stinging a bit, and it's hard to work this way."

"I'll be over in a moment to see it. We'll need to change the dressing anyway."

If she noticed Jake's scowl when she turned back around, she didn't give any indication. A tiny dimple formed at the corner of her mouth as she smiled. "It looks like everything's set on our end. You'd best be on your way."

Jake needed to be on his way—away from her. Somehow the helpless, prissy woman from the train station had turned into an opinionated, independent taskmaster. In a way he wished he could stick around to watch her whip the motley crew into shape. But for now, he needed to go round up their tracker.

At the last moment he decided to go on foot so he could melt into the trees. He felt sure their pursuer advanced alone. Thoughts of the interesting woman he escorted kept interrupting his concentration. He was pleasantly surprised to see how well she'd adapted to every change that came her way. Any other woman would have turned heel and headed back to Pennsylvania after the train robbery. Instead Abbie continued to push on, no matter what trials the journey brought her way. He was mighty impressed.

The crackle of a stick up ahead brought his thoughts back to focus. He slipped farther into the woods and waited as the unsteady gait of a large man—or possibly a bear, considering all the noise being made—approached. He rested his hand on

his gun where it rested in its holster on his hip and prepared to draw. He saw a flash of color through the trees. Now he had his physical sign.

"Don't take another step." Jake stepped from the shadows and held out his gun.

The man froze and about tipped off his feet. Sweat beaded on his forehead, and his eyes were glazed with fever. Though he led a horse, he traveled on foot. He rested against the horse as he stared warily at Jake.

"Why are you trailing us?" Jake took a step closer.

"I'm trailing Miss Hayes, not you." He stopped and took several deep, pain-filled breaths. "After the Indian attack—when you showed up—I needed to know she was in good hands."

"She's in good hands." Jake narrowed his eyes and moved forward again. "How do you know Miss Hayes?"

"I met her the day she arrived at the station."

"And just happened to run into her again at the attack?"

The man shook his head. "No. I rode with Bert."

"How'd you survive the attack? No one else did, save Abbie. Miss Hayes." Jake was close enough now to see the dried blood on the man's shirt. From the volume of it, he'd bled heavily at some point.

"I left the night before."

"Boggs?"

"Yes." He heaved several breaths and glanced up at Jake. He wobbled on his feet. "How'd. . .you. . .know?"

"Miss Hayes mentioned you."

The man tipped forward, and Jake grabbed him. "Do you think you can get back up on your mount?"

"Don't know. Hurts too bad."

Jake sighed. He came out here to flush out their pursuer and instead ended up mollycoddling him.

It took every bit of strength Jake had, but he finally got Boggs up on the horse and was able to lead him back to their camp. His crew had everything set up. Abbie stirred something in the pot over the fire and glanced up at his approach.

Upon seeing Boggs, she darted over to grab her bag and met them on the near side of the fire. "Set him down here." She laid out several blankets and motioned to them.

Red and Scrappy worked as a team with Jake to lower the man to the bedroll.

"Mr. Boggs!" Abbie's gasp of surprise told Jake what he needed to know. Boggs must have befriended her, which didn't surprise him based on his ranch hands' reaction to the woman. "What on earth happened to you? I thought you'd have collected your family by now and be well out of danger's way."

"I couldn't leave you. I tried to go, but I couldn't leave you at Bert's mercy. I know. . .how he is." He gasped in obvious pain. "As I returned to our site, I ran into a warrior. He stabbed me and left me for dead. He was intent on attacking the encampment, so he didn't take time to make sure. I managed to get to camp, but I passed out again. I saw you leave with these men and have followed you since, wanting to make sure you were okay."

Jake watched the interaction with interest. Abbie could take the crustiest of men and calm them.

She shushed Boggs. "There'll be enough time for talk later. Right now I want to tend to your wound."

"Too late." Boggs waved her away.

"Let me be the one to decide that." She motioned for Red and Scrappy to roll him on his side, and she gently cut the back of his shirt. Her face crinkled with concern. "Grub, I'm going to need some hot boiled water."

"I'll collect some water." Scrappy grabbed a small bucket and hurried off to a stream they'd located in the woods. He reappeared a few minutes later, water in hand. Grub took it and put it over the fire. In the meantime Abbie laid out the items she'd need. When she got the water, she dipped a clean cloth into it and cleaned the open wound. Boggs grabbed onto the blanket and moaned.

"The angle is good." She spoke to Boggs as she worked. "You did lose a lot of blood, but I think once I sew you up you'll be fine. It's going to be tender. The outer area is a bit red, but I'll give you something to prevent infection."

She stitched him up and saturated the area with salve before wrapping it in fresh bandages. "He won't be able to travel for a couple of days."

Jake's jaw worked. "We can't afford to sit here."

"Then I'll stay put with him, and we'll join you in a few days."

"No."

"No?"

"I'm here to escort you to the ranch, not to leave you in the forest with a stranger while rogue Indians roam the area."

"Then leave one of your men with me. We'll be fine."

"You didn't seem to think I'd be fine earlier when I went to see who was following us."

"Then you do admit you knew someone was following us."

"I admitted it already! Stop talking in circles. You're not staying behind and that's that. We'll have to figure out a different solution." He ran his hands through his hair. The woman exasperated him. They couldn't afford to sit tight. It wasn't safe.

ten

Jake allowed Boggs two days to recuperate before they hit the trail again. Abbie suggested a longer wait, but even Boggs insisted he was well enough to move on and that it wouldn't be safe to wait any longer. They left at dawn and planned to stop in Nephi for supplies before the final leg of the trip to the ranch. In midafternoon they approached the outskirts of town, and the horses picked up speed.

"I think they must know they'll get a good meal at the livery at the rate they're moving forward." Abbie laughed. "And I have to admit, a solid meal at a regular table sounds mighty good to me, too."

Her enthusiasm dulled, though, as she realized the ramifications of her journey and how much easier it would have been on all of them had it started here.

Jake pulled up beside her. His brown eyes, full of concern, studied her. "Hey, Doc, why did you get so quiet all of a sudden?"

She felt her mouth contort into a wry smile. "I just realized this is where my original train destination was to end. If my trip had gone as originally planned, so many things wouldn't have happened the way they did."

"It was hardly your fault. How were you to know that Bert would plan such a ruse and lie to you as he did?"

Abbie nibbled on her lip. "Still. I walked right into his plan. You'd think I'd have thought things through better. I blindly trusted a stranger and look where it got me. I'm an educated woman. I'm supposed to use my knowledge and think things

through in a way that reflects that education."

"But Bert manipulated the situation, correct? How were you to know? You can't continue to berate yourself for things that are out of your control."

"You're right." She sighed. "And it's not like I can change any of it now. I can only use the experience to avoid such situations in the future."

They rode along in silence, the town looming bigger and bigger on the horizon. This is where Jake had planned to pick her up. And where her trunk hopefully awaited her.

"Will we have a way to transport my trunk—if it indeed made it down here—to the ranch?"

"I left a wagon at the livery. We can bring your trunk and any other supplies that we'll need with us from here."

"Good."

Jake pulled ahead, and Abbie studied him from her place behind him. He sat tall in the saddle, and his quiet strength inspired confidence within her that he'd keep her safe. Apparently his ranch hands felt the same way, based on the constant respect they showed him. Hank, who they explained had only recently joined the group, was the only one reticent with his approval, but Abbie figured that could be explained by his need to grow to trust his new boss.

She returned her attention to Jake. He wore his dark hair pulled back with a brown leather strap, where it lay against his tan neck. His white shirt, rolled up at the sleeves, contrasted nicely against the deep brown of his skin. His feet rested casually in the stirrups, and she wished she had his ease in the saddle. Though she'd become more skilled, she continually tensed her body to stay in place, which caused more aches and pains than she wanted to think about each night when they finally dismounted from their day's trek.

The two-day break, though tedious, had been a welcome relief from the horse's back. She tried to mimic Jake's casual stance and nearly fell from the saddle.

"I'm not sure I can catch you if you fall off, Doc." Boggs' quiet laugh sounded from over her left shoulder. "I'd hate to tear open the wound you so nicely sewed up for me."

"I'll keep that in mind and try not to challenge your healing." She grinned over her shoulder. The man had become her self-declared protector.

The warm spring sun felt good as it shone upon her back. The blue sky stretched endlessly before them, and she marveled at the mountains in the distance. Jake had told her that they'd pass through them on their way to Mount Pleasant. While Boggs recuperated, she'd explored their immediate vicinity with Jake or one of the hands always nearby. The trees, streams, and open area spoke quietly to her heart. She didn't know what the future held, and she'd need to discuss her options with Jake at the soonest opportunity, but for now she held onto the dream that somehow she could still stay out here and help treat the local families as a physician. Jake spoke often of his relationship with the Lord, and she tucked the tidbits away for further contemplation.

She again felt a pang of guilt over her happiness. She hadn't properly dealt with her grief over Caleb's death and didn't want to succumb to it in front of these kind men. Though they were caring, they wouldn't know what to do, so she forced the grief away. She'd been trained to hide her emotions when dealing with her patients. Some of their situations were heartbreaking, and she'd learned to put a shell around her emotions as a way to deal with the deaths of small children or men and women who met their end too soon.

Hank rode up beside her and pinned her with his glare.

She returned his gaze with raised eyebrows, and he shook his head and rode on.

Boggs leaned forward in the saddle and rested an arm on his thigh. "What did you do to that one to make him so full of animosity?"

Abbie shrugged. "I have no idea. At first he seemed semi-friendly, then he changed and hasn't said anything kind to me since. But for the life of me, I can't think of a thing I did to deserve his anger."

"Some men don't need a reason." Boggs shrugged. "Just stay away from him, okay? Something about him sets my nerves on edge."

"I completely intend to stay away from him, don't you worry."

They arrived at Nephi and left their horses at the livery. Jake checked on his wagon and asked that they have it ready for them upon their return. He and Abbie walked to the train depot and asked about her trunk. She was thrilled to find it waiting for her.

Abbie smiled up at Jake, unlocked the trunk, and ran her fingers lovingly over her medical books. Everything seemed to be accounted for.

Jake returned her smile.

"You'll send it over to the livery?" Abbie verified with the stationmaster.

"Will do, ma'am. We'll make arrangements to get it over there right away."

Jake led her down the bustling walkway and toward the restaurant. They ate alone, and she felt comfortable in his presence. Jake had a knack for making her feel relaxed.

"I'll escort you to the store and head over for the horses and wagon while you shop." Jake held the door open as they exited the eating establishment. They walked leisurely along

the boardwalk. Several carriages bounced along the dusty road beside them. He placed her hand on his arm and led her across the street to the mercantile. "Take your time. I'll round up any of the hands I find on my way over, and we'll meet you back here."

"I thought you needed supplies, too."

"I placed my order for supplies when we passed through before. I'll pick them up when I return for you."

Abbie stood inside the door for a few moments and let her eyes adjust to the dim interior. She smiled as she surveyed the well-stocked shelves. A small table covered with checkers sat near a small stove. Several chairs surrounded it. The rest of the store was packed with supplies of every kind.

"May I help you, ma'am?" A robust woman stood before her, a warm smile on her face.

"I'm sure you can, but it will take me a few minutes to figure out all I need." Abbie laughed. She felt as if she'd been away from civilization for months instead of a couple of weeks and wanted to savor the experience of walking through the narrow aisles.

The woman appraised her in return. "You've been traveling?"

"Several long days by train and a week by horse." Abbie wrinkled her nose. "It's that obvious?"

"You don't exactly look like you just stepped out of the hotel. Your dress is a bit disheveled. I'd be lying if I said otherwise."

"My trunk continued on without me, and I've just now caught up with it. I could use a few new lightweight dresses for the rest of my journey. Do you have any ready-made dresses for sale?"

"We sure do!" She gestured for Abbie to follow her. "Right over here. We have several that should fit you." She stepped

back and studied Abbie's outfit. "Perhaps you'd like something that isn't quite so austere?"

Abbie glanced down at her full, dark skirt and jacket. Her scuffed boots peeked out from below her hem. The outfit worked well in the city, but out here it did feel rather oppressive. She nodded.

The storekeeper chose several dresses, and Abbie fingered the soft material. "This would feel heavenly after the stifling heat we've endured on the ride down."

"While you were traveling by coach?"

"No, by horse."

The woman's eyebrows raised in surprise. "You rode horseback in those fancy clothes? You must have sweltered at times." She dangled the dresses in front of Abbie. "These will be much better suited for riding, and you'll love the airiness of the fabric."

"I hope so. That sounds delightful."

"Come over to this storage room, and you can try them on."

Abbie stepped into the small room as the door to the shop opened. She closed the door behind her, but could still hear the shuffle of the new shoppers' feet. As she unbuttoned her jacket, she heard Grub's voice and Scrappy's response. She smiled. By the time she was finished, they'd probably be done, too, and they could all leave to meet Jake together.

"I'm telling you, the petticoat doctor ain't what she appears to be."

Hank's words froze Abbie in place. She tried to get her fingers to move, but they wouldn't cooperate. What was he thinking saying such a thing? She realized she'd inhaled a breath and held it, and now she forced herself to release the air from her lungs.

"What're you talkin' about, Hank? You ain't liked Doc

since she joined us, but we ain't seen no reason to back up your claims."

Dear, precious Scrappy. She wanted to give him a hug.

"I heard rumor that she planned that Indian attack on Bert and his men."

Red's voice carried through the thin wooden walls as a chair scraped on the floor. "That can't be true, and I won't have you bad talking Doc. She's not here to defend herself. It ain't right. You're just jealous because her intentions seem to be toward Jake instead of you."

Abbie felt her face flame. She didn't have intentions, did she? She enjoyed Jake's company, but only because he was kind. It wasn't any different with Boggs. She appreciated their protective instincts after years of looking out for herself. Though she did have to admit she felt drawn to Jake in a way she didn't feel with Boggs. But the realization that Red and possibly the others had sensed it made her blush with embarrassment.

And here she stood holding the most beautiful pale green dress in her hands. She couldn't deny that when she first saw it she wondered what Jake's reaction would be when he saw her in it. Time was running out, and she slipped out of her skirt and blouse and slipped the light cotton garment over her head. It fit perfectly. After the heavy wool of her other garments, she felt light and carefree in this new one.

"I could care less if Jake gets all her attention, if you know what I mean." Hank's guttural laugh knocked the air out of her. She closed her eyes and again held her breath, waiting for Red's response. "But rumor had it back in Salt Lake City that our good doctor told Bert he'd be sorry, and now he and all his companions are dead. And there she waltzes out from behind a rock without so much as a scratch."

"I've seen no sign of Doc being anything but kind and caring.

Bert and his men kidnapped her. They met their demise at their own hand. It had nothing to do with Miss Hayes."

Abbie wanted to hug Grub, too. And she wished Boggs had entered the store with the others instead of waiting with the horses. He'd have set Hank straight in a moment.

Hank's voice intruded on the thought. "Fine. Think what you want. But I don't trust her, and I'd advise you all to rethink where you place your trust, too."

"I think we have." Red's voice, surprisingly strong for a man who Jake said ran from any altercation, finished the discussion.

She heard Hank stomp to his feet and slam out the door.

"Doc ain't like that," Scrappy said, sounding sad.

"No, she ain't," Grub agreed. "Don't you worry about it, Scrap."

"She's taken right good care of us," Red finished. "Hank's had something bothering him from the moment he joined us. Jake isn't happy and plans to release him as soon as we get back to the ranch."

The men's voices quieted. Abbie jumped as a knock sounded on the storeroom door. "I have a towel and some wash water for you, dear."

Abbie heard the hands get to their feet and mutter farewells to the storekeeper. The outer door opened and closed and only after silence settled over the area did Abbie open her door.

"Oh, honey, you look beautiful in this dress. It softens your rough edges."

"Rough edges, huh? I'm Abbie Hayes, by the way. If you're going to be so blunt, I guess we'd best know each other by name."

"Madeline Costner. My husband and I own the store. And I didn't mean any offense by my statement."

"None taken." Abbie surveyed herself in the blurry mirror in the room. The storekeeper was right. With her hair pulled back

so severely and the oppressive, heavy dress, she had looked hard and unapproachable. This dress softened her and made her look and feel more feminine. She turned with a smile. "I like it."

"What about the others?"

"I'll take all three. And I'll need new bonnets to match, too." As she thought back, she couldn't remember a time she hadn't worn black, brown, or tan. The pastel blue, green, and pink dresses brought her back to her childhood when she'd tagged along with Caleb and he'd tugged her matching ribbons from her braids. If the garments brought back even a touch of those carefree days, they were well worth the purchase. "Do you mind if I wear this dress now?"

"Not at all. Hand me your other outfit, and I'll wrap it for you." She raised an eyebrow as Abbie handed it over. She held it out by her fingertips. "On second thought, I'll wrap it separately from the others. It's a mite dusty."

Abbie laughed and closed the door, returning her gaze to the mirror. One by one, she pulled out her hairpins. She ran her fingers through her unruly curls and then twisted the strands back up into a softer style, allowing a few tendrils to drape casually around her face. The change in her appearance was drastic. She smiled. The men would likely walk right past her and wouldn't even know it. She snatched up the towel and scrubbed the travel dust from her face. The action made her cheeks glow with color. Her eyes appeared brighter and reflected the green of her dress.

Her first thought was to wonder what Jake would think. The thought reminded her of Hank's accusations, and her heart sank. Jake might not think anything at all. Or he might believe Hank's lies and think Abbie did indeed have something to do with Bert's death. And if she searched her heart, she knew he was right. She inadvertently did.

eleven

Jake returned to pick up Abbie and walked right past her before looking again and stepping back to stare. "Doc?"

She nodded, a blush filling her cheeks. Her eyes darted to look off into the distance beyond his shoulder. She refused to meet his gaze.

"Wow. You look. . ." He stopped short of telling her she looked beautiful. From the expression on her face, she wasn't in a mood to be fussed over. But the difference from the stodgy woman at the train station and this one that stood before him was remarkable. "Different."

"Oh. Thank you." She glanced back at him and something akin to disappointment filled her eyes.

He'd gambled with his words and lost. He'd said the wrong thing.

She quickly tried to cover her reaction and forced a smile to her face. "I'm ready when you are. Let me just get the things I bought."

"I'll get them." Jake hurried over to the counter where a brown paper-wrapped package waited. "The wagon is just out front. At least from now on you'll travel in style."

Abbie nodded, gathered her skirts in one hand, and headed out the door.

He followed, ruing his doltish response. "Doc. . ."

She turned around to look at him, her features a mask of innocence. "Yes?"

He pulled his hat from his head and stood on the boardwalk,

wondering why he hadn't just let the uncomfortable moment pass. She stared at him and nibbled on her lower lip. He should have just bustled her out to the wagon and been done with it. But she did look pretty, and it suddenly seemed important to him that she knew.

Two men passed by, jostling him as he stared awkwardly at the beautiful woman. They tipped their hats at Abbie, bidding her a good day, and she responded to them with a pleasant grin. He silently fumed. Suddenly he wanted all her attention on him. He wanted her to respond to him—and only him—with her flirtations.

"Jake?"

"What?" He didn't realize he'd been glaring at the two men as they walked down the walkway until she interrupted his musings. He sent them one last glare for good measure and returned his gaze to her. "You look beautiful." He snarled the words.

Her laugh circled the air around him. "Thank you. I think."

"You think?" He'd just uttered the hardest words he'd ever had to say in his life, and she "thought" she thanked him?

"I'm not used to having compliments snarled at me." She fussed with the delicate lace at her wrist.

She had tiny wrists. How had he missed that before? Somehow in her matronly garb she'd appeared much more sturdy and self-sufficient. Now he found himself wanting to do everything for her.

"I didn't mean to snarl. When those nefarious men so blatantly flirted with you, my compliment got all mixed up."

"Jake! They didn't flirt!" Her face turned several shades of red. "They were simply being friendly." She pinned him with her green eyes. "Honestly. The things you say. I never can get my bearings when you're around."

He grinned. She might put on her scientific front, but underneath she apparently felt just as muddled around him as he felt around her. He'd take that as a good sign.

Whoa, buddy! He stopped that line of thought in its track. There needn't be any muddling or befuddling or anything else when it came to Abbie. She was Caleb's sister. He had an obligation to get her to her brother. He didn't need any romantic interests to distract him from his mission. The last thing he needed to do was moon around because of some female.

He wiped off the grin and cleared his throat. "We'd best be on our way."

Confusion clouded her eyes, and with her expression perplexed, she nodded and headed for the wagon. Before she could even reach for the handhold, he'd swept her up and onto the seat. He registered as he let go that his hands fully circled her waist.

"Oomph." She gasped and glared at him for a moment before leaning forward to fluff her skirts. She sent him another glare and settled back onto the hard wooden surface, arms folded defiantly across her chest. "I'd appreciate it if you'd warn me next time before you manhandle me in such a way."

"Manhandle?" he stalked to the other side and climbed up beside her. "I merely lifted you to your seat as any gentleman would, including either of those two men you batted your eyes at a moment ago. Would you chastise them for doing their duty as a male?"

Abbie's eyes narrowed, and she huffed out a breath. "I didn't bat my eyes at them. They tipped their hats and greeted me, and I in turn responded. If they'd dared to touch my waist as you just did, I'd have pounded them with my reticule for taking such a liberty with me."

He smirked. "Yet you didn't pound me. Interesting." He could tell his words irritated her further. He sent her an innocent smile. He'd taken a liking to riling her up.

"Of course I didn't pound you. I—I. . ." She stopped to gather her thoughts. "You're my escort to the ranch. I can't afford to alienate you."

"Right."

She shifted on her seat and turned toward him. Her raised left eyebrow quirked and quivered. "What's that supposed to mean. 'Right'?"

"I think you might have liked the feel of my hands on your waist. *That's* why you didn't 'pound' me." He raised his eyebrow back, but held his steady—no nervous twitches there—which gave him the upper hand. "You know I made a commitment to your brother. I'm not going to abandon you on the streets, no matter how snide or biting your comments can be. And surely you know that. Therefore I have to assume that you appreciated my gallant attempt to assist you onto the bench."

"I know nothing of the sort." She faced forward and pulled her skirt closer to her legs. "But what I do know is that the men are waiting for us up ahead and from the looks on their faces, they're curious as to what has us sitting here wasting time talking."

Irritated, Jake looked over and saw the men sitting on their horses just as she said at the edge of town. Scrappy waved. Jake waved back. He gathered the reins and urged the horses forward.

Abbie glanced at the wagon bed. "Oh!"

He slowed.

"You have my trunk!"

"I do."

"Thank you."

Her charming grin dispelled his irritable feelings, but he wasn't about to let her know that. He forced out a grumpy, "You're welcome."

They joined the men. Boggs had waited with Hamm and now placed him in the wagon beside the trunk. He winked at Abbie, but Jake noticed none of the others would meet Abbie's eyes. He sent her a questioning glance and noticed that she stared at Hank with pain-filled eyes. What had Jake missed?

"Hey, um, Doc?" Scrappy's voice pulled her attention from Hank. "Can I speak to you for a moment?" He glanced at Jake. "Uh. In private?"

What on earth could Scrappy have to say that Jake, his boss, couldn't hear? It was downright disrespectful.

"Scrap. Anything you need to say to Doc can be said in front of me." They needed to remember who was in charge of this trip.

Scrappy sent Jake a sideways glance and peered anxiously up at Abbie. He lowered his voice. "Doc?"

Abbie looked around and pointed to a stand of trees up the road. "We'll meet you over there."

His face relaxed, and without a further look at Jake, his *boss*, he hurried back to his mount.

"I need my men to respect me, Doc, or nothing will be done correctly."

"We mean no disrespect, Jake, but a patient's confidence needs to be respected. If he needs me to speak to him in private, as his physician, I need to honor that. So do you."

Jake mumbled under his breath, but directed the wagon toward the trees. "Make it quick, please. We've wasted enough time in town. We need to find a place to set up camp before nightfall."

He watched as she dropped gracefully to the ground. She picked up her black bag and carried it off to meet with Scrappy. After some furtive hand movements on his part, she opened the bag and pulled out a small container. She dispensed an amount to him, and he disappeared behind the trees. Abbie slowly meandered back Jake's way, and he wanted to bellow at her to hurry. But with Scrappy behind the trees, they couldn't exactly rush off. He knew his frustration was due to the fact that Abbie had ingratiated her way into the hearts of all his men, while seeming to hold him at arm's length.

Scrappy reappeared and hurried to his mount. He led it their way and asked if he needed to assist Abbie onto the wagon. She sent him a charming smile and thanked him for the courtesy, but Jake hurried to her side and helped her into place. Jake choked back his comment and just stared at her with questioning eyes before hurrying back to his place beside her.

Abbie narrowed her eyes at him. "What?"

"What what?" Jake slapped the reins on the horses, and they moved forward.

"You look like you just swallowed a sour lemon."

"No I don't."

"How can you say you don't when you have no mirror? I'm looking at you and can see it plain as day. You, on the other hand, can't possibly see your sour face or countenance. It's ridiculous to assert that you can."

"It's my face. I can certainly assert anything about it that I want."

She snickered, the sound completely incongruent with her prissy outfit.

"Now you're laughing at me?"

"I can't help it. You sound like one of my disgruntled pediatric patients back home."

How many times could one woman insult him in a few moments' time? "Anything else?"

"No." She sat demurely upon the bench, her hands folded in her lap. "By the way, it's a chafing problem."

"A chafing problem?" He couldn't keep up with her rambling thoughts.

"Yes. Sometimes a small rash, if left untreated, can grow to cause a person a great deal of pain and irritation. That, in turn, can make a man cantankerous."

Jake was horrified by her newest topic. From time to time a man might get a small rash from being in the saddle too long, but it certainly wasn't any of her business either way. "I don't have a chafing problem. My problem is that you seem to be undermining my authority with my men."

She stared at him.

He tried to stare back, but couldn't meet her eyes with the present topic under discussion.

"My comment referred to Scrappy's medical issue. The saddle has caused a rash on the back of his thighs."

"Huh? Oh. Of course."

"He said I could tell you, since you're *the leader* and all."

"Good. Good. I appreciate that." Jake shifted in his seat.

She pointedly glanced down and back up with a guileless smile. "Are you sure you don't have an issue we need to discuss, too? I have plenty of salve."

"This topic is highly improper."

"Not really. Not for me." She sighed. "I'm sorry. My whole adult life has been centered on the hospital, my training, and my patients. I'm not used to social situations." Her eyes clouded. "I didn't mean to offend or to say anything improper."

Again he shifted. Her medical observations made him uncomfortable. Her personal observations made him more uncomfortable. Everything the woman did suddenly made him uncomfortable. And instead of just stating the fact, she'd made him nervous and now thought he had a chafing rash. Next time a pretty woman turned his head, he'd keep his thoughts to himself. And he'd stick with the innocuous word "different" instead of the all-telling word "beautiful."

"Hank!" Jake ignored her and spurred the horses on.

Abbie placed her hand upon his arm, a look of alarm passing across her features. "What do you need with Hank?"

"I'm going to switch out with him for a while and take the lead. I need to see what's up ahead."

"No, please! Anyone but Hank."

He didn't miss her panicked tone and urged the horses to slow. "What did Hank do to you?"

"Nothing."

"Doc. If something inappropriate or offensive was said or done to you by one of my hands, I need to know. And if it helps, he's already on his way out of my employment. He'll be let go as soon as this trip is over."

She stared straight ahead, and he studied her, waiting for her response. Her brow furrowed in concentration. "I overheard him at the general store."

"Overheard him say what?"

Her face contorted, though she gave a valiant attempt to keep her tears at bay. "He said I'm responsible for Bert and his gang's death. He tried to convince the other hands to turn their trust from me."

"Scrappy showed you otherwise."

"I'm not sure what you mean."

"Did the hands know you were there, in the store? Did

they know you'd overheard?"

She shook her head. "No, I was in the storeroom with the door closed."

"You think it's coincidental that Scrappy just now had a chafed area bothering him? He's not been in the saddle all afternoon. If he had a problem earlier, wouldn't he have told you about it at that time?"

He watched as Abbie turned her attention toward Scrappy, who clowned around in the saddle as always. "He sure doesn't look to be in pain."

"That was his way of showing his confidence in you."

Her face transformed with her smile. "But. . .chafing? He couldn't come up with something other than that?"

"Apparently not. But regardless, his trust is fully in you, and I can assure you Red and Grub feel the same way."

She looked up at him through lowered lashes. "And you?"

"My trust is with you, too." He chuckled. "If I ever have an issue with chafing, you'll be the first to know."

"I'm honored."

Her teasing grin told him otherwise, but he let the issue rest. "And about his other comment? We've already discussed that and put the topic to rest, haven't we?"

"To an extent."

He sighed. "To what extent?"

"I still prayed for them to leave me alone, and they died. How can you explain that?"

"Sin."

"Sin?"

"You run hard enough from God, and eventually sin will catch up with you. Bert and his gang were long overdue their day of reckoning."

"So you're saying it was coincidental?"

"Pretty much." He held the reins loosely in his left hand and watched her worry her skirt with hers. "God likes us to speak to Him through prayer, to petition Him, but He's not a magic genie ready to do our bidding."

"So when we pray, He won't always answer?"

"Oh, He'll answer. Just not always in the way we want."

"Bert's death wasn't what I wanted. I just wanted to get away from him."

"I know." He reached over and pushed a tendril of hair under her new bonnet. "And God knows."

"But if He doesn't answer our prayers specifically, why are we to petition Him? It's confusing."

Jake dug deep for words that would help her understand. He sent up a quick prayer for guidance.

"As a small child, did you ever petition your ma or pa for something?"

"Of course."

"Did they give in every time you asked?"

"No, of course they didn't."

"Why not?"

He watched as she contemplated his question. "Well, I'd always want more than my share of peppermint sticks when we'd go into town, and they'd say no because it wouldn't be in my best interest."

"Exactly. But you were allowed to ask."

"I suppose I was."

"That's how it is with God. We can pray and ask and petition, but He sees the bigger plan and knows when to say yes, when to say no, and when to say not now."

"But I asked Him to rid me of the gang, and He did say yes. So that goes back to my request causing their deaths."

"Not necessarily." Jake rubbed his forehead in frustration

and gave the matter some more thought. "Did you pray and ask, 'Smite them down in my very path, Lord'?"

She gasped. "Of course not!"

"Then you didn't cause their death. You didn't ask God to take their lives. You only asked Him to get you out of that situation. The attack could have been coincidental, and it could have been God answering your prayer, but correct me if I'm wrong, you didn't personally ask God to kill them."

Peace flowed across Abbie's features. "No, I didn't ask Him to kill them."

"And also correct me if I'm wrong, but Scrappy seems fine with your doctoring skills, even to the point of possibly concocting a false ailment—an ailment most men would rather die from than ask a petticoat doctor for assistance with. No tough cowboy likes to admit his thighs are chafed from sitting in the saddle."

She laughed. "You're correct."

"The men all stick together. If Scrappy trusts you, they all trust you."

"All except Hank."

"Hank doesn't enter into it. He hasn't fit in since day one, and I wish I'd seen it before we left."

She nodded her acceptance. It was never easy to watch a person die. Surely as a doctor she'd seen her share of death. And in her case, as a physician, it had to be even harder to watch helplessly as everyone around you died a terrible death and you couldn't do a thing to save them. Even with that, he thought she'd truly let go of her responsibility in the other men's deaths. But even as he acknowledged the fact, a dark foreboding settled into his chest.

twelve

After their Hank discussion, Jake stayed in control of the wagon and kept Abbie close to his side. She enjoyed his company, but his mood seemed to become more sober with every mile that passed. She counted her blessings that Hank kept his distance. She'd become accustomed to sleeping under the stars, and now that they had the wagon, she made a bed in the back and slept even better at night. And with her trunk in her possession, she had access to all of her personal items. Though she tucked her new dresses aside for her future home, she didn't have to wear the stuffy outfit she'd arrived in.

Abbie hadn't yet faced her emotions regarding her kidnapping at Bert's hand, the massacre, or anything else. She continued to keep her feelings carefully tucked away until she could examine them in private. The time would come—a time when the men didn't lurk everywhere nearby—when she could deal with all that the trip had brought her. She wanted to talk to Jake about Caleb, but the minute she did, she knew she'd fall apart. And she refused to fall apart in front of her new friends.

In the meantime, she determined to focus on the good in her life and to enjoy each new experience the journey brought her. In that way, everything would be perfect, if Jake would only open up to her again. The sun peeked over the horizon with the clear promise of a new day. Abbie closed her eyes and deeply inhaled the fresh air. The crisp blue sky went as

far as her eyes could see, filled with fluffy white clouds.

"You seem to be in a good mood this morning."

She opened her eyes to see Jake surveying her with a grin.

"As opposed to. . .?" She raised her eyebrows. "I try to keep my mood pleasant all the time."

He nodded. "I've noticed. And I appreciate it. The men seem to reflect your mood, and they've been much more relaxed in your company."

"All except for you." She hoped her bluntness wouldn't cause him to shut down on her again. "You've been more distant as the days have gone by. Ever since we left Nephi and I commented on Hank. I didn't mean any offense."

Jake squinted his eyes and tilted his head her way. "Why would I be offended by your comment? I asked you to share about what happened with him."

"I don't know. He works for you, and I felt that perhaps I spoke out of turn. Why else would you grow so silent?"

"I can promise my moods have nothing to do with you."

"That's not what I meant." Her hand flew to her mouth. Did he find her too outspoken? The last thing she wanted was for him to think she felt responsible for his every mood. "I didn't mean to imply. . ."

He waved her away. "It's not you. I've had this feeling. I'm trying to stay focused."

A chill ran up her arm. "What kind of feeling?"

"Nothing I can back up. It's more of a foreboding, and I don't usually pay much thought to that type of thing. I've spent time in prayer and have tried to ignore it, and the oppression hasn't gone away. It's probably nothing, but just in case it is discernment and God's giving me an advance warning, I want to be prepared."

Abbie studied his profile. "You've felt this way for days?

Why haven't you shared with me before now?"

"I didn't want to upset you. Especially if I'm wrong. You've been through enough."

"And what if you're right? Don't you think I deserve to know what we're up against?"

"That's just it; we don't know what we're up against. It's only a feeling."

"A feeling you don't often have."

He swallowed. "Yes."

"So we have to assume there's something to it." She stared into the thick trees that ringed the mountain beside them. Anyone could hide there and watch as they passed, and they'd be none the wiser. "I'm tougher than I look."

He nodded, and his mouth quirked into a grin. "I've noticed."

"Two of us can watch more carefully than one."

"That's true."

"Do the other men know?"

"Yes."

"So I'm the only one who wasn't told, which allowed me to babble on when you could have focused better without my constant chatter."

"I wouldn't say you 'babble on,' and I happen to enjoy your chatter."

He didn't look her way. Instead he looked pointedly in the other direction, but her heart did a little jig at his words. "You do?"

"Yep."

A rustle to their left had Jake's full attention. He didn't slow their pace, but Abbie could sense a subtle change as his wariness increased. "What is it?"

He didn't answer. He whistled a strange sound as if spurring on the horses. But he'd never used that whistle—at least

that Abbie had ever heard. The horses picked up speed. She reached up and held her bonnet on her head with one hand while bracing against the bench with the other. She looked ahead and noticed Scrappy and Grub sat higher in their saddles. A casual glance backward showed Hank and Red also on alert. Boggs rode alongside them to her left. Abbie shifted in her seat and watched the trees but couldn't see a thing out of place.

She didn't dare speak. Her heart pounded with fear. Unknown fear that weakened her knees with all the unanswered questions. She'd lived through one attack. She knew what the aftermath looked like. She forced her thoughts—and the shaking—to stop. She'd just told Jake to let her in on his concerns, and she wouldn't fall apart and prove that he'd been right to keep her naively blasé to what was going on.

She studied his handsome profile. Though he remained silent, his face betrayed his concern. His lips pressed down into a firm, straight line. "If I tell you to move, I don't want you to question me. Get into the bed of the wagon as quickly as you can and take up the rifle that's behind this seat."

"Okay."

"You remember how to shoot?"

"Yes." He'd insisted she practice with each of his weapons. After the events of the past week, she didn't hesitate to agree. Though she'd been a good marksman as a child, she'd not handled a gun in years. Jake's instruction quickly brought back her technique.

"Good. If we come into gunfire, you have to shoot back."

"Oh." Shooting at trees was one thing. She hadn't thought about shooting at living targets.

He risked a glance at her. "What?"

"I hadn't thought that part through."

"What part?"

"Shooting at someone."

"You didn't think our target practice was so you could shoot a tree in case of attack?"

"I didn't really think about it all that much. I just enjoyed being near. . ." Flustered, she let her voice drift off. She'd almost admitted she let him train her because she enjoyed being near him. "I enjoyed the lessons."

"The lessons were intended as preparation in case of an attack."

"I'm a physician. I took an oath to save lives, not take them."

"I understand that. But there comes a time, possibly today, when you have a choice. You can take a life or lose your own."

"That sounds selfish. Why would my life be worth more than the person who might shoot at me?"

"Because you're a good person, and you're needed. If someone evil is intent on killing you, you need to defend yourself."

She hugged her arms around her waist. "I'm not sure I can."

"Then what if someone plans to hurt Scrappy? Or Red? Or Grub? Boggs—or even Hank?"

Or you?

The thought passed through her mind, and she knew in an instant she'd do whatever it took to protect any of the men— even Hank, but especially Jake—from any evil adversary that set his sights on her new friends.

"I'll do what I have to do."

"Thatta girl." He tightened his hold on the reins. "I'm going to slow for a moment. Get over the seat as fast as you can, but be careful. We can't afford to stop and scrape you off the ground."

She narrowed her eyes and glared. Though his expression didn't change, a hint of humor resided there.

"Go!" Jake slowed slightly and grabbed Abbie's arm, keeping her steady as she moved.

Holding tightly to the back of the seat, Abbie swung her leg over the back and ducked down to do as Jake had instructed. Her heart beat a staccato rhythm against her chest as she leaned against the rough planks and lifted the rifle into her arms. She suddenly hated the cold weapon. Only a little bit hesitant, she prayed she'd not need to use it. Hamm squealed with excitement that she'd joined him and snuggled against her legs. She welcomed his warm body against hers. Scrappy had taken a liking to the piglet and had insisted on caring for him until they retrieved the wagon. She'd missed her little pet.

She held her nerves at bay by talking to the runt. "Looks like Scrappy did a good job of keeping you alive and out of Grub's cooking pot."

Hamm squealed, and she quickly covered his snout, not wanting the men to get distracted by his grunts and squeaks.

Jake spurred the horses on, and Abbie dared a peek over the sidewall. She saw movement in the trees, but only a brief glimpse. She settled with her back against the bench and rested the rifle on her skirt.

She watched as Red lifted his weapon and took aim toward the trees and shot off a warning round. Abbie jumped and closed her eyes. Several yells rang out from the trees, and Abbie dared a quick look forward as more gunfire joined in with Red's. Both Scrappy and Grub shot toward the trees. Silence filled the air as the wagon bounced along the hard path.

"Stay low for a few more minutes."

"I'm not in any hurry."

She heard Jake's quiet chuckle. "Good."

Red pulled alongside the wagon on the left while Hank did the same on the right.

"I think we scared them off. That'll gain us some time."

"Thanks, Red." Jake didn't change his pace. "You okay back there, Doc?"

"I'm dandy; thanks for asking." Her backside wouldn't agree, but hopefully she'd be back in her seat beside Jake before long—if her legs would still cooperate after all the bouncing around.

Hank looked away, but she thought she saw the first hint of a genuine grin on his face as he turned. He didn't look half bad when he smiled.

After another thirty minutes with no further sightings, Jake pulled the horses to a stop. Boggs, Grub, and Scrappy circled around to join them as Jake spoke.

"I think we're clear for now, but I don't want to take any chances. It's obvious where we're headed."

"Could you tell who it was?" Scrappy kept a white-knuckled grip on his reins.

"I didn't get a clear view, but I'm guessing it was the same Indians who attacked Bert and his gang."

"Why would they be after us?"

Jake shook his head. "I wish I knew. With the majority of tribes on the reservations down south, I'd have to guess this band contains some of the disgruntled few who are holding out."

Abbie stood on shaky legs and got her footing. She stepped over the side of the wagon and placed her foot on the sideboard before allowing Jake to assist her back onto the seat beside him. "But why would they attack us? Why Bert and his men?"

"I guess because they're angry and we're all easy targets. Other than that, I don't know. Why did Bert and his men

do the things they did? As the Bible says, we live in a fallen world."

"You look upset, Doc." Grub shouldered his way past Hank and surveyed her with worried eyes.

"Things like this don't exactly happen in Pennsylvania."

"Yeah." Jake also looked her way. "I guess they don't."

"So what's next?" Red still looked nervous, though he'd rested his rifle on his lap.

"We continue on and put some distance between us." Jake's expression didn't show his anxiety, but Abbie's trained eyes didn't miss the nervous jiggle as he held the reins. "But I don't want to move into an ambush."

"Could we take an alternate route?" Abbie searched the road ahead but couldn't tell anything about the terrain up ahead or the passes through the mountains.

"Not any that would be convenient. They'd all take us days out of our way." The jiggle moved to his leg. "There's a pass we all used to use, but it's fallen apart and no one can get through anymore."

Abbie thought back to one of the articles she read coming out on the train. "I think I may have an idea."

thirteen

Jake, Grub, Red, Scrappy, Boggs, and Hank stared at her expectantly. She hesitated. What if the plan didn't work? She'd spoken without thinking, a tendency that often got her into trouble back East.

She felt a flush creep up her face. "I read an article on the train coming out. There was a group of settlers a few years back that came upon a seemingly impenetrable cliff. They ended up blasting their way through."

"Blasting their way?" Scrappy scratched his head. "You mean they blew it up?"

"They were at the top of the cliff. It was steep. They had to blast it down to different levels so they could lower their wagons down the side."

"Doc?"

"Yes, Hank?"

"I don't know if you noticed, but we don't exactly have any cliffs around here. We're actually at the bottom of the hills."

Abbie pinned Hank with her gaze. For a few moments there, she'd thought he was softening toward her. "I'm well aware of the fact that we don't have cliffs, Hank, but thanks for clarifying." She didn't know what she'd done to rub the man wrong, but she'd had enough of his snide remarks. As if speaking to a child, she enunciated her next words for Hank's benefit. "My point is, maybe we can find a pass, an older one that isn't often used, and as this gang chases us through, we could blow the opening behind us."

130

"Doc, that's a good idea." Abbie saw both admiration and amusement in Jake's eyes. "I think I know of a perfect spot not too far away."

Grub stared into the hills. "I think I know the place you're thinking of. Will the wagon make the trail?"

"It'll be tight, but I believe it will. I don't think we have another choice."

"Sure we do." Hank glared at Abbie. "We could always stay on the well-traveled path and hope whoever is behind us changes direction."

"And if they don't?" Jake's eyes targeted Hank. "What then? We sit and let them attack us like they did Bert and his gang? I'm sure you're aware we picked up a case of dynamite in Nephi to use at the ranch. One wayward shot and we'll be blown sky high. I don't intend to sit around and let that happen."

Hank winced. "There's no guarantee they're still after us."

"You saw the aftermath—from *afar*. We laid the men to rest. We saw each and every wound."

Abbie watched with interest. Apparently his patience with Hank had run out about the same time as Abbie's.

"I saw all that I needed to see," Hank retorted.

"Boss, I don't want to see that again. I vote we go with Doc's idea." Scrappy pushed his scraggly hair from his face and nodded at Abbie.

"I second the idea." Grub glared at Hank.

Red didn't speak, but stepped closer to Abbie's side and squinted his eyes at Hank with an unspoken challenge. Boggs joined him.

"Looks like you're outvoted, Hank." Jake leaned down to pluck a long piece of grass and put it between his teeth as he surveyed the trail ahead of them. "We'll continue as we're going. The pass isn't far ahead. We won't reach it tonight, but

can camp just below. First thing in the morning, we'll make our way up the mountain and put our plan into action."

This was the only part of the plan Abbie didn't like. "What if we're attacked as we sleep?"

"We'll keep watch. The location I have in mind has good visibility in all directions. There's no way the Indians got ahead of us, so we'll only have the lower area to watch. If we can't see them on this overcast night, they shouldn't be able to see us. There's a clearing they'll have to cross to get to us. We'll camp just on the other side of it."

Abbie felt the air whoosh out of her mouth. "That sounds fine." She couldn't stand a repeat of the other attack. Especially when she hadn't cared for the other men at all, and even with Hank's sour disposition, she cared about each of these men.

Jake raised the reins in preparation to move out.

Scrappy pulled his battered hat from his head and worried it with his hand. He sent Abbie an apologetic look before returning his gaze to Jake. "Um, boss? One thing."

"Sure, Scrap. What is it?" Jake stilled his hands.

Again Scrappy looked over at Abbie.

"Go ahead." Her forehead creased as she wondered what he didn't want to say in front of her.

"The canyon we're entering. Isn't it where the massacre happened?"

"That was a long time ago."

Jake's eyes also slid over to Abbie. He didn't elaborate.

She placed a hand on his forearm. "What happened? I need to know."

"I was only a boy. A small group of unarmed immigrants cut through the canyon, Salt Creek Canyon, and they were attacked by Indians. Only one man escaped and made it to Ephraim alive."

She swallowed. "Oh."

"They used a tomahawk on the lady of the group."

Why Scrappy felt led to share that little tidbit of information, Abbie didn't know. But she'd have been fine without it. His words brought back more memories of the attack on Bert's gang. Her breathing hitched, and Jake turned his eagle eyes her way. She quickly concealed her emotions.

"Then I'd best be extra cautious."

Jake nodded approvingly at her and urged the horses on, not allowing time for any of the others to comment. About an hour into the journey, they began to slowly make their way up the steep side of a mountain. Small groupings of trees hid their progress. Even Abbie's untrained eyes could tell the trail had seen better days.

"It's not used much, is it?"

"No, not any more. There's a quicker way to Mount Pleasant now."

She sat in silence and worried her lip.

"What is it?"

"I'm just wondering. . ." She looked over at him. "Maybe you should have listened to Hank and taken that more traveled route. Surely we would have seen others. And there's safety in numbers."

"The other path isn't exactly well-populated."

"The story you told. . .did they ever capture the Indians responsible?"

"I don't recall." His dark eyes stared into the trees beside them.

"Then maybe. . ."

"If you're thinking what I think you're thinking, you're wrong. Those Indians are long gone. This attack might have been modeled after the original. But whoever these men are,

I think they're a renegade group."

"How can you be so sure?"

"It doesn't happen that way anymore. And my instincts tell me otherwise."

"Your instincts are never wrong?"

"Never." He glanced at her with a wry grin. Her heart sped up at his nearness. The setting sun glistened off his black hair, and she could see her reflection as his brown eyes looked into hers. He was extremely handsome. "At least, not yet."

She quirked an eyebrow in response, and he laughed. His levity broke her tongue-tied mood.

"Let's hope that instinct doesn't let us down now, hmm?"

❧

They reached their destination at dusk. A small stand of trees sheltered them, and with practiced ease, they set up the most basic of camps. After a dinner of cold biscuits and dried beef, everyone but Abbie settled onto the ground. She slept in the wagon, and Jake sat protectively upon the seat, his rifle posed on his lap.

"I won't sleep a wink with you so close." Her voice, while quiet, sounded loud to her own ears.

His soft laugh drifted her way. "Are you that intrigued by me then?"

She huffed. "I'm not intrigued at all. I'm simply not used to sleeping with a rifle pointed over my head."

A moonbeam drifted through the trees and shone down on him as he stared at her. "Not even a little bit intrigued?"

He sounded disappointed.

"Maybe a little." She smiled in the dark, glad he couldn't see her expression as well as she could see his.

A grin tipped up the corners of his mouth. "Good."

She waited, but no other comment was forthcoming. Though she had no intention of sleeping, the security of his presence relaxed her enough to do just that.

ॐ

The next morning they woke at dawn. Red and Jake went ahead to survey their trail. Abbie gathered their supplies while the men loaded the bedrolls onto their mounts.

"Wouldn't it be easier to put your things in the back of the wagon? Then you wouldn't have to secure them each time we break camp."

Boggs smiled. "A cowboy needs to be ready at all times. If we had our supplies in the wagon and something happened to separate us, we'd be up a creek."

"Oh, I hadn't thought of that." Another lesson learned for the city girl.

They were ready by the time their scouts came back.

Jake secured Steadfast to the front of the wagon and climbed up beside Abbie. They took the lead and the others fell in behind.

"How'd you sleep, Doc?"

"Just fine." She kept her gaze forward, embarrassed by their late-night conversation.

She could feel his stare.

"Did anyone ever tell you that you snore?"

She gasped and turned to face him. "I do not!"

Though his eyes were tired, a teasing smile lit up his face. "You most certainly do."

He looked very much like the dangerously handsome man she remembered from the train station. Though he tossed out playful banter, she saw that his wary eyes never ceased to search the area around them.

"You're trying to distract me with your teasing."

"What teasing? I'm merely stating a fact."

"I don't snore."

He raised an eyebrow her way. "You can hear yourself sleep?"

"I'd know."

"How?"

"My roommates would have told me."

"Would they now?" The eyebrow went higher.

He grinned, and she held back a sigh of contentment. How wonderful it would be to have such a good-natured man by her side for life. The thought caught her off guard. Never before had she given thought to a future with a husband. Her choice in becoming a doctor limited her prospects. Most men she'd met didn't like the idea much of a wife with more book knowledge then they had. Though she knew her education would most likely prohibit her chances of marriage, she hadn't realized until now just how severely her life would be affected. She'd never before met a man like Jake.

After she finished medical school, she'd suddenly realized how restricted her options were. Though she could continue with her work at the hospital, without her training schedule she'd suddenly felt adrift and very lonely. The offer from Caleb came just in time to give her direction. But what would she do now? She didn't belong on the ranch without her brother.

"Hey, Doc, why the sudden scowl?" Jake's words went from teasing to gentle.

She hadn't realized her thoughts were so clearly written on her face. Horrified, she felt the tears she'd held back form behind her eyes. She whipped her head around to face the empty landscape. The dry ground in this part of their journey matched the dryness in her heart.

"Doc?" Jake didn't slow their pace, but his soothing manner cajoled her to look his way. "You're crying! I didn't mean. . ."

She waved his words away. "It's nothing you did."

How could she explain? No way would she admit to him that she'd looked at him and saw a future that wouldn't be hers.

"As soon as I see to my brother's affairs, I'll head back to Pennsylvania. All this will have been for nothing."

"See to your brother's. . ." He stared at her, perplexed. "He didn't bring you all the way out here just to watch you leave again."

"Watch me leave?" Now she felt confused. "But Bert said he was. . ."

"Dead? No way." The smile returned. "Your brother is alive and well and anxiously awaiting your arrival."

A wave of emotion passed through Abbie. Laughter won out. "He's alive?" She stared at her companion in wonder. "All this time. . .I thought. . ." Again she laughed.

"I'm sorry, Doc. I had no idea."

"You never spoke of him."

"Neither did you."

"I couldn't. I knew I'd break down if I tried." She stared hard at him. "You mean it? He's all right?"

"He will be by the time we return. He did have a run-in with Bert. He had a hard time of it, but he pulled through. He's doing better, but wasn't up to the trip to meet you. I just assumed you knew."

"No. But I'm so glad to hear you say it now."

"Better late than never."

"Yes." She couldn't stop smiling. "I have a home."

Jake scowled. "Of course you do. Even if something had happened to Caleb, I'd have made sure you had a place to live."

"I wouldn't have expected you to."

"Caleb would have."

She wondered if Caleb was the only reason. Would he have

done it of his own accord? She shook away the silly question. Without Caleb, he wouldn't have known about her.

After a few moments of silence, Jake spoke again. "All this time, since the station, you thought you had no home?"

"Yes."

"Yet you never brought it up."

"What good would it have done?"

"I could have put your mind at ease."

"I didn't know that at the time."

His forehead creased as he watched her.

"What?"

"You're not used to leaning on others, are you?"

She shrugged. "I've not had much experience with that."

"Why didn't you come to Caleb immediately? After you lost your parents?"

"I tried." Wistfully, she wondered how her life might have been different if she had. "I didn't know where he was. He left when I was fourteen." She contemplated the thought. "I was busy with my training, and it took me a long time to track him down. But I wouldn't trade the way things turned out. I enjoy doctoring."

"I can tell." He surveyed their surroundings and relaxed slightly in the seat. He propped a worn boot in front of him on the wagon's frame and rested his right wrist on his leg. "May I ask you something?"

Intrigued, she smiled. What could he possibly want to know? How her training had come about? How she'd fared in her classes? "Sure. Ask anything."

"Why didn't you ever marry? If you had, you'd surely have several children by now."

Anything but *that*!

"My question offended you."

She fanned her warm face. "No. But it certainly caught me off guard. I thought you'd meant to ask me about my work."

He laughed. "So family never entered into your thoughts?"

She shrugged. "Perhaps at some point, but then. . ." She let her voice drift off. What could she say? That no one ever cared enough to ask? More accurately, she chased off each suitor before they had a chance to ask. The right man hadn't come along. Only after accepting that his daughter faced a future as an old maid had her father reluctantly agreed to let her pursue her studies.

"Then. . .what?"

"It just never happened."

"Good."

Again she whipped her head in his direction. "Good?" Her heart picked up in tempo. Did he feel a connection with her, as she did him?

"You would have missed this whole adventure."

"Oh." Her voice faltered. So he didn't feel it. She cleared her throat and continued. "Of course. To miss the adventure. . . that would never do."

She forced a smile.

His countenance changed, and his lips parted. Lips that commanded her attention. He seemed to be on the verge of saying something important when Hank's sarcastic call broke into their conversation.

"Hey, boss. Maybe you ought to ride over here and take a gander at this view."

Hank and Red had moved ahead during their discussion and now waited at the top of a rise.

"We'll talk more later." Jake spurred the horses on, and they pulled up alongside the men. Boggs, Scrappy, and Grub joined them.

Abbie bit back a groan as she surveyed the scene. Barren cliffs blocked their path, and the small opening they needed to pass through was filled with huge boulders. If their pursuers were indeed on their tail, they'd be trapped.

Hank swung off his horse and dropped to his feet. "This is what we get for listening to your precious Doc."

"That's enough, Hank." Jake jumped down to join him. "We've all had enough of your complaints and whining, and I won't stand here and listen while you verbally attack Doc."

"He has a point." In this situation, Abbie had to agree with the caustic man. Guilt threatened to drown her. She couldn't bear to be responsible for the massacre of the men she'd grown to love. She cared about each and every one of them—even Hank with all his abrasive ways.

"We said we'd likely have to blast our way through before closing it back off. What did you expect to see?" He paced a few steps nearer Hank. "But your attack on Doc won't help anything. I've had enough of that."

"And I've had enough of you mooning over the doctor while making poor decisions that affect the rest of us."

Before anyone could stop him, Jake reared his arm back and punched the man. Hank stumbled backward and landed on his backside. Red and Grub jumped forward to stop him as he bolted to his feet. He struggled, but they held tight.

"You'll be sorry you did that."

"Really?" Jake fisted his hands at his side and moved close to the man. "The way I hear it, you accused Abbie of saying those same words just before the attack on Bert and his gang."

"I don't know what you're talking about."

"Yeah. I think you do. I heard that's what you told the other hands back at the general store in Nephi."

Hank glared at the other hands. They each shrugged.

"It wasn't them, Hank. It was me." Abbie hopped down from the wagon and joined the men. "I was there." She forced the quiver of anger from her voice. "Every man at that camp died. I had nothing to do with their deaths."

Hank winced.

Boggs walked up beside her. "Abbie didn't do a thing to hurt any of them men in the gang. She even saved one man's life. I won't hear talk about her like this again."

Abbie redirected their attention to the matter at hand. "So we blast our way through the opening. The settlers I mentioned needed to work their way down the cliffs. We just need to go through."

The men followed her lead and moved forward as one.

"I think it will work, Doc." Jake climbed a few boulders, testing them for stability. They didn't budge. He climbed higher and peered over the top. "They're stacked on top of each other, but aren't very wide." He worked his way back down and jumped to the ground beside them. With hands on hips, he backed away and looked at the mound from several angles. He sent Abbie a grin. "It'll work."

The men moved into action. Boggs moved the horses a safe distance away as Jake led the wagon and Abbie over to Boggs' side. Scrappy pulled some burlap bags from a crate in the wagon's bed and cautiously carried them to the pile of rocks. Hank refused to help and surveyed the action from afar, his feathers still ruffled.

As they surveyed their handiwork, Abbie noticed the approach of someone from down below.

fourteen

The tuft of dust grew larger as their pursuers came closer. Abbie's heart pounded. From this vantage point, she could identify them as Bert's killers.

"Hurry! They're coming!" She yelled the words, but the men didn't pay her any attention. They were too focused on setting the charges in place. Jake's hair brushed against his collar, and he tucked it haphazardly behind his ear. He held a wick in his lips for a moment, his face a study of concentration, while he carefully worked with a stick of dynamite. He pulled the wick free and pressed it into the paper-wrapped stick. He set it aside and repeated the process.

Abbie glanced over her shoulder and saw that their pursuers were moving steadily closer. They weren't going to have time to blast the rocks out of the way and get through the opening before facing the impending attack.

Boggs prepared the animals and held them securely at his side. When the blast came, it would be up to him to keep them from bolting. Scrappy and Grub assisted Jake with the dynamite, placing it securely as directed. Red had cautiously climbed over the wall of rocks and disappeared from sight, presumably planting a few sticks on the far side. If all went well, the blast would completely clear their path. Abbie didn't want to think about what would happen if their path remained impassable.

Hank worked at the farthest edge, securing the explosive into a crack between the cliff wall and rocks. He'd have the

hardest time getting back and through the opening safely. Abbie had been told to remain with the wagon, but she grabbed hold of her skirts and ran forward to snatch a stick of dynamite from the pile Jake had set behind him. She chose the one with the longest fuse.

She knew enough about the explosive to be cautious. She held it gently in the palm of her hand and reached for a match. Jake and the others were busy unwinding long lengths of wick so one fuse could be lit to blow the entire area.

Abbie might have been invisible for all the notice they gave her. With shaking hands, she struck the match. It lit and went out just as quickly. She hurried back over to get a few more. She laid them carefully beside her on the wagon's tailgate. Again she carefully struck one and this time shielded it from the slight breeze. The flame caught and grew tall. Stepping away from the wagon, she held it under the fuse, whispering a prayer for their safety and for success.

Sparks flew from the wick, and it disappeared far more quickly then she'd expected. She stepped backward, swung her arm back, and hauled her arm forward with all her might. Covering her eyes, she peeked through her fingers to watch as it hurled end over end and arced down the mountainside. Midair, just before it reached the other men, it blew. She watched as their horses reared, spewing the riders in all directions before hoofing it back down the trail. The men scrambled to their feet and took off in pursuit.

Only then did Abigail think to look over at the men she rode with. They all stood with mouths agape, their skin void of all color, staring at her in horror. Jake got his bearings first and stalked up to her.

"Wh–wh–," he sputtered, the word not fully releasing from his angry lips. "*What* do you think you're doing?"

She pointed downhill and saw his eyes register the scene below.

"That's them?" His brown eyes pierced hers. "Why didn't you say something?"

"I did! I yelled. I walked right behind you, and you were so focused on what you were doing that you didn't hear."

Jake didn't respond. He finished his assessment, hurried over to pick up the fuse, and continued to unroll it. "Let's go! We don't have much time before they catch their mounts and regroup."

Red had climbed to the top of the pile at the sound of the explosion, but now dropped back out of sight. Scrappy headed over to help Boggs with the animals while Grub took Abigail by the arm and led her back to the wagon. "Get down below the bed. After the percussion dies out and you're sure no rubble will come your way, head for the seat and be ready to go."

He handed Hamm to her, and she wrapped him securely so he wouldn't escape. He lay shivering in her arms from the first explosion as it was. She slid under the wagon as Grub had instructed and crooned quietly to the pig.

"Grub?"

He ducked his head and peered at her. "What?"

"What if the horses startle?"

He grinned. "They didn't a minute ago when you tried to blow apart the mountain."

She rolled her eyes. "I didn't try to blow the mountain. I only meant to detain them and buy you some time."

"Which you did."

"But the horses? This explosion will be much closer."

"I think they'll be fine. Watch carefully and roll fast if they startle." He saluted her and hurried off to join Jake. They discussed the plan and resumed their positions.

Abbie held her breath as Jake lit the fuse. He ran her way and dove down beside her. As the explosion rocked the hillside above them, he held her close and placed his upper body protectively over hers. She sneezed as the air filled with dust and smoke. He pulled her face against his shirt, which, since he'd rolled in the dust to get under the wagon, didn't help much.

But she relished the stability and closeness of his warm chest. She felt safer at that moment than she had in a long, long time. She clutched his shirt and took comfort in the rhythmic beat of his heart.

Unfortunately, the moment passed much too quickly.

"Let's go!" Jake rolled back out, secured Abbie in his firm grip, and dragged her along with him. She scrambled to her feet, and he assisted her—and Hamm—onto the wagon. Scrappy, Boggs, and Grub already moved through the newly opened pass. Red appeared safely on the other side, laying the last few sticks of dynamite in the hopes that they could reclose the opening before the other men arrived.

"Hurry, they're coming!" Abbie watched behind them as their pursuers resumed their trek up the hilly mountain. Their fast pace didn't bode well. She'd bought her group some time, but she'd raised their enemies' ire in the process.

Hank rounded the edge of the remaining boulders, assisting Red with the extra sticks. "Hank, c'mon!" Jake jumped onto the wagon and urged the horses through.

Abbie couldn't help herself. She scooted over to his side and clutched a piece of his sleeve in her hand. Jake didn't seem to mind. She felt his muscles bunch as he adjusted the reins and guided their mounts forward. After they were a safe distance from the explosives, he slowed and handed the reins down to Grub.

Hank's voice followed them. "Light the fuse. I'll be right behind you. I want to make sure everything is set."

Concerned, Abbie touched Jake's arm. "You can't light it until he's through."

"We can't afford to wait. He'll be fine." Jake slipped to the ground, leaving Grub to assist her.

"Jake, it's *dynamite*," she called. "You can't be sure. We can't take the chance."

"He'll be fine, Doc. We talked over the plan, and he'll be right behind us. Red scouted the area and told Hank exactly where to go as soon as he passes through. The repercussion shouldn't affect him at all."

Abbie had learned a lot during the past few weeks. And the main thing she learned was that she wanted Jake's—and Hattie's—strong confidence in their future. If this plan didn't work, one way or the other Abbie and the men would likely meet their Maker. She intended to meet Him as one of His chosen children.

God, the other times I've talked to You, the results haven't been exactly what I wanted. She hesitated, not wanting to hurt His feelings. *I mean, I appreciate all the help You've given me, but I didn't mean for Bert and his gang to be killed. I'm just learning the ropes of how prayer works, and, as I'm sure You know, how You work. I understand now that I didn't "pray" the others dead, but if possible, I'd like a nicer ending from now on.*

"Move it, move it, they're gaining on us!" Scrappy's panicked voiced interrupted her prayer.

She glanced up, willing Hank to rush through. He didn't appear.

I want to make things right with You. I need to make things right with You. Jake's been explaining how a relationship with You works, and I want that. I want to know You're guiding my choices

and watching over me in all situations. And especially in this one.

"Abbie, get under the wagon, *now!*" Jake knelt beside the fuse and watched the opening for Hank.

Abbie bent down so she and Hamm could return to their safe haven.

I give You control of my life. I believe, Lord. I've watched Jake's quiet faith, and I want to experience that for myself. I hear Caleb has become one of Your followers, too. I want to see my brother again soon, but if I can't, I want to be sure I'll see him in heaven. Please watch over him for me in the meantime if something goes wrong in the next few moments.

"Hank, where are you?" Jake sat posed with one knee on the ground and with the wick and a match in hand. He'd be ready to run as soon as he lit the match. The fuse would sizzle its way to the explosives, and if all went well, they'd be safely on the far side of the cliffs from their enemies.

Hank's voice carried from between the cliffs. "I'm coming. Jake, light the fuse!"

Lord, get Hank safely through this. Please make him hurry. I want him to have a chance with You. I haven't been very nice to him. I don't want that on my conscience. If You'll give him another chance, so will I.

Though she still felt anxious about their present situation, she also felt a cloud of peace descend. No matter what, she'd be all right. At worst, she'd be in her Creator's presence. And at best, she'd have a chance to meet her brother and see what the future brought with Jake. Her hand nervously thrummed against the hard-packed dirt.

Even under the circumstances, Abbie felt her face crease into a smile. She'd done it. She'd turned her life over and was now a follower of Christ. No matter what happened, she'd be okay.

Jake lit the fuse. Abbie held her breath. Hank moved into sight, but stumbled as something from behind rocked his body, knocking him off his feet. A flow of blood ran down the front of his arm as he fell. It was obvious that Hank wouldn't make it through the pass before the explosion. Abbie scrambled out from under the wagon. Time slowed. She screamed as she rushed forward. This had been her idea. She wouldn't be responsible for another man's death and live to tell about it. It was one thing for her to meet her Maker on this day, but quite another for Hank to meet his. She wasn't sure he was ready. And she wasn't ready to see him die before she'd had a chance to share her newfound joy in her Savior. Hank had to live.

Abbie tripped and fell. Jake pulled out his pistol and shot at the wick. He missed. Hank pulled himself frantically along the ground. Jake shot again. This time the wick stopped glowing. Abbie gathered her skirts and headed his way. Jake tackled her and held her down.

"Stay back. It could still blow. I'll get him."

Abbie pushed to her knees and watched Jake move cautiously forward. Another gunshot rang out from the other side of the opening. A bullet whistled over her head.

"Doc, stay down!" Jake hit the ground. He continued to inch forward on his stomach, nearing the injured man. Boggs now stood beside her and covered the men with his rifle, shooting over Jake's head through the opening in the cliffs. She heard a scream of pain from the far side.

Jake had reached Hank's side. Just as Abbie breathed a sigh of relief, she heard a rumble from overhead. The percussion of gunshots along with the earlier blast created an avalanche that effectively blocked the pass but now tumbled down onto Hank's helpless form. Jake was trapped beside him.

fifteen

"Jake!" Abigail tried to rush forward, but Boggs held her back.

Scrappy and Grub hurried over to Jake while Red dropped down on his knees beside Hank.

"Jake." A sob tore at her throat. She had to help him. She tried to shake out of Boggs' grip.

Hank lay motionless nearby, held captive by the pile of rock.

"I need to get to them."

"Now, Doc, you need to settle down. We'll stay over here where it's safe. It won't do us any good for you to get injured. Grub and Scrappy will bring them to you."

He had a point. They hurried to the wagon, and she jumped up onto the wagon's bed where she'd stashed her black bag. Boggs tugged her trunk out of the way and lowered it to the ground. Hamm squealed at all the noise.

"I'm off to help Red." Boggs hurried away.

When she had her supplies ready, she glanced up to check on the men's progress. Jake, supported by Scrappy, walked her way. He was alive and well. She closed her eyes with relief and thanked God for his safety. Grub joined Red and Boggs, and all three worked to dig Hank out. She saw Hank's foot move. He, too, had survived. She prayed his injuries were as minor as Jake's appeared to be. She couldn't do anything with Hank until they freed him, so she turned her attention to Jake.

"You scared me." She skewered the man with a glare.

He grinned. "I sort of scared myself there for a few minutes."

"Well get on up here and let me look you over."

"I'm fine, Doc. I need to go help with Hank."

She narrowed her eyes at Scrappy. "Don't let him move an inch until I've given my approval."

"Yes'm." His eyes widened, and he shifted nervously back and forth on his feet. "Um, boss. . ."

Jake sighed. "It's fine, Scrap. You head on over and help the others while Doc fusses over me."

Scrappy didn't wait to be told twice.

"I'm not fussing."

Jake hopped up to sit on the tailgate of the wagon. "What do you call it then?"

"An examination."

Dirt smudged across his forehead, and his face had several small scrapes and bruises. His shirt was torn, but otherwise he looked intact.

"How do you feel?"

"Like I came out on the bad side of a wall of rocks."

She poured astringent on a clean cloth and began to clean his wounds.

"Ouch!" He tried to pull away, and she gently tugged him back.

"Do you hurt anywhere?"

He snorted. "I hurt everywhere."

She tossed the cloth aside and placed her hands on her hips. "You're not going to make this easy. Do you want me to do a full examination?"

His gaze became wary. "What's that supposed to mean?"

"A full examination." She enunciated each word carefully. "I'll check every part of your body. Twice if need be."

"Whoa." He jumped to his feet and waved a hand in the air. The effect would have been more successful if he hadn't wobbled and grabbed the wagon for balance. "I'm fine, Doc. Nothing's broken. I have no gaping wounds for you to sew up. Sorry to disappoint."

"I hardly *want* you to be hurt." She grasped his chin and looked into his eyes and felt a jolt travel up her arm. She tried to ignore it. He was her patient after all. "Look into my eyes."

"My pleasure." His mouth formed into a foolish grin as he squinted his dark eyes and peered into hers. "How do I look?"

Breathtakingly handsome. But she wasn't about to tell him that. His pupils looked fine. She covered his eyes with her hand and was glad he couldn't see the tremble he brought on.

He leaned close, his face only inches from hers.

Her breath hitched. "Will you let me concentrate?"

"I thought I was."

Though he seemed okay, his unusually flirtatious actions made her think he'd suffered a small concussion in the fall.

She quickly moved her hand and watched his pupils tighten to small pinpoints in response to the light. He squinted, still way too close. As she studied his eyes, his pupils dilated, and she saw hunger replace the humor.

"I think a kiss would make me feel better."

His eyes began to close.

Abbie panicked. She'd never kissed a patient and wouldn't start now, but all reason seemed to escape her. She *wanted* to kiss him.

"You're concussed."

He paused and stared at her. "I'm what?"

"You hit your head and have a concussion."

"That's what your exam tells you?" He reached up and twisted a strand of her hair around his finger.

"It's what your actions tell me." She busied her hands with reorganizing her instruments. If she didn't look at him, maybe he wouldn't have such a hold on her.

"Hey, Doc."

"Yes, Mr. Maverick?"

His deep laugh told her the formal title didn't throw him off.

"I'm not 'concussed.'"

His words stayed her hands. She didn't dare look at him. She waited until she heard him walk away before she turned around. The ranch hands had almost cleared the debris from Hank's inert form, and Jake hurried to help them without a backward glance.

Jake had flirted with her, she was sure, and she didn't know what to make of it. She'd had official suitors back East, but they were painfully formal and nothing ever came of their attentions. With Jake things were different. He made her heart beat faster, her breath hitch, and her knees feel weak, almost as if she had an affliction. She smiled a secret smile. If she had to suffer an affliction, this is the one she'd choose to have.

"Doc, we're coming your way!"

She shook off the silly notions and focused on her newest patient. The men carried the unconscious man over and positioned him in the wagon. She settled beside him and began her exam. "I'm afraid he's suffered a few broken ribs. I'll need some strips of cloth to secure them. He also has some pretty nasty gashes. He'll need stitches. Grub? Could you boil some water for me?"

Grub hurried away to do as she asked.

The other men hovered nearby.

She gently cut away Hank's shirt.

Jake squatted opposite her on the wagon bed. "What can I do to help?"

He sounded suspiciously normal all of a sudden. She raised an eyebrow at him. He shrugged.

"Find something for them to do. I don't need an audience, and I doubt Hank will appreciate waking to see them all gathered around staring at him."

"Scrappy, see what you can do to help Grub. Red, keep an eye on the passage. It closed back up and looks unstable, so stay off the rocks. But just to be on the safe side, make sure we don't have any surprise visitors. And Boggs. . ."

"I'll take care of the animals."

"Thanks."

The men scattered, and Jake resumed his place at Hank's far side. "Now tell me what I can do to help you."

The thought of him so close sent her nerves into a dither, but she knew she needed his assistance. She set him to work cleaning the surface wounds while she cleaned the deeper wounds and stitched them up.

"Hank." She checked his eyes and saw no response.

Jake leaned an elbow on his knee, his face full of concern. "What do you think?"

"His pulse is weak, but steady. His worst injury seems to be the ribs, but I don't think they punctured a lung. His breathing is strong." She frowned. "But I have no idea why he hasn't regained consciousness."

"Could he have suffered a head injury?"

"Definitely." Diagnosing in these conditions, where so many things were unknown, was her least favorite part of her job. "But I see no signs of a blow to his head. You suffered a bigger bump than him."

"What else could cause the unconsciousness?"

"He could have internal injuries. I have no way to care for him out here if that's the case. I can't very well do surgery."

Jake pulled his hat from his head, his expression troubled. "Wouldn't there be signs?"

"Yes. In most cases. And I don't see any at this point. I'll keep watch, but so far there's no bruising on his abdomen or back and nothing on his chest to show anything like that. That's encouraging. But only time will tell. I have him as stable as possible for now."

"Then continue to stabilize him as well as you can, and we'll head out immediately. We can reach the ranch in two more days, one if the conditions remain steady."

By conditions she assumed he meant they didn't run into Bert's killers.

The men packed up, and Boggs helped Jake lift her trunk back in beside Hank's still form.

"I'll ride back here with him." Abbie settled her skirts around her. Hamm pressed close against her side.

❧

Jake spurred the horses on, wishing they had a smoother path. The jolting wouldn't make Hank's trip any better. As they traveled, he had a lot of time to think. More time than he wanted. He wished Abbie were sitting beside him instead of back with Hank, but he knew the other man needed her more.

He hadn't missed the fact that Abbie's soft hands gently skimmed over Hank's body during her examination. The unconscious man didn't know what he was missing. She hadn't examined Jake that thoroughly. He felt a tinge of jealousy and grimaced. In all fairness, she'd threatened to do just that, and he'd waved her away. Maybe he should have taken her up on it.

And what kind of man felt jealousy over such a thing? Abbie was only doing her job. Maybe he had a touch of a

concussion after all. Why else would he be dwelling on the good doctor and her bedside manner?

He needed to focus on something else. Their homecoming. He always loved coming home to the ranch, and this trip was no exception. More than ever he craved the stability and consistency of their ranch. Home. His home. Caleb's home. And now Abbie's home. He pictured her in the ranch house, cooking meals and cleaning, and the domestic image put marriage on his mind. He shook it off.

Would she cook and clean? After all, she was a medical doctor. He frowned. His thoughts had returned to the beautiful doctor sitting in the wagon behind him.

"Jake! Slow down."

Jake reined in the horses and motioned for the others to stop. He jumped down and hurried to her side. "What is it?"

"Hank. I think he's coming around."

She caressed the man's cheek, and Jake fought off his urge to scowl. The man had been nothing but trouble the entire trip, and now he lay on Abbie's lap while she caressed his cheek. Life could be so unfair.

Jake rested his arms on the wagon's side and waited. The other men paced around behind him.

A low moan escaped Hank, and Abbie's face lit up with a smile.

"Hank." Again she caressed his cheek. "Can you open your eyes?"

His eyes fluttered open and closed.

"That's it," she crooned.

She'd never crooned over Jake's injuries. With him she acted more like a ruthless taskmaster. He allowed himself to scowl this time. The action made him feel better. "Hank! Doc said to open your eyes."

Jake hadn't meant for his command to come out quite so loud or harsh, but at least Hank opened his eyes.

"There you go." He gently pulled Abbie's hand from Hank's face. "You can stop touching him now."

She smirked. "Jake, are you feeling all right?"

"I'm feeling fine. But the man doesn't need you mollycoddling him after all he's been through."

"I'm not mollycoddling him. I'm using a caring bedside manner."

Jake didn't even want to think of her at Hank's bedside. Ever. Especially looking like she did right now. Her hair blew freely in the wind, the long blond strands pulled loose from the day's events. Her delicate hands lay primly in her lap, and her features crinkled into a look of amusement at his expense.

"No doctor I know would caress a man's cheek to wake him up," he growled.

"Well, I suppose not since all the doctors you know are likely male."

"That's just my point. You aren't male, so you don't need to be doing—," he fluttered his hand, "that."

"I'd do the same for any of my patients, Jake, including you."

The thought had his face warming.

"If you all don't mind my interrupting, could someone please explain what's going on?"

Hank's words interrupted their verbal sparring.

"Of course!" Abbie turned her full attention on her patient, promptly dismissing Jake.

Jake renewed his vow to fire the man the moment he was healed. He half listened as Abbie filled in Hank on the avalanche and his injuries. As she talked, she examined the man.

Hank muttered something Jake couldn't quite make out.

Abbie's chatter quieted. "What did you just say?"

Hank tried to sit, but she stilled him with her hand. A hand Jake suddenly wanted to claim as his own—in marriage.

"Bert. He's my brother."

Jake's thoughts suddenly diverted from Abbie to Hank. He clenched his teeth and gathered his thoughts before he spoke. "Bert, the man who kidnapped Doc, is your brother." He didn't question; he stated the fact.

"Yes."

"You were in cahoots with him all along."

"Yes."

"Is that why you hired on?"

He nodded, grimacing in pain.

"And the reason you were 'sick' and slowed us down?"

"Yes."

Jake wanted to punch him. "If you hadn't slowed us down, Abbie never would have been kidnapped. And Bert. . ." He stopped, realizing what his next words would have meant to Hank.

"Go ahead, boss, say it. Bert wouldn't have been killed."

So Hank had been living his own personal hell. Jake had been there plenty of times himself. He sighed. "It wasn't your fault."

"Yeah. Thanks. That doesn't bring my brother back, though, does it?"

So now Jake knew where Hank's bitterness came from. Self-hate was a harsh emotion.

"I blamed you, Doc. I figured if you hadn't—I don't know—existed, I guess, things wouldn't have turned out as they did."

"Why are you telling us this now?"

"I almost died back there." He shifted and gasped in pain. "I thought I saw God. Then I felt unbearable pain. It was so

bad, I thought God had sent me away. To. . .the other place. Then I realized He'd just left me here on earth." He looked up at Abbie. "Then I felt your hand on my cheek and heard your soft voice and thought maybe I'd gone to heaven after all."

Jake loomed over the man, his stance meant to intimidate.

Hank laughed harshly as he looked at Jake. "Yeah. And then I saw you and knew I surely wasn't in heaven."

"Very funny."

Abbie snickered.

"I figure if God spared me from what I deserved, a brutal death like my brother experienced—though the way my ribs feel, I'm not sure I was spared anything in this case—God must have other plans for me."

"I bet He does, Hank," Abbie soothed.

So when had she become such a theologian? Jake echoed her words sarcastically in his mind before feeling chastised. Hadn't he wanted Abbie to grow closer to God?

As if reading his mind, she looked over at him, and her soft lips curved into a serene smile. "I made my peace with God, Jake. I prayed about my salvation and turned my life over to Him."

"You did?"

"I did."

Jake couldn't stop grinning. "I'm glad to hear that."

"I thought you might be." She glanced back at Hank. "I prayed for you, too."

"That so?" Hank narrowed his eyes. "I think it's probably a good thing. I'd like to hear more later."

"We can sort this all out when we get to the ranch." They'd lost enough time for now. They wouldn't make it in by nightfall, but if they got back on the trail, they'd reach the ranch by midmorning. "Doc, is he stable enough to travel?"

"Hank? What do you think?"

"I want to get home. That is, if I still have a place there."

"Of course you have a place. Right, Jake?"

Abbie looked at him, her green eyes captivating, and he couldn't refuse her. He was in trouble. He already dreaded telling Caleb all that had happened while Abbie was under his care. What would Caleb think when Jake admitted that in the process of botching up the entire trip, he'd fallen in love with Caleb's baby sister?

sixteen

"The ranch lies just beyond that ridge up ahead."

Abbie's heart beat in anticipation. "I can't wait to see it. To see Caleb."

"Scrap?" Jake called. "Ride ahead and tell Caleb of our arrival."

Scrappy, looking relieved to be free of the stressful journey, spurred his horse and hurried out of sight.

The midmorning sun rose high as they traveled the last few miles. Hank had pulled through and lay snoring in the wagon's bed. He hadn't talked much since the previous afternoon when he'd cleared his conscience, but the few times he did speak, his manner was kind and relaxed.

Jake slowed the horses and looked at her. "About the ranch, Doc. I've not been totally up front about—"

"Well, it's about time." Caleb's rich voice interrupted whatever Jake was about to say. His teasing words met them as they cleared a rise that overlooked the ranch. "I send you off on a six-day trip, and two weeks later you mosey back—that's just great!"

"Caleb!" Abbie slid down from the wagon before it had completely stopped and threw herself into her big brother's embrace. "I thought you were dead."

"Dead?" He looked over her head toward Jake. "What made you think I was dead?"

Scrappy hovered in the background.

"Bert Sanchez told me as much. Let me look at you."

She held him at arm's length and stared. His features were stronger. He'd filled out. His blond hair had darkened, but the long, sun-bleached strands gave him a rugged look that hadn't been there when he'd left the city. "Where's the prissy city boy who walked out of my life all those years ago?"

A grin transformed his face as he wrapped his arm around her neck and bumped his forehead up against hers. He stared into her eyes. "Now, little sister, let's get one thing straight. I ain't never been a city boy, and I never will be. That's the whole reason I came out here when I did. The city was smothering me. But here? A man can breathe with all this open space."

"I'm beginning to see what you mean." Abbie exchanged a look with Jake. "Now that I have the train robbery, the kidnapping, the massacre, and the explosion behind me, I'm starting to see the better side of living out here. The city. . .it was boring in comparison. Noisy, dirty, crowded, and did I mention. . .boring?"

Caleb stared hard at her for a moment then threw his head back with a wild laugh. "That's my Abigail. You might be a fancy doctor these days, but I'm glad to see you haven't lost your imagination and spunk." He looked at Jake who still rested on the seat of the wagon. He watched their exchange with an air of amusement. "Growing up she was a tomboy to beat all tomboys. She gave our parents fits. She gave most of the neighborhood bullies fits."

"Caleb, some things are better left in the past."

"Well, at least now you're making restitution by patching people up instead of sending them to the doctor in a coma."

Abbie sucked in her breath. "That only happened once."

Jake choked on his laugh. Abbie glared. Caleb smirked.

"But was it ever an event when it did happen."

"Tell me about it." Jake leaned forward, much too eager to hear the story at her expense.

"I don't think this walk in the past is necessary. We need to get Hank settled in." Abbie folded her arms across her chest and tapped her foot with exasperation.

"I'm fine. I want to hear the story." Hank, now fully awake, lounged against the wagon's sidewall.

Caleb used a walking stick to move closer to the other two men, completely dismissing Abbie's request.

"It was the year I left." *Now* he turned her way. "What were you, eleven? Twelve?"

"Almost fifteen."

"Fourteen then." He returned his attention to his rapt audience. Now Red, Grub, and Boggs had joined the cluster.

She glared at them. "I treated every one of you and will treat you again in the future. You really want to think about your actions."

Abbie's threat went unheeded, and a couple of the men actually shushed her.

"Though a tomboy at heart, she'd clean up right pretty when our folks forced her to attend town events." He winked her way. She flushed and rolled her eyes. "The suitors would come out of the woodwork."

"Suitors? They were mere boys."

"I think fending them off is what sent our pa to an early grave."

"It was not! He died of a weak heart, and you know it."

"What *weakened* his heart, hmm?"

"Nothing I did."

"Anyway. . .she'd ride up all haughty and pretty and the men—boys—would absolutely flock. Most of them would scatter by a well-directed look from my father or myself." He

laughed. "But there was one in particular who continued to give Abbie a hard time. He'd stay at a respectful distance if one of us were around, but one day I had to run back inside the church after a town meeting to find my hat—"

Abbie interrupted. "Ha. You snuck around behind the church to steal one more kiss from Penelope Myers."

"While I was gone, Petey Piker snuck up to the wagon and tried to do some stealin' himself."

"He was a despicable boy."

"I'll agree with you there. If you hadn't put him into a coma, I surely would have."

"So Doc really let him have it, huh?" Scrappy sat so far forward on his saddle he looked like he'd topple over the front at any moment.

"Scrappy, if you break your neck at my expense, I won't doctor you up."

He scooted back a few inches, and Abbie released her breath. She still held her arms protectively crossed at her chest, though, as if that would protect her from her brother's story. How charming that he'd jumped right back into his annoying brotherly ways. She fumed and huffed, willing him to hurry up.

Jake stared at her, much too pleased with the present events.

"Oh she let him have it all right. As rumor has it, he climbed up beside her and tried to steal that infamous first kiss all the males were vying for."

"And she was only fourteen?" Jake sounded impressed and sent her a look that said just that.

"Fourteen but looking like she was sixteen."

"Wow, Doc, I guess you've always been pretty." Scrappy's awe was palpable. "So what'd you do, punch him?"

"Nah, she's too much of a lady. You wouldn't punch anyone, would ya, Doc?" Grub held his horse by the reins and munched a piece of jerky.

Abbie opened her mouth to answer, but Red interrupted. "I bet she whipped out a pistol and shot 'im right then."

"I did no such thing!"

Jake seemed way too amused by all the comments. She'd ask him the reason later.

"Nah." Caleb had their full attention and dragged the moment out. "She did carry a pistol half the time, though our parents would have died on the spot had they known. She wore it strapped around her thigh. She could outshoot the best of us *city boys*. And she had been known to punch a few boys back in her younger days."

"I think I'll head on down to the ranch by foot. It didn't seem to wind Caleb too much. He seems to have plenty of gumption for talking after his long stroll."

They were so attuned to Caleb's words that no one even noticed she'd spoken.

"C'mon, Caleb. Tell us. What'd she do next?" Boggs spoke to Caleb as if he'd known him all his life.

"Well, he climbed up on the wagon bed, taking her by surprise. When he leaned in for the kiss. . ."

Abigail remembered that horrible moment and shivered with disgust.

"She screeched for the horses to pull out."

"Wow, did she throw him off?" Red sent her a look of raw appreciation.

"Not at that moment. He clung for dear life, having been caught off guard. He would have been fine if she hadn't suddenly jerked back the reins." This time his expression held a touch of pride as he stared at her, his baby sister. "Poor Petey

didn't expect it and went flying headfirst over the front."

"And then she ran him down?" Scrappy almost drooled with anticipation.

"Not according to Abbie, right, sis?" He looked back at the men. "According to the story she told, the horses spooked and ran him down of their own accord."

"So you really ran over a helpless man. Doc, I'm stunned."

Jake didn't look stunned. The teasing glint remained in his eyes. He also looked intrigued and. . .charmed? Regardless, she had no intention of letting them all continue to tell stories at her expense.

She turned and stalked off toward the buildings of the ranch. She heard the group disperse. The men each tipped their hat as they passed. The wagon rolled by at a fast pace, and she looked up in disappointment. Caleb held the reins.

"Doc."

Jake's quiet voice called to her from behind. Slowly, she turned.

He stood in the same spot where Caleb had been while regaling them with stories.

"C'mere."

They met under the cooling shade of a juniper tree.

"You let Caleb take the wagon."

"Yep."

"Now we really have to walk."

"Looked like you were doing just that anyway."

"So why'd you stay behind? Surely you're eager to get home? If you'd stayed on the wagon, you'd have been there by now."

"I thought about asking you to hop back on, but in your present mood, I was afraid you'd turn me down in front of my men." He chuckled. "And I didn't want to take a chance you'd reject me and try to run me down."

He moved closer. His brown eyes crinkled at the corners where laugh lines betrayed his attempt to be serious. His dark hair blew freely in the breeze, and she wanted to tame it. The strands reflected the wild heart of the man who wore them, a heart she longed to capture.

Her breathing hitched. "Why would I want to run you down?"

They were mere inches away now.

"Because," he whispered. "You knew I'd do this. . . ."

He leaned forward and dusted his lips across hers. She closed her eyes and smiled. He kissed her again. This time his lips lingered, and the kiss intensified. Her entire body went weak, and she was grateful that his strong arms surrounded her, keeping her firmly on her feet.

"I've wanted to do that for a long time." He leaned his forehead against hers, the effect completely different from Caleb's brotherly move. Jake's mouth remained an inch away from hers. She could feel his breath mix with hers.

"I wouldn't have run you down."

He leaned back so he could see her eyes, keeping her tucked securely in the circle of his arms. "What was that? I'm afraid I didn't hear you."

She could tell by his twinkling eyes that he had.

"I said I wouldn't have run you down." She couldn't look him in the eye. "I saved that kiss, from all those years ago, just for you."

This time his eyes registered surprise. "All those suitors and all this time. . .and you saved your kiss for me?"

"I did. I didn't care for any of those suitors. I care about you."

"Oh." For the first time he seemed to be without words.

"Petey almost ruined it for you."

"I should hunt him down and punch him."

"Nah." She laughed. "He met his match in his wife. There's nothing you could do to make him any more miserable."

"Then justice has been served. Twice. After you put him in a coma—"

"My *horses* put him in a coma."

"I'd have thought he'd pick a mild-mannered woman to marry and live out his years."

"That was always Petey's problem. He never did learn from his mistakes."

His mirth abated, and he studied her, his eyes warm. She shivered at his intensity. "I know we've not known each other long...."

"I feel like we've known each other a lifetime."

"We've been through a lot the past two weeks."

"And I'd love to go through a lot more, as long as you're by my side."

"I need to speak to your brother. Though we're partners in the ranch—"

She interrupted. "Partners?"

"Yeah, partners. I tried to tell you that just before we ran into Caleb."

"I thought you were the foreman." She grinned.

"Does it matter?"

"Nope."

"So you don't mind if I talk things over with my partner?"

"What things?"

She knew from his expression he aimed to give her a hard time. "Things like which, if any, of the cattle took ill while I was gone. Did our supplies come through? How is the newest litter of kittens in the barn? That type of thing."

"Oh, that's all?" She punched him softly in the arm and turned to walk from beneath the branches of the tree.

He grabbed her by the arm. "Other than one other little detail." He pulled her back into the circle of his arms.

"And what would that be?" She held her breath.

"How would he feel about my getting hitched with his pretty little sister?"

"Oh."

"Just 'oh'?"

"What if he says no?"

"He's not going to say no."

"How can you be so sure?"

"I can be very convincing."

"I can imagine."

He knelt down on one knee, and a tear coursed down Abbie's cheek. He reached up to wipe it away. "Aw, Doc, don't cry."

"I can't help it. These are happy tears."

"Think you can hold back the happy tears until I've actually proposed the question?"

"I'll try." Now her tears coursed freely down her face.

A rumble of laughter sounded from his chest. "I'm in trouble."

"The best trouble of your life." She dropped to her knees to stare into his eyes.

"You've got that right." He cleared his throat, his own eyes misting suspiciously. He searched her eyes. "Doc?"

"Yes?"

"Will you do me the honor of becoming my wife?"

"I will."

They kissed to seal the agreement under the juniper tree.

❧

Caleb hadn't seemed too surprised at Jake's marriage request. His only requirement was that they have the ceremony soon so he could be released from the burden of watching out

for his wayward younger sister. Jake and Abbie were all too willing to appease him.

A few short weeks later, they stood beneath the very tree where he'd proposed and now said their vows. When they were done, he pulled her into a deep kiss and spun her around to face their witnesses. He held her close against his chest. Along with the preacher, his motley band of misfits comprised their entire wedding party—and guest list—but Abbie didn't care. Between them, her brother, and Jake, she had everyone dear to her in attendance. They gave their well wishes and slowly drifted off, leaving her alone with her groom.

"So, wife. What do you think?"

She remained where she was, leaning back against his chest. "What do I think about what?"

"All of it. The journey. The ranch. Me."

"I wouldn't trade the journey for anything. It led me to you."

He rested his chin on her head. "Hmm. Good point."

"The ranch—" She surveyed the buildings and pastures below them. She saw the men going about their chores. They were her family now. She no longer felt so alone. "Is simply breathtaking. I can't believe I get to live and work here forever."

"And me?"

She turned in his arms. "There are no words with enough depth and meaning to describe my feelings and love for you. If there are, I certainly haven't learned them."

"Really?" He glanced down at her. "With all the book learning you've put in?"

Grinning, she nodded. "Really. Hard to believe, but true." Happy that he embraced her status as physician instead of resenting her schooling, she laid her head against his chest and listened to the beating of his heart.

"Well, I suppose you could try to *show* me in actions what

your words can't seem to say."

"I'll keep working on the words." She met his kiss with her own. "And as for the actions, that's exactly what I plan to do, every day, in every way I can, for the rest of our life together. I love you, Jake Maverick."

"And I love you, Abbie Maverick. And by the way. . ."

"Yes?"

"Those words you just stated said everything I need to hear. You don't have to study any further."

"I guess sometimes the simplest words say all that we need to hear."

"Yep." He took her hand, and they headed down the hill, ready to start their new journey.

A Letter To Our Readers

Dear Reader:

In order that we might better contribute to your reading enjoyment, we would appreciate your taking a few minutes to respond to the following questions. We welcome your comments and read each form and letter we receive. When completed, please return to the following:

Fiction Editor
Heartsong Presents
PO Box 719
Uhrichsville, Ohio 44683

1. Did you enjoy reading *The Petticoat Doctor* by Paige Winship Dooly?
   ❏ Very much! I would like to see more books by this author!
   ❏ Moderately. I would have enjoyed it more if

   _____

   _____

   _____

2. Are you a member of **Heartsong Presents**? ❏ Yes ❏ No
   If no, where did you purchase this book? _____

   _____

3. How would you rate, on a scale from 1 (poor) to 5 (superior), the cover design? _____

4. On a scale from 1 (poor) to 10 (superior), please rate the following elements.

   ____ Heroine   ____ Plot
   ____ Hero   ____ Inspirational theme
   ____ Setting   ____ Secondary characters

5. These characters were special because? _____

_____

_____

6. How has this book inspired your life? _____

_____

_____

7. What settings would you like to see covered in future
   Heartsong Presents books? _____

_____

_____

8. What are some inspirational themes you would like to see
   treated in future books? _____

_____

_____

9. Would you be interested in reading other **Heartsong
   Presents** titles? ❏ Yes ❏ No

10. Please check your age range:
   - ❏ Under 18   ❏ 18-24
   - ❏ 25-34   ❏ 35-45
   - ❏ 46-55   ❏ Over 55

Name _____

Occupation _____

Address _____

City, State, Zip_____

PRAIRIE HILLS

Three women challenge their
historically meek and needy
roles. . .but will doing so deafen
them to the call of romance?
Contributing authors
are Paige Winship Dooly
of Florida, Linda Ford
of Alberta, and Susan May
Warren of Minnesota.

Historical, paperback, 352 pages, 5³/₁₆" x 8"

Presents

P R E S E N T S

If you love Christian romance…

You'll love Heartsong Presents' inspiring and faith-filled romances by today's very best Christian authors…Wanda E. Brunstetter, Mary Connealy, Susan Page Davis, Cathy Marie Hake, and Joyce Livingston, to mention a few!

$10.⁹⁹

When you join Heartsong Presents, you'll enjoy four brand-new, mass market, 176-page books—two contemporary and two historical—that will build you up in your faith when you discover God's role in every relationship you read about!

Mass Market 176 Pages

Imagine…four new romances every four weeks—with men and women like you who long to meet the one God has chosen as the love of their lives…all for the low price of $10.99 postpaid.

To join, simply visit www.heartsong presents.com or complete the coupon below and mail it to the address provided.

- -

YES! Sign me up for Heartsong!

NEW MEMBERSHIPS WILL BE SHIPPED IMMEDIATELY!
Send no money now. We'll bill you only $10.99 postpaid with your first shipment of four books. Or for faster action, call 1-740-922-7280.

NAME_____

ADDRESS_____

CITY_____ STATE _____ ZIP _____

MAIL TO: HEARTSONG PRESENTS, P.O. Box 721, Uhrichsville, Ohio 44683
or sign up at WWW.HEARTSONGPRESENTS.COM

AUTHOR'S NOTE

SUBSTANTIALLY SHORTER AND DIFFERENT VERSIONS OF CHAPTERS 2 (with Joseph Schaefer), 3, and 4 (with Charles and Nancy Knight) were published in the Heldref Publishing educational weather magazine *Weatherwise*.

The photograph on page 163 is used with kind permission of the Southern New England Telephone Records, Archives, and Special Collections at the Thomas J. Dodd Research Center, University of Conneticut Libraries.

Chapter 1
FREAKS OF THE STORM

ITEM: On a foggy October morning in 1947, wildlife biologist A. D. Bajkov and his wife were peacefully eating their breakfast at a small restaurant in the town of Marksville, Louisiana. Suddenly the waitress, glancing out the windows, yelped in surprise, "Quick, look! Fish are falling from the sky!" Bajkov—a trained scientist—immediately dashed outside to collect and study the bizarre occurrence. He discovered to his amazement that literally hundreds of fish were falling around the city. Indeed, falling fish had actually hit one of the clerks at the Marksville bank and two other local merchants as they walked to their businesses. As part of his investigations, Bajkov determined there were areas along Main Street "averaging one fish per square yard." He wrote that so many had fallen that automobiles and trucks were running over them and importantly, "fish also fell on the roofs of houses."

ITEM: When a rare November tornado ripped through the town of Great Bend, Kansas, in 1915, people witnessed an abundance of nature's oddest happenings. In one of the strangest, the tornado flew five horses a quarter of mile from their barn, landed them unhurt, all together—and, on top of it all, they all were still hitched to the same rail! In another instance, witnesses found as many as forty-five thousand migrating ducks dead at a nearby bird sanctuary and battered ducks reportedly fell from the sky as far as forty miles northeast of that refuge. In the town of Great Bend itself, residents found an iron water hydrant reportedly full of wooden splinters and discovered only one small wall remaining of the Riverside Steam Laundry, which was built of stone and cement block—yet two nearby wooden shacks were utterly untouched by the tornado. A dresser from a destroyed home was uncovered as a mere mass of splinters, but salvagers found its fragile mirror lying unbroken against a fence some distance away.

ITEM: The Great Hurricane of 1938 caused great damage and distress along the Eastern Seaboard, particularly on Long Island but it also left its share of strange sights: Pieces of flat boards and blunt sticks of wood were driven through the walls of houses like nails while residents discovered chickens with their feathers plucked completely by the wind. A small cottage reportedly drifted off in the tidal wave and made landfall on another person's property several hundreds yards away. Although the small house came to rest upside down, residents found that not a single windowpane in it was broken. Apparently, they even stumbled upon a fresh egg, whole and uncracked, that was resting gently on a pile of debris from a smashed kitchen.

NATURE IS POWERFUL. ON OCCASION, IT ALSO CAN BE INCREDIBLY weird. While we are awed by the unimaginable power of a tornado ripping a house into splinters, we find it difficult to reconcile that terrible power with accounts of tornadic winds safely carrying people and animals hundreds of feet through the air. Similarly, the relentless flood waves of hurricanes have killed millions of people and destroyed whole cities, yet they also have led to the cessation of war and even the creation of an entirely new country. Lightning has brought massive death and destruction across the globe by striking munitions depots or oil refineries, but, conversely, a lightning strike once cured a French priest of paralysis in the sixteenth century and, more recently, apparently cured an Oklahoma City woman of the symptoms of multiple sclerosis.

Such odd happenings in relation to weather were tagged in the first part of the last century with the phrase "freaks of the storm." Webster's dictionary defines the word *freak* as "a sudden and apparently causeless change or turn of events, the mind, etc.; an apparently capricious notion, occurrence, etc." In times past, newspapers rushed to press with stories sensationalizing the "freaks" of the latest tornado, hurricane, or lightning strike. Occasionally, that rush to supply public curiosity led to huge exaggeration. As severe weather historian Thomas Grazulis wryly speculated, tornado damage stories—such as an iron jug that was blown inside out or the rooster that was blown into a narrow-necked bottle such that only its head stuck out—are undoubtedly fictional. Yet even the exaggerations point to the great public interest in the odd and bizarre and it is well known that even exaggerations tend to have at least a kernel of truth in them. For example, while there are embellished stories of babies being safely carried up to seventeen miles from where they were first lifted by the twister, there are undeniably true stories of babies being carried safely by tornadoes several hundred yards or more.

Is there a way to distinguish between gross exaggerations and true accounts of odd weather? Some might suggest that reputation and quality of either the actual observer of the event or the honesty of the recorder of the event is critical to that determination. For instance, one of the very few personal accounts of being inside a tornado is that of William Keller of Greensburg, Kansas. His story was published in the prestigious government weather journal *Monthly Weather Review* and, as a notice on his account's believability, Keller was described as a man whose "reputation for truthfulness and sobriety is of the best. Apparently he is entirely capable of making careful and reliable observations." While Mr. Keller's veracity has been deemed unquestionable, other people with more "colorful" backgrounds have also compiled many weird weather observations. In this survey of unusual weather, it is certainly necessary to "watch the watchers" and look at the character of those people—in some cases, quite eccentric—who have documented strange weather.

Charles Fort, Compiler of the Weird

Over the past century, the word *fortean* has been applied frequently to weird weather events, as well as other eccentric and exotic phenomena such as UFO research and paranormal abilities. *Fortean* is a tribute to an early collector of all accounts of the unusual, Charles Fort. Fort was the eldest of three brothers whose father owned a wholesale grocery business in Albany, New York. According to his rather limited biography, he mentioned being beaten as a child—circumstances that may have shaped his sharp rebellion against accepted science and convention and likely influenced his philosophy and writings. Upon reaching adulthood, Fort married simply and lived off a meager inheritance. He occasionally sold articles to magazines and newspapers in the New York area. However, most importantly, Fort spent innumerable hours in the New York Public Library (and later in the British Museum) documenting and archiving tens of thousands of odd physical anecdotes. He later published these accounts in a sequence of four books (*Book of the Damned* in 1919, *New Lands* in 1923, *LO!* in 1931, and *Wild Talents* in 1932) that even today form the foundation of most paranormal research libraries.

Fort primarily culled his accounts of weird and unusual phenomena from either newspaper accounts or from the scientific journals of the day. In the nineteenth and early twentieth century, many scientists—and a number of enthusiastic amateur observers—published notes on any odd or unusual physical event they witnessed in the world's leading science journals, such as *Science* and *Nature*. Today, for the most part, that practice has vanished—these journals now are almost exclusively limited to reporting science discoveries and theories in the modern science manner, specifically with multiple testing and reproducible results. Yet, in those earlier days, many science journals were filled with observations of "blood rains," strange hail, weird lightning experiences, and the innumerable oddities of tornadoes. For decades, Charles Fort sat in the New York Public Library and assembled thousands of such observations. Actually, he collected them several times—on at least two occasions, he literally burned his entire compendium of handwritten notes because, as he wrote, "they were not what I wanted." Then he would reconsider and once again begin the whole process of searching the library collection and painstakingly jotting down relevant notes.

One of his favorite bizarre science topics involved reports of falling fish and frogs. As a sample, Fort described the following events, extracted from science magazine and journal reports:

- A fall of a tremendous number of little toads, which were supposedly only "one or two months old" that occurred near Toulouse, France, in 1804.
- A fall of little frogs in London after a heavy storm in 1838.
- A famous fish fall at Mountain Ash in Glamorganshire in 1859.
- A tremendous deluge of rain that was termed "one of the heaviest falls [of fish] on record" in 1850

India such that the ground was found "literally covered with fishes."

- A fall of hundreds of small fishes, identified as sand
  eels, in Hindon, England, in 1918.

Unfortunately, his high-quality, meticulous journal searches for
descriptions of odd and unusual events in nature were coupled
with an apparent distain for traditional science and its methods.
As potential explanation for such events as falling fish and frogs,
he suggested that a vast ocean orbits in space near Earth, a
"Super-Sargasso" space sea filled with odd creatures and materials that, as he put it, occasionally has its bottom "dropped out."
It is debatable as to whether Fort actually believed his hypothesis,
was trying to be amusing or tongue-in-cheek, or, by suggesting
such an absurd idea, was heaping scorn and disdain onto traditional science.

That apparent scorn for conventional science has undoubtedly caused his writings to drift into the realm of science skeptics.
Consequently, "fortean" has expanded beyond the description of
any unusual or strange natural event to representing observations
from such fringe topics as "Ufology" and paranormal activity.
This link to the occult, combined with the fact that study of
Fortean events relies so heavily on public observation, which
today's scientists find to be subjective, irreproducible, and therefore potentially unreliable, has commonly caused Fort's style of
research to be dismissed by modern scientists.

Scientists of past times—particularly those in astronomy and
weather—were, however, much less hesitant to study and document odd weather. Indeed, some of the most famous scientists of
the past have been instrumental in recording freaks of the
storm—but equally often failed to question the reliability of their
sources. Three of the most famous have been François Arago,
Camille Flammarion, and Charles Tomlinson.

One of the great archivists of meteorological oddities, Dominique Francois Jean Arago. (Original watercolor painting by Day, courtesy AIP Emilio Segré Visual Archives, Knapp Collection.)

François Arago, Consummate Observer

François Arago was a brilliant French physicist and director of the Paris Observatory in the early nineteenth century. In the world of science, he is undoubtedly best known for his discoveries in magnetism and optics (he was an ardent advocate of the hotly debated wave theory of light) as well as for his astronomical observations (for instance, he is credited as the discoverer of the Sun's chromosphere, a thin reddish layer of the sun's atmosphere normally visible only during a total solar eclipse). Early on in his career, it is evident that Arago was also a meticulous observer. Once, the story goes, he traveled to Spain just to complete measurements needed to establish a universal standard of length in the metric system (and on his return journey to France, he was shipwrecked and almost imprisoned in Algiers). Later, as director of the Paris Observatory, he suggested to his student Urbain Jean Joseph

LeVerrier that he study irregularities in the orbit of Uranus—a suggestion that eventually led to the discovery of the planet Neptune.

As a keen observer and recorder of phenomena, Arago also compiled a great amount of information on different aspects of weather. Indeed, he wrote that he was "engaged both by taste and by duty in meteorological studies" although he was strongly against the idea of using those observations to actually forecast the weather. His interest and devotion to meteorology is seen in his 1855 book entitled *Meteorological Essays*. In it, he particularly focused on aspects of thunder and lightning and related a number of very odd anecdotes about the weather. Here is a brief sample of the more bizarre anecdotes that Arago related:

- In Swanborough, Sussex, lightning struck a reddish colored ox with white spots early in September 1774. According to Arago's source, no hair was left on the white spots while the red part showed no injuries.
- In the summer of 1787, two persons who had taken shelter under a tree were struck by lightning. Arago noted, "Portions of their hair were thrown to the top of the tree. An iron circle belonging to a sabot of one of the poor victims was also found after the event caught in a branch very high up."
- Arago also recounted the bizarre lightning strike tale of a naval officer by the name of Rihouet onboard the British ship-of-line *Golymin* in 1812: "In going round the ship after the accident, I was accompanied by an officer and the master gunner." As they conducted their survey, the trio found to their profound astonishment "no trace of fire, but a complete overturning of [the bread-room] contents; more than twenty

thousand biscuits had been tossed about." In addition, either the officer's razor or his beard had become damaged by the strike: "The next day when I wanted to shave myself, I found that the effect of the razor upon the beard was to pull it out by the roots, instead of cutting it; and since that time I have had no beard. The hair on my head, my eyebrows, and eyelashes, and generally all the hair on my body, successively came out in the same way by the roots, and did not grow again."

Arago received a huge number of honors both during and after his life. The French scientist was elected as a Fellow of the Royal Society, as a Fellow of the Royal Society of Edinburgh, and as a recipient of the Royal Society Copley Medal. His fame as a scientist even in modern times has led to a lunar crater being named after him as well as commemoration on the Eiffel Tower.

Camille Flammarion, People's Astronomer and Psychic Researcher

Camille Flammarion was the "Stephen Hawking" of his day—one of the great popularizers of astronomy for the nineteenth century. Born in France in 1842, he began early on to demonstrate a passion for astronomy and science in general. Equally early in his life, he was recognized as a genius. At the young age of sixteen, he authored a five-hundred-page technical book entitled *Cosmologie Universelle,* and through that accomplishment became an assistant of Arago's talented understudy, Urbain Jean Joseph LeVerrier, at the Paris Observatory. After a short time, Flammarion started his astronomical career by cataloging the occurrence of double stars, eventually publishing a catalog listing more than ten thousand of the stellar phenomena.

The great popularizer of astronomy and archivist of odd weather events, Camille Flammarion. (Photo by Stebbing, Paris, courtesy AIP Emilio Segrè Visual Archives, Brittle Book Collection.)

In astronomical history, Flammarion is best known for his hypothesis that the red color of Mars might be due to vegetation and, indeed, he claimed that it was likely that Mars was inhabited by "a race superior to our own." In partial support of that theory, he published several trendy books, including *Popular Astronomy*, which sold over one hundred thousand copies in France as well as being translated into a popular English edition. In 1877, Flammarion founded the Astronomical Society of France.

Most importantly for weather research, Flammarion published a book entitled *The Atmosphere* in 1871. In that book, he recounted a number of very odd and unusual anecdotal accounts involving weather, particularly lightning. A sampling of his anecdotes shows a rather unquestioning acceptance of what many modern scientists would term blatantly impossible weather occurrences:

- In France in 1838, according to Flammarion, three soldiers sought refuge from a violent thunderstorm under a linden tree. Some peasants, seeing them stand motionless long after the storm had passed, and receiving no reply to their calls, touched them on the shoulder. Incredibly, according to Flammarion, the bodies instantly crumbled to fine ashes. He noted that the soldiers' clothing was not torn, and their faces wore a natural appearance.

- In an equally bizarre fashion, the French scientist wrote that a lightning bolt hit a miller's assistant on January 20, 1868, while he was at a windmill at Groix. "The lightning struck him, and split him from his head downwards in two."

- And still another rather unbelievable lightning occurrence related by Flammarion: "A stranger near the Pont de l'Erde, on the Quai Flesselles, was enveloped by a flash of lightning, but preceded on his way without experiencing any ill effects." The man had a wallet with two separate pockets—one containing two pieces of silver in one compartment and a ten-franc piece of gold in the other. When the man opened his wallet, he found that "a coating of silver taken from one of the silver pieces—a franc—had been transferred to both sides of the ten-franc piece. The franc, slightly thinner, especially over the moustache of Napoleon III, was in parts slightly bluish. This transference of the silver on to gold was made through the skin of the partition of the compartments."

In the later years of his life, Flammarion shifted his focus to psychic and metaphysical research. In particular, he became fascinated by death and near-death experiences and began collecting many accounts of such events. This compilation eventually led to the publication of a three-volume set entitled *Death and Its Mystery*.

Most strangely (at least compared to modern scientists), Flammarion enjoyed an immense popularity among the general public and almost fanatical devotion from his supporters. One of Flammarion's ardent followers—perhaps "groupie" might be a better word—donated to him a complete observatory and estate for Flammarion's exclusive research and study. Even more bizarre is the story, compiled by David Darling in *The Universal Book of Astronomy*, of a devoted young French woman who died of tuberculosis. Although the woman had never actually met Flammarion, she made a startling request as part of her will. She appealed to the widely admired scientist through her last testament that a large piece of her own skin be removed from her body, tanned, and used to bind a copy of his next book. Consequently, Flammarion instructed his publisher that the first copy of his book *Lands of the Sky* was to be bound in the lady's skin with a gold-embossed inscription on the front cover: "Pious fulfillment of an anonymous wish/Binding in human skin (woman) 1882."

Charles Tomlinson, People's Educator

A contemporary of Flammarion, English scientist Charles Tomlinson is best remembered as a scientist who strived to make science available to the world. As opposed to Flammarion's rather flamboyant style, Tomlinson assumed a much more traditional scholarly persona. He wrote books, published professional papers, and penned many letters to the major English newspapers and magazines of his day. In particular, one of Tomlinson's pet peeves was the popular conception that lightning somehow "imprinted" the images of nearby trees onto the bodies of those struck by lightning. Once in 1866, the *London Times* wrote a rather sensational account of a boy struck dead by lightning and described that rescuers found

THE

RAIN-CLOUD

AND THE

SNOW-STORM:

AN ACCOUNT OF THE NATURE, FORMATION, PROPERTIES,
DANGERS, AND USES OF RAIN AND SNOW

IN VARIOUS PARTS OF THE WORLD.

BY CHARLES TOMLINSON, F.C.S.,

LECTURER ON SCIENCE, KING'S COLLEGE SCHOOL, LONDON.

PUBLISHED UNDER THE DIRECTION OF
THE COMMITTEE OF GENERAL LITERATURE AND EDUCATION,
APPOINTED BY THE SOCIETY FOR PROMOTING
CHRISTIAN KNOWLEDGE.

LONDON:

SOCIETY FOR PROMOTING CHRISTIAN KNOWLEDGE;

SOLD AT THE DEPOSITORIES:

77, GREAT QUEEN STREET, LINCOLN'S INN FIELDS; 4, ROYAL EXCHANGE;
48, PICCADILLY;
AND BY ALL BOOKSELLERS.

Title page of one of the books by the English meteorologist and archivist of
weather events, Charles Tomlinson.

burned onto his body "a perfect image of the tree [under which he had taken cover], the fibres, the leaves and branches being represented with photographic accuracy." Tomlinson immediately responded with a detailed explanation of how such marks were not created as some kind of magical lightning photography.

British weather historian and contemporary of Tomlinson, G. J. Symons, recounted in the magazine *Knowledge* a similar diatribe of Tomlinson against a Cuban professor, Dr. Andrés Poey, who was one of the great hurricane researchers of the late nineteenth century. Symons wrote that when "Professor Poey brought out a complete memoir" on the subject of lightning imprinting, the publicity for it was "too much for Mr. Tomlinson, and the result was the insertion of two papers 'On Lightning Figures,' " in the *Edinburgh New Philosophy Journal* in which Tomlinson basically ridiculed Poey's rather fanciful notions of lightning imprinting.

During his lifetime, Tomlinson wrote over fifty books as well as published over a hundred technical papers and notes. Most importantly, he was a compiler and synthesizer of scientific knowledge. His chief scientific accomplishment *A Cyclopaedia of the Useful Arts,* is a masterful compilation of the nineteenth-century state of science, technology, and industry. But Tomlinson's primary interests remained the variations and oddities found in weather and, to that end, he assembled a tremendous number of observations. Most of these he discussed in a series of books (written around 1860) on various aspects of the weather; *The Rain-Cloud and the Snow-Storm, The Thunder-Storm,* and *The Dew-Drop and the Mist.* A sample of these observations gives an indication of his talents in collecting and analyzing anecdotal evidence:

- In *The Rain-Cloud and the Snow-Storm,* Tomlinson presented an account of a hailstorm that he personally witnessed in Leipzig: "It is no exaggeration to say that the stones were of the size of hen's eggs; some were larger." He described some of the hailstones, which he personally had examined, as having "an internal nucleus of perfectly transparent ice of the form of a very flat spheroid, surrounded by semi-opaque ice, radiating to the circumference." According to Tomlinson, the fifteen-minute hail-storm consisted of "only a few perfectly round hail-stones; most were more or less flattened, with a circular outline more or less perfect; some were loaf-shaped, some egg-shaped; others resembled small brain-stones, with similar deeply-indented convolutions."

· In *The Thunder-Storm,* Tomlinson described a seem-ingly impossible lightning oddity—but a phe-nomenon for which we now have supporting photographic evidence: "On the 17 September, 1772, the lightning, which fell on a house at Padua, pierced a pane in a window on the ground-floor with a clean round hole, such as a gimlet would make in wood."

· In *The Rain-Cloud and the Snow-Storm,* Tomlinson described one of Charles Fort's favorite weather phenomena, a fish shower: "About noon, the wind being in the west, and a few distant clouds visible, a blast of high wind came on, accompanied with so much dust as to change the tint of the atmosphere to a reddish hue." The wind had similarities to a tor-nado or downburst: a damage path that was only four hundred feet wide and the ability to fell large trees. However, as Tomlinson noted when the storm had passed: "The ground, south of the village, was

found to be covered with fish, not less than three or
four thousand in number. They all belonged to a
species well known in India, and were about a span
in length. They were all dead and dry."

And yet, occasionally, Tomlinson himself appeared to slip
into a rather accepting attitude as seen in this account from *The
Rain-Cloud and Snow-Storm*: "Indeed, there is one instance on
record of iron having been actually seen to fall from the atmosphere, namely, that which took place at Agram in Croatia, on 26
May, 1751." He wrote that, around six o'clock in the evening
under a clear sky, "a ball of fire was seen, which shot along, with
a hollow noise, from west to east, and, after a loud explosion
accompanied by a great smoke, two masses of iron fell from it in
the form of chains welded together."

The Modern Archivists: Corliss, Lane, and Grazulis

With the publication in the middle of the last century of Fort's
books on weird nature—and his scathing rejection of modern
science—the study of strange natural events was by-and-large
restricted to tabloid-style magazines, such as *FATE* and *Fortean
Times*. Then, in the 1970s, a science writer named William R.
Corliss initiated a massive compilation of unusual natural phenomena. Corliss began as a technical writer with an unques-
tioned scientific background, including a bachelor's degree in
physics from Rensselaer Polytechnic and a master's degree in
physics from the University of Colorado.

His passion and curiosity for unusual phenomena led Corliss
to assemble a massive database of geophysical anomalies, which he
termed the Sourcebook Project. Corliss privately published,
under the auspices of the project starting in the 1980s, a number
of books and catalogs involving geophysical anomalies. According

to Corliss, the project was designed for several purposes. First, he sought to provide libraries and individuals with a comprehensive collection of first-hand accounts of unusual natural phenomena (something not comprehensively done since the days of Fort). Second, he wanted to pose a challenge to the scientific community to investigate these oddities and, third, he planned to "beguile the casual browser."

Corliss divided his data into anomalies associated with basic scientific disciplines:

- Archaeology (e.g., reports of fossil footprints of humans found in situ with dinosaur tracks);
- Astronomy (e.g., observations of mystery flashes on the Moon or Mars);
- Biology (e.g., accounts of strange animals and creatures);
- Chemistry (e.g., oddities such as cold fusion and transmutation of elements);
- Geology (e.g., reports of "singing" sands and earthquake predictors);
- Mathematics (e.g., studies on prime numbers and math's linkage to the real world);
- Psychology (e.g., reports on psychic abilities and such mental deviations as those displayed by idiots savants);
- Physics (e.g., reports of unexplained gravity deviations and characteristics of subatomic particles);
- And, most importantly, for this book, meteorology. Corliss's meteorology topics focused primarily on lightning, hail, tornadoes, fogs, and rains. Corliss attempted to categorize his various weather accounts into types, such as clear sky rains, giant snowflakes, anomalous hailstones, and so forth.

In a similar fashion and about the same time, tornado historian Thomas Grazulis, through his own venture (the Tornado Project), started work on a massive archive of every significant tornado to have struck the United States building on the records of past giants in the study of tornadoes, John Park Finley and Snowden Flora. One of the prize possessions in my own library is Grazulis's tornado compilation recorded in what my meteorology students fondly refer to as "The Big Green Book"—an eight-pound, 1,450-page tome entitled *Significant Tornadoes*, published in 1992. While it is an absolute treasure trove of useful information for researchers investigating tornadoes, it is a bit pedantic for the general public. In order to list the thousands of tornadoes that have occurred over history of the United States, Grazulis was limited, for the most part, to giving only the most basic information about a given tornado: its date, time, intensity, location, and a concise sentence or two regarding its damage.

A third example of modern weather archivists is the meticulous researcher Frank W. Lane. Other than his two meteorology books mentioned below, Lane is best known for his animal naturalist books, such as *Kingdom of the Octopus, Nature Parade,* and *Animal Wonder World*. However, to the delight of a large audience interested in the workings of the atmosphere and the Earth, Lane published his 1965 book entitled *The Elements Rage* in which he detailed many of the odd and bizarre happenings associated with geophysical phenomena. Specifically, he examined the state of the science in a number of disasters, such as hurricanes, tornadoes, waterspouts, hail, avalanches, lightning, floods, earthquakes, and meteors. Being an incredibly thorough researcher, Lane actually took over six years to investigate his subject and wrote over two thousand letters to scientists and other specialists around the world. Indeed, he recruited over eighty people to read drafts of his research before he published it. The book was such a success that it went through four editions in Great Britain and was published in five other countries, eventually leading to an updated sequel *The Violent Earth,* in 1986.

As a key point to his success, Lane took a very unthreatening approach in his writing. Although he strove to address the latest scientific advances in each type of phenomena, he also addressed the oddities, such as tornadoes' ability to lift trains (as seen in Fergus Falls, Minnesota, in 1919 and in Moorhead, Minnesota, in 1931), the enigma of ball lightning, and the oddities of fish falls.

The three modern researchers mentioned above should be considered representative of modern weather and disaster archivists. But for completeness, I must also mention the works of many other great archivists, such as Russian geoscientist D.V. Nalivkin, or hurricane compilers Douglas, Tannehill, and Long- shore, or Kansas's renown climatologist Snowden Flora, British weather writer Paul Simmons, the incomparable weather histo- rian David Ludlum (founder of the *Weatherwise* magazine), the master Canadian weather historian David Phillips, or modern Fortean archivists, such as John Michell, R. J. M. Rickard, and Jerome Clark. All of these people have collected incredibly useful weather information although sometimes the focus and audience of their efforts was markedly different. Scientists such as Nalivkin, Tannehill, or Flora had a quite different agenda, for example, than the more popularizing tone set by Douglas, Michell, Rickard, or Clark.

Modern Freaks of the Storm?

All of the archivists mentioned above have a fascination with the oddities of nature. Many of those oddities—at least with regard to weather—have been nicknamed in past newspapers, science jour- nals, books, and weather records, the "freaks of the storm." Through diligent and thorough study, particularly over the past few decades, scientists have begun to identify, research, and understand a number of those freaks of the storm.

Research of these unusual aspects of weather has led to some surprising breakthroughs. We now know that there is a scientific explanation behind many of the anomalies identified by authorities such as Corliss or Lane, or even older archivists such as Fort. Take, for instance, the occurrence of straight-line thunderstorm winds—a radial outflow of wind from the center of a massive thunderstorm cell. This type of devastating event now has been linked to a specific new type of weather event called a "microburst." Microbursts are often visible in desert regions as one hundred mile-per-hour walls of dust and sand winds blast outward of a central point. A brilliant meteorologist by the name of Dr. Ted Fujita first identified these phenomena by comparing damage patterns between the atomic destruction of Hiroshima and Nagasaki to odd radial destruction patterns that he found in areas hit by very severe thunderstorms in the American Great Plains.

In a similar fashion, older archives of strange lightning events contain many accounts of "rocket lightning"—strange flashes that shot upward from a thunderstorm into space. Now we have photographic evidence from the Space Shuttle and other orbital platforms that such lightning can and does occur. A whole new set of lightning terminology—blue jets, sprites, and elves—and supporting theories have been developed to address these oddities.

But given all of our incredible improvements in weather research and technology, do freaks of the storm still occur? Does Nature still have the odd trick up her weather sleeve? In the following pages, you will discover that odd happenings that continue to defy immediate explanation still occur—even as recently as this century. Take, for example, the very first hurricane-strength tropical cyclone to be identified in the South Atlantic Ocean in 2004—an occurrence previously thought by many to be impossible, or the world-record-size rain droplets possibly as large as one centimeter (0.4 inch) recorded over Brazil or the uncracked eggs found scattered near a demolished truck in a Nebraska 2004 tornado.

Undoubtedly some of these odd curiosities—even the modern ones—can be explained away as exaggerations or outright hoaxes, but they also reflect weather's very real strangeness and capriciousness as well as our impressions of it. In each of the following chapters, I have created a number of basic categories of weather oddities and selected an assortment of interesting (and, hopefully, entertaining) anecdotes to present their basic nature. This book contains well over five hundred different—and odd—stories of unusual weather from my archive of eight thousand entries. Its chapters were written with input and insight from some of the very best scientists in meteorology. However, please be aware that anomalies and oddities are often viewed by different people in very different manners. Some scientists like their worldview to be "tidy." They therefore occasionally have difficulty in accepting or sometimes even addressing some of the most bizarre and likely exaggerated weather anecdotes. Consequently, my interpretation of these "freaks of the storm" should not be taken as necessarily an endorsement from any of the great scientists with whom I have collaborated in the development of this book or whom I mention in this book. Any errors, inaccuracies, or misconceptions should be attributed directly to me while the credit for a deeper appreciation and understanding of weather and its oddities undoubtedly is a tribute to them.

Each individual chapter also contains a section on general safety recommendations for each given type of weather. These safety recommendations are not meant to be used as the sole definitive guidelines for protection from these various types of weather but rather as starting points for readers to develop their own disaster-readiness plans. Sometimes our best weather safety advice changes. At one time, for instance, we recommended taking cover in the southwest corner of a basement during a tornado. Additional study now suggests it is much better to take shelter on the lowest floor (a basement is best), in the center of the house, and in a small room, such as a bathroom or closet. Consequently, given the occasional changes in safety recommendations, you are strongly encouraged to always get the most up-to-date safety information and recommendations for each of the weather types discussed in this book from official sources, such as the Red Cross, the Federal Emergency Management Agency, the National Weather Service, and other disaster management organizations.

So, with those caveats addressed, draw the curtain back and let the show begin . . .

Boys, girls, ladies, and gents, step right up! Come one, come all! Be entertained, be amazed, and be frightened! Encounter the outlandish, the odd, and the weird . . . the Freaks of the Storms! Step right up and hear the strangest plethora of wind, rain, and storm stories ever to be assembled in one place.

Do you have the courage to hear the creepy story of "Ice Spear of Death"? Can you endure the tale of the "Lightning Strike that Ignited a Man's Stomach"? Have you the willingness to witness the cattle "Herd Shot around the World"? Do you have the nerve to learn the secrets of the horrifying "Rains of Blood" or the macabre "Killer Fog of Pennsylvania"? Are you brave enough to learn the gruesome details of the "Tornado Crucifixion" or bold enough to discover the intriguing secrets of the "Hurricane Pig"?

The Weird. The Bizarre. The Unusual. It's all here . . . so, boys and girls, ladies and gents: Prepare to enter the baffling world of . . . the Freaks of the Storm!

Chapter 2
TORNADOES

A TORNADO IS ONE OF NATURE'S MOST VIOLENT CREATIONS. IT can materialize in what seems like an instant, carry out an extraordinary amount of damage over a small area, and then abruptly vanish back into its parent thunderstorm. A tornado can terrify us but it can also invoke a feeling of awe at the power and majesty of nature. As Snowden Flora, a tornado expert of the first half of the last century, remarked, "Passing through one of these storms is an experience never forgotten."

Formally, a tornado is defined as a violently rotating column of air that hangs from the clouds of a severe thunderstorm and is in contact with the ground. Yet, within this broad definition, there are several oddities that can confuse the situation a bit. For instance, meteorologists now realize that larger tornadoes will sometimes have smaller vortices, termed "suction vortices" rotating around them. Or sometimes a whirling vortex might not actually contact the ground; so we created the term "funnel cloud" for a severe vortex that has not yet touched down from a thunderstorm. However, from my personal experience, it can sometimes be difficult to determine if a funnel cloud actually is in contact with the ground. Since a funnel is composed of swirling air, which may or may not be made visible with condensed water and debris in it, a tornado that appears "only" to be a funnel cloud (no apparent funnel touching down) may actually have winds that are doing damage on the ground.

To create a tornado, one first needs a thunderstorm, preferably a supercell or rotating severe thunderstorm, from which the most destructive and deadly tornadoes often descend. Such a severe storm (and the generation of any potential tornadoes from it) is fundamentally controlled by a basic physical principle: warm air rises. Consequently, the basic recipe for the creation of a tornado requires three critical ingredients that help to promote the maximum uplift of warm air. First, moisture is needed to serve as the fuel for the storm. When water vapor (a gas) is condensed into water (a liquid), the release of heat supplies energy

A single, large (F5) tornado composed of two rotating smaller tornadoes called suction vortices. Image taken on April 11, 1965 in Elkhart Indiana by Paul Huffman. (Photo Courtesy of National Oceanic and Atmospheric Administration/Department of Commerce Photo Library Historic NWS Collection.)

that then warms the air and helps uplift. Second, a large difference in temperature over a short distance enhances the uplift of warm air, which is comparatively light, over heavier cold air. Third, wind shear—the changes in wind speed and direction with height—can lead to the spinning and uplift of air as well. But, beyond these rather broad ingredients, the specifics of actual tornado formation are still relatively unknown to meteorologists. Simply put, we can't predict far in advance precisely when and where a tornado will touch down. However, with continued study in the field by storm scientists and improvements in our theories of tornado formation, we are improving our abilities.

After a tornado strikes and people begin to pick up the pieces that it left, often the first aspects of a tornado that impact society involve how much damage it caused. In the middle of the last century, Dr. Ted Fujita created a scale (now called the F-Scale in his honor) that ranks tornadoes based on how much damage they do. When Dr. Fujita first developed his scale, he established thirteen classes—F0 being the weakest and F12 being the damage class linked to winds of Mach 1, the speed of sound. Practically, however, his tornado scale ends at F5 damage with top winds of 320 miles per hour. The reasoning is fairly straightforward; winds of 320 miles per hour will destroy a structure down to its foundation, so there is no way to distinguish damage caused by higher speed winds (remember, the Fujita scale is linked to damage, not directly to wind-speed measurement). So, practically, no tornado damage can be determined to exceed F5.

After hearing about the overall damage, we also often hear curious and sometimes unbelievable accounts of the freaks of the tornado and its passage. After culling innumerable newspaper accounts, science journals, books, and weather records, these oddities begin to separate themselves into certain repeatable categories. In this chapter, with the input of top tornado forecasters,

Don't be fooled! This is a photo of a tornado—
not a funnel cloud—touching down near Denver
Colorado (notice the debris on the horizon).
(Photo Courtesy of Larry E. Evans.)

I have selected twelve of those categories to demonstrate the
bizarre and unusual aspects of tornadoes, such as human and
animal carries by tornadoes, strange "inside tornado" personal
accounts, and even some of the most gruesome stories of tornado
passage, including "natural crucifixion." But to end on an upbeat
note—as with Pandora's Box, where the final occupant of the box
was Hope—I have included a final thirteenth section on basic
instructions on how to survive a tornado.

(1) Chicken Plucking

One of the most common features of early tornado stories is
mention of tornadoes' bizarre ability to pluck the feathers right

out of a chicken. Time after time, old accounts of tornadoes describe "chickens . . . stripped of their feathers and carried long distances" (an 1879 Kansas tornado) or "thirty chickens . . . stripped entirely of their feathers and found sitting in the poultry house, stiffly at attention. All were dead" (a 1943 Michigan tornado). Indeed, even pictures of deplumed chickens have appeared nationally, such as the occurrences documented by two top meteorologists Galway and Schaefer in a 1979 issue of the popular weather magazine *Weatherwise*. In that article, they wryly noted, "While it is not the mission of the National Severe Storm Forecast Center (NSSFC) to record tornadoes which deplumed fowls, enough events of this phenomenon have been documented over the past one hundred and forty years to warrant its acceptance."

But how does a tornado deplume a chicken? Scientific attempts to answer that question date back to 1842. In that year, a well-known meteorologist named Elias Loomis performed a bizarre—but widely reported—experiment that undoubtedly would not pass through the rigid scientific review process of today. Basically, Loomis endeavored to determine the precise wind speed needed to defeather a chicken. For his instrument of choice in this "scientific test," he employed what he termed "a gun of two inches calibre." First, he filled the gun with five ounces of black powder, and then added a recently killed chicken as the bullet. Because the chicken was much bigger than the barrel of the gun, Loomis needed to shove the chicken into the gun using "considerable force," with the result that the chicken was, he scientifically recorded, "somewhat bruised." He then pointed the gun straight up and fired. The experiment caused chicken feathers to be shot up twenty or thirty feet, and they were immediately scattered by the wind.

When Loomis retrieved a few pieces of the chicken shrapnel, he found the feathers to have been pulled out of the chicken cleanly—that is, little skin was still adhering to them. The main chicken body, according to Loomis, was torn into innumerable small fragments. Indeed, he could only find a part of the whole chicken. He concluded, "A fowl, then, forced through the air with this velocity [he computed the speed at 341 miles per hour], is torn entirely to pieces; with a less velocity, it is probable most of the feathers might be pulled out without mutilating the body." He lamented in his writings that if he could have only found "a suitable gun," he could have experimentally determined the minimal velocity to cause defeathering. However, he "presumed" the necessary plucking speed "to be not far from a hundred miles per hour."

A few years later in 1890, another highly recognized meteorologist named H. A. Hazen declared, "There seems very little doubt" that chicken defeathering is a result of lightning rather than being blown by the winds. Hazen linked tornadic chicken plucking to the strange weather finding that (as I will discuss later in Chapter Three) many people struck by lightning in the past were discovered to be naked—that is, all of their clothes were stripped from them. He suggested that a similar explanation could be employed to explain defeathered chickens found after tornadoes.

Today, we believe that defeathering is primarily a stress reaction by the poultry; something called "flight molt." Flight molt probably first developed as a survival mechanism for the flightless birds. Through this molting ability of the chicken, an attacking predator is only able to grab a few of its feathers as opposed to the whole chicken. And chickens aren't the only fowls to experience this panic molt. In 1883, George Clinton Smith wrote in *Popular Science Monthly* that a tornado plucked a full flock of geese of their feathers and deposited them "in a hedge-fence, giving it a complete coating."

Occasionally, tornadoes can cause more than just defeathering. G.T. Meaden wrote in the British *Journal of Meteorology* that 136 pink-footed geese in 1978 were killed by a tornado in England. When autopsies were performed on five of the geese, it was discovered that the birds were not singed or burnt (such as might be created by lightning), and there were no pellets with the bodies. All of the birds had apparently died of trauma caused by hitting the ground (or buildings) at great force and all had ruptured livers and hemorrhaged lungs, which could have resulted from hitting something or, Meaden reasoned, perhaps due to decompression caused by the tornado. The conclusion reached at the time was that the birds had been swept up to great heights by the storms and died before they actually hit the ground.

(2) Planes, Trains, and Automobiles

Man-made objects have often suffered greatly from the passage of a tornado. Many historical accounts address how massive objects, such as trains, have been strangely treated by tornadoes. For instance, an old *Weatherwise* article recounted the odd tale of a hobo who was aboard a freight train on the track at Tonica, Illinois, when tornadic winds propelled it safely along the rails to La Salle, twelve miles away. The tornado's capricious movements can be vertical as well. The *Literary Digest* magazine reported that in 1920 an Illinois tornado lifted a freight car, packed with fifteen hundred pounds of unidentified cargo, forty feet into the air and deposited it into the side of a train station. One of the more infamous train-tornado encounters was that between the passenger train *Empire Builder* and an F3 tornado (referring to the ranking of the famous Fujita tornado damage scale of F0–F5, with F5 being the worst) on May 27, 1931, in Minnesota. The tornado hit the train almost at right angles and lifted five of the coaches, each weighing about seventy tons, off the track. One coach was carried eighty feet and laid in a ditch. But, conversely, an older account of a Union Pacific Railroad engine being picked up, turned around in midair and set down on a parallel track, facing in the opposite direction is apparently a tall tale—at least, I haven't been able to confirm it.

Automobiles are also not exempt from a tornado's wind. Because of the air space between the bottom of the vehicle and the ground, cars and trucks are particularly easy for tornado winds to lift. For example, a weather observer by the name of Lyman in Minnesota recounted the story of a Minnesota tornado that "split open a tree, jammed in an automobile, and clamped the tree shut again" in 1919. The Palm Sunday Tornado Outbreak of 1965 produced damage that Indiana Sheriff Woody Caton described to a *Times* reporter as looking "like a giant auto-crushing machine had simply chewed the place up." He said that the twister had "seared paint off cars, squeezed them together like accordions, or exploded them as if by dynamite."

According to an article in the fortean magazine *FATE* by Paul

The wreckage of the Empire Builder, a passenger train bound from Seattle to Chicago, after being hit by a tornado. (Photo Courtesy of NOAA Photo Library Historic NWS Collection.)

Steiner, a 1966 Mississippi tornado reportedly lifted a mother and her two-year-old daughter in the family Volkswagen into the air and carried it a staggering seventy feet through the air. Finally, the tornado dropped the small car on the top of the local electrical company building. Amazingly, the Volkswagen sustained only a couple of dents in the hood and miraculously neither the mother nor her daughter was injured. On the other hand, some tornadoes apparently are only interested in certain parts of cars. For instance, Snowden Flora reported that a 1942 Oklahoma tornado selectively ripped off only one of the wheels of a car. But the tornado wasn't so kind to the house next to the car; the entire four-room frame house was completely blown away, leaving only the front porch and a small wooden bench that had been leaning against the house.

Tornadoes don't just dislike cars; some of them apparently

The awesome power of a 1980 Nebraska tornado demonstrated as a 2 inch by 4 inch board shot through a car windshield. (Photo Courtesy of Dr. Merlin Lawson, University of Nebraska.)

have an aversion even for roads. J. L. Stanford, in his 1987 book *Tornado (Accounts of Tornadoes in Iowa)*, mentioned a twister in 1964 that literally peeled several hundred feet of Highway 10 five miles north of the town of Herreid, South Dakota. And, finally, some tornadoes don't even like the ground. A 1928 twister in Greensburg, Kansas, literally plowed a two- to three-feet-wide ditch through a field of wheat. Witnesses reported that the dirt was thrown over on each side of the furrow just as if a farming plow had made the trench.

Airplanes have also suffered at the winds of a tornado. A couple of incidents related by expert meteorologist Joe Schaefer of the Severe Storms Forecast Center prove the point. First, in May 1953, a Lockheed Constellation flying near Houston in clouds northeast of a thunderstorm experienced something that might be equated to a tornado. During a twenty-five-second period, the plane's altimeter went up and down from 12,000

A damage evaluation committee poses next to a 1 inch by 5 inch board which was driven through a 2 inch by 6 inch post by the infamous Tri-State Tornado in 1925. (Photo Courtesy of National Oceanic and Atmospheric Administration/Department of Commerce Photo Library Historic NWS Collection.)

feet up to 16,500 feet, then down to 2,500 feet and back up to 4,000 feet. During the ascent portion, the plane was upside down, and could not have mechanically maintained an indicated air speed of 170 knots. The rate of climb was pegged at six thousand feet per minute. On that day, tornadoes were reported near San Antonio, Baton Rouge, and Corpus Christi. Did the plane actually encounter a tornado in midair? No one can say for sure what happened. Nevertheless, the account does make for interesting reading.

Second, in November 1963, a DC-8 flight from Houston to Mexico City underwent an uncontrollable incredibly fast dive, flying at nineteen thousand feet just south of Houston. The plane was climbing through clouds on the north side of a radar echo. The airspeed indicators both went to zero before the dive. To get out of the dive, the pilot was forced to reverse the thrust of the jets while in the air.

Substantial damage can even be done to aircraft on the ground by the passage of a tornado. For example, one of the more costly tornadoes ever to hit the United States was one that destroyed an air force base in Texas in 1952. That tornado caused forty-eight million dollars worth of damage by leaving one hundred and six heavy B-36 bombers in tattered shreds on the runway.

(3) Weighty Transport and Fragile Transport

The destruction of a fleet of military bombers attests to the power of a tornado—but tornadoes have also demonstrated their awesome muscle in other ways throughout the years. For example, a rare tornado in India in 1838 drove a long stalk of bamboo completely through a five-foot thick wall, covered with masonry bricks on both sides. In a similar fashion, in 1896, the chief of the Weather Bureau, Willis Moore, observed one of tornado history's most bizarre happenings the day after a mammoth

twister struck St. Louis, Missouri. The head weatherman personally witnessed that a two-by-four-inch pine plank had been
rammed right through a solid iron girder supporting the Eads
Bridge. In his own words, he "saw a two-by-four pine scantling
shot through five-eighths [inch] of solid iron on the Eads
Bridge, the pine stick protruding several feet through the iron
side of the roadway, exemplifying the old principle of shooting a
candle through a board."

A shovel that has been shot six inches into a tree during the massive St. Louis Tornado of
May 27, 1896. (Photo Courtesy of National Oceanic and Atmospheric Administration/
Department of Commerce Photo Library Historic NWS Collection from the 1922 book
The New Air World by Willis Luther Moore.)

A 1912 tornado in Syracuse, New York, according to a weather observer in *Monthly Weather Review,* lifted a home from its foundations, turned it part way around, then abruptly flipped the building completely upside down. When the winds finally dropped the house, amazingly, it was almost on its former site but now with its roof pointing downward into its basement. Also, miraculously, after their topsy-turvy adventure, the family inside escaped unharmed from a window by crawling on the ceiling.

In terms of massive, it is hard to top the 1927 tornado in Hutchinson, Kansas, that turned over a five-ton Caterpillar tractor and then rolled it a remarkable five hundred feet. Even more impressively, a 1970 Texas tornado, according to a Texas Tech University meteorologist, apparently pushed and rolled an eighteen-ton cylindrical liquid fertilizer tank measuring forty feet long and eleven feet in diameter, for over half a mile. As final demonstration of tornadic power, a meteorologist analyzing an 1877 Mount Carmel, Illinois, tornado reported that the tornado slammed a normal brick into a house through its outer wall, through the interior wood, through the plaster, then across two rooms (an amazing distance of twenty-seven feet), and then finally lodged the brick in a rear wall . . . all without even breaking corners off the brick!

And yet, oddly enough, tornadic winds can sometimes be as gentle as a mother's hands. While the winds of the catastrophic F5 Xenia, Ohio, tornado completely demolished a whole farmhouse and its entire contents, it also left three quite fragile items completely intact: a box of Christmas ornaments, a mirror, and even a case of eggs! Similarly in the great Tri-State Tornado of 1925, a survivor recalled that nearly two weeks after the tornado, his brother, who was helping clean up debris, found a box of eggs—and "as unbelievable as it sounds, not one egg was broken." In still a third analogous story, a reporter for Lincoln *Journal-Star* wrote that prior to a tornado strike on Hallam, Nebraska, in 2004, a man had been driving home after buying four dozen eggs from a family there. After encountering the tornado and having his pickup truck rolled perhaps eight times by the gale winds, the man and his neighbors afterward still found "four or five of [the eggs] . . . hadn't even been cracked."

In another tornado-egg instance, I contacted a well-known meteorologist (and one of the founders of the National Weather Association), S. Joe Rigney, who had been a weatherman at Scottsbluff, Nebraska, in 1951 when a tornado passed over a prairie farm. According to Rigney, the twister had destroyed the farmstead, even spearing a steer with a piece of lumber but it also created a bizarre oddity in the farm's chicken coup. In the Weather Bureau's damage assessment afterward, Rigney discovered that a bean had been embedded one-inch-deep in an egg without having cracked the shell—and meteorologist Joe Schaefer

Bean imbedded 1 inch in egg

An old photograph purportedly showing an egg that has been penetrated by a bean, taken near Scottsbluff Nebraska by S. Joe Rigney in 1952. (Photo courtesy of Joe Rigney, United Airlines, and the Linda Hall Library of Science, Engineering & Technology in Kansas City.)

and I even uncovered an old copy of the photograph of that bean-pierced egg!

According to Earl V. Bower, an early Weather Bureau cooperative observer, an F2 tornado that hit Kansas in 1913 tore up an apple tree nearly a foot in diameter by its roots and broke it into pieces "while a beehive within three feet of the tree was not even turned over." Then there is the story first reported by meteorologist W. J. Humphreys, in his 1937 book *Weather Rambles,* of a Connecticut F4 tornado in 1917 that is said to have picked up a glass jar of sweet pickles, which the twister later dropped (without breaking) in a ditch some twenty-five miles away.

(4) Flying People

If a tornado can sometimes carry a glass pickle jar for twenty-five miles without breaking, it might not be too surprising to find accounts of babies, children, and even adults being carried safely by tornadoes. Although the 1955 F5 tornado that hit Udall, Kansas, a small town southeast of Wichita, did kill or injure over half of the population of that rural community, there were also some weird stories of safe transport that were recorded in *Time* Magazine: A retired railroad worker was actually sucked out of his house and out of his shoes—and into a tree where he sat unharmed while the storm raged about him. Conversely, a husband and wife simply knelt in a back bedroom when the tornado struck—but then emerged to find that the rest of their house was completely gone. A local barber in Udall apparently was a sound sleeper—he was thrown out of bed, through the window, and into the street—while he still slept!

William Bixby, in his 1961 book *Havoc,* tells the story of two men, named "Bill" and "Al," who once had an adventure (tho' perhaps not "excellent") near Higgins, Texas, (close to Texas's eastern border) in April of 1947. Bill was visiting Al when they heard a roar. When Al opened the door to see what was happening, the door was ripped from his hands. He was abruptly picked up and carried over the treetops. Subsequently, Bill went to the door to investigate Al's abrupt disappearance, and he found himself thrown about two hundred feet from the house. His buddy Al, tossed a few yards away, had started back to the house and stumbled across his friend Bill encased in painful barbwire. Al carefully unwrapped Bill as the winds continued to howl. Then, because of tornadic winds unrelentingly whirled around them, they crawled rather than walked back to the house. Upon the two friends' return, they found that literally all of the house's walls had disappeared. Fortunately, Al's wife and two children were uninjured, huddled on a couch. Bizarrely, the only other piece of furniture left on the floor was a lamp.

Even more strangely, Sioux Falls, South Dakota, television meteorologist Jeff Trobec, in his 1995 book *State of Extremes,* related the story of nine-year-old Sharon Weron, her horse, and a South Dakota tornado. On the afternoon of the first of July in 1955, Sharon was riding her pony through the grassland prairie. Suddenly a thunderstorm built over the area and she turned her horse quickly back toward her home. Unfortunately, as she galloped to within a few hundred yards of her farm, a tornado struck. She and the pony were whipped into the air, over a hill, and across a valley. The girl's mother briefly saw them both airborne, being carried over a second hill by the tornado. Apparently, the pony and the youngster ended up being carried over three fences and dropped about one thousand feet from where they were first picked up by the twister. Sharon later recalled that she landed like an airplane, "on her tummy, grabbing onto weeds to stay on the ground." Sharon admirably survived the trauma—I recently have had the wonderful opportunity to speak with her— and she said that she had even been asked to do a reenactment of the incident for a BBC show.

The incredibly fortunate Sharon Weron astride one of her horses. The young Ms. Weron and her horse were carried a thousand feet through the air safely by a South Dakota tornado in 1955. (Photo Courtesy of Sharon Fischer.)

Babies have also been carried by tornadoes. Canadian weather historian David Phillips, in his 1998 book *Blame It on the Weather*, tells the tale of a Saskatchewan family returning home in 1923 when a tornado picked up their baby girl from a buggy. After a long ten-hour search, the girl was found asleep in a shack two miles from the point where the buggy had been upset. Likewise, in St. Louis in 1927, an automobile mechanic watched the walls of a baker's shop across the street split wide open and tumble outward as a tornado passed. Incredibly, he then saw a three-year-old baby girl sail out through one of the cracks of the building. The child was later found unharmed in a vacant lot several blocks away from the bakery.

(5) Flying Animals

If a tornado can lift cars and people large distances, it should come as no surprise to discover many accounts of animals being carried through the sky. Indeed, tales of flying cows actually date back to the Middle Ages. In 1563, William Fulke, in his book *A Goodly Gallerye (Book of Meteors)*, wrote, "Auicen says that a whole calf fell out of the air and some would make it seem credible, that of Vapors and Exhalations, with the power of the heavenly bodies concurring, a calf might be made in the clouds. But I had rather think that this calf was taken up by some storm of whirlwind and so let fall again, then agree to so monstrous a generation."

More recently, Sir Graham Sutton recounted a Kansas tale of "a herd of cattle emulating the nursery rhyme and taking off for the moon 'looking like gigantic birds in the sky.' " When Frank W. Lane contacted the Kansas City weather office about this story, meteorologist Donald House responded, "We have been unable to verify the legend you refer to in your letter, but we believe it is within the realm of the possible." He wryly added that if a herd of cows did thus become airborne they would probably refer to it as "the herd shot around the world." Snowden Flora recalled in an early issue of *Weatherwise*, "Several years ago in Norton County, Kansas, a tornado struck a herd of steers, drawing them up to a great height. Persons who saw them reported they looked like gigantic birds."

Sometimes, tornadoes will fly animals that don't normally need help in that capacity. As example, according to A. H. Godbey, in his 1890 book *Great Disasters and Horrors in the World's History*, newspapers reported following a massive twister strike on Louisville, Kentucky, in 1890 that "at Baird's drug store on Market above Ninth [Street], two bird cages with the birds were blown in through the skylight. The cages were not injured, and the birds are as full of song as ever."

Undoubtedly one of the strangest "flying animal" tornado stories concerns an 1899 Missouri severe F4 tornado that was reported in a concurrent issue of *Century* Magazine. Three people, Miss Moorehouse, Mrs. Webster, and her son, were caught up in the storm, and carried nearly one fourth of a mile, and let down so gently that none of the three were seriously injured. Miss Moorehouse told an amazing tale of the tornado's winds: "I was conscious all the time I was flying through the air and it seemed a long time. I seemed to be lifted up and whirled round and round, going up to a great height, at one time far above the church steeples, and seemed to be carried a long distance." She recalled that as she was hurled through the air literally "being whirled about at the sport of the storm, I saw a horse soaring and rotating about with me. It was a white horse and had a harness on. By the way it kicked and struggled as it was hurled about I knew it was alive." She recalled at the time fervently praying that horse didn't smash into her and, miraculously, "it did not." She finished her astounding account by noting that the tornado tossed her back on the ground "unharmed, saved by a miracle." The young boy also recalled that at one time the horse, which his mother had seen, "was directly over me, and I was very much afraid I would come in contact with its flying heels."

It was discovered later that the white horse belonged to a teamster named Cheney, living in the southeastern part of the city. Its teammate was found dead near the wrecked barn in which both horses had been placed. Bizarrely enough, beyond being well plastered with mud, the white horse was uninjured by his fantastic tornadic flight.

Such events aren't limited to the United States. Canadian weather historian David Phillips stated that, after a tornado hit a Saskatchewan farm in 1946, a milk cow was found alive but stranded on its back. Literally, its four legs were sticking straight up in the air with its horns anchoring it firmly to the ground. According to Phillips perhaps somewhat tongue-in-cheek, the farmer did not continue to milk the cow "for fear of sour milk."

(6) Inside a Tornado

As noted in the stories above, a few extraordinarily lucky people have been safely carried by tornadoes. An even smaller number of people have claimed to have seen the inside of a tornado. The most famous of "inside tornado" stories is that of farmer Will Keller. In a 1930 article in *Monthly Weather Review,* he was described as "a man apparently between thirty-five and forty years of age. His reputation for truthfulness and sobriety is of the best. Apparently he is entirely capable of making careful and reliable observations."

Keller's description of the interior of a tornado has become one of the standards in tornado meteorology:

> . . . At last the great shaggy end of the funnel hung directly overhead. Everything was still as death. There was a strong gassy odor and it seemed that I could not breathe. There was a screaming, hissing sound coming directly from the end of the funnel. I looked up and to my astonishment I saw right up into the heart of the tornado. There was a circular opening in the center of the funnel, about fifty or one hundred feet in diameter, and extending straight upward for a distance of at least one half mile, as best I could judge under the circumstances. The walls of this opening were of rotating clouds and the whole was brilliantly visible by constant flashes of lightning, which zigzagged from side to side. Had it not been for the lightning I could not have seen the opening, not any distance up into it anyway. Around the lower rim of the great vortex small tornadoes were constantly forming and breaking away. These looked like tails as they writhed their way around the end of the funnel. It was these that made the hissing noise. I noticed that the direction of rotation of the great whirl was anticlockwise, but the small twisters rotated both ways—some one way and some another. The opening was entirely hollow except for something, which I could not exactly make out, but suppose that it was a detached wind cloud. This thing was in the center and was moving up and down.

Retired army captain Roy S. Hall also had this type of unique encounter with a Texas tornado in 1948 and described it for *Weatherwise*. He described the tornado as something that "had billowed down from above, and stood fairly motionless save for a slow up and down pulsation." The funnel was curved with the concave part facing toward Captain Hall. Within a short moment, he was "inside the tornado itself! It resembled the interior of a glazed standpipe." The core, he wrote, extended for well over a hundred feet upward and demonstrated a marked swaying motion that caused it to bend slowly to the southeast. The bottom of the funnel, he recalled, "was about 150 yards across. High up it was larger, and seemed to be partly filled with a bright cloud which shimmered like a fluorescent light." He described the entire funnel cloud as a bizarre set of stacked rings, "each moving independently and causing a wave to ripple from top to bottom." When the crest of each pulsation reached the bottom of the spinning column of air, Hall noted, "the funnel's tip snapped like whip."

(7) Sounds of a Tornado

One of the most common features discussed by tornado survivors is the noise—and, very often, an almost trite description of its sound is given—"the sound of a freight train." That well-known description actually dates back to the early 1800s. Eminent meteorologist J. P. Espy, for example, recounted the cacophony of the New Haven, Connecticut, tornado of 1839 as "a heavy rumbling noise . . . not unlike the passing of a long train of railway cars, which was audible in every part of the city." Yet, with this incredible roar of "a thousand trains crossing [a] big bridge at once" as some have referred to it, other noises are often drowned out. Early tornado historian William Ferrel noted, during an 1875 South Carolina tornado, "at least five thousand trees in the village were scattered in every direction. The roar of the wind was such that the tremendous crash was heard by no one." In a similar fashion, David A. J. Seargent's fascinating 1991 book on Australian tornadoes *Willy Willies & Cock-eyed Bobs*, told the story of a family caught in their house during a 1959 tornado in New South Wales, Australia. The family, according to Seargent, was so overwhelmed by the deafening roar of the tornado that they did not even hear their own roof being blown off.

Now, with the advent of video cameras, many people have heard the roar of a tornado. Yet, the very first sound recording of a tornado occurred fairly recent, having been made with the infamous Xenia tornado in 1974. That recording, produced by Thomas Yougen who had turned on his tape recorder as the tornado approached and then passed over the city, was played on national television following the event. Another survivor of the Xenia tornado perhaps more graphically described the Xenia

LEFT: A branch from a tree that was rammed through the iron Eads Bridge during the massive St. Louis Tornado of May 27, 1896. RIGHT: Close-up of the branch through the bridge. (Photo Courtesy of National Oceanic and Atmospheric Administration/Department of Commerce Photo Library Historic NWS Collection from the 1922 book *The New Air World* by Willis Luther Moore.)

twister's sound as "a piercing shriek, like the sound of thousands of nails being wrenched from the boards they anchor."

(8) Coincidence

Everyone has heard of weird coincidences, of seemingly separate events somehow strangely linked together, and the past literature attests to the fact that tornadoes produce their share of bizarre coincidences. Tornado historian Thomas Grazulis, for example, cited the 1895 example of two separate teachers killed by a single tornado in two distinctly different schools in Iowa. Reminiscent of a Ripley's oddity cartoon, Grazulis continued the coincidence by noting that the two teachers killed were actually brother and sister. In another instance, an El Dorado, Kansas, tornado threw a woman sixty feet out of her house and safely deposited her next to a phonograph record of the song "Stormy Weather." And more recently, in 1996, a drive-in theater in St. Catharine's, Ontario, was struck by a tornado apparently as it was showing the blockbuster tornado movie *Twister*. And, perhaps suggesting that nature was trying to make a point, I present an unconfirmed story communicated to me by a fellow meteorologist of a gentleman who lost his first wife in the Ganesville, Georgia, tornado of 1903 and, only three short years later, lost his second wife in the subsequent Ganesville tornado of 1906.

According to a 1920 issue of the *Literary Digest* (quoting a New York *Tribune* report), a tornado struck a church just as a minister was saying to his congregation that they should "be prepared, for you know not when you will be called." At that very moment, the roof caved in, the steeple collapsed, and three people, two women and a child, were killed by the tornado debris.

(9) Tornadoes and Electricity

As our knowledge of tornadoes has increased, so has the quality of our observations. Many early accounts of tornadoes are filled with curious observations of "electric" or "fiery" tornadoes (for instance, see Captain Hall's account above). For many years, research meteorologist Bernard Vonnegut (brother of the famous writer Kurt Vonnegut) was one of the leading advocates of a linkage between tornadoes and electricity. For instance, he described a 1965 Ohio tornado in the journal *Science* as having a "beautiful electric blue light" and a "ball of orange lightning [which] came from the cone point of the tornado." A classic description by a weather observer named Floyd Montgomery of a "luminous" tornado in 1955 even appeared in *Weatherwise*. He viewed the tornado as having a "fire up near the top of the funnel [that] looked like a child's Fourth of July pinwheel" and described the colors of that "fire" as being "the same color as an electric arc welder but much brighter, and it seemed to be turning to the right like a beacon lamp on a lighthouse."

Even earlier accounts attempted to link tornadoes and electricity using damage assessment; nineteenth-century meteorologist, Robert Hare, for example, claimed that the "parched and scorched" nature of the vegetation following an 1835 New Jersey tornado "conclusively proved" that electricity is fundamental to tornado formation. An observer to the 1890 Louisville, Kentucky, tornado described it as "balloon-shaped, twisting an attenuated tail to the Earth." He said that the tornado emitted "a constant fusillade of lightning, and seemed to be composed of a lurid, snake-like mass of electric currents, whose light would sometimes be extinguished for a few moments, making almost intolerable darkness."

However, in contrast to these early reports, today's sophisticated meteorological equipment, which can triangulate exact positions of lightning, does not indicate marked or significant electrical activity inside of tornadoes. Were these old "electrical tornado" observations therefore merely instances of people—

upon hearing other people say they saw lightning in tornadoes—reporting what was then expected of them? What would you say if you had just experienced a tornado and a reporter asked you, "Was there a lot of lightning in the tornado?" Whatever the real explanation, abundant "lightning in a tornado" does make for a more exciting news or science story—but doesn't appear to be true.

(10) Long-Distance Transport

One tornado oddity that is currently being investigated is exactly how far materials can be transported by tornadoes. According to the University of Oklahoma Tornado Debris Project, the current record-holder for longest-known debris transport is a personal check that traveled 223 miles from Stockton, Kansas, to Winnetoon, Nebraska, via a strong F3 tornado in 1991. As for movement of larger objects, William Ferrel cited an 1877 Illinois tornado that carried "the spire, vane, and gilded ball of the Methodist Church" a distance of 15 miles. Meteorologist W. J. Humphreys, in his 1937 book *Weather Rambles,* wrote of a 1932 South Dakota major F3 tornado that tore a 200-pound, 6-inch-wide, 13.5-feet-long steel I-beam from a highway bridge, carried it an eighth of a mile, and finally drove it endwise squarely through the heart of a 15-inch diameter cottonwood tree some 20 feet above the ground. The tree was splintered at the point of exit (but not entrance) and was not split or topped over. Incredibly, the steel I-beam, which protruded two feet out of the tree, was so bent that its two ends actually pointed in the same direction.

(11) The Risqué

Sometimes modesty and the accouterments of civilization suffer mightily at the hands of nature. Such was the case for a couple of young women during the Great St. Louis tornado of 1896. Julian

Curzon related such a story told by a reporter in the 1896 modestly named book *The Great Cyclone at St. Louis and East St. Louis, May 27,*
1896: Being a Full History of the Most Terrifying and Destructive Tornado in the
History of the World. The reporter described the plight of three ladies
during the twister as "very embarrassing." As the storm slammed
into the city, the three women were enjoying a ride in an open-
air cable car. They were in a quandary. Should they stay or should
they go? Eventually, the rapid advance of the storm and lack of
any nearby shelter dictated that the ladies remained where they
were on the cable car. But then the reporter stated "the unprin-
cipled wind began to take unwarranted liberties" with the ladies
and they decided to risk an attempt to get to shelter. Unfortunately they were wearing large skirts and the tornado winds blew
under their clothing. With ominous "rips" as the seams of their
dresses parted, the storm winds proceeded to disrobe the women,
carrying "sections of garments . . . bodily away." According to the
reporter, the women did get to shelter before they were completely unclothed. "But," he concluded, "in those awful few minutes even Peeping Toms had something else to indulge their
prying propensities, and the ladies had no cause to blush."

A Midwestern insurance agent suffered a similar fate in the
Palm Sunday Outbreak in 1965 when the tornado sucked him out
of the house. The next thing he remembered was that he "was
sliding out into the street with no clothes on." When the man
stood up, he saw that his entire house had been destroyed by the
tornado. His wife yelled from the now open-air basement that
she was all right but was stuck in the wreckage. Luckily, a neighbor
ran to the man's rescue with a pair of old pants and then both
men quickly dug out the man's wife. Government meteorologist
Finley reported that a Delphos, Kansas, tornado in 1879 caused
particularly severe suffering to women. He recounted that "in
every instance they were entirely divested of their garments, and

left perfectly at the mercy of the flying debris that filled the air."
The tornado, combined with heavy rain, so matted the hair of the
female victims with mud that "their heads had to be shaved in
order to clean them, or, as one gentlemen remarked who witnessed the scene, 'it seemed as if the mud belonged there
naturally, and that the hair was but a mere usurper.'" Apparently, the mud was so prevalent that it filled the victims' eyes and
ears to the point that when rescuers arrived, the victims didn't
initially see or hear them.

(12) The Gruesome

It must be remembered that tornadoes are quite deadly. Injury
and death by such a formidable force of nature can be graphic
and gruesome. A bizarre case of natural crucifixion proves the
point. According to the *Literary Digest,* a devastating F4 tornado
that hit Georgia in 1932 tossed—and impaled—a farmer onto a
barbed wire fence. He hung spread-eagle in the fence in an
uncanny semblance to the Roman crucifixion practice until some
time later when he was discovered. Although he was quickly transported to a hospital, he later died of his injuries.

Unfortunately, women are not exempt, either. Jay Robert
Nash, in his 1976 book *Darkest Hours,* recounted a macabre story
from the Waco, Texas, tornado of 1953. Two men were driving
home when their car was caught by the tornado and lifted into the
air. Seconds later they were set gently down on the street again.
But then the shaken driver turned to his passenger and pointed
to the new gruesome hood ornament on their car. The badly
mangled body of a woman was draped over the car's hood.

Thomas Grazulis recounted an even more gruesome story that
he took from Georgia newspapers of the time. In 1875, following
a tornado in Covington, Georgia, rescuers discovered a man
named Andrew Tillman injured—but alive—in the wreckage of his

outhouse. Doctors attending Tillman determined that several pieces of bone literally had been driven into the man's brain. They managed successfully to extract these bone fragments— along with, the reports said, a tablespoon of the man's brains! Surprisingly, the old news report ended with the comment that, following the bizarre operation, Andrew Tillman was doing well.

In the 1899 Kirksville tornado, survivors made a grisly discovery in a treetop. They found the scalp of a woman with its hair intact—yet no person was found near it. A second human scalp was found three miles from the city underneath a bridge. And, finally, sometimes, weird death can happen even if not caused directly by the tornado. An issue of the *Monthly Weather Review* published an extract from the *Sylacauga Advance* in Alabama of a very strange death resulting from a 1920 tornado. Apparently, when the twister struck the farmstead of Mr. Will M. Baker near Hackleburg, a small town northwest of Birmingham, Alabama, its winds dislodged a loaded shotgun hanging on one of the walls. The gun hit the floor and fired, thereby fatally killing the young Mr. Baker.

(13) Safety: How to Survive a Tornado

Before the tornado season begins, two critical actions should be accomplished for people living in a tornado-prone area. First, you should either have a tornado cellar or designate a room in the home that will serve as your primary tornado shelter and practice having all family members getting there quickly in response to a tornado threat. That shelter ideally should be a separate tornado cellar but otherwise you should select a room (a) on the lowest floor of the house (a basement is best), (b) in the center of the house (to put as many walls between you and the tornado as possible), and (c) be a small room (such as a closet or bathroom).

Second, all members of your household should know the crucial differences between a tornado watch and a tornado warning. The National Weather Service issues a tornado watch when the conditions for producing tornadoes are present in a given area. Consequently, a tornado watch means that you should "be alert and aware" but not panic. You should listen to news (television or radio) and take the weather in consideration in planning activities during that day.

A tornado warning is issued by the National Weather Service when a tornado has been sighted either visually by a storm spotter or by radar. At that time, you should take immediate cover. If at home, go to your designated shelter. If outdoors, try to get into a building, if possible. If that isn't possible, you should quickly lay in a ditch or low-lying area. If driving, don't try to outrun it! Tornadoes can travel at amazing speeds and make unexpected turns. Get out of the car and take shelter in a building, if possible. Again, if none are available, get into a ditch or low-lying area. Contrary to a rather famous tornado video, do not stop under an overpass or bridge—such structures are extremely dangerous as tornadic winds can be funneled into them. Consequently, tornado winds can literally pop you out from the overpass or the whole structure can be picked up and dropped on you.

If you are in a large building, such as a school, shopping center, church, theater, or office building, avoid large rooms with wide-span roofs, such auditoriums, large classrooms, or cafeterias. Get to the lowest level of the building (again, a basement is preferable) and into an interior small room, such as a bathroom. If a small room is not available, you should crouch along the walls of a hallway with your hands positioned to protect your head and neck.

Chapter 3
LIGHTNING

IGHTNING HAS ALWAYS BEEN AN AWE-INSPIRING SIGHT throughout human history. We now have a fairly good scientific appreciation of this strange phenomenon. Normal lightning begins as negative charges (electrons) are ripped from the top of the cloud usually via raindrops and accumulate in the lower regions of the thunderstorm. This sets up an increasingly large electrical potential in the cloud with negative charges in the bottom and positive changes in the top and on the ground under the storm. Given the physics principle that states opposite electrical changes attract, nature tries to bridge the gap between positive and negative charges by sending out a stream of electrons from the bottom of the cloud through air toward the positive charges. If this electron flow moves close enough, a flow of positive charge (protons) progresses toward the electrons and an electrical arc is induced, connecting the two. At that point, an electrical circuit is completed, the channel becomes illuminated, and we see the flash. As subsequent streams of electrons flow through the channel, it becomes reilluminated, giving the flickering characteristic we often see with lightning. This whole process takes only a fraction of a second to complete.

Even though a lightning strike transpires over a period of only milliseconds, its effects are long-term—indeed, they have been recorded throughout the history of mankind. For thousands of years, stories of lightning miracles, lightning injuries, and odd types of lightning, such as rocket lightning or ball lightning have amazed and baffled scientists and the public alike. In this chapter, I have collected anecdotes involving some of the stranger aspects of lightning, which I have categorized into twelve "odd" categories. As with tornadoes, the final section in this baker's dozen involves general safety guidelines for lightning.

(1) Lightning and History

Lightning has occasionally played a leading role in shaping human history. A good example of this is a story told by G. D. Freier in his 1992 book *The Wonder of Weather,* regarding the present location of Vatican City. At the end of the thirteenth century, the papacy had been moved to Avignon in France and many Frenchmen were elevated to cardinals so as to ensure that its location would remain in France. But when English, Spanish, and German cardinals objected to paying tithes to a French-based church, the School of Cardinals was called together to establish, once and for all, the papacy's location. As the cardinals were voting, lightning struck the electoral chamber and set it on fire. Thinking that this was a divine sign from God, the cardinals immediately voted to move the papacy back to Rome whereupon Gregory XI was made pope.

De Fonvielle, a nineteenth-century lightning historian, recorded that when the Goths, under the rule of Alaric, besieged Rome in AD 410, the commander of the Roman's guard, as a last resource, listened to the propositions of certain Etruscan wizards, who stated that they could draw down lightning upon the enemy. But their attempt ended in a most disastrous failure—no lightning and no enemy deaths—and the Eternal City of Rome was indeed sacked by Alaric and his barbarians.

Conversely, in AD 174, when renowned Roman Emperor Marcus Aurelius was attacking the barbarians in Germany during a hot summer, he found his infantry completely surrounded by mounted warriors. Seeing their advantage, the barbarians settled for a long siege, expecting to capture the Romans easily as the result of the summer heat and their growing thirst. So the barbarians, with their superior numbers, posted guards to keep the Romans from reaching any water source. After a short time, the Romans began to suffer from fatigue, wounds, the heat of the sun, and above all, thirst. In desperation, Marcus Aurelius called upon his wizard, an Egyptian named Arnuphis, to do something. Arnuphis apparently crafted powerful weather magic and, the historians tell us, soon after he began, a massive rainstorm built over the area and cool, wet rain fell over the Romans.

When the rain poured down, initially all of the Romans turned their faces upward and simply let their parched mouths fill with rain; indeed some even held out their shields and others seized their helmets to catch more of the water. Of course, the barbarians, as they watched the Romans scramble for the rainwater, realized that the storm was the perfect time to finish off their enemy. But, according to the ancient historians, Marcus Aurelius's Egyptian wizard then transformed the rainstorm into a thunderstorm. And, the barbarians—being on horses and thus taller than the Roman infantry—were particularly susceptible to the lightning strikes. Numerous thunderbolts fell upon the ranks of the barbarians and they were "consumed by fire and dying." Miraculously to the barbarians and to their foes, "the fire, on the one hand, did not touch the Romans." The result was that the Romans won the battle and legend has it that that victorious Roman legion henceforth became known as the Thunderbolt Legion.

Addressing an even more pivotal event in history, Dr. John D. Bullock put forth a fascinating theory regarding lightning and one of the early fathers of Christianity in his 1994 scholarly article in the medical journal *Survey of Ophthalmology*. The biblical book of Acts records that Saul of Tarsus—a notorious persecutor of early Christians—experienced a dazzling vision of Christ while on the road to Damascus. Indeed the vision was so overwhelming that Saul was struck blind by the light. He was cured three days later by a Christian doctor named Ananias in Damascus. Immediately, Saul renounced his prior life, converted to the upstart religion of Christianity, and in an incredible reversal of roles actually becomes one of its major proponents, taking for himself the name of "Paul." From Acts 9:3, 8—9, 17—19:

> And as he journeyed, he came near Damascus: and suddenly, at midday, a light from heaven, brighter than the sun, flashed around him . . . And Saul arose from the earth; and when his eyes were opened, he saw no man: but they lead him by the hand, and brought him into Damascus. And he was three days without sight, and neither did eat nor drink . . . And Ananias [laid] his hands on him, said, "Brother Saul, the Lord Jesus who appeared to you on the road by which you came has sent me that you may regain your sight and be filled with the Holy Spirit." And immediately something like scales fell from his eyes, and he regained his sight. Then he arose and was baptized, and took food and was strengthened.

Bullock reviewed the story from a physician's perspective and suggested that Saul's conversion on the road to Damascus might have been the result of being struck by lightning. Bullock gave nineteen separate indicators from Paul's injuries, recovery, and later, career which are consistent with the experiences and injuries of many lightning victims. For example, Bullock theorized that Saul's blindness may have been "caused by bilateral corneal burns" created by the instantaneous evaporation of moisture from the eyes due to the lightning's heat. The return of Saul's vision after three days, according to Bullock, may be attributed to a "debridement" (or "peeling"), by Ananias, of "the 'scale'-like, opaque corneal epithelia" that had been burned. And, Bullock contented, Paul's marked personality change from a violent persecutor of Christians to a devoted and fervent preacher may be attributable to a type of neurological injury that some modern lightning survivors have experienced following a lightning strike. Dr. Bullock did, however, suggest that his theorizing should not diminish the miracle of Paul's conversion. He affirmed that Paul's encounter on the road to Damascus can still be regarded as a miracle regardless of whether it occurred supernaturally or as the result of a lightning strike.

(2) Lightning and Clothing

One of the oddities sometimes evident with lightning strikes is the effect that lightning has on clothes and shoes. Because of what might be called the "vapor explosion" effect—the immediate conversion of body sweat into steam when struck by lightning—the resulting explosion of steam will literally blow the shoes and clothing off of the unfortunate victim. For example, Camille Flammarion reported in 1868 that seven people took refuge under a huge ash tree during a French thunderstorm. One of them, a woman, was killed by the strike and "the clothes of the woman who had been killed were torn into many shreds, many of which were found clinging to the branches of the trees."

Similarly, meteorologist George Hartwig reported, in his 1887 book *The Aerial World,* that when the mayor of a city in France

The "vapor-blasted" hiking boot of an unfortunate hiker who survived being struck by lightning. (Photo courtesy of Sheryl Olson.)

in 1869 took refuge under a high poplar tree during a thunder-storm, "soon after he was killed by lightning, which stripped him completely, with the exception of a single shoe." In another instance in 1855, both Flammarion and Hartwig reported that a man was struck by lightning near Valleriois, France, and stripped naked. According to witnesses, all that could be found of his clothes after the strike were a few shreds of cloth, a shirtsleeve, and some pieces of his hobnailed boots. The man was uncon-scious for ten minutes, then awoke, complained of the cold, and inquired curiously how he happened to be naked.

Even today in an era of less and looser clothes, many victims of lightning are still found shoeless because of the vapor explosion effect. In 1959, the *Miami Herald* reported (as related by P. E. Viemeister in his 1961 book *The Lightning Book*) that a crewman seated in the clear plastic nose of a Navy P2V patrol bomber had his shoe set on fire when lightning struck the plane as it was flying at seven thousand feet. When interviewed, the man didn't recall what had happened. All he remembered was that all of a sudden his feet hurt and, when he looked down, his right shoe was burning. Later, the ground crew discovered that lightning had sheared off some of the rivets on the plane and damaged the tail. The crewman was treated for minor burns and shock.

(3) Animal Strikes

Many of us are increasingly more aware of the effects of lightning strikes on people, via media stories, the medical efforts of lightning injury specialist Dr. Mary Ann Cooper, and an extraordinary support group of lightning survivors (www.lightning-strike.org). Far fewer people realize that lightning also inflicts deadly hits on animals as well. For example, Flammarion reported that a 1672 lightning strike electrified a lake in Zirknitz, Switzerland, such that local residents collected an astounding eighteen wagons of dead fish out of it. A hundred years later, meteorologists noted that lightning fell on the Doubs River in Besançon, France, killing all the pike and trout. The river's waters were subsequently covered with dead fish, their stomachs floating upward.

A portion of the 835 sheep killed in Utah by a single stroke of lightning at the top of Pine Canyon in the Raft River Mountains of Box Elder County in northwestern Utah. (Photo courtesy of National Weather Service and Utah Center for Climate and Weather.)

Larger creatures also aren't immune to the lethal power of lightning. In 1939, according to Utah meteorologists Dan Pope and Clayton Brough, a single stroke of lightning struck and killed an incredible 835 sheep that had bedded down on top of Pine Canyon in northwestern Utah. Apparently, the sheep were all huddled around a single tree in the area when lightning hit that tree. The electrical charge proceeded to pass from one sheep to another through their wet bodies. Only fifteen sheep (out of a flock of 850) survived, as did the sheepherder who was asleep in his tent. Tomlinson mentioned a similar, but even more deadly, occurrence in 1888 when a single lightning strike in Ethiopia killed two thousand sheep.

I have a somewhat odder animal-kill story, given to me by respected lightning researcher Ron Holle from a rare, privately published book of news stories gathered by nineteenth-century lightning enthusiast H. F. Kretzer. According to one news story, "several gentlemen were sitting in front of a store," in 1891 in Nashville, Tennessee, "when one of the party observed a large turkey-buzzard that was sailing majestically across the sky." The apparently bored gentlemen were idly watching the buzzard's soaring "when suddenly, just as it was opposite and above them, they were blinded by a flash of lightning, which seemingly exploded on the back of the buzzard." Recovering from the shock of the brilliant flash, they set about to find the buzzard. Sadly the majestic bird was no more; all that was left of the avian raptor were a few black tail feathers that fluttered pathetically to the ground.

Even in more modern days, animals are struck and killed by lightning. A single atmospheric electric discharge killed forty-seven head of cattle in 1924. According to junior meteorologist W. E. Maughan in the *Monthly Weather Review*, the forty-seven cows had crowded together under the branches of a single large willow tree in Hancock, Minnesota, when the fatal strike had occurred. In

2003, according to the National Climatic Data Center (the primary climate and weather data archive for the United States), lightning killed a six-year-old giraffe named Betsy at a large theme park attraction in Florida. Although the park was equipped with lightning rods, the storm struck with too little warning to bring the animal inside. In Chapter Thirteen, I present the details of an even larger animal-killing lightning strike when I relate the shocking death of "Old Pitt" the circus elephant.

One of the strangest stories of animal lightning is the anecdote associated with the great American scientist Benjamin Franklin (and recorded by noted lightning experts R. H. Golde and W. R. Lee in the *Proceedings of the Institute of Electrical Engineers, London* and by I. B. Cohen in his 1941 book *Benjamin Franklin's Experiments*). Franklin performed a lightning experiment in which he electrocuted a turkey—specifically, he "killed" it by applying an electric shock directly to its head. Amazingly, the revolutionary scientist then revived the turkey "by repeated blowing into its lungs," and, when he set the turkey down on the floor, it "ran headlong against the walls." Many researchers regard this odd experiment as one of the first cases of artificial respiration being used in treatment after an electric shock.

(4) Ball Lightning

Following Benjamin Franklin's early discussions of lightning, one of the first researchers into the mysteries of lightning was Professor G. W. Richman. He was also—unfortunately—one of the first researchers to encounter the phenomenon known as ball lightning. In 1753, he built what he termed an "electrical gnomon," consisting in part of an ungrounded lightning rod erected upon the top of Richman's house. At the height of the storm, a fist-sized glowing ball appeared at the end of the rod and floated through the laboratory. The ball of lightning detonated as it approached Richman, instantly killing him.

Hundreds of personal accounts of ball lightning have been told over the past three centuries. One of the most cited is the story of the "cat-like" ball of lightning striking a tailor's shop in Paris back in 1843. The owner of the shop recounted that, during a thunderstorm, a fireball the size of a human head emerged from the fireplace. Although the ball was luminous, it emitted no heat as it hovered above the floor. A member of the French Academy of Sciences who was present in the shop described the ball as a good-sized kitten rolled up into a ball and moving without showing its paws. A few moments, the ball passed up through a chimney flue and detonated with a thunderous explosion.

An illustration of the strange phenomenon known as ball lightning descending into a room from the book *The Aerial World,* by G. Hartwig, London, 1886. (Photo Courtesy of National Oceanic and Atmospheric Administration/Department of Commerce Treasures of the NOAA Library Collection.)

Camille Flammarion was particularly fascinated by ball lightning and collected a number of anecdotes of its particular nature. For instance, one interesting account of ball lightning recorded by Flammarion is attributed to the abbé Lazzaro Spallanzani, who was the first to discover how bats can fly in complete darkness. Spallanzani stated that, on August 29, 1791, a globe of fire "about the size of a billiard" materialized before a young peasant girl in a field near Pavia, Italy. The fireball literally danced around her feet, then made its way up her clothes, and finally emerged from her bodice. The presence of the lightning ball beneath her petticoats caused them to "blow out like an umbrella." Fortunately, the frightened girl was not seriously hurt, although the globe exploded with an angry roar soon after it escaped her clothing. A medical examination showed a minor burn extending from the right knee to the middle of her breast. The girl's chemise was torn in two and there was a hole through her bodice where the ball had emerged.

Enough cases—many recorded in fortean literature—have been cited that most experts are willing to admit that ball lightning does exist. Consequently, in true scientific fashion, many researchers have proposed a variety of theories to explain this apparently rare phenomenon with new hypotheses being constructed almost monthly. For instance, within the last few years, scientists have suggested that ball lightning might be a phenomenon called a magnetostatic plasmoid, or a localized stored energy outside an ionized region, or even perhaps most unlikely a miniature black hole. No single theory of ball lightning has, as of yet, gained universal acceptance by the science community.

(5) Coincidences of Lightning

Lightning often seems to occur at auspicious or disastrous times. For example, in AD 306, the father of the Catholic patron saint of lightning victims, St. Barbara Dioscorus, was enraged beyond modern comprehension when his daughter converted to Christianity without his permission. Incredibly, the infuriated father not only ordered his own daughter's beheading but decided to personally carry out Barbara's death sentence himself. Appropriately, God issued His own stern judgment just moments after the decapitation, for Barbara's father was fatally struck and killed by a stroke of lightning . . . and Saint Barbara's link to lightning was insured for all of history.

An even more telling lightning vendetta recounted in many fortean books and magazines is the story of Major R. Summerford, a British military officer. In February 1918, the major was knocked off his horse while fighting in Flanders by a stroke of lightning and temporarily paralyzed from the waist down. Consequently, he retired and moved to Vancouver (some sources say Alabama), but then in 1924, as he was fishing with two friends, lightning struck him again and paralyzed his entire right side. Through two long years, Summerford managed to recover his mobility but, when in 1930 a third lightning strike struck him, he was left permanently paralyzed. The unfortunate lightning-prone man died two years later. But the story wasn't over—in 1934, during a severe summer thunderstorm, lightning struck the cemetery in which he was buried and destroyed a tombstone. Of course, that tombstone marked the grave of Major Summerford.

The epitome of lightning coincidence stories must be the trials of Forest Park Ranger Roy Sullivan. Ranger Sullivan earns a unique place in history by having been struck an amazing seven different times by lightning during his life. Number One: In April 1942, he lost a big toenail to lightning; Number Two: In July 1969, his eyebrows were blown off; Number Three: In July 1970, his left shoulder was seared; Number Four: In April 1972, his hair was set on fire. (This episode caused him to start hauling a bucket of water around with him in his car.); Number Five: On August 7, 1973, he was out driving when lightning hit him on the head through his hat, set his hair on fire, again, knocked him ten feet out of his car, went through both legs and knocked his left shoe off; Number Six: On June 5, 1976, the strike occurred and hurt his ankle; Number Seven: On June 25, 1977, the last lightning hit him while he was fishing. Ironically, Mr. Sullivan actually died in 1983 by an apparent self-inflicted gunshot wound.

(6) Lightning Figures

As mentioned in the introduction, scientists have long engaged in debate about odd markings that sometimes appear on the skin of lightning victims. Until the twenty-first century, most people, including scientists and doctors, believed that lightning created a "photographic" impression of the surrounding landscape—trees, birds, etc.—on the victim.

Andrés Poey, director of the Meteorological Observatory at Havana, Cuba, and a founding father of modern hurricane observation and forecasting, was particularly fascinated by this idea of "lightning imprinting." He published a classic article on this topic in the journal *Athenaeum* in 1857 that listed twenty-four distinct cases of what he termed "the photographic effects of lightning." For instance, Poey related that the image of a palm-leaf hut and its surroundings, residing an astounding 350 yards away from the lightning strike location, was found etched on some dried leaves of a palm tree in the plantation at St. Vincent. According to Poey, the image was so perfect that it appeared to be more like an engraving than anything else.

In another example, Poey cited a French newspaper from September 1857. The paper reported that lightning struck both a cow and a peasant girl who had taken refuge under a tree during a storm. The cow was killed by the strike but the girl recovered. However, when rescuers reportedly loosened the girl's dress "to induce respiration, a distinct image of the cow was observed upon her breast."

According to Poey, even the great Benjamin Franklin had reportedly heard of cases of lightning imprinting. The Cuban meteorologist said that Franklin wrote to the Meteorological Society of London about an incident he remembered forty years before (other sources say only twenty years). Franklin recalled the case of a man who saw lightning strike a tree near him as he stood at his door during a thunderstorm. Apparently, according to Franklin, the man was affected by the strike for, when revived, he was "very much surprised to perceive on his breast a facsimile of that tree."

Despite many critics of lightning imprinting (such as Charles Tomlinson), some doctors still ascribed, even in the "enlightened" twentieth-century, to this common—yet mistaken—view that lightning could miraculously burn an image of the surrounding landscape onto a victim. For instance, an English doctor examined the burns received by a London man who was killed by a lightning strike in 1919. The doctor stated, as reported in *Monthly Weather Review,* "From the right shoulder and across the chest and down to the lower of the front of the abdomen impressions of branches and leaves [of nearby trees] were clearly imprinted on the skin, showing like an X-ray plate how certain rays of light were impeded by the branches and foliage, whilst others made the contours of these."

Today we have identified these strange treelike wounds found on some lightning victims as "Lichtenberg" figures or sometimes called "feathering marks." A Lichtenberg figure is the pattern produced by electrons shot out from an electrode under high voltage. These marks don't break the surface of the body but rather display a branching or treelike pattern on the skin. Similar patterns have been observed on animals struck by lightning.

The markings don't appear to follow blood vessels or nerve pathways and probably are similar in nature to bruises. Doctors have noted that these lightning-induced blemishes often turn a darker color and disappear after a few hours or days after the strike. Not all lightning victims show Lichtenberg markings and, according to lightning expert Dr. Mary Ann Cooper, their appearance is not necessarily a sign of the severity of the lightning strike. Many—if not most—lightning victims actually do not display any visible signs of injury. As I discuss in the last section of this chapter, one of the most frequent physical trauma associated with lightning is cardiac arrest.

(7) Jewelry

A related type of wound associated with lightning is the injury where skin is in contact to heated metal hit by the electrical charge. Many lightning victims have received burns due to metal necklaces burned into the skin, or when belt buckles, coins, or backpacks are rapidly heated to burning temperatures. Victims of direct strikes in the open are often carrying or wearing something metal. Reports exist of victims carrying umbrellas or golf clubs, wearing jewelry, necklaces, hearing aids, or even having, in one very unusual instance, a metal tracheotomy tube.

The previously mentioned Cuban hurricane expert (and lightning story archivist) Andrés Poey's set of very bizarre lightning branding stories published in *Athenaeum* also contained several stories of this type. For example, according to Poey, the body of a man killed by lightning in 1836 was found to have an impression of six rings, "which seemed the more distinct in that the rest of the man's own skin was very dark." The ring impressions overlapped each other and were of different sizes on the body. They also corresponded "exactly with those of the gold coins which he had on him . . . as the public official who examined his body and all the witnesses were able to testify." French meteorologist W. De Fonvielle discussed a similar situation at about the same time in his 1867 book *Thunder and Lightning*, when lightning struck a young lady who wore a silver necklace. "The lightning was not content with having ruptured the coquettish ornament; it tore away some particles from each of its tiny beads." He reported that, when the girl was picked up from the floor, "her skin was found to be marked with little black lines corresponding to each of the silver beads of her ornament."

The severity of such metal-related burns is likely a function of the metal (such as its weight, thickness, and type) rather than a characteristic of where the metal actually was located on the body. One thing that we have learned regarding lightning injuries is that metal worn close to the head or in the hair doesn't increase the likelihood of being hit (unless perhaps it projects far above the head, thereby substantially increasing the person's height).

Yet, odd stories of lightning injuries still persist. In 1999, the Reuters News Agency reported that two women were killed by a bolt of lightning in London's Hyde Park when their underwire bras allegedly acted as electric conductors. Amazingly the experience apparently wasn't even unique. The coroner purportedly declared that this was the second time in his examination of over fifty thousand deaths where lightning had caused death by striking the bra's metal underwire. In a similar fashion, the BBC of London in 2003 reported that a woman became temporarily blind and badly blistered by a lightning strike that seemingly was centered on her tongue stud.

(8) The Preposterous

As if lightning wasn't an impressive enough event, people (or their historians) throughout the ages have been tempted to embellish their lightning tales. Many bizarre and frankly preposterous lightning injury stories have proliferated through history. One of the strangest is what the lightning injury specialist Mary Ann Cooper calls the "crispy critter" myth. Its greatest advocate was the nineteenth-century meteorologist Camille Flammarion who collected many stories related to the alleged frying ability of lightning. For instance, he related the story of three soldiers in Vic-sur-Aisne, France, who had taken refuge under a linden tree during a thunderstorm. As they stood under the tree, lightning blasted it. Peasants, coming to the rescue, touched the three stationary soldiers and discovered to their amazement that the "bodies instantly crumbled to fine ashes." Such stories appear to be complete fabrications in that, in reality, lightning tends to flash over the outside—not burning through—a victim's body and has never in modern times been scientifically observed to ignite spontaneous human combustion.

Yet, many examples of the "crispy critter" myth exist in literature:

- Nineteenth-century lightning story archivist W. De Fonvielle, in his 1867 book *Thunder and Lightning*, recounted the French historian Le Laboureur's story of how lightning, having penetrated through a small window in the department of the Dauphin, killed a young squire in the antechamber. "The electric fluid appears to have consumed the whole of the inside of his body leaving nothing but the skin, which, was, however, as black as coal."
- Jerome Cardan (also known as Cardanus) wrote that eight harvesters, taking their noonday lunch under a maple tree during a thunderstorm, were killed by one stroke of lightning. When approached by their companions after the storm had cleared away, they seemed to be still enjoying their lunch. Reportedly, one was

raising a glass to drink, another was in the act of taking a piece of bread, and a third was reaching out his hand to a plate. There they sat as if petrified, in the exact position when lightning struck them.

- François Arago related the story of lightning in 1775 striking a dappled horse in Glynd, England, whose hair then came off on all the white spots with the slightest touch while the other parts had "its usual adherence."

- Two nineteenth-century meteorologists mentioned that some oxen were struck by lightning near Nymwegen, Holland, in 1838 and, upon examination, locals discovered that the oxen's bones were shattered into thousands of fragments "as if rent by fulminating powder."

- J. Rouyer wrote in an 1884 issue of *Knowledge* of the peculiar effects of a 1781 lightning strike. The bolt struck the chapel door of the Commandery of St. John near which a woman and three children had taken refuge. According to Rouyer, the woman was "suffocated" by the lightning such that her body was frozen in place, as was also one of the children.

Actually, this last anecdote isn't quite as preposterous as many of the "crispy critter" genre. Given the specifics of the story, it is likely the woman and child were most likely killed by one of the primary causes of lightning death—heart attack. Such an affliction would create symptoms that might appear similar to death by "suffocation" to the more medically limited people of the eighteenth century.

The two closest modern equivalents to the "crispy critter" myth also involve strange lightning strikes. The first is the bizarre story told by Derek Elsom in a 1989 issue of the science magazine

New Scientist. Lightning struck a golfer in Ireland as he carried a bag of golf clubs on his shoulder. It completely burnt his clothes, went through his metal-studded shoes and shot out of the furled umbrella he was holding into the ground like a fiery missile. But surgeons discovered that his most amazing injuries were the half dozen perforations in his bowels, a condition that medically is called peritonitis. How did such perforations occur? Apparently the lightning had superheated the gases in his bowels and those gases had literally exploded. Even given the severity of his internal injuries, the volatile golfer recovered and within six months was back playing his favorite game.

The second is a news story, collected by Thomas Grazulis in an update to his massive volume *Significant Tornadoes,* about a Florida man who was seated on his toilet when lightning struck a tree near his house. The lightning strike produced a massive surge in the water of a septic tank buried nearby, which traveled through the pipes and into the bathroom toilet of the house. The force of the electrically propelled water reportedly knocked the sixty-nine-year-old man off the toilet and into the air. The man was treated and released from a local hospital for an elevated blood pressure . . . and a reported "tingling" in his lower extremities.

(9) Thunder

We now know that thunder is basically the rapid expansion of air by a lightning strike. Thunder cannot occur without lightning. As Mark Twain so aptly wrote, "Thunder is good, and thunder is impressive, but it is lightning that does the work." When a lightning strike occurs, the air around it is ionized and superheated to an incredible fifty-four thousand degrees Fahrenheit—a temperature five times hotter than the sun. This sudden heating and ionization causes the air to expand so fast that the air forms a shock wave. We experience that shock wave as thunder. Since a lightning bolt normally consists of several very short-duration streams of electric current flowing down to the ground, multiple shock waves are created. These multiple pressure waves create the rumble effect of thunder in that each shock wave takes a slightly different amount of time to reach us. Actually, the fact that the lightning flash and the thunderclap are two results of the same event has been known back to ancient times. The Roman historian Seneca explained that we see lightning's flash before we hear thunder's bang "because our eyesight is swift and greatly outdistances our hearing."

Obviously given the power of lightning and its linkages to the ancient gods, the ability to create thunder would be a powerful means for priests to control their congregations. In ancient Egypt, the priests of the Temple of the Labyrinth made an interesting device to mimic the sounds of thunder. Pliny the Elder described the Temple in detail, noting that when the priests opened the

An illustration of St. Elmo's Fire on mast of a ship at sea in *The Aerial World,* by Dr. G. Hartwig, London, 1886. (Photo Courtesy of National Oceanic and Atmospheric Administration/Department of Commerce Treasures of the NOAA Library Collection.)

doors, "a thunder sprung up terrible within." The Greek engineer Hero gave a most interesting—and plausible—explanation for the sound. He suggested that a cord, hidden from direct view of visitors to the temple connected the door to a pulley that was attached to a large and rather strange trumpet. The mouthpiece of the trumpet, a large hemispheric bowl, was suspended above a cistern of water. When the door was opened, the trumpet and its mouthpiece were submerged into the water. As the water pressed out the air in the mouthpiece, the air was forced out through the trumpet and, behold—the god's thunderous voice spoke!

But before we pat ourselves on the back for our post-industrial knowledge of thunder, even in more recent times, there have been strange, and frankly unbelievable, notions about the booming sound. J. D. Canton, in an 1858 article in *Scientific American*, wrote that it was well known to dairy men and housewives at the time that a violent thunderstorm would turn sweet milk to sour. Common thought even in the early part of the last century said that thunderstorms could, on occasion, produce the same effect on beer. Today, more scientists would likely argue that such a souring is merely a coincidence of timing. That is, milk (or beer) souring is most likely to occur on hot summer days—and that is exactly the type of weather in which thunderstorms are likely to form.

Thunder has often played a role throughout our history, even in our entertainments. For example, George Stimpson, in his 1946 book *A Book About a Thousand Things*, recounted that the phrase "stealing one's thunder" is linked to the production of one of Shakespeare's great plays. In 1709, a somewhat untalented but mechanically innovative playwright named John Dennis created a novel method of simulating thunder in his play *Appius and Virginia*. Prior to Dennis's innovation, stagehands had simply pounded large bowls to mimic the booms of thunder. Dennis, however, created a means of producing more resonating thunderclaps by rapping on "troughs of wood with stops in them." Unfortunately, Dennis's writing didn't match his engineering. His play was a miserable failure and quickly closed, much to the disappointment and disgust of the bad-tempered dramatist (for instance, he once called famous critic Alexander Pope a "hunchbacked toad"). A few weeks later, as Dennis watched a performance of Shakespeare's *Macbeth,* he was infuriated to hear his improved thunderclaps being used in the play. The frustrated playwright reportedly exclaimed, "That's my thunder, by God! The villains will not play my play but they rattle my thunder!"

(10) Lightning Cures

A few stories exist of extraordinary lightning "cures"—lightning strikes that miraculously cause a remission or cure of some ailment. In 1930, the magazine *Literary Digest* listed a number of lightning cures that it claimed were mentioned in a medical journal:

- An African-American woman, who suffered from anemia, "apparently of the pernicious and sometimes incurable type," regained her normal health after being struck by lightning.
- An elderly woman was inexplicably returned to a "normal condition of young womanhood," following a lightning strike.
- A North Carolina man suffering from facial paralysis and apparently unable to close his eyelids was cured by a stroke of lightning.

Paralysis was the ailment associated with one of the first lightning cure stories. In 1782, a priest for the household of the Duke of Kent in England reportedly was cured of his paralysis following a lightning strike. As recounted in many newspapers, Edwin

Robinson of Falmouth, Maine, is a more modern recipient of lightning strike's benefits. Mr. Robinson had lost his sight and hearing after suffering a traffic-related head injury in 1971. However, nine years later, Robinson was walking out into his yard with his aluminum cane, looking for his pet chicken when a thunderstorm forced him to take shelter under a poplar tree. A moment later, he was struck by lightning and was completely knocked out. When he regained consciousness some twenty minutes later, he felt extremely groggy and went back to his house for a nap. Soon after, he found his central vision was back (although he still couldn't move his eyes); and the next morning he could hear perfectly without his hearing aid (which had been burnt out by the lightning)—even his hair started to grow back. He later appeared on a national morning talk show to retell his wondrous story.

In one instance, the cure for a lightning strike apparently came directly from the gods. Missionary E. T. C. Werner, in his 1825 book *Myths and Legends of China,* wrote of a very strange Chinese legend. The legend stated that an old woman living in the Chinese village of Kiangsi had suffered a broken arm after being struck by lightning. Soon afterward a mysterious Voice boomed out from above and said, "I have made a mistake." At that point, a small bottle filled with a strange liquid fell from the clear air, and the Voice again spoke to the woman, "Apply the contents and you will be healed at once." The old woman did so—and her lightning-damaged arm swiftly mended. The other villagers, seeing this miraculous cure and obviously regarding the bottle and its contents as a divine medicine, decided to steal it away and hide it for future use. When they attempted the theft, however, they discovered that even several of them together could not lift the magic bottle from the ground. Then, the legend concluded, the bottle abruptly rose up on its own and vanished into the air.

Even animals are not apparently immune to the random curative processes of lightning. According to the great astronomer and meteorologist François Arago, a valuable sick horse belonging to a French lieutenant colonel, was one of a number of animals struck by lightning in 1842. Reportedly, prior to the lightning strike, the animal had acquired several deadly lesions on its body and the veterinary surgeons of the time had recommended that the horse be put down. Incredibly, however, the day after the lightning episode, the horse's health markedly improved and, in a short couple of weeks, according to Arago, it was quite out of danger.

At this point, before you get too excited about such marvelous lightning "cures," it is wise to remember François Arago's final words concerning these supposed lightning-induced remedies. He said—and modern scientists would undoubtedly agree—that the risks of a lightning strike far outweigh any hope of a miraculous cure and so we should "dare not . . . venture to recommend any one to tempt a thunderbolt in the hope of experiencing its curative powers."

(11) Unclassifiable Lightning Oddities

Sometimes, lightning "just happens." Take, for example, the 1985 story reported in the *Daily Express* and archived by the *Fortean Times* of a young Brooklyn woman who was killed while talking to her mother on a public phone. Lightning struck a flowerpot on a ledge eight stories above the woman, causing it to crash onto her head. Her mother, left on the telephone, had to be informed by a passerby as to the tragedy that just happened. In a similar fashion, the journal *New Scientist* reported that a British schoolgirl was killed in 1974 when a lightning strike hit and vaporized a tree that she was walking past. She was hit by a flying piece of its bark and died from a fractured skull. A third bizarre coincidence is discussed by Paul Jones in a National Safety Council 1943 pamphlet entitled *Public Safety*. According to the pamphlet, a soldier was literally welded into his sleeping bag when lightning struck the bag's zipper and melted it. When freed, the uninjured soldier reportedly said, "Now I know what a baked potato feels like."

Lightning even apparently ended a potential love story in 1989 when two rhinoceroses were mating under a large isolated tree in South Africa. According to John and Nancy Seff's book *Our Fascinating Earth,* the tree was abruptly struck by lightning and witnesses reported that both rhinos were briefly knocked unconscious by the blast. When they awoke, the rhinoceroses staggered to their feet, stared at each other for a long moment as though contemplating the shocking consequences of mating during a lightning storm and then abruptly ambled away in opposite directions.

An odd lightning story reported in a 1961 issue of the Manchester *Daily Union* (and recounted in fortean authors Frank Edwards's book *Strange World,* and Vincent Gaddis's book *Mysterious Fires and Lights*) concerns the strange problems of a house in Alstead, New Hampshire. A violent stroke of lightning struck the house during a severe thunderstorm. When the firemen arrived, the house initially appeared normal electrically; the firefighters found no fire, no blown fuse or even a short circuit. However, they did find that the house's walls were incredibly hot to the touch. They continued to spray the house with water—apparently to no effect—until around midnight. The walls finally cooled off and the firemen were able to return to their station. No scientific explanation for the hot walls was given.

According to a 1960 story in newspaper *Missourian* (and collected by P. E. Viemeister in his 1961 book *The Lightning Book*), lightning struck a power line connected to an electric clock of Columbia, Missouri, and the clock actually began to run backward. Evidently the lightning had triggered a power surge that fused some of the clock's wiring. This apparently reversed the magnetic field of the clock motor and caused the hands to turn in the wrong direction. In a similar fashion, Vincent Gaddis (in *Mysterious Fires and Lights*) reported, quoting a UP news article, that following a lightning strike on a house in Mexica, Texas, in 1945, the family discovered their house's entire wiring was completely fused and relinked. As an example, the report claimed that, when the radio was turned on, the bedroom lights flickered on and, if the bedroom light switch was flipped, a floor lamp in the living room lit up. Eventually a complete rewiring of the house had to be undertaken.

(12) "New" Lightning: Sprites, Jets, and Elves

In the last fifteen years, a whole new field of lightning—high-altitude lightning—literally has taken the science world by storm. As part of this new field, an odd set of previously unstudied types of lightning, given colorful names like blue jets and red sprites, have been scientifically identified, photographed, and researched. All of these "new" lightning types occur far above the storm, instead of below it.

Although anecdotal "freak" reports of high-altitude lightning have existed in the literature for over a century, there was no systematic scientific inquiry into those accounts. One of the earliest stories of one of these new types of lightning actually first appeared in the science journal *Nature* back in 1885 and described a series of vertical lightnings jetting up from thunderstorms in Kingston, Jamaica. Since that time, many others, particularly pilots, have observed strange lightning flashes occasionally shooting out of the top of storm clouds.

With the advent of video cameras, space-based satellites, and shuttles, we have begun to document—and understand—these strange upward "rocket" shots of lightning. Bernard Vonnegut was one of the first to propose space-based investigations of these new lightning types. One type of the first of these "new" lightnings has been named *sprites*. Sprites are huge upward blasts of reddish hue into the upper atmosphere. They have been measured as traveling upward to altitudes over fifty miles high, but only lasting a tiny fraction of a second. Sprites rarely appear alone but instead tend to occur in clusters of two, three, or even more.

Although a few images of sprites were taken by aircraft and even by space shuttles in the early 1990s, researchers flying over thunderstorms in the Midwest in the summer of 1994 are generally credited as being the first to scientifically identify and photograph sprites. Professors Davis Sentman and Eugene Wescott of the University of Alaska used special low-light-level cameras aboard two jet aircraft to photograph these oddities. Sentman described the flashes as resembling fireworks on the Fourth of July, similar to Roman candles.

Our best explanation for sprites involves the density of the air in relation to the strength of the electrical field. If the upper part of the atmosphere is sufficiently electrified after an unusually powerful lightning flash from below (what is termed a "positive" cloud-to-ground lightning flash), electrons can travel through the extremely low-density air very quickly. When the electrons collide with the molecules in this region, the excited air molecules release that energy as a blast of red light.

A second lightning oddity, called a *blue jet,* was identified at the same time as sprites. Blue jets are distinct from sprites and were first observed using low-light television cameras. These lightnings are harder to observe visually than sprites because they tend to occur much lower in altitude (observed only below twenty-five miles in altitude). Blue jets emit a deep-blue light and move upward in narrow cones with unbelievable speeds of over three hundred times the speed of sound. These upward lightning flashes don't appear to be linked to lower level lightning but do occur over lightning storms producing hail. Although theories to explain them are still being formulated, blue jets appear to be created by a rapid accumulation of a large amount of positive electrical charge near the cloud top.

Elves is the term applied to a third type of new lightning. Although the name fits nicely into mythological nomenclature used for these high-altitude phenomena, "elves" actually stands for "Emissions of Light and VLF perturbations due to EMP Sources." Elves are very high-altitude, pancake-shaped layers of reddish glow. In essence, they are the visual "bang" of the electrical fields created by exceptionally intense conventional lightning from below. Imagery from space shuttle flights indicates that elves are the result of strong interaction between the electromagnetic pulse from lower lightning strokes and the ionosphere above. Elves occur at roughly the same time as sprites but they tend to form first and don't even last as long as sprites.

We continue to study and learn about these new high-altitude lightning types. In 2001, researchers recorded a "blue jet"-like flash above a thunderstorm around Arecibo Observatory in Puerto Rico. The blue flash shot up ten miles from the cloud top in a branching, conical manner upward toward the ionosphere but then it somehow morphed into more of a sprite event than a blue jet.

And our scientific discoveries of lightning progress even with more "normal" lightning. In 2002, Professor Joseph Dwyer and colleagues published a technical report in the journal *Science* that, during rocket-triggered lightning experiments, they had detected high-energy radiation in "normal" triggered lightning. In other words, they had chronicled the existence of minuscule amounts of radiation at extremely short wavelengths, such as those of X-rays and gamma rays, in their lightning bolts.

(13) Lightning Safety

Authorities have created an excellent standard for outdoor safety from lightning storms that they have nicknamed the "30-30" rule. That safety guideline refers to two separate time periods, specifically 30 seconds and 30 minutes. First, 30 seconds: If the difference between the lightning strike and the thunder clap is less than thirty seconds (meaning the strike is closer than six miles), lightning is close enough to be a threat and one should seek shelter immediately. Second, 30 minutes: One should wait a full thirty minutes after seeing the last lightning flash before leaving shelter—this is due to the unfortunate fact that more than half of all lightning deaths occur after the center of the thunderstorm has actually passed the area!

If you are outdoors, you should avoid open high ground, avoid isolated large trees, and, if possible, find a safe shelter, such as an enclosed car (not a convertible) or a house. Once in a shelter, avoid using electrical devices, such as computers, appliances, or televisions, avoid talking on landline telephones (cell phones are generally safe), and avoid taking a shower or bath as a lightning strike can hit a water line and use it to conduct electricity into the house. If someone is struck by lightning, call emergency services immediately. The most likely injury from a lightning strike is cardiac arrest, so you should apply CPR to the victim if necessary. There is no danger to you in rendering such aid. Lightning victims are not electrified, so you can apply first aid without fear of electrocution.

Chapter 4

HAIL

IMAGINE SOLID CHUNKS OF ICE FALLING FROM THE SKY. HAIL IS
fortunately a relatively rare phenomenon that has mystified
and amazed people throughout history. Yet, that relative
rarity, its infamous carnage involving people, animals, and
property, and its influence on history, religion, and society have
led to many odd accounts of hail, some of which continue to defy
explanation.

The formal definition of hail requires an ice particle with a
diameter exceeding five millimeters. Generally, hailstones begin
their lives as ice forms on "seeds" of small frozen raindrops or
soft ice particles referred to as *graupel*. The size of hailstones usually increases with the intensity of the thunderstorm cell from
which they spawn. As an illustration, hail experts state that a
"golf-ball-sized" hailstone would require over ten billion supercooled droplets (microscopic water that remains in a liquid state
far below 32°F) to be accumulated (compared to the million
droplets needed for a typical raindrop). Consequently, a hailstone of this size must remain in the storm cloud for at least five

to ten minutes. Hail grows almost entirely from the process of these supercooled cloud water droplets colliding with the hailstones as the icy stones fall, or are suspended, through the cloud.

The categories of this chapter on the oddities of hail involve such strange stories as the "the fake hail story that prevented a war," the gruesome story of the "human hailstones," and, in counterpoint, the strange "winter in June" festival thrown by Pasadena, California, residents after a major hailstorm. The last section of this chapter involves the general steps you should consider taking to be safe during a hailstorm.

(1) Hail and History

Stories of hailstorms date back to the very early explorations of our continent. In what is perhaps the first "official" hail report recorded in North America, legendary conquistador Francisco Coronado described, as recorded in G. P. Winship's edited 1990 book *The Journey of Coronado, 1540–1542,* a severe hailstorm that struck his expedition in an area of what is now Texas in 1541. Coronado recounted that, while his company was bivouacking one summer afternoon, a huge thunderstorm built up over the plains and moved over the Spaniards' camp. The severe storm struck the conquistadors with incredibly high winds and hail. Coronado wrote that, over a very brief period of time, a huge number of hailstones fell with the size of some iceballs larger than bowls. The conquistador described the area as being covered "two or three spans or more deep" by the massive hailstones. In addition to dumping an enormous amount of ice, the storm was apparently incredibly destructive, even to a temporary camp such as that of the Spaniards', because "the hail broke many tents, and battered many helmets, and wounded many of the horse, and broke all the crockery of the army."

One of the most significant hail events in history is described in the Bible. The Israelites, led by great warrior Joshua, had routed the Amorite army in a surprise night attack and were pursuing the fleeing enemy when, apparently, a hailstorm tipped the balance even more in favor of Israel. From Joshua 10:11: "And as they [the Amorites] fled before Israel, while they were going down the ascent of Beth-horon, the Lord threw down great stones from heaven upon them as far as Azekah, and they died; there were more who died because of the hailstones than the men of Israel killed with the sword." Such severe Middle Eastern hailstorms have been reported in more modern times. D. V. Duff, in his 1936 book *Palestine Picture,* mentioned that he personally had seen cattle killed by pounding hail in the region.

Probably the most bizarre hail story is a fake report of a hailstorm that actually prevented a war in 1757. Meteorologist C. F. Talman, in a 1931 article in *Nature Magazine,* recounted that there was much excitement in Berlin in 1757 over rumors of an impending war. In order to divert the people's attention from this, King Frederick the Great caused a completely fake news story to be published in the realm's newspapers about a hailstorm at Potsdam. According to the misinformation, hailstones of the Potsdam storm were enormous, supposedly "as big as pumpkins," and were said to have killed hundreds of cattle. The medieval propaganda machine worked. The public attention focused on the hail story to the exclusion of all else . . . and the war fever abated.

Unbelievably, a deadly hailstorm can even led to peace. In the spring of 1360, English King Edward III's army in France encountered a terrible thunderstorm near Chartres, France. The English army was preparing to attack the French when a severe storm plummeted the English with hail the size of "goose eggs." According to Sir John Froissart, a historian of the time, the hailstones were "so prodigious as to instantly kill six thousand of his horse and a thousand of his best troops." After the storm,

Edward III sprang from the saddle, stretched arms toward the Church of Our Lady at Chartres, and vowed to God and the Virgin Mary that he would no longer object to peace proposals between the English and French.

(2) Absurdly Big Hailstones (Megacryometeors)

History has given us two basic types of so-called *megacryometeors* (absurdly big ice stones) that greatly exceed the size and weights of the official hailstones mentioned above. The first type is likely the result of *regelation*—the somewhat complex process of melting and amalgamation on the ground of many hailstones so that a single ice mass results. For example, in Salina, Kansas, an 1882 newspaper report appeared in the *Saline County Journal* with the following story lead: "Considerable excitement was caused in our city last Tuesday evening by the announcement that a hailstone weighing eighty pounds had fallen six miles west of Salina, near the railroad track." The facts of the story were that, on that Tuesday afternoon, a railroad work crew had been laboring on the track several miles out of town when a severe hailstorm abruptly sprang up over the prairie and literally battered the work crew almost senseless. The foreman of the crew, Martin Ellwood, claimed that the entire party was plummeted by massive hailstones of the weight of four or five pounds. Immediately, the work crew dashed back to Salina to escape the thunderstorm but, as they traveled, the ice missiles increased in size. Finally, when they neared the city, Ellwood's work crew abruptly stumbled upon a huge mass of ice weighing, in the foreman's estimate, a full eighty pounds.

The newspaper article asserted that "Mr. Ellwood's statement is straightforward, and he . . . is known to be a reliable, honest man, and cannot possibly be a party to a fraud." The "hailstone" was brought into the city and put on display in the window of a local merchant who saved it from dissolving by placing it in saw-dust. Scientifically, the most likely explanation for an eighty-pound ice chunk—even given in the 1882 paper—is it formed by the regelation of ice, or ice that fell, melted, and then refused into a single mass.

Similarly, the so-called "elephant hailstones" in India recorded by Dr. George Buist in 1855 were likely also formed by regelation. Buist recorded four occasions for which it was reported that "remarkable masses of ice, of many hundred pounds in weight" fell on India. The largest, an ice mass that fell near Seingapatam in the end of the late 1700s, was purportedly to have been the "size of an elephant" and took a full three days to melt. A second huge ice stone nearly a cubic yard in size fell in Khändeish in 1826. The third big fall was a massive con-glomerate of hailstones, twenty feet in diameter, which fell at Dhärwär in India. Buist's fourth elephant hailstone was an immense block of ice, consisting of fused hailstones, which was found in a dry well that was eighty miles south of Bangalore. Again, the best scientific explanation for these "elephant hail-stones" is that they were regelations of hailstones that merged together once they were on the ground.

It is also possible that this is the type of event described by the medieval English historian Reverend Thomas Short when he wrote that in June of AD 824 there "fell out of the Air in Burgundy, a Board of ice 15 foot long, 7 broad, and 2 thick." The good Rev-erend described a similar event that occurred 180 years later in Herbipolis "wherein such a prodigious Piece of Ice fell, that when broken into four Quarters, four Men could not carry it."

A second type of megacryometeor apparently does not require a hailstorm. These ice stones have been documented as falling "out of the clear sky" and can reach enormous sizes. In the his-toric records, we have the classic tale of the massive hailstone of the Isle of Skyre in 1849. The *Times* of London reported that a farm owned by a man named Moffat experienced a curious phenomenon one Monday evening in August of 1849. Following a loud blast of thunder, an "irregularly shaped mass of ice, reckoned to be nearly 20 feet in circumference, and of a proportionate thickness, fell near the farmhouse." The size of the stone was such that no measurement of its weight was made; however, the reporter did note that if the stone had actually fallen on Moffat's house, "it would have crushed it, and undoubtedly have caused . . . death." Interestingly, the *Times* reported that no other hail or snow events were witnessed in the surrounding area.

Although many meteorologists have tended to ignore these megacyrometeors because the physics causing them quite frankly isn't understood, some basic studies have been published. In particular, meteorologist J. E. McDonald collected many instances of these odd atmospheric iceballs (some of which he published in *Weatherwise*). For instance, he reported that, on January 16, 1953, in Whittier, California, Mrs. Catherine Martin and her son witnessed a chunk of ice thirteen by sixteen inches that struck their garden, half-burying itself, and narrowly missing the pair. Again, in February of 1953, "50 pounds fell near LaGuardia Field" in New York City. This was followed in April of 1954 with "10 pounds" of ice falling near Idlewild, New York, and a large ice chunk hitting the home of Mrs. Edna Lewis in Los Angeles. Reportedly, neighbors heard a crash like an explosion and discovered the driveway between the two houses littered with big splinters of ice. The ice chunks had also knocked a fifteen-inch diameter hole through the Lewis house.

McDonald recorded a 1953 news story stating that a used-car lot in Long Beach, California, was hit by chunks of large ice. An employee told the Los Angeles *Examiner* that, as he was just finishing polishing one of the cars on the lot, and was walking away from it, he suddenly heard a sizzling sound. He said, "I looked up and saw the air full of big shiny stuff plunging down." A big piece of ice that purportedly appeared to be the size of a man smashed down on that car and ice flew all over the lot.

Many might suggest that such modern ice stones are the result of aircraft deicing or related aircraft equipment (e.g., a leakage from onboard toilets). In some cases, such an occurrence might indeed explain the ice. In June 2003, the Associated Press recorded that a California man won a lawsuit against American Airlines for damages to his boat by falling "blue ice" from an airliner. Conversely, in November of 1959, falling "white" ice tore a twelve-by-eight-inch hole in a house's shingled roof in Whittier, California, and cracked plaster of the ceiling under the attic space. Sheriff deputies estimated about twenty-five pounds of ice were found in the attic and gave an explanation that this was undoubtedly ice broken loose from deicing gear of some aircraft. Meteorologist McDonald carefully checked weather records and determined that it was "entirely impossible to explain the source of the Whittier ice-fall in terms of deicing gear action."

Indeed, one of these strange falling megacryometeors apparently almost hit a weather expert. On April 2, 1973, meteorologist Dr. Richard Griffiths, then a postgraduate student at Manchester University, was nearly hit by a block of ice that fell to shatter at his feet. He had been on his way on Burton Road to buy a bottle of whisky when he noticed a single flash of lightning. Since he was a registered lightning observer for a research association, he made careful note of the time: 7:54 P.M. He bought the whisky, and as he started out at 8:03 P.M., the ice chunk hit. The block of ice, Griffiths later estimated was 4.5 pounds (roughly two kilograms). His careful analyses revealed that the piece of ice was made up of fifty-one layers of ice separated by layers of trapped air bubbles. Reportedly, it did not resemble known hailstones in that its ice crystals were larger and its layers were far too regular. Its composition, according to Griffiths, was simply "cloud" water.

Griffiths also eventually excluded the possibility of aircraft icing by making "enquiries at the engineer's department at the airport." He determined that no plane in the air at the time reported any icing on their wings and the meteorologist claimed that the engineers denied "quite categorically" that there was any icing on any of those aircraft. There is no way to tell, however, if the strange event was possibly a prank played on the unsuspecting meteorologist graduate student by fellow classmates.

More recently, in January of 2000, at least fifty different megacryometeors fell over Spain, including one that hit a car in Tocina, a village close to Seville. The ice chunk broke into two pieces, one weighing 1.2 kilograms [2.6 pounds] and 1.7 kilograms [3.7 pounds]. A panel of Spanish scientists postulated that the massive ice balls were created in the stratosphere by abnormal cooling of the localized region. Research meteorologist and hail expert Dr. Charles Knight noted, however, that "solid ice cannot form in the absence of thick, highly visible clouds."

Megacryometeors continue to fall. As recently as February of 2005, the Decatur *Herald and Review* reported that a huge ice slab "about the size of a concrete block" smashed into the backyard of a couple living in Decatur, Illinois. Examination of the ice proved it was clear and white—not the "blue" of an airplane's chemical toilet—and a spokeswoman of the Federal Aviation Administration dismissed the possibility of the ice falling from an airplane's wings. So, the mystery of megacryometeors—nature's enormous ice chunks—continues.

(3) Shapes

As stated earlier, hailstones begin their lives as ice forms on "seeds" of small frozen raindrops or soft ice particles referred to as graupel. Normally, as supercooled (tiny water droplets that remain in a liquid state far below 32°F) cloud droplets collide into the forward sides of the hailstones, the hailstone takes on the common conical or pyramidal shape of small hail. However, when a hailstone grows to about an inch or more in diameter, it almost always begins to tumble. This tumbling causes the hailstone to morph into an oblate spheroid (somewhat grapefruitlike) form. At the same time, these larger hailstones often collect more water than they can freeze to the main body, and so the excess water may begin to flow over the outside of the icy stone, with some of it partially freezing at points on the outer surface. This can produce iciclelike protrusions on the hailstone's surface, and these appendages will, in turn, influence the direction and speed of tumbling.

Consequently, the resulting shapes of big hailstones can be very complicated and, in many cases—as noted below—not well understood. An additional shape-changing effect is that large hailstones may actually break apart while in the air. Experts suggest that this

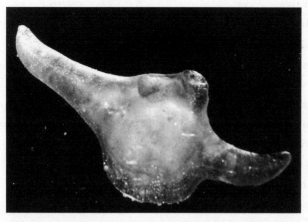

An oddly shaped hailstone from an Oak Ridge Tennessee hailstorm. Note the ice perturbations could give more superstitious people an impression of "horns." (Photo Courtesy of Dr. Charles Knight, National Center for Atmospheric Research.)

fracturing is likely the result of continual freezing and expanding of trapped water in the hailstones. So, given the tumbling, the water flow, the fracturing, and other processes occurring in large hailstones, it isn't surprising that such hail can fall in very odd shapes.

For instance, in the mid-1800s, the science journal *Scientific American* reported that a correspondent from Illinois observed three separate hailstorms that he termed "remarkable" for the size and peculiar shape of the hailstones. In one of the storms, the hailstones fell in the form of "square chunks," apparently resembling ice cubes. The report noted that some of these odd hailstones killed a variety of chickens, pigs, and other small animals. Hailstones, which battered Oak Ridge, Tennessee, in 1968 and subsequently described in *Monthly Weather Review,* were rare in that they resembled starfish and daggers with long and symmetrical spikes. A meteorologist who examined them described some of the stones as having spiraled arms while others had lobes on the end of the spikes. But he concluded, "Perhaps the most striking shapes were in the form of perfect crosses, or daggers." Other examples of hail with appendages or spikes include the occurrence of spiked hail in 1886 in the Dakotas, in Pennsylvania in 1889, and in Sydney, Australia, in 1971.

Variations on the concept of oblate hailstones and their formation include several reports of "platelike," "disclike," "pyramidal" or "conical" hail found in historical reports. Less common but perhaps also related to the basic oblate nature of hailstones are the accounts of "Saturn-shaped" hailstones (having equatorial rims so that they resemble miniatures of the planet Saturn) that fell in 1888, knobbed hail in 1918 in Britain, or actual doughnut-shaped hailstones of Hot Springs, Arkansas, in 1948. Oblate hailstones do often have hollows on their large faces—somewhat like doughnuts but generally not with complete holes.

As mentioned above, hailstones with icicle appendages can occur. For instance, *Monthly Weather Review* reported that a hailstorm at Oswego, New York, in 1889 had a few hailstones, which "were found, measuring one-and-a-half inch by one inch; they were of clear ice, very irregular in formation, and resembled the fragments of icicles." Similarly, Reverend Thomas Short, the English historian, described a severe hailstorm back in 1714 as "a dreadful Storm of Hail five Inches about, with 20 Icicles depending on some of them, and near an Inch in Length." Even more bizarrely, hailstones that fell over Lübeck, Germany, in 1392 apparently resembled human faces with pointed beards—yet one might see, with a bit of imagination, how a spike on a hailstone, such as one of those photographed at Oak Ridge Tennessee, might be interpreted as a "beard" or "horns."

The strangest account of an icicle fall is that given by West German newspapers in January 1951 and recounted by many fortean sources. Reports from those papers stated that a spear of ice, which measured six inches in diameter and six feet long, "fell from the skies" and skewed a carpenter who was working on the roof of a house in Kempten near Düsseldorf.

(4) Killer Hail

Yes, hail can kill. Even in the United States, a few people have died by hail. At Moore, Oklahoma, during a severe thunderstorm in April of 1893, one hailstone struck a child on the head "breaking its skull." Another child, a fourteen-year-old boy, was killed by hail while working in a field near Laredo, Texas, on May 21, 1928. Despite these two stories that were reported by meteorologists and were published in government publications of the time, such as *Monthly Weather Review*, the three deaths "officially" attributed to hail in the United States occurred in 1930, 1979, and 2000. The first (acknowledged by weather historian

Snowden Flora in his 1956 book *Hailstorms of the United States*) happened near Lubbock, Texas, on May 13, 1930, when a farmer,
thirty-nine years of age, working in a field, was caught in a
sudden hailstorm and before he could reach shelter, he was
beaten so violently by the hailstones that he died within a few
hours. The second death (discussed by Pat Hughes and a colleague in *Weatherwise*) occurred when a small six-month-old baby
was struck by a large hailstone in July 1979 and died a few days
later in Fort Collins, Colorado. The third most recent death
(mentioned in the National Climate Data Center's *Storm Events*
database for March 2000) was of a nineteen-year-old man in
Lake Worth, Texas, who was struck by "softball"-sized hail while
trying to move a new car out of danger from the ice missiles. The
young man died the following day of severe head injuries.

Hail has proven far more deadly in other parts of the world.
During a severe thunderstorm in Kostov, Russia, in 1923,
twenty-three people perished after running into their fields to
save their livestock. Reportedly, hailstones may have weighed
between one and two pounds. A Rumanian 1928 May Day festival, mentioned in the next year's issue of *Literary Digest,* proved
deadly when six children were killed and ten other persons
injured by hailstones "the size of hen's eggs." In 1930, a hailstorm over the Siatistic district in Greece killed twenty-two
people and injured another twenty-nine.

By far, the most deadly of modern hailstorms have occurred in
India. In 1888, hailstones as large as "goose eggs and oranges" or
even cricket balls were recorded to have killed 246 people (230
at Moradabad and sixteen at Bareilly) in India. Some victims were
directly pounded by hail and others were buried in the large
drifts of several feet of hail and died of cold exposure. More than
sixteen hundred animals were killed. One account of this storm
by an Englishman living in the area, J. S. MacIntosh, related, "A

terrific storm of hail followed, breaking all the windows and glass doors." He noted that the destructive hail was confined to a relatively small area, only about six or seven miles around Moradabad. The Englishman stated that at least two hundred and thirty people were killed in the storm and that the majority of those deaths were directly caused by the hail. On the whole, he said, those who were outside when the storm hit were "simply pounded to death by the hail." Even more distressing was MacIntosh's comment that "more than one marriage party were caught by the storm near the banks of the river, and were annihilated." Some scientists are of the opinion that those who perished by the hail hadn't been killed directly by the blows of the hailstones but rather killed by being knocked down by the wind and hail, buried in the hail, and ultimately perished through the combined effects of cold and exhaustion.

Unfortunately, even in this modern day, people are still being killed by hail. In April 2005, a severe hailstorm in Sichuan Province killed eighteen people and injured another twenty-five according to the *China Daily*. Nearly twenty-eight thousand homes reportedly were damaged by the massive hailstorm.

(5) Animal Kills

Of course, in addition to humans, many types of animals, living their entire lives in the outdoors, are even more vulnerable to the dangers of hail. After a hailstorm with stones as large as cricket balls hit Naini Tal, India, in 1855, Charles Tomlinson recounted, "No bullocks were killed, but a monkey was, and three human beings were knocked down." In 1867, another Indian hailstorm pounded a country district near the village of Bellary. Hailstones reportedly as large as coconuts and mangoes killed two men, nearly twenty-five hundred sheep and eight cattle in one township alone. In a report to the Royal Meteorological Society in 1937, Sir George Simpson stated that when in India, he had received a report of a hailstorm killing buffaloes over a large area. More recently, biologist Allen G. Smith, writing in an issue of *Audubon Magazine,* estimated that a 1953 hailstorm, which traversed a 140-mile-long and five-mile-wide path near Balerta, Canada, killed over thirty-six thousand waterfowl of various species. In the same hailstorm, a six hundred-pound hog was literally battered to death because it was caught out in the open, away from shelter.

In the United States, weather historian Snowden Flora reported that a hailstorm, which hit Rapid City, South Dakota, in July 1891, contained massive hailstones that killed sixteen horses. Reportedly, some horses were blinded and others were so seriously injured that they had to be put down. Similarly, a weather observer, George Loveland, wrote in *Monthly Weather Review* that an August 1917 hailstorm near York, Nebraska, killed hundreds of chickens and fatally injured young pigs and calves. He stated that the hailstones so pounded any unfortunate horses and cattle caught in the open pastures that, when later discovered, they were entirely covered with blood and huge lumps. Witnesses purportedly found scores of rabbits dead in the fields, and one farmer picked up over four hundred hail-struck grackles (birds) in a space of about three hundred by three hundred feet. Even in recent times, newspapers have written of antelope being killed by hail in Wyoming.

(6) Hail Protection

Methods to stop hail have been proposed for not only decades but even for centuries. For instance, in ancient Greece, the philosopher Seneca derisively reported on the "hail guards" who were appointed by the state for a small town near Corinth. He wrote that he found it incredible that the village actually employed sentries—so-called hail guards—who were paid out of public funds to simply stand around the city and watch for hail. Mockingly, he noted that when such hail was sighted, the response from the citizenry wasn't for safety but rather for divine appeasement. People of Cleonae, he wrote, didn't run to their houses to get protective clothing or to take cover but rather they dashed to the temple to offer an appropriate sacrifice, such as a lamb or a chicken. Consequently, Seneca wondered if the people really expected that once the hail gods had tasted blood, the storm's terrorization would be satisfied and it would move off in another direction.

To ensure the point was completely made, Seneca continued, "Are you laughing at this? Here is something to make you laugh even more." According to Seneca's sources, if there wasn't a convenient lamb or a chicken to sacrifice to the hailstorm, a Cleonae citizen simply pricked his finger with a pin and "sacrificed" his own blood. Seneca cynically wondered how the hail magically ascertained the value of the man's blood. Why would a hailstorm be as willing to turn away from the fields of such a "pricked" man, he argued, as it would from the fields of a man who had appeased it with more expensive sacrifices of a lamb or chicken?

According to meteorologist C. F. Talman, in a 1936 issue of *Natural History,* European peasants during the reign of Emperor Charlemagne in AD 800 erected tall "prayer poles" in their fields as safeguards against hail events. A small strip of a parchment carefully inscribed with a prayer against hail was attached to the top of each pole. Even by 1899, superstitions still ruled many areas with regard to hail. Flammarion, in his 1901 occult book, *The Unknown,* recounted the odd story of "the hail cross." At the end of the nineteenth century, near Albertville, in Savoy, a priest was asked to bless a new huge cross, the Cross of la belle Étoile. Such a blessing was required because the old cross had been burned to ashes by angry inhabitants of a neighboring commune. Those residents apparently believed that the cross worked just a bit too well for the village of Mercury-Germilly above which it stood. The neighboring villagers thought that, because of the protection of Mercury-Germilly's cross, the frustrated hail was pushed into their nearby unprotected village.

An Italian professor of mineralogy at the end of the nineteenth century stated that it was conceivable that the formation of hailstones could be prevented by injecting smoke particles (to serve as condensation nuclei, or the "seeds" of raindrops) by means of cannons fired at thunderstorms. This, he reasoned, would lead to rain rather than hail. His theory led to the creation of the famous hail cannons of Europe. The premier example of these cannons was the Stiger Hail Gun, a cast-iron muzzle-loading mortar (as discussed in Jack and Marcia Donnan's interesting 1977 book *Rain Dance to Research*). The Stiger Hail Gun's muzzle was over an inch in diameter, used a load of nearly a third of a pound of black powder and designed to be fired vertically into the air. There was no bullet or cannonball to the Hail Gun; instead, when it was fired, the Hail Gun produced a bizarre whirling ring of smoke and gas. Its explosion was powerful enough, however, to splinter sticks and even kill small birds that were caught in its blast path.

An additional modification of the Hail Gun included the installation of metal extensions onto the muzzles to act as sounding boxes and make even more noise. This innovation was attributed to the conjecture that somehow loud sounds caused the clouds (and therefore the hail) to dissipate. Stiger eventually deployed thirty-six of his Hail Guns in Austria by the end of the nineteenth century. Then something weird happened. For scientists, the occurrence of "negative results"—having nothing happen during the experiment—is, in general, the bane of research. In this instance, and likely due to simple chance, no damaging hail fell in Austria during the year in which the Hail Guns became "operational." People, of course, attributed the lack of hail to the operation of the Hail Guns—and, by 1900, seven thousand Hail Guns were sold and placed in northern Italy alone.

However, within a couple of years, serious doubts were raised about the effectiveness of the cannons. One problem was their safety—in Venice and Brescia alone, the Hail Guns accounted for seven deaths and seventy-eight injuries. Another problem involved their effectiveness. Were they actually working to impede hail? Consequently, as Cleveland Abbe in *Monthly Weather Review* recounted, a professor of physics at the Royal University at Rome, Dr. Blaserna, was personally appointed by the Italian president to investigate the effectiveness of hailshooting.

Blaserna first selected the area of Castelfranco in Venetia to test the hail suppression hypothesis, using 222 cannons. Each of these cannon was capable of sending a "vortex ring" of smoke over ten feet in diameter. Later, a cannon sending up a vortex forty feet in diameter was subsequently added. As a further test in 1906, another two hundred and fifty broadsides were fired by over two hundred cannons at Aulagne and researchers at Rome exploded a series of one-ton bombs with no discernible results. As a result, Blaserna's report given before the Royal Academy that year explicitly stated that hailshooting in Italy was not effective.

But that didn't stop the practice. For instance, a later Italian hail-reduction practice involved firing explosive "hail rockets" into potential severe thunderstorms. Such rockets were thought to "make hail soft." While there is no rationale for this method or for the hail cannons, some people took these protective meas-ures quite seriously. Indeed, even in 2005, the government of China was still detonating thousands of rocket charges to "force hail to change into rain."

As another way of coping with the ice menace, some states began to issue hail insurance by the start of the twentieth century. Such insurance was not only risky for the farmer but for the insurer. When the state legislature of North Dakota enacted hail insurance in 1911 for farmers of the state, the losses during the first year exceeded the premiums by nearly eighteen percent, and the state actually had to prorate all losses at seventy cents on the dollar.

Today, people still try to come up with ways to prevent hail damage—even on the spur-of-the-moment. Canadian weather historian David Phillips, in his entertaining 1998 book *Blame It on the Weather,* told the story of frantic motorists in Calgary, Alberta, who were plummeted by "orange-sized" hail in 1996. Apparently, some desperate motorists even attempted to bribe gas station attendants with as much as fifty dollars to let them drive their cars into covered service bays. In a more proactive manner, according to an article in *New Scientist,* Nissan Motor Company recently employed sonic boom generators to protect cars from hail at its factory at Canton, Mississippi. From an agricultural standpoint, commercial hail nets that capture—or at least impede—hail before the ice stones can damage crops have been used in many regions around the world to protect high-value crops.

(7) Human Hail and Other Hail Inclusions

While the core or nucleus of a hailstone is often a soft ice particle known as graupel, on rare occasions, more exotic "seeds" are used. In 1882, according to *Monthly Weather Review,* the reputable foreman of the Novelty Iron Works factory in Dubuque, Iowa, found two small living frogs embedded in two large hailstones that fell during a terrific hailstorm over the city. In another instance, the same meteorology journal reported that during a severe thunderstorm at Vicksburg, Mississippi, in 1894 "a remarkably large hailstone was found to have a solid nucleus, consisting of a

piece of alabaster from one-half to three-quarters of an inch."
At the same time in nearby Bovina, "a gopher turtle, six by eight
inches, and entirely encased in ice, fell with the hail."

As recounted by a number of sources, including the famous
A. D. Bajkov who opened this book, an Essen Germany professor
experienced in 1896 a hailstone that was "the size of a hen's egg"
but which amazingly had encased a completely frozen fish within it.
The German professor wrote that the hailstone containing the fish
"was picked up in my presence so that there can be no doubt of the
fact." He described the fish as a crucian carp about two inches
long. The medieval historian Reverend Thomas Short reported

Yes, it is indeed an actual ladybug embedded in a hailstone—photograph
taken in Nebraska in May 2003 showing a. U.S. quarter in upper left corner
demonstrates size of hailstones. (Photo Courtesy of Theresa A. DeBoer.)

that locals in 1713 Hungary were pelted by "Hail with Worms, and winged Beetles, within the Hailstones." A slightly more scientific study by John Hopkins Hospital (and discussed by *Scientific American*) identified a huge number of bacteria living in the interior of large hailstones, which fell during an April 1890 thunderstorm. They suggested that the number of bacteria in these ice stones ranged from an astounding four hundred to seven hundred specimens to the cubic centimeter.

One of the more bizarre hail stories is told of a gliding competition just before World War II (although sources disagree on the exact date) when five "Hitler-inspired" German glider pilots were forced to bail out and parachute into a thunderstorm over the Rhön Mountains. As they were thrown up and down through the storm by the tremendous updrafts and downdrafts, ice began to encase them in much the same manner as hailstones. As the only survivor recounted, the consequences were dreadful. Instead of falling gently downward, the parachutes were filled to bursting point by the gusting winds and violently shot upward. The attached pilots were carried into increasingly colder and higher layers of cloud. However hard they tried to steer their storm-whipped parachutes, they could not escape the howling force of the gale. When the winds eventually crashed them into the ground, all five pilots were literally covered by layers of ice. Unfortunately, only one of the glider pilots survived and even he lost three of his fingers and suffered frostbite on his face.

Sometimes embryos of a hailstone can be bits of the regional landscape. For example, in 1686 England, a local resident reported to the old science journal *Philosophical Transactions* that "this City and Country round about, is filled with Reports of raining Wheat about Warminster." The resident wrote, "It was confidently affirmed (and backt by several, who affirme they had seen it) that those Grains were found in the Hails, as Seeds in Comfits." Much more recently, a volcano off Iceland produced clouds (from heated sea water) that subsequently produced hail. Ships stationed nearby were hit with hailstones containing tiny volcanic bits in their centers.

(8) Strange Composition and Color

The water that comprises the ice of a hailstone is usually fairly clear and clean. Even so, for many years, people were taught that hail water was unsafe to drink. For instance, in a 1764 issue of *Gentleman's Magazine* (contrary to usage in modern times, this was a mild-mannered magazine), the advice given to a traveler to Spain was never let a flock of sheep "approach a rivulet or pond after a shower of hail, for if they should eat the dewy grass, or drink hail water, the whole tribe would become melancholy, fast, pine away and die, as often happened." The Spanish sage continued that hail water was so harmful that "the people of Molina will not drink the river water after a violent shower of hail, experience taught the danger." Conversely, nineteenth-century meteorologist D. P. Thomson recounted that the British in India had found an innovative use for hailstones: "Dr. A. T. Christie observed very large hailstones fell . . . the quantity was so great, that a sufficient supply was obtained for the cooling of the wine of a military mess for several days."

Occasionally, impurities are introduced into hailstones. Most commonly, these impurities are basically dirt. As hail experts Charles and Nancy Knight demonstrated in a *Bulletin of the American Meteorological Society* research article, an Oklahoma hailstone was found that contained bright red-orange dirt. Although the first thin-section did not reveal how the dirt might have entered the hailstone, a second thin section clearly showed a channel through which the muddy water entered the stone after it had fallen to the ground. Such channels may account for stories of "red" or "blood" hailstones such as fell in Italy in 1873 or in Russia in 1880.

There still remain inclusion oddities such as the Mississippi hailstones of 1871 (and reported in *Scientific American*), which a local paper said were flavored with turpentine. The Mississippi paper hastened to assure readers that the amount of turpentine in the hailstones was not sufficient to be used as a medicine. Another hailstone inclusion covered by *Scientific American* was the New Jersey hailstorm of 1874 that, according to a Professor Leeds, consisted of hailstones tainted with carbonate of soda. A witness to the hailstorm, who had picked up one of the large hailstones after storm and licked it, said that the hailstone tasted so intensely bitter that he immediately spit it out. Finally, a *Scientific American* report (and other records at the time) stated that an 1821 Irish hailstorm contained hailstones that were mixed with iron sulfate. One might speculate that perhaps these "iron" hailstones originated in part from the pollution of nearby factories.

One of the strangest hailstorms occurred in India in 1893 where, according to the respected science journal *Nature*, witnesses discovered hailstones that inexplicably were not even cold to the touch. Still more strangely, the reports continued, when the hailstones were licked or put into the mouth (as was the custom in India—in contrast to the Spanish report above), the "ice" apparently tasted like sugar.

(9) The Sound of Hail

Falling hail can shriek in such a distinctly unique fashion (in much the same manner as a tornado's infamous freight train sound) that it creates a lasting impression on the witness. Noted meteorologist Elias Loomis, in his 1879 *Treatise on Meteorology*, compared the "peculiar cracking noise preceding the fall of hail" to "the noise of walnuts violently shaken up in a bag." He noted that some had attributed the sound to the rapid speed at which the hailstones fell through the air, while others had "ascribed it to feeble electrical discharges from one hailstone to another, for electricity always attends the progress of a hailstorm." However, French meteorologist J. N. Plumandon, a contemporary of Loomis, suggested a more plausible theory that the "noise associated with hail is from the combined sound of hailstones falling on surface objects (e.g., leaves, roofs, etc.)."

Of course, oddities still exist. The Columbia, Missouri, hailstorm of 1911, according to a short report in *Nature,* contained large hailstones that battered the city's windows, walls, or pavement and "exploded with a sharp report, so loud as to be mistaken for breaking window panes or a pistol shot." The hailstones literally shattered upon impact in a multitude of tiny fragments and scattered in all directions, so that observers reported the area looked "like a mass of 'popping corn' on a large scale." Russell Rolo, in his rare 1893 book *On Hail,* recorded that "on July 10, 1863, Mr. Watson and several other persons [experienced] a fall of hail succeeded by the peculiar hissing and boiling sounds of the escape of electricity from their hatchets, stocks, and hands."

(9) Most Hail Accumulation

Massive hail falls can lead to ice accumulations of such magnitude that snowplows are sometimes needed to remove them. For example, according to a 1925 *Monthly Weather Review* report, an Iowa hailstorm produced hail to a depth of two to four inches, which was then washed from the adjoining fields into a creek by a torrential fall of rain. An observer recorded, "About 1 [and] 1/2 acres were covered with hail to a depth of from 2 to 4 feet."

Similarly, on May 7, 1865, a violent storm burst over the Aisne district of France, causing immense damages. According to witnesses (cited in Rolo's book and by Flammarion), the valleys of the Somme and the Scheldt were pelted with so many hailstones that the ice lay five yards deep upon the ground. Hailstones were still visible five days after, and, at some places, formed such a solid mass that they acted as a dike to keep back the

Aerial photograph of Selden Kansas after a massive July 1959 hail-storm caused summer to become winter for the Great Plains city. (Photo from the files of the *Norton Kansas Daily Telegram*.)

water. In one place, a mass of ice, which formed from the hail, was said to be a mile and a quarter long and about two fifths of a mile broad, amounting to twenty-one million cubic feet.

One of the better-documented big accumulation hailstorms hit Selden, Kansas, in July of 1959. According to a report by the Norton, Kansas, *Daily Telegram* and related in the journal *Monthly Weather Review,* the storm lasted an amazing eighty-five minutes and produced hail depths in open areas of eighteen inches with drifts to four feet. Indeed, hail that had accumulated on a truck weight scale, which measured ten by forty-five feet, weighed twenty-eight thousand pounds or an astounding 62.2 pounds per square feet. As evidence of how massive this hailstorm actually was, snowplows weren't enough to clear the streets—they simply couldn't move the icy mass—and so bulldozers were called in. According to one resident, "The hail began and just didn't stop."

(10) Miracles and Hail Martyrs
Sometimes people see what they wish to see in hailstones—particularly if it involves religion. For example, following a 1907

edict by the local government forbidding a religious procession
through the town of Remiremont in France, an apparent miracle
occurred—perhaps showing divine wrath at the restrictive edict. A
number of fortean books have recounted the wondrous story
published in 1908 issue of a British science journal called the
English Mechanic and World of Science. The local abbé said that he had
been drawn into witnessing the miracle when his housekeeper
brought in some of the very oddly shaped hailstones. According
to the abbé, each of the ice stones was shaped in the form of the
bust of a woman, who was wearing a garment much like a priest's
robe. Perhaps not surprisingly given the religious controversy
that had gone on prior to the hailstorm, the good abbé described
the image on the hailstone as an identical likeness to the Virgin
of the Hermits for whom the procession through the town of

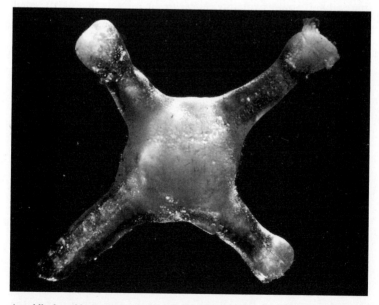

An oddly shaped hailstone from an Oak Ridge Tennessee hailstorm. Note the ice perturbations could give more superstitious people an impression of a "cross" and may be the
type of hailstone associated with medieval stories of "falling crosses." (Photo Courtesy of
Dr. Charles Knight, National Center for Atmospheric Research.)

Remiremont had been banned. Later, the abbé collected the signatures of fifty people who had seen the extraordinary hailstones and were "thoroughly convinced of the truth of their observations."

As another linkage between hail and religion, two famous Christian martyrs, Emeterius and Chelidonius, have gained a local reputation for hail protection in the city of Calahorra, Spain. In olden days, when a hailstorm threatened the city, the town's clergy immediately undertook a five-step invocation: They made a procession to the church, put lighted candles on the altar, then sang a hymn to these martyrs, chanted the antiphona, and, finally, sung the praises of these martyrs. Supposedly, by the time this was finished, the hailstorm would be vanquished by the power of the martyrs (of course, one should realize that hailstorms don't normally last too long anyway). The reason for the martyrs' supernatural hail power probably relates to the miracle that occurred at their beheading. When the executioner cut off their heads, a ring of one of the martyrs and a handkerchief of the other purportedly were taken up into a cloud and brought to Heaven. According to Aurelius Clemens in his book *The Crown*, everyone who was present saw this, and so far as the sight of eyes could follow, the people watched the gleam of the gold ring and the brightness of the linen with an astonished gaze.

(11) Bird Kills

Often, with our concern of the effect of hail on crops, livestock, people, and property, we don't think about the consequences of hail on birds. Yet, hail can wreck havoc on the avian community. A scientist reported in *Science* of a hailstorm with hailstones described as the size of "hens' eggs," which hit Baton Rouge, Louisiana, in 1933. In the aftermath of the severe hailstorm, the scientist was most amazed at the enormous destruction of bird life. He stated that the campus of Louisiana State University was littered with carcasses of birds that had been battered by the hail. Indeed, areas outside the immediate Baton Rouge area apparently showed an even heavier mortality. In the Baton Rouge suburb of Istrouma, one man collected twenty-six bobwhites over an area that was approximately five acres in size. Other people confirmed his findings—a vast variety of dead birds, including "meadow larks, sparrows, mocking-birds, Virginia cardinals and other birds" were collected in the area as a result of the storm.

In a similar fashion, three condors became "iced up" in a California thunderstorm in October 1938. According to W. W. Wenstrom's 1942 book *Weather and the Ocean of Air,* two of the condors crashed to the ground and were killed, while the third, wounded by the hail, flew falteringly away. British newspapers reported the story (which was subsequently recounted by the *Fortean Times*) of a flock of frozen ducks that fell from the sky above Stuttgart, Arkansas, in November 1973. The head of the State Game and Fish Commission suggested that the plunging fate of the ducks was consistent with the problem of airplane "icing." He hypothesized that the ducks simply had reached a colder part of the atmosphere and, at that point, moisture had frozen onto their wings. That caused the flock to come crashing down into the ground. Indeed, many of the residents of Stuttgart actually ate the storm-killed ducks for dinner.

In a related fashion, Mike Stark of the *Billings Gazette* reported on a massive bird kill in Yellowstone National Park, Wyoming, caused by a sudden snow squall. Ornithologist Terry McEneaney estimated that over forty thousand ducks and hundreds of other birds were disoriented by the May 2005 snow squall and flew into the buildings. Hundreds of grebes—a water species of bird—likely became confused in the early morning storm and mistook parking lots and roads for water, crashing down onto the pavement.

(12) Pasadena's Hail Fun

As seen in the previous categories, generally hail is regarded as a major economic and social problem. Hailstorms have caused crop damage, animal deaths, and even injuries to people. Renowned weather historian David Ludlum, however, recounted in *Weatherwise* the details of a very rare "holiday" summer hailstorm that hit Pasadena, California, in 1884. This hailstorm created an almost festival springlike atmosphere around the city in a manner reminiscent of the "frost fairs" of London, England.

Normally, Pasadena is a quite hot and dry place in the summer months. This extraordinary thunderstorm proved that common impression false. First, it dropped an immense amount of ice in the form of two-inch diameter hailstones, covering the ground to a depth of nearly two inches, and, second, the hailstorm cooled the California town down tremendously. So, rather than dwell on the extensive damage to the area's hay crop, everybody proceeded to make "the best of it." For instance, a large number of boys—and men—partook in some "lively snowballing" while others concocted makeshift "snow sleds" (perhaps "hail sleds" might be a better phrase) from dry goods boxes and other crates. Some people actually hitched up their confused horses to some of these sleds to go on impromptu (and improbable) June sleighrides in Pasadena, California. Later in the evening of the "hail day," one couple even gathered up enough of the hailstones to make homemade hand-cranked ice cream. From all reports, for a brief June day in Southern California, people used a normally despised hailstorm to make "a merry evening of it."

(13) Hail Safety

Although the National Weather Service does not specifically issue hail watches or hail warnings, large hail is one of the primary criteria used to issue Severe Thunderstorm Watches or Warnings.

The National Weather Service issues a Severe Thunderstorm Watch if conditions necessary for the creation of a severe thunderstorm are present for a given area. A severe thunderstorm is defined as a storm that can produce strong winds, heavy rain, and large hail—generally three-fourths of an inch in diameter or larger. As with a tornado watch, a Severe Thunderstorm Watch is designed to alert the public to potential danger. Normally watches are issued for areas approximately 150 miles by 200 miles. When a watch is active, you should plan your activities (particularly those that are outdoor) with the weather in mind and keep information sources (such as television or radio) nearby. A Severe Thunderstorm Warning is given when a severe thunderstorm has been observed in your area and you should take immediate action to protect life and property.

When hail is falling and you are driving, you should generally stop driving—pull to the side of the road, under a bridge or overpass (be aware, however, that hailstorms are often associated with thunderstorms that can produce tornadoes; overpasses are very bad shelters for tornadoes), or under a gas-station awning. Do not leave your car while it is hailing. Your car gives reasonable protection during a hailstorm. However, you should stay away as much as possible from the car windows. If you are in a well-constructed building during a hailstorm, stay there as large hail falling outside can cause serious injury. If you are caught outdoors with no immediate shelter, try to protect your head as much as possible.

Chapter 5

RAIN

R AIN IS NORMALLY ONE OF THE FIRST THOUGHTS THAT COME TO mind when we mention "weather." Most of us think of rain as a fairly common and straightforward event. The physical processes to form a raindrop, however, are actually quite involved. Raindrops are created by one of two processes, depending on the temperature of the clouds in our atmosphere. For *warm* clouds—those clouds whose temperatures are above freezing—rain is produced through a vast number of tiny collisions of microscopic water droplets. At its center, each droplet has a core called a *condensation nucleus* upon which the water collects. This nucleus is exceptionally small, only on the order of tens of a millionth of a meter. As the microscopic droplet containing the condensation nucleus falls through the cloud, it collides and coalesces with other droplets. Common condensation nuclei include minuscule specks of sea salt, pollen, ash, or dust. This is the reason why our cars are often dirty *after* a summer rainstorm— each raindrop contains millions of tiny condensation nuclei, many of which are simple dust and dirt particles. Once the water runs off or is evaporated, the dirt is left.

The size of the raindrop is a function of how many collisions have occurred. Thin stratus clouds tend to generate smaller droplets, resulting in drizzle. Thicker clouds are more likely to produce larger droplets of rain. The critical element of this model of raindrop formation is the necessity of a warm cloud.

Cold clouds—those clouds with tops that are below freezing— create rain by a slightly different process. In a cold cloud, ice crystals exist in suspension with a multitude of supercooled droplets (microscopic water that remains in a liquid state far below 32°F). As the ice crystals collide with the supercooled water, the water instantly freezes onto the droplet, normally on one of six sides, given the underlying molecular structure of the ice crystal. If a sufficiently large number of collisions occur, the crystal aggregate becomes a snowflake—and, if that flake melts before it hits the ground, it becomes a raindrop.

Other issues than those involving raindrop creation, such as "how much rain," "how little rain," "how frequently is the rain," "how intense is the rain" are what we want answered on our evening newscasts. But occasionally nature decides to play a few tricks on us by giving us rain in different colors, having strange additions to our rainfall such as fish, frogs, and even snakes, or blasting us with incredibly intense cloudbursts. In this chapter, I have categorized odd rainfalls into twelve basic categories—and added a thirteenth that addresses the general safety concerns associated with rainfall.

(1) Blood Rains

Colors often evoke specific emotions and feelings in us. Red, as the color of blood and warning, frequently induces a sense of fear in many people. This contrasts to the more soothing normal colors found in nature, such as blues, greens, and whites.

Occasionally, nature's normalcy fails and oddity abounds; even rain itself sometimes falls with a "dreadful" red tint. In those instances, many believe that Higher Powers are sending a clear message of fear and terror. If bloody events can indeed occur, one would expect that historians would undoubtedly record such red rain showers—and they have.

Romans, in particular, carefully noted occurrences of blood rains. As early as in the reign of Rome's legendary founder, Romulus, mention is made of blood falling from the skies. The ancient historian Plutarch wrote that soon after the legendary

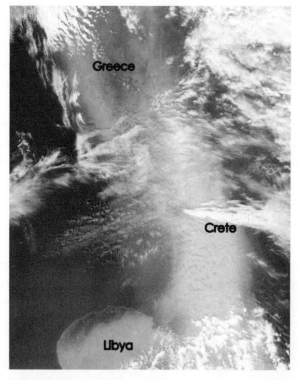

The origins of a Blood Rain: A satellite image of Saharan dust moving over the Mediterranean Sea and into Europe on April 17, 2005. This particular storm subsequently created a pronounced yellow haze over Greece, which caused problems with air and sea transportation. (Image Courtesy of MODIS Rapid Response Project at NASA/GSFC.)

Romulus conquered the Fidenae, a deadly plague broke out in Rome, mysteriously causing sudden death without any previous sickness. And, as if that wasn't enough trauma for the people, Plutarch added, "There rained blood, too, in the city" so that fear of the great gods was added to their sufferings. In a list of dreadful omens occurring in Rome in 181 BC, ancient historian Livy cataloged a shower of blood falling in the precinct of Vulcan and Concord of Rome. In response, the Senate decreed that the consuls of the city should sacrifice full-grown victims to the gods.

Saint Gregory of Tours, famous medieval bishop and historian, recorded a strange rain occurrence happening in France in the seventh year of King Childebert's reign, around AD 582. He stated that on Easter Sunday, the whole sky above the city of Soissons seemed to catch fire and in Paris "real blood rained from a cloud." This blood, the saint claimed, fell on the people's clothes and so stained them with gore that people immediately stripped them off in stark horror. In an even more bizarre occurrence, medieval historian Reverend Thomas Short in his chronology of historical weather events registered a strange red rain in AD 775 in Constantinople, ". . . if some Historians are to be credited, little red Crosses fell from the Air on their Children."

The French philosopher Peirese was one of the first scientists to rationally explain blood rains. Frank Cowan, in his fascinating 1865 book *Curious Facts in the History of Insects (Including Spiders and Scorpions)*, communicated Peirese's story as told by his biographer Pierre Gassendi.

According to Gassendi, nothing in the whole year 1608 pleased Peirese more than that he was able personally to observe a "bloody rain" and determine its cause. He found that "great drops" of the blood rain "were plainly to be seen, both in the city itself, upon the walls of the church-yard of the church." Throughout the summer, Peirese studied the problem and then inadvertently stumbled upon the cause of the French blood rain. He discovered that, after a caterpillar that he had captured for study had metamorphosed into a butterfly, the box in which the caterpillar resided contained "a red drop as broad as an ordinary sous or shilling." When Peirese realized that at the same time other butterflies were maturing around the city, he deduced that the red "blood" stains found around the city likely were the result of those butterflies. The French philosopher theorized that other blood rains such as those recorded by Gregory of Tours might also be the result of butterflies.

Butterflies can't explain all bloody rains, however, since butterflies swarm only at certain times of the year and blood rains have been reported in every season. People, therefore, have proposed alternate theories to explain the occurrence. In a major explanation of the phenomenon, many scientists have discovered that some blood rains are the result of particles such as red sand. On October 9, 1764, it was recorded that a red rain resembling blood fell on the public in the Duchy of Cleves and created a panic among the superstitious. When a sample was sent to a local scientist, however, he concluded the red rain was caused "by particles which has been raised into the atmosphere, by a strong wind" and the rain "was no way hurtful to mankind or beasts."

In a similar fashion, the famous naturalist Charles Darwin encountered a strange phenomena onboard the HMS *Beagle* as the ship traveled across the Atlantic during his famous voyage around the world. Darwin recorded in an 1897 edition of his *Journal* that the air onboard ship became hazy around the Verde Islands. He speculated that the haziness was "caused by the falling of impalpably fine dust." He even managed just before landing at Porto Praya to fill a little packet with the brown-colored fine dust off the ship. Darwin hypothesized that the dust "is produced, as I believe, from the wear and tear of volcanic rocks, and must come from the coast of Africa." His theory of African origin for the dust, however, was put into doubt by C. G. Ehrenberg, one of the leading scientists of that time. Ehrenberg supported a South American origin for the dust because he thought that some of the organisms in Darwin's samples could only have a South American origin.

Today we know that Darwin was absolutely correct; these particular blood rains that hit the Verde Islands, Great Britain, or Europe are indeed the result of huge Saharan dust storms. We now have records in modern times of reddish Saharan dust being picked up by windstorms over the African desert, carried across the Mediterranean Sea, dumped on Italy or Greece (accounting for the numerous blood rain events there), transported across Europe and then often deposited on Great Britain. Modern-day blood rains include:

- An estimated two million tons of fine red mud that poured down all across Europe in April 1926. Early twentieth-century meteorologist Charles Talman observed that the European newspapers and the scientific journals referred to this event as a "shower of blood" but used the expression in a "purely conventional sense."
- Red rain that fell on the Italian Rivera on March 23, 1937.
- A red rain that fell in the region of Fontanella near Bergamo in Italy in April of 1942.
- Western Scotland's red-colored rain that was believed to be dust blown from the Sahara Desert and fell in March of 1977.

While most scientists are satisfied with the Saharan dust (and occasional butterfly residue) explanation, a visually related phenomenon found in the Arctic—red snow—has a quite different explanation. That type of occurrence will be discussed in Chapter Eight, addressing the oddities of snow.

(2) Yellow Rains

Yellow rains also commonly appear in historical records of the past three thousand years. The problem with yellow rain is that, often in the minds of especially superstitious people, the color yellow is associated with sulfur—and sulfur is directly linked to the Devil. Respected nineteenth-century meteorologist David Purdie Thomson reported on an English yellow rain in the late spring of 1804 that "created fear in the minds of the people, especially as it was phosphorescent."

Even the United States has had its share of yellow rains. H. L. Eades observed in the journal *Scientific American*, "that the days of miracles have not yet passed." He wrote that, on the night of March 12, 1867, many Kentucky residents experienced a heavy fall of rain, which was comprised of water and an unknown "yellow substance." Eades wrote that the residents of Bowling Green, believing the yellow rain "to be sulfur, are somewhat alarmed," because they supposed that it might be a forerunner to "that great fire in which sinners expect to find themselves ensconced in a coming day!"

The fear of devilish yellow rains is clearly seen in Richard Proctor's description of a German occurrence recorded in an 1886 issue of the science journal *Knowledge*. He said a heavy evening rainfall in Munich had "brought down a quantity of sulphur" such that all nearby pools and streams contained streaks of yellow mud, "of the primrose tint proper to the substance, which Satan claims peculiarly as his own." He cynically wrote that "the old women of both sexes, with their accustomed brilliancy, recognized the approaching end of the world in this terrible phenomenon." These "foolish people," after smelling the yellow mud and believing that it reeked of "the Devil's favorite odor," declared that "the end of the world had been especially announced for the year 1886." They did this, according to Proctor, "for the exquisite reasons that Easter day falls later this year than it has for more than a century, and that the year both begins and ends with a Friday."

Yet, many learned people as far back as the seventeenth century correctly suggested that the substance that causes rain to be tinted yellow is nothing more than the pollen of flowers and trees—pine trees, in particular. A scientist who was asked to comment on an English yellow rain in June 1879 noted that it "was taken by the general masses to be a fall of sulfur. It was said by the imaginative to smell 'awful like brimstone' and to presage the end of the world." However, when he examined yellow dust from the "sulfur" rain under a microscope, he found it to be nothing more than pollen from nearby Scots fir pine trees.

In a related fashion, an 1883 Illinois tornado apparently coated a family, whose house was completely torn away by the winds, "with a gummy substance, which would not wash off!" The author of the report speculated that the gummy substance might have been formed from the sap of trees and excretions of leaves leaking from the torn shreds of foliage in the tornado's path.

(3) Other Colored Rains

Rains tinted the color of brown are usually linked to mud. As far back as the time of the Roman Republic (101 BC) the historian Livy recorded that, during the consulship of Gaius Marius and Manius Aquilius, it rained mud on the Roman district of Aventine. More recently than the days of the Roman Empire, a massive shower of mud fell on a passenger train in Nevada early in March 1879, according to the Winnemucca, Nevada, *Silver State* newspaper. The passenger train literally inched along the tracks due to an hour-long fall of mud so thick that the train wheels, unable to get traction in the slimy muck, kept slipping on the rails. One witness observed that the cars looked as if they had been repeatedly dragged through a mud hole.

The correct cause-and-effect was given for these massive mud rains in an analysis of the mud rains that occurred over the Atlantic Seaboard states in April 1901. A writer to the journal *Science* described a mud shower in New Haven, Connecticut, that caused "ladies who attended the ball game that afternoon [to have] their clothes badly spotted." The *Science* editor responded to this report by noting that "vast quantities of dust must have been taken up by the wind on the dry western plains, and that it was precipitated with the rain over the States farther east."

People have also witnessed other types of colored rains. Ancient historians recorded a fall of black rain over Constantinople that may have been linked to an eruption of Vesuvius in Italy. Similarly in 1755, near a volcanic island of Iceland, sailors witnessed a fall of black dust. They described it as resembling "lampblack" but smelled strongly of sulfur. Apparently farmers working in nearby Icelandic fields had their clothes, even hands and faces, blackened by the rain. Yet the observers correctly linked the rain to "some extraordinary eruption of [the volcano] Hecula." Similar black rains have occurred in areas next to coal mines as, for example, with the black rains of Worcestershire, England, in 1846 where witnesses commented that the black rain "smelled of soot, and probably was impregnated with carbonaceous matter from the coal fields adjoining."

Other substances have also tinted rainwater. In 1846 in Shanghai, China, an "olive-gray powder" fell on the city that at first appeared to be "hair," but more thorough examination determined it to be a kind of algae. A strange, undetermined crumbly greenish-black substance fell on Mighei, Russia, during a rainstorm in 1889. There have even been gold rains! In 1930, a science reporter wrote in the magazine *Popular Science Monthly* about the odd finding following massive dust storms in California that purportedly deposited tons of dirt over Los Angeles. According to the report, an assayer scooped up some of the dust and examined it. The man "found gold and silver dust which had come hundreds of miles from desert regions in the interior."

Finally, one of the odder colors noted in the history of colored rains is white. Many so-called "milk rains" have been documented in times of the Roman Republic. One of the earliest is one that apparently fell in 124 BC in the Rome suburb called the Graecostasis, where Greek and other foreign ambassadors lived. Livy described that not once but twice, during the consulship of Servius Galba and Marcus Scaurus of the Roman Republic, milk rained from the sky.

Historian John Swan suggested a strange unlikely cause for milk rain in his 1643 book *Specvivm mundi*. He hypothesized that the milk rains resulted when "the vehement heat of the sun shall either draw milk from the udders of cattell, and shall mix it with the other parts of the cloud; . . . so that it may look something white, then will the drops look as it rained milk."

Flammarion logged a remarkable fall of milky rain in Chambéry, France, on March 31, 1847, and gave a more logical answer for it. He first described the rainwater as being saturated with a milky substance, giving the appearance of thin clay particles and noted that people's clothes exposed to this milk rain were bespattered with whitish spots. But then he went one step further, analyzed the white spots and reported—thereby giving the most probable scientific explanation for milk rains—"the chemical composition of this dust showed predominance . . . from the Sahara."

(4) Fish Falls

Charles Fort, noted archivist of the odd and paranormal, loved stories of fish falls. He collected hundreds of anecdotes regarding the unusual phenomenon. This included such tales as a major fish fall in India in 1830 and the "Great Stickleback Fish Fall" of 1859. In the first event, nine separate people offered official depositions regarding a singular fall of fish in India. They all reported that fish were seen first in the sky, like a flock of birds, descending rapidly to the ground but that the fish, even the large ones, were all dead and some of them were actually rotten and mutilated.

The second event also involved a detailed personal account. In this case, the description was given to the Reverend Aaron Roberts by a lumberman John Lewis (subsequently reported and discussed in a wide variety of media including the *Annual Register* and *London Times*). He affirmed that he had been getting out "a piece of timber, for the purpose of setting it for the saw, when I was startled by something falling all over me—down my

An engraving of a fish fall during a Renaissance storm that appeared in *Der Wunder-reiche Uberzug* [sic] *unserer Nider-Welt*. . . . by Erasmus Francisci, 1680. (Photo Courtesy of National Oceanic and Atmospheric Administration/Department of Commerce Photo Library Historic NWS Collection; Archival Photography by Steve Nicklas, NOS, NGS.)

neck, on my head, and on my back." When he put his hand up to his neck, he was shocked to discover the "something" were little fish. He continued, "By this time, I saw the whole ground covered with them. I took off my hat, the brim of which was full of them." They were all alive and covered the ground in a long rectangle of about eighty yards by twelve yards around the mill.

Fort took great glee in mocking an official explanation for the Lewis fish fall given by Dr. Gray of the British Museum. Gray concluded that, upon reading all evidence about the fish fall, it was likely only a practical joke. The British scientist suggested that one of the lumberyard employees had probably thrown a bucket of fish and water upon Lewis, who then thought fish had fallen from the sky. Most scientists of the time agreed with Gray.

As late as 1946, the debate raged through the science community as to whether fish could indeed fall from the sky. At that time, E. W. Gudger of the American Museum of Natural History was one of the prime proponents of the reality of fish falls. In the 1920s and 1930s, he had published a series of articles recounting many anecdotal accounts of fish falls, including the two above that were described by Charles Fort. In addition, he related accounts of fish falls in many other regions around the world. He chronicled as a sampling:

- In North America, Mr. S. W. Narregang of Houston, Texas, told Gudger that while living in Aberdeen, South Dakota, in 1886, he had observed, following hard rains, many small fish on the roofs of office buildings, including his own.
- In Australia, distinguished ichthyologist J. Douglas Ogilby reported that a rain of fish had occurred at a farm near Cooper's Plain in 1906. Following the event, Dr. Ogilby actually exhibited some of the little fish with one specimen remarkably still alive.

- In South Africa, at Newcastle in April 1909, a Mr. Nesbit found hundreds of fish of the species *Barbus gurneyi* on wet ground with "some alive and unhurt, some dead and some smashed almost to a pulp."

- In Malaysia, an English engineer wrote to Gudger of a very hot day when he and his wife were caught in a terrific thunderstorm. According to his letter, the couple soon were walking in water well over their ankles, and the nearby fields of hard-baked dirt quickly flooded to a depth of several inches. Then they discovered to their astonishment a plethora of small fish about an inch and a half long were swimming in the water. The engineer stated that the fish were not mudfish and noted that any fish that might have been dormant in the ground (which are common in Malaysia in the dry season) did not have time to escape because no mud had formed.

In direct opposition to Gudger, science skeptic Bergen Evans believed that it was very unlikely that fish could fall from the sky. The two researchers entered into a rather heated (at least for scientists) exchange via letters in the journal *Science*. Following Gudger's presentation of a number of anecdotal stories of fish falls, Evans replied with the argument that no trained observer has yet witnessed any showers of fish actually coming down out of the sky. The debate abruptly changed in 1949 when wildlife biologist A. D. Bajkov recounted in *Science* the story of the Marksville, Louisiana, fish fall given in the first chapter of this book. Following Bajkov's article, scientific opinion of fish shifted into an acceptance that such a phenomenon *could* occur. The problem was to determine *how* it could occur.

Theories for explaining fish falls have abounded for centuries. Pliny the Elder, for example, believed that frog and fish showers could be explained in that frog and fish seed in the soil is miraculously brought to life by rain. By 1550, Jerome Cardan, famous Italian physician, mathematician, and astrologer, proposed that a whirlwind or waterspout could lift up fish and deposit them some distance away. German scientist Baron von Humbolt observed in the 1690s that, when underground vents in the volcanoes of South America were opened via earthquakes, they could occasionally emit water, mud . . . and fish. Von Humbolt observed, "This [is] the singular phenomenon that furnishes the fish which the inhabitants of the highlands of Quito call 'Preñadilla.' " As noted earlier, Charles Fort offered in the past century the bizarre explanation of a "Super-Sargasso" space sea filled with odd creatures and materials that, as he put it, sporadically has its bottom dropped out.

Observational evidence of a more logical explanation, that of a waterspout lifting fish out of water and depositing them elsewhere, date as early as 1889. In that year, a Dutch scientist's brother witnessed a waterspout form during a heavy storm over the River Meuse and hang down from a heavy bank of clouds. The brother recounted that the spout then began to retract itself back into the cloud, whereupon a great quantity of water fell from the storm, bringing with it a large number of fish.

More recently, a waterspout near St. Petersburg, Florida, made a terrific roar in 1952 as it passed over the shallow water of Big Bayou, according to G. H. T. Kimble in his 1955 book *Our American Weather*. He wrote that witnesses observed a huge wave five feet high rushing ahead of the waterspout. They then watched the waterspout strike land and literally cause the ground to explode. Trees, sand, and other debris shot skyward into the waterspout's funnel. But the witnesses also mentioned that one seven-inch long fish fell from the sky an astounding ten miles from where the spout hit land.

Gudger—an advocate of the waterspout theory—presented the compelling story of Mr. E. A. McIlhenny, owner of a seafood cannery on Avery Island, Louisiana. As Gudger recounted in the journals *Science* and *Natural History,* McIlhenny was aboard one of his oyster-dredge boats in the Vermillion Bay in 1921 when he and his crew saw a big thunderstorm developing over the bay. As they watched, one thunderstorm cell about three miles from them developed a funnel cloud and formed a very crooked waterspout. Apparently the waterspout didn't touch down for a long period as McIlhenny said that the cloud reabsorbed the waterspout and moved rapidly toward their boat. When the thunderstorm was only about a quarter of a mile from them, it abruptly released a massive downpour of rain.

McIlhenny recalled that, within minutes of the start of that massive cloudburst, his oyster boat was so swamped with water that the entire crew immediately started bailing to keep the boat afloat. The water, he said, was "as salty as if it had been dipped up from the sea in buckets." But with regard to the falling fish debate, the sailor's next observation was critical. Along with the salty rain from the waterspout, McIlhenny claimed that between thirty and fifty native fish, each with a length of between two and three inches, fell on the boat. According to the oyster boat captain, that type of fish tended to swim in large shoals at the surface of the water. McIlhenny concluded, "Those which fell in our boat were lively and had evidently been drawn up by the waterspout and let down in the cloud bursts."

Most scientists have accepted the possibility of waterspouts or strong winds picking up fish and dropping over land. However, there still remain some difficulties in assigning tornadoes or whirlwinds as the sole cause of these falls. One of the most popular criticisms (initially brought forth by the great scientific skeptic Charles Fort) is the apparent high selectivity of these falls of fish. Reports of fish falls tend to mention only the given type of fish itself and do not mention any other aspects of their environment (for example, weeds, other types of fish, etc.) falling with the fish. Even today, the odd selectivity of fish falls remains a difficult aspect to explain scientifically.

(5) Falls of Frogs and Toads

There are almost as many reports of frog falls as there are of fish falls. Remarkably, these events don't even have to take place near a swamp or ocean. The respected science journal *Scientific American* reported in 1873 that a Kansas City thunderstorm produced a shower of frogs as extensive as to have "darkened the air and covered the ground for a long distance." Even the London *Sunday Times* in 1977 reported that local authorities believed freak whirlwinds caused a rain of frogs in the Moroccan Sahara.

The witnesses of such falls include respected members of the community. A well-known British newspaper columnist for the London *Sunday Express* observed a frog fall in 1969 in Buckinghamshire, Great Britain, as she was traveling to a dinner party. She recalled that hundreds and thousands of little frogs cascaded down from the sky and fell into her car's doors and windows. The bizarre spectacle caused her to be late for her party but she found a couple of frogs still residing in her baggy pants to prove her story's authenticity.

Fundamentally, the cause for such events—as with fish falls—is regarded by most scientists to be whirlwinds, tornadoes, and other types of strong winds. Another potential confirmation of that theory is the account given by the Associated Press following the passage of Hurricane Isabel in September 2003. A reporter

interviewed a man in Berlin, Connecticut, who surprisingly discovered hundreds of tiny gelatinous eggs falling onto his back deck
during the passage of Isabel. When he took some of the eggs to a
nearby state university, one of the scientists there identified them
as frog eggs. Interestingly, the biologist speculated that the eggs
likely originated from warmer locations such as North Carolina
and so reasoned that they were picked up by Hurricane Isabel. He
said that it was unlikely the frog eggs had originated locally because
Connecticut frogs don't lay eggs so late in the year.

(6) Falls of Seeds, Nuts, and Manna

Weather archivist Charles Tomlinson discovered a "wondrous"
account in the Minutes of the British Royal Society for 1661: "On
Saturday last [May 20, 1661], it was rumored in this town [War-
wick], that it rained wheat at Tuchbrooke, a village about two miles
[away]." Many of the residents of Warwick immediately headed
toward Tuchbrooke to see the oddity and purportedly observed
great quantities of wheat "on the way, in the fields, and on the
leads of the church, castle, and priory, and upon the hearths of
the chimneys in the chambers." Many of the locals believed that
the material was indeed wheat that had been brought to the area
"by starlings; who, of all the birds that we know, do assemble in the
greatest numbers; and do, at this time of the year, feed upon these
berries; and digesting the outward pulp, they render these seeds
by casting, as hawks do feathers and bones."

But can it really rain seeds or nuts? An English publication
called the *Golden Penny* for 1897 cast a vote in favor of seed rains
when it reported, "Some days ago the province of Macerata in
Italy was the scene of an extraordinary phenomenon." The
report stated that just before sunset, a huge number of "blood-
colored" clouds invaded the skies above the province. Shortly
thereafter, a thunderstorm developed, "and immediately the air

became filled with myriads of small seeds." The news account stated that "seeds fell over town and country, covering the ground to a depth of about half an inch."

A good test for the validity of such odd events is the occurrence of any modern reports. A number of fortean sources, as well as Lyall Watson's scientific book *Heaven's Breath*, recount that, in February 1979, a strange occurrence struck the residence of Mr. and Mrs. Roland Moody in Southampton, Great Britain. As Mr. Moody recalled, he heard a "whooshing sound" on the windows but didn't pay much attention to it. When the sound repeated a bit later, he glanced up at the window and found the window covered with a huge mass of mustard and cress seeds. Even more bizarrely, the seed rain continued to fall five or six more times that day—and so much of it fell that he and his wife both could smell the crushed mustard and the cress seeds on their shoes when they went outside.

Some people have suggested that falls of seeds, nuts, and lichens may explain the wondrous "manna from heaven" events described in the Bible. In Chapter Sixteen of the Biblical book of Exodus, the starving Israelites fleeing from Egypt were miraculously saved: "And it came to pass, that even the quails came up, and covered the camp: and in the morning the dew lay round about the host. And when the dew that lay was gone up, behold, upon the face of the wilderness there lay a small round thing, as small as the hoar frost on the ground. And when the children of Israel saw it, they said one to another, it is manna: for they knew not what it was. And Moses said unto them, this is the bread which the Lord hath given you to eat."

Several accounts exist of more modern "manna falls" in the Middle East over the last couple of centuries. In 1920, *Scientific American* reported that the British Consul in Jerusalem claimed that "manna is found now in the regions of upper Mesopotamia,

Kurdistan, and along the Persian frontier" and fell there "in the form of dew during September, October, and November." The consul affirmed that the manna was actually collected and stored by locals to be used as a food in the winter or shipped to Baghdad for sale. Reportedly, the manna was described as sweet tasting and often used as substitute for sugar or honey. In a similar vein, the European science journal *Nature* stated in 1891 that after a Middle Eastern fall of "small yellowish spherules that were white on the inside," the local villagers made the seedlike material into a bread that was deemed of "good flavor and easily digestible." The *Nature* news item stated that botanists, who analyzed samples, determined the substance to be lichen and that the fall was the result of having "been caught up by a waterspout and carried along by the wind."

(7) Snakes, Snails, and Shells

As fish and frogs are normally associated with water, perhaps accounts of their falling with rain (after being whipped into the air by wind) aren't totally unbelievable. But, occasionally, larger water-related creatures have been reported to fall from the skies. Of those, snakes are one of the more common species. William Ruggles of South Granville, New York, in a letter dated August 6, 1860, wrote to *Scientific American* that during a late afternoon rainstorm while standing on a flat rock, he "heard a peculiar noise" near his feet and, when he looked down, "I saw a snake lying as if stunned by a fall from an immense height." The foot-long, gray-colored reptile appeared stunned but alive, according to Mr. Ruggles—at least until the man applied "a blow to the head" of the snake. He wrote that he had previously heard of similar falls of animals, "but now, judging from ocular demonstration, I verily believe that his 'snakeship' had never before seen South Granville, or, indeed, any other part of terra firma."

Some cases of snake falls may be explained by the fact that

An engraving of a snake fall during a Renaissance storm that appeared in *Der Wunder-reiche Uberzug* [sic] *unserer Nider-Welt. . . .* by Erasmus Francisci, 1680. (Photo Courtesy of National Oceanic and Atmospheric Administration/Department of Commerce Photo Library Historic NWS Collection; Archival Photography by Steve Nicklas, NOS, NGS.)

nobody actually saw the snakes plummet from the skies, giving rise to the more likely hypothesis that they came up from the ground. From an 1877 issue of the science journal *Monthly Weather Review*: "Concerning the reported shower of snakes at Memphis [Tennessee] on the fifteenth [of January 1877], the following is taken from the observer's report: 'Morning opened with light rain; 10:20 A.M. began to pour down in torrents, lasting fifteen minutes, wind SW.; immediately after the reptiles were discovered crawling on the sidewalks, in the road, gutters, and yards of Vance street, between Landerdale and Goslee streets, two blocks; careful inquiry was made to ascertain if anyone laid seen them descend, but without success; neither were they to be found in the cisterns, on roofs, or any elevations above the ground . . . I heard of none being found elsewhere; when first seen they were a very dark brown almost black; were very thick in some places, being tangled together like a mass of thread or yard.' " This suggests that the snakes likely came out of the ground after the rain and did not actually fall with the rain.

Shells and snails have also fallen from the skies. In 1869, a scientist named John Ford exhibited very small snails to the Philadelphia Academy of Natural Sciences that he stated fell in a rainstorm at Chester, Pennsylvania. According to Ford, a witness of the storm—the editor of the Delaware County *Republican*—had observed the very odd fall of snails from the very state, and, to use the editor's own words, "it seemed like a storm within a storm."

Science writer Edward Teale reported in a 1935 issue of *Popular Science Monthly* on a 1930 seashell shower that occurred over Danville, Virginia. Seashells, he claimed, fell from the sky and rattled on the roofs of houses during a severe thunderstorm. Given that Danville is over two hundred miles from the coast, the winds that kept the fragments aloft must have been very great indeed. More recently in 1984, according to Derek Elsom in the journal *New Scientist,* a strong rainstorm included a fall of hundreds of tiny winkle shells and starfish on a gas station in England. But the closest that such creatures—and indeed many of them apparently were still alive in their shells—could have originated from was the North Sea some thirty miles away.

(8) Cloudless Rains

Although to many it might appear as impossible, several accounts exist of cloudless rains—rains that occurred without need of clouds. Indeed, the phenomenon of cloudless rains even has its own name, *serein*. The most famous of this type of event is the incredible Charleston, South Carolina, cloudless rain of 1886. Starting on early October of that year, people began to notice that a particular area of Charleston—specifically the area between two trees near Ninth and D streets—was experiencing a regular but strange rainfall every afternoon after 3:00 P.M. After a couple of weeks of this, a Signal Service (a predecessor of the modern Weather Service) observer was dispatched to the location. He stated in his report published in *Monthly Weather Review*, "I visited the place and saw precipitation in the form of raindrops at 4:47 and 4:55 P.M. while the sun was shining brightly. On the 22d I again visited the place and from 4:05 and 4:25 P.M. a light shower of rain fell from a cloudless sky . . . Sometimes the precipitation falls over an area of half an acre but always appears to center at these two trees and, when lightest, occurs there only."

Like frog and fish falls, cloudless showers are not limited to coastal areas. A. W. Greely, in his 1888 book *American Weather*, recounted the story of a Midwestern cloudless rain. On June 30, 1877, residents of the small town of Vevay, Indiana, (located between Cincinnati and Louisville) witnessed a heavy cloudless shower, lasting five minutes. The raindrops were reportedly of a huge size such that, when they were caught on a sheet of blotting paper, the individual drops made circles two and a half inches in diameter.

Can such events be explained? A couple of possibilities exist. Often, cloudless rain isn't truly "cloudless." Strong winds can sometimes carry rain many miles from where the storm actually originated so that, to observers, it might appear that the rain magically appeared from clear skies above them. Also, some trees will secrete a watery sap under warm conditions that might be mistaken for rain.

(9) Cloudbursts

E. L. Hawke chronicled in a 1952 *Nature* article a description of an odd storm that hit the town of Oxford. The story was told originally in a 1682 pamphlet by Richard Harrison. Harrison said that a "sudden and violent tempest" over Oxford produced raindrops that were "thick, strong, and ponderous." Eventually, these drops "followed one another so closely that they seemed one continued spout or stream." Similarly, William Ferrel, in his 1904 book *A Popular Treatise on the Winds,* wrote that a local Montana weather observer in the 1890s learned of a cloudburst that destroyed eight hundred head of sheep. According to the observer's report, the storm "exploded at the head of Dry Run Creek and came pouring down in a solid wall thirty-two feet high, carrying off nearly the entire herd, and almost drowning a herder. The carcasses of the animals are strewn along the river for a distance of sixteen miles below the scene of the disaster."

Scientific American in 1849 supplied the common nineteenth-century explanation for such immense rainfalls in its description of an event in Alpine, Georgia. The journal wrote that "a Water Spout, of immense size," collapsed over the area and created "an impression in the earth thirty feet deep and forty or fifty feet wide." The report continued that the Water Spout wiped out a multitude of giant trees and incredibly even wrenched several multiton rocks from the hillside. In a similar fashion, Robert Bentley, in a 1907 summary of war weather events in the *Quarterly Journal of the Royal Meteorological Society,* said that the Emperor Charles V in 1541 suffered a major defeat when "an immense waterspout" burst over his military camp and caused a huge loss of life.

Today, we now know that cloudbursts commonly are not associated with waterspouts but instead are associated with severe convective thunderstorms—the kind of storms that is produced through great surface heating—and specifically those thunderstorms that tend to remain stationary over a given spot for a long period. A few years ago, I was retained as a forensic weather expert to evaluate a terrible cloudburst event in Arizona. The northern part of that state consists of many beautiful canyons, including the massive Grand Canyon. Smaller canyons, called slot canyons, feed into the Grand Canyon and are formed through the scouring action of intense flash flooding.

One slot canyon in particular, Antelope Canyon near Page,

Arizona, was the site of a cloudburst disaster. On a late summer afternoon in 1997, a group of European tourists climbed down a series of ladders to the deep and narrow sections of the slot canyon. At nearly the same time in the upstream region, which feeds water into Antelope Canyon, an isolated thunderstorm only a few miles wide suddenly produced one and half inches of rain in less than ninety minutes—a massive amount of water for the arid Southwest. That water was funneled into the very narrow Antelope Canyon until it became a surging ten-foot wall of water and debris that tore through the little canyon. The flash-flood water swept through with a force so strong that it ripped the clothes off the victims and hurled them miles downstream near the canyon's confluence with Lake Powell. One person, the tour guide, managed to escape death by grabbing an overhanging branch but, unfortunately, none of the European tourists survived. A colleague of mine, a noted expert in western river systems, termed the event a "geologic"-scale occurrence—meaning the canyon itself was partially reshaped by the rushing waters of this storm.

No waterspout caused this cloudburst. Incredibly, the actual area where the tourists themselves were located received a mere trace of rainfall. The water that cascaded through the canyon came from a single isolated severe thunderstorm several miles away. Fortunately, with new weather technology such as Doppler radar and satellite imagery and, most importantly, a growing scientific understanding and communication of such events, we can hopefully prevent such disasters from occurring in the future.

(10) Cobweb Showers

The air is critical to the dispersion of many creatures of the Earth. Certain species of spiders, for example, will spin their webs to create tiny natural balloons or parachutes that the winds can lift and carry far from their place of origin. A number of older weather and insect historians (including F. Cowan, C.

Tomlinson, and C. F. Talman, as well as reports in the journal *Nature*) have recounted historian Gilbert White's description of a web shower in the eighteenth century: "About nine an appearance very unusual began to demand our attention, a shower of cobwebs began falling from very elevated regions, and continuing, without any interruption, till the close of the day." White described the cobwebs as consisting not only of "single filmy threads; floating in the air in all directions, but perfect flakes of rags; some near an inch broad, and five or six long." According to the historian, even later in the day when the fox-hounds attempted to hunt, the dogs, "blinded and hoodwinked, were obliged to lie down and scrape the cobwebs from their faces with their fore-feet."

The noted naturalist Charles Darwin also observed a web rain onboard the HMS *Beagle* in 1832. He recorded in his journal for October 31, 1832, that during the evening, a strong wind blowing from the coast all the ropes with a "gossamer" web. Indeed, Darwin managed to capture a few of the spiders amidst their webs and speculated that the tiny aeronauts must have traveled at least sixty miles from the coast to the *Beagle*.

In a similar fashion, *Scientific American* in 1881 reported that residents of coastal Wisconsin experienced one of history's most massive spiderweb showers. Witnesses observed cobwebs measuring over sixty feet long floating over Lake Michigan and descending from a great height. In some places the spiderwebs were so thick "as to annoy the eye." More recently, in 2002, the Associated Press reported that residents of Santa Cruz, California, apparently were concerned with a similar fall of massive cobwebs from a cloudless sky. Fortunately, local police were able to reassure citizens based on information from a local biology professor who stated that fibrous strands falling from the sky were simply wispy floating spiderwebs.

(11) Military Meteorology: Deborah and Napoleon

One of my favorite stories involving rain concerns a biblical story
that I first heard described in weather terms from a fellow professor, University of Delaware geographer Russ Mather. The
story involves the meteorological prowess of the Israelites around
1200 BC when the prophetess Deborah was the de facto ruler of
the fragmented Israeli people. As the biblical story opens, she
watched with growing concern an alarming buildup of a large and
hostile Canaanite army under the command of an experienced
general named Sisera. Such an army, she reasoned, could easily
split and destroy the loose confederation of Israelite tribes
existing in Palestine at the time by driving a wedge eastward across
the great Plain of Esdraelon (near Haifa).

After conversing with God, Deborah declared that the Israeli
confederation needed to assemble a single unified militia to
oppose Sisera and his army. But she also understood that, even
with a united army, the tactical situation was potentially catastrophic for her fragmented people. In particular she was concerned with the formidable strength of Sisera's nine hundred iron
chariots—an awesome force that rendered Sisera's army nearly
invincible. Nevertheless, Deborah assembled her troops under her
chosen military leader, Barak, in the vicinity of Mount Tabor
located at the headwaters of the Kishon River. Then, as we learn
from the biblical Song of Deborah, God tipped the scales in favor
of Israel by forming a severe rainstorm near the river—specifically
the field of Edom where Sisera's chariots had to pass—just before
the battle was joined. In Judges 5:4: "Lord, when thou went out of
Seir, when thou marched out of the field of Edom, the earth trembled, and the heavens dropped, the clouds also dropped water."

It is likely that Deborah and Barak comprehended exactly what
this heavy rain would do to the soil conditions in the Kishon
River Valley. Not only did the river flood, carrying away many
of Sisera's troops, but the muddy conditions over the fields

rendered the iron chariots virtually useless and then a flash flood ensued to wash them away. In Judges 5:21: "The river of Kishon swept them away, that ancient river, the river Kishon." Indeed, the general himself was forced to abandon his chariot in the mud and flee on foot. Mather wryly noted that Deborah's obvious mastery of a subject that could now be called "military climatology"—combining the knowledge of geography, including the topography and drainage of the Kishon Valley, and climatology, led to a stunning victory that eventually helped to consolidate the Israelite tribes into a single nation.

Rain was also a deciding—but hostile—factor in Napoleon's invasion of Russia. In a 1907 fascinating article on war weather in the *Quarterly Journal of the Royal Meteorological Society,* Richard Bentley revealed the tragic effects of a tremendous rainstorm on the emperor's army. Following a hot summer, the French troops were marching through Eastern Europe when they encountered a devastating and long-lasting rainstorm. Reportedly, hundreds of horses perished in the storm and its muddy after-effects. One writer claimed that there were no less than ten thousand dead and dying horses lying by the roadsides of Vilna alone and, within a week period, over twenty-five thousand troops had to be treated for various ailments linked to the incessant wet conditions. As the Napoleon's army marched eastward, one of his generals vividly described how any westerly wind bore with it a "gruesome pestilential smell" from the scores of decaying bodies of men and horses left behind.

(13) Hatfield, the Moisture Accelerator

As will be detailed in a later chapter concerning snow oddities, modern technical rainmaking originated with Vincent Schaefer's experiments for the General Electric Laboratories in 1949. Prior to that, there were a number of less scientific "precipitators" and "moisture accelerators," particularly in the western United

States, who made their livings by "creating" rain through very secret methods. Even the person best known for his breakfast cereal company, C. W. Post (or "Postum Post," as some called him) tried to "shake" rain from the sky in Battlecreek, Michigan, by exploding bombs. Most of these "precipitators" were flim-flam men . . . but others had far greater success.

Undoubtedly, the supreme rainmaker of the early twentieth century was Charles Mallory Hatfield of San Diego, California. According to the detailed expose given by Clark Spence in his 1980 book *The Rainmakers*, Hatfield started his adult life as a sewing machine salesman but quit that job in 1902 to begin his illustrious career as a rainmaker. As his initial job, he accepted a commission of fifty dollars from a farmer to "precipitate moisture" near Los Angeles in 1903. Reports are that Hatfield first built a wooden platform that stood about twenty feet off the ground for his rain-making experiments. On that platform he then placed large

The monument (in the shape of San Diego County) erected at Lake Morena near San Diego in honor of Charles Hatfield the Rainmaker. (Photo by author.)

holding tanks in which he mixed a secret set of chemicals that he claimed would induce rain. Apparently Hatfield's work in that initial job succeeded beyond anyone's expectations—the farmer reportedly even paid Hatfield an extra fifty dollars in appreciation for the rain that Hatfield "produced."

After that opening success, the Great Precipitator, as Hatfield came to be called, conducted more than five hundred rainmaking contracts in and around Los Angeles over a period of twenty-five years, with fees steadily increasing. Within a couple of years of his start, Hatfield took on a four-thousand-dollar commission to fill the Lake Hemet reservoir—promising four inches and "delivering" more than seven. His chemical releases were followed by eleven inches of rain that raised the water level in the reservoir by twenty-two feet and, according to the testimony of the operators, gave them the biggest bargain they ever had. Popularity for the rainmaker began to swell. Merchants even began marketing "Genuine 'Hatfield' Umbrellas" when they heard the Precipitator was coming to their area.

Hatfield's greatest—and most infamous—rainmaking adventure came in 1916 when he and his brother Paul were commissioned by the San Diego City Council to end a drought in Southern California and fill the Morena and Otay reservoirs. San Diego's contract with the rainmaker stated that Hatfield would receive a fee of ten thousand dollars if he succeeded in producing rain to fill the Morena reservoir within one year but the Great Precipitator would receive nothing if he failed. Nevertheless, the Hatfields set up their twenty-foot platform near the reservoir and began a series of rainmaking procedures. On January 1, 1916, Hatfield launched his first rocket of hydrogen and zinc smoke. Nine days later rain began to fall in San Diego. And it kept raining. By January 19, the Morena Reservoir was filled to its capacity for the first time since its construction.

And it continued raining. Water began to spill over the top of the dam; highway bridges and railroad tracks were washed out; telephone and telegraph lines were disrupted.

And it kept raining. The San Diego River overflowed its banks. Thousands of people had to be evacuated from flooded areas of San Diego.

And still the rain fell. On January 26, a record daily rainfall of 2.41 inches occurred over the San Diego area. Both the Morena and Otay dams ruptured and at least twelve people, maybe as many as fifty, were killed. Property damage in the millions of dollars was recorded. By this time, the surging floodwaters had turned the tide of public opinion strongly against the great rainmaker. A front-page cartoon in the *San Diego Union* depicted a mad farmer chasing Hatfield into the bay. Rumors had it that lynch mobs combed the city for Hatfield in every hotel and boarding house.

The San Diego City Council's reaction was even more disappointing to Hatfield. They flatly refused to pay the ten-thousand-dollar fee they had agreed upon, even though he had quite obviously fulfilled his part of the contract. After all, the Morena reservoir had been filled. But, according to the councilmen, they had hired Hayfield to save San Diego not to submerge it. So they offered Hatfield the practical choice of assuming legal and financial responsibility for the inevitable lawsuits from the flooding, or leaving town with no pay and declaring that the rain was "an act of God." Hatfield wisely chose the latter option.

The rainmaker died in 1958 at the ripe old age of eighty-two, at his home in Pearblossom, California. But his memory lives on. A marker, ironically erected with the cooperation of San Diego County at the edge of Lake Morena, continues to commemorate Charles Hatfield's great—if still infamous—rainmaking escapade for the southern California city.

(13) Rain Safety

Excessive rain can produce flooding. There are two basic types of flooding. The first is river flooding, or the inundation of areas next to a stream or river. The second type is flash flooding, or flooding created within six hours of an extreme rainstorm, or from a dam failure, or an ice jam. In contrast to "flooding," flash flooding is not limited to river areas but to any area subject to inundation by heavy rains.

Flash flooding is particularly dangerous because of the speed with which it can occur can be life threatening. Consequently, the National Weather Service has developed an extensive flash flooding watch and warning system. Specifically, a flash flood watch indicates that the day's weather conditions are favorable for the occurrence of flash floods. Consequently, people in a watch area should pay close attention to local media for news and information and make preparations to evacuate to high ground if necessary.

A flash flood warning indicates that flooding is imminent or is occurring. If a warning is issued, you should take immediate steps to preserve your life. The most basic advice is to head to higher ground and avoid areas prone to flooding. In particular, do not attempt to cross (either by driving, swimming, or walking) any flooded areas. Most flood fatalities are caused by people attempting to drive through water, or people playing in high water. A critical point that many people don't realize involves the buoyancy that moving water has on a vehicle trying to drive through a flooded area. In essence, running water can cause the vehicle to act as a boat. If a car is going through water that is moving only ten miles per hour, every foot of water depth displaces fifteen hundred pounds of the car's weight. That means that only two feet of water moving at ten miles an hour can float virtually any car.

Recently, in the Phoenix, Arizona, area, even a Hummer—the commercial version of the "all-terrain" military Humvee—attempted unsuccessfully to cross a flooded road following heavy rains in the area. Consequently, the driver and his young children passengers needed to be saved by a professional fire-and-water-rescue team. This and other such incidents have led Arizona state legislators to enact what has been termed the "Stupid Motorist Law," which states that, if a motorist drives around marked barricades to cross a flooded road—and then has to be rescued from that situation—the motorist can be charged with the entire costs of the rescue. More important than the legal and financial liability, such stupidity endangers not only the life of the motorist and passengers but the rescuers as well.

Chapter 6
HURRICANES

A HURRICANE IS ONE OF THE MOST INTENSE STORMS THAT OUR planet can produce. The recipe for cooking up a hurricane requires relatively specific ingredients. First, hurricanes can only form in warm tropical waters. In the Atlantic, they often start as small disorganized clusters of thunderstorms moving off the western coast of Africa—sometimes these clusters are even the remains of Saharan dust storms. But even though hurricane birth requires warm waters, these storms can't form right at the equator because they also need the spin imparted by the Earth's rotation—what scientists term the Coriolis Effect—something not experienced directly at the equator. Hurricane formation also necessitates relatively calm winds throughout the atmosphere. Too much wind shear—the change in wind speed and direction with height—can quickly tear a hurricane apart. Consequently, while in a given year many tropical disturbances may form in the Atlantic or Gulf of Mexico, only an average of seven to ten such disturbances will reach the critical hurricane wind strength of seventy-four miles per hour or greater.

A close-up of a one inch by four inch board driven through the trunk of a royal palm 30 feet above ground level by the winds of Hurricane Andrew in 1992. (Photo Courtesy of National Oceanic and Atmospheric Administration/Department of Commerce Photo Library Historic NWS Collection.)

All hurricanes tend to have a circular shape with a diameter normally less than four hundred miles and most possess a relatively clear area in their center called the eye. The severe danger zone of a hurricane is the immense donut-shaped ring of thunderstorms surrounding the eye, termed the eyewall. This region is the location of the hurricane's strongest winds—and the normal place for the storm's greatest damage. In the 1960s, two researchers, Saffir and Simpson, devised a method for ranking the strength of hurricanes based on the damage that the hurricane creates. Their hurricane hierarchy ranges from a Category One hurricane with winds in the eyewall of 74 miles per hour to 94 miles per hour, to a Category Five hurricane with eyewall winds in excess of 154 miles per hour.

Hurricanes are known by a variety of different names around the world depending on what specific region of the world in which they occur. While "hurricane" is the name given to such storms in the Atlantic and western Pacific oceans, they are called *typhoons* off the west coast of Asia and around Japan. In the Bay of Bengal and along the coast of India, such storms are often referred to as *cyclones*. Around the Philippines, they are sometimes called Baguios. The most basic name for these massive spinning sea storms is *tropical cyclone*. In this chapter, I examine some of the odder stories involving tropical cyclones. These include the strange history of how hurricanes came to be named, some of the remarkable stories of both human survival and tragedy during these storms, and even the ghoulish story of hurricanes and floating coffins. To end on a more upbeat note, I discuss some of the recommended safety considerations for hurricanes in the last section.

(1) Gaining New Lands

Although hurricanes and tropical storms are generally regarded as completely destructive with little or nothing to redeem them, tropical cyclones have also been the background cause for some of the most important discoveries in history. In 1609, a hurricane drove a flotilla of nine English ships off course as they traveled across the Atlantic Ocean to Jamestown, Virginia. One of the ships, the *Sea Venture,* eventually ran aground on Bermuda—until then an undiscovered island. The fifty-four survivors of the wreck, including the flotilla's commander, Sir George Somers, banded together to establish the island's first permanent settlement. Although different modern sources debate the actual first publication, it is irrefutable that within a few short years after the hurricane, a number of stories about the *Sea Venture*'s riveting adventures abounded in the English press.

One of them, based on a long letter by William Strachy to the

wife of the governor of Virginia Colony, is related by Stanley
Rogers in his 1932 book *Twelve on the Beaufort Scale* and subsequently by Majory Stoneman Douglas in her 1958 book *Hurricane,*
and makes fascinating reading. As the fleet commenced to suffer
the "dreadful Storm," Strachy vividly described the classic elements of a hurricane: a ferocious wind that pounded the ships
with terrible and unceasing wails, a thick darkness so ominous
that, to the eyes of the sailors, the very "hell of darkness" had
come upon them, and mammoth sea waves of gargantuan height.
Strachy's ship, the *Sea Venture,* quickly became separated from the
fleet as the gargantuan storm continued to hold the ship in its
watery grasp. For an entire day, howling winds tossed the small
ship about the raging seas and thundering waves smashed into the
deck timbers. The ship's crew and the passengers were left
shaken, bewildered, and began to believe that not even in their
wildest imaginations could the situation possibly get any worse
. . . yet it did.

By the second day, colossal waves heaved upward by the hurricane periodically engulfed the *Sea Venture*—covering the vessel
from stem to stern like a huge liquid blanket. Unsurprisingly, the
ship began to leak. Everyone—even gentlemen who, Starchy wryly
noted, throughout their lives "had never done hours of work
before"—struggled to keep the ship afloat by manning hand
pumps. Yet, despite their best efforts, water filled the ship to at
least two decks deep as the storm continued to rage. Waters
flooded into their kitchen galley and storeroom, making it
impossible to get to the provisions or water. Strachy noted with
some irony that the struggling crew and passengers needed continually to pump manually gallon after gallon of water out of the
floundering vessel merely to stay afloat yet they did not even have
a single drop of drinkable water to relieve their growing thirst.

Then, just before noon of the third day in the storm, Captain
George Summers, who heroically had held the wheel throughout

the tempest, cried out, "Land!" Shortly thereafter, the *Sea Venture* ran aground between two rocks where it became firmly wedged. With prose that would be a credit to any modern adventure novel, Strachy wrote that they had landed on "the dangerous and dreaded Island, or Islands of Bermuda." What followed were another ten months of incredible exploits (even including three mutinies) before the group was eventually rescued.

The story so captured the public imagination that it is very likely William Shakespeare incorporated some of the more vivid hurricane descriptions for his play entitled *The Tempest*. Storm historian Marjory Stoneman Douglas stated, "Surely *The Tempest* is the loveliest thing ever to come out of a hurricane."

Other discoveries and unexpected landfalls have also been linked to hurricanes. Even the Pilgrims' *Mayflower* may have encountered the fringes of a hurricane. As the *Mayflower* was enroute to the New World and the Virginia colony, it encountered a violent storm and was knocked far off course. While some historians believe that the storm alone was to blame for the *Mayflower*'s course deviation, others suggest that the *Mayflower*'s captain, for reasons of his own, deliberately misplaced the Pilgrims and simply used the storm as an excuse.

(2) Losing Land: The Other Isaac's Storm

Many people have heard and read of the extensive destruction of Galveston Island in the Great Hurricane of 1900, an event regarded as the worst natural disaster ever to hit the United States. A ghastly six thousand people—a seventh of the entire population of Galveston at the time—died as a result of that terrible hurricane. Erik Larson, in his compelling book *Isaac's Storm*, vividly documented the ineffective efforts of weather expert Isaac Cline and the U.S. Weather Bureau to predict hurricanes and warn the public prior to that storm.

Far fewer people have heard the bizarre story of another Isaac's storm. In that instance, a weatherman's incredible dedication to his duty during a hurricane's passage may have been the fundamental reason for the complete destruction and eventual abandonment of an entire town! Although understandably some accounts vary as to the specific circumstances of the disaster, the basic story begins in 1886 when the U.S. Weather Service was part of the Army Signal Corps. At that time, the Signal Corps maintained a weather station in the small Texas coastal town of Indianola. On the evening of Thursday, August 19, Captain Isaac A. Reed, a husband and father of two children, was in charge of that weather office as a massive hurricane struck Indianola.

Throughout the long night as the hurricane slammed into the coastal town, Reed labored to carry on his weather observations. By 3:00 A.M. in the morning, he finally decided to slog across the flooded street to the government telegraph office to dispatch his latest wind and rain readings. In the telegraph office, an assistant customs agent by the name of T. D. Woodward, and the telegraph operator had taken refuge in an interior room from the raging hurricane and were actually trying to sleep through the storm's fury. Reed roused them and asked the telegraph operator to rapidly transmit his vital hurricane observations to Washington.

Unfortunately, by that time, the pounding of the storm had rendered the telegraph inoperative. The three spent a frustrating hour trying to repair the delicate instrument but when the winds began to tear at the roof and walls, they feared the telegraph building would soon collapse, and so they struggled back across the street to the weather office. Through a monumental effort against the storm's winds and waves, they eventually reached the sturdier government building.

Once again back at his post, Captain Reed returned to his weather observations. Unfortunately, he discovered to his dismay that the hurricane had ripped out the wire attached to his wind sensor with a final recorded wind speed of about seventy-two miles an hour at about 3:30 A.M. As the morning progressed, the wind continued to grow. Still Reed maintained his duty—taking air pressure measurements and visual observations as the hurricane continued to howl around them. The darkness, combined with the rain, made his job extraordinarily difficult—so much so that finally Reed took the fatal risk of lighting a small flickering kerosene lamp to help him read his instruments.

Shortly after 5:00 A.M., the captain completed a set of weather observations and carefully worked his way downstairs to the front porch of the building. There he discovered that the telegraph operator and Woodward, the customs agent, had been joined by a local doctor. For five minutes, the four stood in awe on the porch watching the hurricane unleash its wrath against their town. Without warning, total disaster struck.

A gust of wind tore into the Signal Office building and with a shriek of ripped lumber, the structure collapsed. Woodward and the telegraph operator struggled to free themselves from the wreckage while at the same time they searched in vain for the diligent weatherman and the doctor. Matters quickly got out of hand. The small kerosene lamp, which Reed had been using to read his weather instruments, apparently had fallen in the building's collapse and, despite the flooding and the rains, the broken wood structure caught fire. Under the unrelenting hurricane winds, the small blaze (and likely other flames as well) was whipped into a massive fire with flames spreading to a nearby building and soon a large part of the town was on fire.

When the hurricane finally passed by the next day, the incredible destruction of storm and fire could be seen throughout the ruins of Indianola. A follow-up government report in the *Monthly Weather Review* stated, "The appearance of the town after the storm was one of universal wreck. Not a house remained uninjured, and most of those that were left standing were in an unsafe condition. Many were washed away completely and scattered over the plains back of the town; others were lifted from their founda-tions and moved bodily over considerable distances. Over all this strip of low ground, as far as could be seen, were the wrecks of houses, carriages, personal property of all kinds, and a great many dead animals."

In a hearing regarding the storm and the destruction of the city, Woodward testified that Reed and the doctor "were killed, drowned, or burned; we don't know which happened first." According to the customs agent, Captain Reed "perished literally at the post of duty, the last observation being taken about five minutes before he was killed." The combination of flooding and the fire damage was so great that the entire town of Indianola was actually abandoned within the next year. It remains today one of Texas's great ghost towns.

(3) Hurricane Transport

Because hurricanes and tropical cyclones can sometimes travel thousands of miles across oceans, occasionally insects, animals, and other odd things can be trapped within them and be carried for an incredible distance. Frank Cowan's fascinating 1865 insect book mentions a sea captain who witnessed an extraordinary swarm of small butterflies with spotted wings shortly after a trop-ical cyclone in the South Pacific Ocean. According to the cap-tain, when the wind veered to the northward, "for one hour the atmosphere was so filled with butterflies as to represent a snow-storm driving past the vessel at a rapid rate." In a similar fashion, the *Fortean Times* reported that government agricultural officials in Brazil were concerned about a massive increase in the African locust population in the northeast regions of South America shortly after Hurricane Gilbert formed in 1988. They believed that the locusts had been blown across the Atlantic by the mam-moth hurricane.

The Great September Gale of 1815 literally brought hundreds of seagulls inland. New England newspapers stated that confused flocks of seagulls were seen flying above Worcester, Massachusetts, a city that is a hundred miles from the nearest coastline, for days following the storm's passage. In September 1961, such weird storm transport caused Hurricane Carla's central eye to become a no-fly zone. Researchers G. E. Dunn and B. I. Miller, in their 1960 book *Atlantic Hurricanes,* reported that hurricane hunter pilots discovered Carla's calm eye was filled with so many birds that the pilots were concerned about flying into the multitude of avian refugees. In an even stranger transport, Robert Gentry wrote in *Weatherwise* that Hurricane Hazel in 1954 dropped green coconuts, pieces of bamboo, and even a cup with the engraving "Made in Haiti" along the coast of North Carolina.

Undoubtedly, one of the strangest transports that I have discovered is the story of "The Church Moved by the Hand of God,"

The frontplate on the Providence United Methodist Church of Swan Quarter North Carolina, a church that was floated by a hurricane's floodwaters into its present position. (Photo Courtesy of the Hyde County Chamber of Commerce)

related to me by the good people of the Providence United Methodist Church of Swan Quarter, North Carolina. In 1876, although the parishioners of what was then the Methodist Episcopal Church South wanted to build a new church on a particular piece of property in the heart of the town, the land's owner, Mr. Sadler, opted not to sell the land to the church. So the congregation subsequently built a small wood frame church with brick pilings on nearby Oyster Creek Road.

In September of 1876, on the eve of the dedication of the church, a torrential hurricane struck the area with high winds and a massive storm surge. Floodwaters of five feet covered the city. By morning the winds and rain had subsided and the miracle occurred. The small church slowly pulled loose from its brick pilings and began to float down the street. It gently bumped into a general store and, when the church reached what is now called Church Street, it took another turn to the left . . . and settled on the original lot chosen for the church. Sam Sadler, the property owner—perhaps realizing that someone was trying to send him an unmistakable message—reconsidered the Church's offer and deeded the lot to the congregation. And, when the church was dedicated years later, the congregation aptly named their church "Providence," a name that lasts still today. Not surprisingly, the parishioners have chosen Deuteronomy 12:5 ". . . the place which the Lord Thy God hath chosen . . ." as their dictum.

(4) Stopping a Hurricane

Can you stop a hurricane? Throughout history, many people have tried a variety of means to undertake exactly that task. In the days of colonial exploration, the Roman Catholic Church decreed that a special prayer *Ad repellendam tempestatis,* should be recited during the hurricane season throughout the Caribbean islands. In addition, many sailors and coastal residents took solace by displaying a Cord of Saint Francis, a short length of rope with three knots with three turns apiece, in their boats or homes as a protective talisman during the hurricane season. According to tradition, if sailors untied the first knot of the Cord, winds would pick up but only moderately. Winds of "half a gale" resulted from untying the second knot. If all three knots were untied, winds of hurricane strength were produced.

Professor William S. Franklin proposed a more mechanistic way of eliminating hurricanes in a 1929 issue of *Popular Mechanics*. Building upon the concept of "hail cannons" and the Midwest rainmakers of the early twentieth century, he suggested immediate production of great steel cone cannons, each a hundred feet high and each capable of exploding a ton or more of gunpowder. The detonations would create gigantic smoke rings that would drift upward several thousand feet into the air. Such particulates, according to Franklin, would be essential in "combating and dissipating hurricanes." He estimated that only "twenty or thirty of the large explosion cones, distributed thinly over southern Florida and on the Bahama Islands would be needed" to eliminate forever the threat of hurricanes to coastal populations.

During the heyday of cloudseeding technology and advancement in the late 1960s, the U.S. military undertook an actual campaign to modify—and hopefully eliminate—coastal hurricanes. They, working together with hurricane researchers, initiated first Project Cirrus and then, a bit later, the more elaborate Project Stormfury, a program where canisters of silver iodide, a cloudseeding agent, were sprayed into a hurricane by military planes. Scientists at the time theorized that by cloudseeding the area just outside the hurricane's intense eyewall, the storm would develop a new larger eyewall outside the old one and therefore weaken the overall storm. The first attempt in 1969 had planes spraying eight canisters of the cloudseeding agent into the area around Hurricane Esther's eyewall. According to a government report, "The seeded portion of Esther's eyewall faded from a radarscope that detects water droplets, indicating either a change of liquid water to ice crystals or the replacement of large droplets by much smaller ones." Similar cloudseeding was done in Hurricanes Beulah and Debbie with mixed results.

In the meantime, a political storm on the ethics of hurricane modification was also building. In 1963, the Cuba government alleged that the massive destruction and death experienced in Cuba by Hurricane Flora was the direct result of the United States' Project Stormfury. Although not officially in response, the researchers implemented strict guidelines as to the type and location of "modifiable" hurricanes. Nevertheless, funding was progressively cut from the program. By 1983, one of the most unique and controversial weather modification attempts in history was disbanded.

In an interesting follow-up to Project Stormfury, Robert Balling, an Arizona State University colleague, and I concluded in a 1997 study published in the journal *Science* that people could indeed modify hurricanes—although they didn't realize that they were doing it! Through a detailed statistical study of hurricanes and tropical storms, we discovered that hurricanes over the past thirty years or so have acted differently depending on what day of the week it occurred. Literally, we determined that tropical cyclones along the Atlantic coast were markedly weaker on weekends than during weekdays.

Why is this important? The reason has to do with the underlying causes of various periodicities or cycles, including natural variations (like the lunar twenty-eight-day cycle) and man-made cycles, such as the seven-day workweek. The weekly cycle doesn't exist in nature—it comes about solely as an artifact of Western Civilization. Consequently, if we discover weekly cycles in such phenomena as hurricanes, it strongly suggests that people might be influencing those phenomena. In this case, we concluded that the inadvertent buildup of pollution from industry and transportation through the five-day workweek along the Atlantic seacoast actually acted in the manner that the creators of Project Stormfury had wanted—the pollution significantly weakened the storms. So even though people hadn't intended to change tropical cyclone strength, nevertheless it appears that, through our pollution, we indeed may be influencing hurricanes.

(5) Naming Hurricanes

The practice of naming hurricanes dates back to early colonial days in America. Many memorable storms were named by the year in which they occurred as for example, the devastating "Great Hurricane of 1780" that hit the West Indies or the "Great Storm of 1703" whose incredible damage of the British Isles was expertly detailed by *Robinson Crusoe* author, Daniel Defoe. As Christianity took hold in the West Indies, memorable Caribbean hurricanes were often labeled with the name of the saint on whose day they struck land. For example, the hurricane that hit Puerto Rico on July 26, 1825, was termed Hurricane Santa Ana, while another hurricane that struck on September 13, 1876, became known as Hurricane San Felipe.

Several claimants have been put forth as the originators of the modern tropical cyclone "naming" system. Australian weather meteorologist, Clement L. Wragge, is one of the best-established holders of the title. As a forecaster in 1887, Wragge began tagging personal names onto Australian weather disturbances from a wide variety of historical biblical, political, and even "alluring" names. For example, according to A. J. Shields and R. G. Gourlay, in a 1975 *Science News* article, Wragge named some weather systems using the biblical names of *Ram, Rakem, Talmon,* and

Uphaz or the ancient names of *Xerxes* and *Hannibal*. Wragge even nicknamed one storm *Eline*, a name that he thought was reminiscent of "dusty maidens with liquid eyes and bewitching manners." Most ingeniously, he gained a measure of personal revenge by christening some of the nastiest storms with politicians' names such as *Drake, Barton,* and *Deakin.* Modern hurricane researcher Chris Landsea noted that, by using such a personal naming system, Wragge could publicly describe a politician (say one who was less than generous with weather-bureau appropriations) as "causing great distress" or "wandering aimlessly about the Pacific."

A second claimant to the title of originator of storm naming is the noted author George R. Stewart. In 1941, Steward wrote the best-selling novel *Storm* in which a junior meteorologist at the San Francisco office of the U.S. Weather Bureau justifies "the sentimental vagary" of naming any long-lasting storm by telling himself that each storm is "really an individual;" that he could more easily say "Antonia" than "the low-pressure center which was yesterday in latitude one-seventy-five east, longitude forty-two north." As Stewart detailed in his novel, "Not at any price would the Junior Meteorologist have revealed to the Chief that he was bestowing names—and girls' names—upon those great moving low-pressure areas . . . At first, he had christened each new-born storm after some girl he had known—Ruth, Lucy, Katherine . . . Of late the supply of names had run short, and he had been relying chiefly upon ones ending in *-ia* which suggested actresses or heroines of books rather than girls he had ever known." Some people suggest that the popularity of Stewart's book—and, in particular, a special pocketbook edition published just for service personnel—inspired navy meteorologists to christen Pacific tropical storms with absent girlfriends or wives names throughout World War II.

Yet other claimants to the throne of first hurricane namer are the media. Canadian meteorologist and weather historian David Phillips suggested that the first Atlantic tropical storm of 1949 was nicknamed by the news media "Hurricane Harry" after President Harry Truman. Phillips also said that a subsequent (and more violent) storm was dubbed by the media "Hurricane Bess" after Truman's rather outspoken wife.

No matter whose claim is considered to be most valid, the relatively informal practice of naming tropical storms became institutionalized in 1950, when the U.S. Weather Bureau identified tropical cyclones of the North Atlantic Ocean using a phonetic alphabet (Able, Baker, Charlie, and so on.). This rather lackluster practice continued until 1953 when the organization switched to using a series of women's names to identify tropical cyclones in the Atlantic. One name for each letter of the alphabet was selected, except for the letters $q, u, x, y,$ and z (given the lack of names starting with those letters). For Atlantic Ocean hurricanes, the tropical cyclone names could be French, Spanish, or English, since these are the major languages of areas bordering the Atlantic Ocean.

As technology and communication improved, tropical cyclones near Hawaii in the Pacific were given women's names starting in 1959 and, beginning in 1960, tropical cyclones in the remainder of the Northeast Pacific basin were also nicknamed with women's names. But coinciding with the growth of the women's rights movement in the 1960s and 1970s, increasing pressure was placed on the world's primary storm-naming organization, the World Meteorological Organization (WMO). Finally in 1978, that group created annually rotating lists of tropical cyclone labels that also included men's names. "Bob" was the first Atlantic hurricane to be christened with a male name on July 10, 1979. Of course, the practice of giving different names to storms in different ocean basins has led to a few rare instances of name-changing storms. For example, in October of 1988, after Atlantic hurricane Joan savagely struck Central America, it proceeded to move into the Pacific and became Pacific tropical storm Miriam.

Beginning on January 1, 2000, tropical cyclones in the Northwest Pacific basin were labeled using a new list of names. The new designations were contributed by all the nations and territories that are members of the WMO's Typhoon Committee and are primarily of Asian origin. These newly selected names have two major differences from the rest of the world's tropical cyclone name rosters. First, the names, by and large, are not personal names. While there are a few men's and women's names, the majority of northwest Pacific tropical cyclone names are of flowers, animals, birds, trees, or even foods while some are just descriptive adjectives. Secondly, the names are not allotted in alphabetical order, but are arranged by contributing nation with the countries being alphabetized.

So, for example, the Cambodians have contributed *Nakri* (a flower), *Krovanh,* (a tree), and *Damrey* (an elephant). China has submitted names such as *Yutu* (a mythological rabbit), *Longwang* (the dragon king and God of rain in Chinese mythology), and *Dainmu* (the mother of lightning and the Goddess in charge of thunder). Micronesian typhoon names include *Sinlaku* (a legendary Kosrae Goddess) and *Ewiniar* (the Chuuk Storm God).

Finally, the lists of names are not static. For example, in many ocean basins, such as the Atlantic and Pacific, tropical cyclone names are "retired" (that is, not to be used again for a new storm) if the storm is considered to be noteworthy based on the damage and/or deaths it caused. This is to avoid confusion with any legal actions or insurance claim activities associated with the storm, and to avoid public confusion with another storm of the same name. So, for example, the world will never again see "Hurricane Andrew," a "Hurricane Gilbert," "Hurricane Camille," or a "Hurricane Katrina."

(6) The Typhoon's Armistice

Tropical cyclones have also played a role in preventing war. When a German naval fleet bombed a native village at Apia, Samoa, early in the year 1889, an American flag had been torn down and burned—along with the American property upon which it had rested. Subsequently, the U.S. Secretary of State fiercely protested the action and ordered three American warships to steam to Samoa and protect American interests. The three ships arrived in Samoa where they were met by three German warships and a British man-o-war, the *Calliope*. Warfare seemed inevitable. Without warning—before actual shooting began—a third combatant went into the fray. An immense typhoon suddenly assailed the island. Thoughts of war were cast aside as all sides joined forced to fight the common enemy.

The typhoon battered the island and the seven warships.

Several wrecked warships in Apia Harbor, Upolu, Samoa after the typhoon of March 15–16, 1889. The *USS Trenton* and the sunken *USS Vandalia* are on the left and the beached German corvette *Olga* at right. (Photo Courtesy of Naval Historical Foundation and the Department of the Navy Naval Historical Center.)

Throughout the day everyone—islanders and sailors alike—
desperately fought the typhoon in a life-and-death battle against
drowning. Yet, in the true human spirit of bravery, an American
crew, even though they struggled to stay afloat themselves, stood
and cheered in admiration at the seamanship of the *Calliope*'s crew
when the British ship passed the American vessel in the harbor.
Later, the *Calliope*'s captain wrote to the American Admiral Kimberly expressing his heartfelt appreciation for the cheers of the
Americans. Kimberly replied in a letter that has since become
famous: "My dear Captain, your kind note received. You went out
splendidly, and we all felt from our hearts for you, and our cheers
came with sincerity and admiration for the able manner in which
you handled your ship. We could not have been gladder if it had
been one of our own ships, for in a time like this I can say truly
with old Admiral Josiah Latnall that blood is thicker than water."

All six of the German and American ships sank and over 150
people died on that day. Undoubtedly, the death toll would have
been considerably higher had not the combatants and island
natives banded together to aid the victims on all sides of the con-
flict. The forced armistice produced by the typhoon eventually
led to the 1889 Treaty of Berlin that granted freedom to Samoa
for many years. Fittingly, hurricane researcher Ivan Tannehill, in
his book *Hurricane,* quoted the stirring words of Robert Louis
Stevenson with regards to this unusual hurricane armistice:
"Thus in what seemed the very article of war, and within a single
day, the sword arm of the two angry powers was broken; their formidable ships reduced to junk, the disciplined hundreds to a
horde of castaways. The hurricane of March 16 made thus a
marking epoch in world history; directly and at once it brought
about the congress and treaty of Berlin; indirectly and by a
process still continuing, it founded the modern navy of the
United States."

(7) Survival: The *Bostonian*

The "Long Island Express" Hurricane of 1938 was infamous for the mammoth destruction it caused along the New York coast but it also produced a number of incredible stories of survival. One of the more dramatic accounts is that of the New York express train, the *Bostonian,* which ran a regular route from New York to Boston. Near Stonington, Connecticut, the train crossed over a low-lying, rather long causeway that separated ocean waters on one side and a tidal estuary on the other. In the 1930s, with no satellite or modern forecasting, the express train with 275 passengers aboard was caught completely unaware on that causeway when the hurricane struck it with full strength. As the train sat unprotected on the track, the pounding waves began to crumble the foundation of the causeway. Disaster apparently loomed for the *Bostonian*'s passengers and crew.

The derailed train resulting from the 1938 hurricane near Stonington Connecticut. (Photo credit: © 1938 The Southern New England Telephone Company. All rights reserved.)

The train crew, however, quickly rose to the monumental task before them. First, they decided immediately to reduce the size of the train. The porters quickly moved all of the passengers into the first car behind the engine, a baggage car. Reportedly, one African-American porter even heroically carried two children on his shoulders through waist-deep water while still assisting a woman who desperately clung to his coattails in the surging waves. Unfortunately, one of the dining-car employees lost his life when he plunged into the storm waters to save a drowning woman.

While the porters labored with their task, others of the train crew struggled through increasingly deeper waters and massive winds to uncouple the baggage car and engine from the rest of the train. They strained against deep surging waters, hardly able to see through the sea spray and waves and often being blown off their feet by the hurricane winds. As one of the crew recalled later, other hazards threatened them as well, "A storm-driven log cracked me in the knee and threw me down, almost submerged [me], but instinct set me on my feet again." While the porters battled against the wind and waves to safely move the passengers, the train crew was succeeding against all odds in uncoupling the engine and jammed baggage car from the rest of the train. When all remaining crew and passengers were safely aboard, the engineer slowly opened the throttle and gently moved the engine forward, pulling the crowded car away from the rest of the train. Yet the worst still lay ahead for the *Bostonian*'s passengers and crew.

For a few hundred yards, the engineer struggled to keep the train on the deteriorating tracks. A faint glimmer of hope began to surface among the desperate crew and passengers as the train continued to lurch slowly along the causeway. Then, suddenly, the engineer's heart fell. On the track ahead lay an incredible sight; the hurricane had washed an entire house onto the causeway! The engineer tenderly eased the train ahead, until the engine was actually touching the house, and

then edged the train forward, pushing the building. The locomotive shuttered under the combined force of the house and
hurricane but it kept advancing—and, importantly, staying on
the tracks—until the hurricane winds abruptly caught the
house, lifted it into wave-whipped water and threw it out to sea.

But safety still wasn't at hand for the *Bostonian*. As the small train
inched its way across the storm-flooded causeway, crates, logs, and
even small boats continued to smash against the engine. Then
something very heavy rammed into the front end of the locomotive.
Through the driving rain, the engineer spied a full-sized sailboat—
likely the sailboat *Ruth* discovered after the hurricane—lying
trapped on the rail tracks. Again he eased the engine up to the
boat and began to push. Nothing happened. Just as the crew was
about to give in to what appeared to be their inevitable tragic fate,
the *Ruth* abruptly snapped apart and floated away. Without a
second thought, the engineer gunned the locomotive and lurched
the train across the remaining few yards of causeway and into the
relative safety of Stonington. They discovered later that the abandoned rear cars of the train on the causeway had been pounded
and overturned by the relentless hurricane waves.

(8) Tragedy: The Bay of Bengal

The worst tropical cyclone of all time hit in the Ganges Delta in
what is now called Bangladesh on November 12, 1970, and generated one of the worst natural disasters of all time. The cyclone
hit the Asian coast with winds up to 150 miles per hour and a sea
wave estimated to be fifty-feet high. Estimates of the dead range
from between three hundred thousand to five hundred thousand
with most either killed by debris or carried out to sea when the
water retreated back to the Bay of Bengal. That vast death toll
exceeds half of the entire population living on the Ganges Delta
at that time!

In scenes reminiscent of the recent terrible 2004 Boxing Day tsunami disaster, cyclone survivors recounted numerous tragic stories of whole families washed out to sea. For example, when the tropical cyclone first hit, a farmer, his wife, and children linked themselves into a human chain. The family struggled against the gale winds toward the house of the farmer's brother. Eventually, they were forced to crawl through the mud and surging waters. When they finally reached the brother's house, the family climbed to its roof, and suffered through hours of misery as the cyclone raged around them. Then, abruptly, the farmer recalled, he heard a roar and a massive wave of water hit them. The roof ripped loose. The farmer managed to grab his youngest son, lunged for a tree, and seized one of its branches.

As the cyclone pounded the delta throughout the seemingly endless night, the farmer clung to the tree branches—and his child—as waves, debris, and even people whirled about in the surging waters below in the tree. Over the wailing winds and crashing waves, the farmer heard faint screams of children as they were swept past but he could do nothing. By the next morning, the wind and water relented and the farmer finally climbed down from his tree. Amazingly, he found his whole family had survived in other trees—his wife covered in blood as she had been forced to clutch a thorny palm tree throughout the storm.

Others were far less fortunate. A reporter for the Pakistan *Observer* reported, "Bodies, which could not be buried, have started decomposing." He said that a bad odor filled the air and the few survivors wandered about without food. The reporter counted nearly eight hundred bodies within a limited area about a busted dam. Another newsman recalled, "I saw at least three thousand bodies littered along the road." Survivors were in shock and wandered aimlessly, crying out the names of their loved ones. The reporter witnessed over "5000 bodies in graves, 100 or 150 in each grave."

(9) Hurricane Storm Surges

By far the most deadly characteristic of a tropical cyclone is the incredible rise in seawater that is drawn up by the fierce winds and extreme low pressure of the hurricane. This massive bulge of seawater is called the "storm surge." When it smashes into islands and coastal low-lying lands, the results can often be catastrophic.

The Bay of Bengal to the east of India has the frequent recipient of deadly storm surges. Part of the incredible destructiveness of these Bengali storm surges involves the geography of the coast. The Bay of Bengal is shaped like a huge funnel with the spout pointing directly at the low-lying delta region of the Ganges River. Consequently, wind-whipped waves and high waters are squeezed into a large dome of water that can completely inundate the region. When that water dome is coupled with an inadequate warning and safety infrastructure, death and destruction are almost assured.

In October of 1737, a forty-foot dome of water cascaded into the northern area of the Bay of Bengal. It completely swept over the islands, the lowlands, and over the mouth of the Hooghly River and River Ganges delta, drowning an estimated three hundred thousand people. The flooding destroyed more than twenty thousand ships of all types.

A famous early hurricane scientist, Henry Piddington of the Imperial East India Company, experienced many of the Bengali tropical cyclones. Indeed, he was the first to coin the word "cyclone" (using as its base the Greek word *kyklos* or "coil of a snake"). In a vivid description of a storm surge, Piddington observed a tremendous disaster arising from a cyclone in December 1789. An entire city, Coringa, was destroyed in one day by the monstrous storm surge of a tropical cyclone. After the waters receded, Piddington wrote, "The sea in retiring left heaps of sand and mud which rendered all search for the property or bodies impossible and shut up the mouth of the river for large ships. The only trace of the ancient town which now remains is the house of the master attendant and dockyards surrounding it."

Even in the Atlantic Ocean, a hurricane's storm surge can be astonishing. In September 1922, the huge fifty-four-thousand-ton Cunard ocean liner *Aquitania* was traveling from Southampton, England, to New York when it was caught in a hurricane. The crew discovered that waves raised by the hurricane smashed ten ports on the ship's B deck. The *Aquitania*'s B-deck was located fifty feet above the waterline!

(10) The Eye of the Storm

One of the greatest oddities of the massive tropical storms and hurricanes is the strange calm region found in these storms' center—the eye. The eye is a byproduct of the colossal donut-shaped ring of thunderstorms, the eyewall, which surrounds the eye. Because the air of the eyewall thunderstorms is so intensely

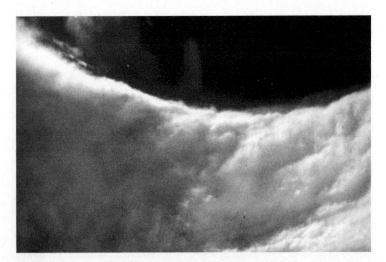

The massive eyewall of a hurricane as seen from one of the hurricane hunter NOAA P-3 aircraft. (Photo Courtesy of National Oceanic and Atmospheric Administration/Department of Commerce Photo Library Flying with NOAA Collection.)

rising, a corresponding downward flow must be created to compensate for the upward motion. The eye provides a place for some of that downward motion. Since descending air leads to dissipation of clouds, the eye is consequently an anomalous column of air that often is cloud-free. Indeed, one can sometimes see all the way down to ocean waves in high-resolution satellite photographs of a hurricane's eye.

A nineteenth-century seaman once described entry into a hurricane's eye to H. D. Northrop (who recounted the conversation in his 1887 book *Earth, Sea, and Sky, or Marvels of the Universe*), "I saw myself, as it were, at the bottom of a crater of an enormous volcano; around me, nothing but darkness; above an aperture and a gleam of light." This small clearing, however, can often lead to oddity and tragedy as seen in the tragic consequences of the 1926 hurricane that struck Miami, Florida.

A huge land rush in the early 1920s created a huge population, who had never experienced a hurricane, building homes along the low-lying Florida coast. When the 1926 September hurricane crashed ashore, many were confused as to the potential severity and danger of the situation. Indeed, as J. R. Nash retold in his 1976 book *Darkest Hours*, when the gale winds howled during a formal party at a hotel in Miami Beach, one of the partiers actually called to the band to play louder because the mammoth storm was drowning out the music. The party atmosphere across the city continued through the night—until as morning broke, an ominous calm descended on the city.

Hundreds of new Floridians stepped outside to view the situation. On all horizons, a ring of huge towering thunderstorms encircled Miami Beach but oddly the sky above the city itself was clear. People, perhaps confused, perhaps inebriated from the parties, perhaps ignorant of the danger, marveled at the spectacle and headed down to the beach for better views. One man—the local meteorologist Richard W. Gray—yelled out for everyone to take shelter again because the worst was yet to come but few paid him any attention. A few minutes later, the other side of the hurricane invaded the city with savage winds and monstrous waves. Over a hundred people died that terrible morning.

Stupidity isn't limited to the coast. A German meteorologist in 1959 told the story of a U.S. Navy pilot who, while attempting the incredibly hazardous task of flying through a hurricane, observed a sailing ship calmly drifting in the storm's eye. And to cap off the odd sight, the pilot reported that the ship's crew all on the deck were happily sunbathing.

(11) The Destructive Power

Examples of the awesome power of a hurricane's winds and waves abound in the literature. As far back as 1825, according to nineteenth-century German meteorologist L. F. Kaemtz, witnesses observed huge cannons on fortress walls high above the waterline that moved hundreds of yards. Along with their small tornadic brethren, hurricanes exhibit the peculiar ability to ram wood through wood. In several cases, such as the Havana hurricane of 1926, the Puerto Rico hurricane of 1928, and even the recent 1992 Hurricane Andrew, wood planks as much as a yard long and two wide have been impaled through mature palm trees.

According to Stanley Roger's 1932 book *Twelve on the Beaufort Scale*, hurricane winds and waves were so strong in the country of present-day Honduras in 1931 as to lift a two-hundred-ton bottom dredger out of the harbor and drop it on the roof of the customhouse. In an even more bizarre display of the power of a hurricane, weather historians tell us that inhabitants of tiny Swan Island in the Caribbean experienced an oddity when Hurricane Janet struck in 1955. Janet's winds, which had been gusting to two hundred miles per hour, abruptly dropped to thirty miles per hour in the short time of only ten minutes. After the storm, residents came out to their beaches to find thousands of dead fish, "almost all with their eyes popped out," apparently caused by the abrupt pressure and wind changes.

Hurricane researcher J. Barnes, in his 2001 book *North Carolina's Hurricane History,* recounted the *Beaufort News'* odd story involving the power of a 1933 hurricane. According to the paper, some men were doing cleanup on Cedar Island after the hurricane had passed when they encountered a forty-pound hog wedged into tree branches about fifteen feet from the ground. Apparently the high storm surge and terrific hurricane winds had somehow deposited the pig into the tree. But the oddest event was yet to come. The men decided that it would be best to yank the hog down in order to prevent the beast's carcass from rotting and causing both stench and disease. When one of the men climbed the tree and began to saw away one of the limbs, the pig suddenly came to life and let out an unearthly squeal that echoed throughout the woods. Understandably, the man on the tree nearly fainted at this unexpected porcine resurrection but after the bewildered men realized that the hog was really alive, they quickly removed it from the tree.

(12) Hurricanes and Coffins

The Floating Coffin of the 1900 Galveston Hurricane is one of the more often-repeated hurricane stories. Most retellings are based on a story penned by Robert Ripley for his famous newspaper cartoons. The tale begins with the birth of the actor Charles Francis Coghlan on Prince Edward Island, Canada, in 1841. When he grew to manhood, he aspired to the stage—and succeeded. Famed actress Lillie Langtry remembered Coghlan as "an exceedingly 'brainy' actor, but an equally temperamental one, giving at times a great performance, and at others a purely mechanical one."

Coghlan's weather notoriety came as he began an American tour in 1899 with his own acting troupe, performing a play that he had penned *The Royal Box*. Before the tour was completed, however, the actor fell ill and died in Galveston, Texas, on November 28, 1899. Coghlan's lead-lined coffin was placed in a granite vault in a local cemetery, although, the legend goes, he had always regarded his true home as Prince Edward Island. The next year, on September 8, 1900, the infamous Galveston Hurricane occurred. Floodwaters poured into local area cemeteries, sweeping coffins out of graves and, although (the legend continues) his family offered a sizable reward, his coffin could not be found. Apparently, Coghlan's coffin had been swept by the massive hurricane and its storm surge into the Gulf of Mexico.

The next part of the tale states that Coghlan's coffin eventually drifted into the Gulf Stream and then floated northward along the coast of the United States until it reached the vicinity of Newfoundland. Finally, in October 1908, several fishermen from Prince Edward Island sailed out to set their nets in the Gulf of St. Lawrence. After a time, the fishermen's nets snagged a large floating box and towed it back to shore. The silver plate on the coffin told the story: Charles Coghlan had finally returned home. The actor's body was subsequently reburied near the church where he had been baptized and the wandering spirit could at last rest.

Unfortunately, truth isn't quite as dramatic as the legend. Waldron Leard, a local Prince Edward Island historian and author of the book *Burial Sites of Interesting People on Prince Edward Island,* told me, "There is no way this story is true as far as Prince Edward Island is concerned. Coghlan was here only briefly as a part of the Actor's Colony. He is not on the charts or in the burial records of the Bay Fortune United Church Cemetery, which date back as far as 1803. There was a woman in the area in the mid-1980's who was a relation of Coghlan's (a daughter, Gertrude Coghlan Pitou) and she stated that the remains that were washed out to sea, were recovered, and reinterred in the Galveston area of Texas. This included her relative. She stated that she could not find the grave. Her visit here was to see the area, which her relative visited, not to visit any burial sites."

So how did the story arise? It might be due to a simple coincidence of names. Charles Coghlan did have a summer home on Prince Edward Island, as did another actor named Charles Flockton. Apparently at about the time as the Galveston Hurricane, Flockton died and was cremated in Los Angeles. His remains were eventually returned to Prince Edward Island for burial at his property on Abel's Cape, Fortune Bay. Indeed, a sundial monument was erected there to mark his resting place. Conversely, Coghlan's remains apparently are not found on the island.

Is the story of a floating coffin even plausible? A news item from the London *Evening Post* for May 16, 1751, suggested that coffins have long floated some distance away from their burial grounds: "We have an account from Hambourg that on 16 April last, about six leagues off the North Foreland [near Kent, England], Captain Wyrck Pietersen, commander of the ship called the *Johannes*, took up a coffin made in the English manner, and with the following inscription upon a silver plate, 'Mr. Francis Humphrey Merrydith, died 25 March 1751, aged fifty-one.' " When the coffin was carried to land and opened, rescuers found another coffin, a lead one, inside. In the second casket, they finally discovered the body of an embalmed elderly man dressed in fine linen. Even official reports of more modern hurricanes, such as Hurricane Agnes in 1952 and Hurricane Diane in 1955, have noted that the heavy flooding associated with these storms have on occasion tore coffins out of their cemeteries and washed them away.

(13) Safety from Hurricanes and Tropical Storms

Before the hurricane season begins (which is June 1 for the Atlantic and Caribbean areas), several critical actions should be accomplished. First, determine if you live in an area that can experience a hurricane. Then, if so, you should learn which are the safe routes inland and where the official shelters are located. Make sure that you have adequate supplies of nonperishable food and water supplies on hand, as well as materials, such as plywood, that will be necessary to properly protect your home. In addition, you should maintain your house and yard by checking for such things as loose and clogged rain gutters or rainspouts and making sure that trees and shrubbery are trimmed.

When a hurricane watch is issued (indicating that hurricane conditions are possible in the area usually within thirty-six hours), you should make sure to (a) listen to the media (radio or television) for official bulletins of the storm's progress, (b) determine that your vehicles are operating and full of fuel, (c) ensure that you have materials to cover all of your windows and doors, (d) check your supplies of batteries, canned food, first aid supplies, drinking water, and essential medications (such as for diabetics, etc.), and prepare to bring inside lawn furniture and other loose, lightweight objects, such as garbage cans, garden tools, etc. If a hurricane watch is issued, people in mobile homes, people who live on the coastline, an offshore island, or near a river or a flood plain, and people who live in high-rise apartments should plan to evacuate.

When in a region under a hurricane warning (indicating that hurricane conditions are expected in the area usually within twenty-four hours), people should, first, closely listen for official bulletins and then follow instructions issued by local officials. Specifically, if you are told to leave, immediately do so by following the official evacuation routes. Once inland and away from low-lying river areas, you should follow one of three options: 1. stay with friends or relatives, 2. go to an inland motel or, 3. travel to a predesignated public shelter outside the potential flood zone.

You should also notify your neighbors and family members or friend and who live outside of the warned area of your evacuation plans. Finally, if you have not been ordered to leave, and are staying inside a well-constructed building, and therefore decide to "ride-out the storm," you should find an interior room or hallway for the duration of the storm—stay away from windows and doors. All of the doors and windows should be closed (and shuttered) throughout the duration of the hurricane.

After the hurricane has passed, be careful of journeying outside. You should continue to listen for official notices and do not enter an area until the whole neighborhood has been declared safe. Be aware that standing water may be electrically charged because of downed power lines. You should also check gas, water, and electrical lines and appliances for damage before using and do not drink or prepare food with tap water until you are certain it is not contaminated.

Chapter 7
HOT, COLD, WET, AND DRY

THREE BASIC ATTRIBUTES OF OUR ATMOSPHERE (SCIENTISTS CALL them *state* variables) are temperature, pressure, and moisture. Their variations, plus changes in air density and wind, create all of our Earth's weather. Theoretically, our atmosphere and its weather can actually be "solved"—and therefore predicted—by a set of mathematical equations that contains those five variables. The very serious complication to a dream of perfect forecasts is the nature of those mathematical equations; unfortunately (particularly for nonmathematical folks) they are second-order, nonlinear, partial differential expressions. Given our current state of mathematics, computers and weather information, we can only approximate such equations—and therefore achieve only approximate solutions. That is one of the primary reasons that we don't yet have perfect weather forecasts.

These state variables of temperature, pressure, and moisture also have been the source of some of the strangest stories in weather history—frozen people, boiled people, drought-induced cannibalism, and poison fogs to name a few. In this chapter, I have collected a wide selection of stories involving these basic weather measures and classified them into twelve categories, along with a thirteenth section that involves general safety recommendations from these types of extreme weather.

(1) Temperature and Thermometers

The invention of the thermometer is commonly credited to the Italian astronomer Galileo (although a few recognize the contributions of Sanctorio of Padua). There is much less agreement as to actually *when* Galileo first created the temperature-measuring device. Some writers state a date as early as 1590 while others say the astronomer invented it as late as 1607. Whatever the case, improvements were made to his basic thermometer design throughout the next century. First, the Grand Duke of Tuscany commissioned a thermometer that was sealed and used alcohol as the expanding liquid. Then a German scientist named Gabriel Daniel Fahrenheit fashioned a thermometer with mercury as the expanding liquid and also created a scale for his thermometer using the average temperature of his native Danzig during the winter of 1709 as its "zero" temperature, 0°F. Finally a Swedish astronomer, Anders Celsius, created a temperature scale using the freezing and boiling temperatures of water as the critical values. However, Celsius actually inverted the numbers on his thermometer such that the boiling point of water was zero and the freezing point was one hundred. Linnaeus later reversed those numbers and created the modern Celsius temperature scale.

As Charles Dudley Warner (not Mark Twain as many suppose) said in an editorial in the Hartford *Courant*: "Everybody talks about the weather but nobody does anything about it." That interest in weather, and particularly temperature, inadvertently led to the world's record for "the most published 'Letter to the

Editor.' " Simply enough, according to trivia expert J. Meyers in his 1979 *Mammoth Book of Trivia,* a reader had written to the Paris edition of the *New York Herald* on December 27, 1899, asking about the difference between centigrade and Fahrenheit thermometers. Due to an editor's mistake, the letter was reprinted on the editorial page of the *Herald.* Outraged at the error and the besmirching of his paper's reputation, the *Herald*'s publisher James Gordon Bennet ordered that the letter was to be published in *every* edition of the *Herald* for the rest of his life as a stern reminder to the newspaper's staff. Consequently, by the time of Bennet's death on May 14, 1918, that simple letter inquiring about differences in temperature scales had been printed more than 6,700 times.

(2) Freezing of the Thames

A majority of the last fifteen hundred years has seen colder weather than we presently have, particularly over England. Indeed, the period from 1500 to 1850 is called "the Little Ice Age" because of the consistently frigid temperatures over Europe and eastern North America. One very visual aspect of that cold is the occurrence of frost fairs on the River Thames in London. Today the Thames doesn't freeze. This is due, in part, to a general increase in global temperatures as the world recovered from the Little Ice Age, in part due to an increase in river flow due to demolition of the old narrow London Bridge, and in part due to the creation of power plants that put warmer waters into the river.

When the River Thames did freeze in the past, it often became a time of great festivals. Merchants would open shops on the ice using booths they sledded onto the ice and the frozen river would be a great beehive of commerce and entertainment. One of the first frozen Thames entertainments was soccer. In 1564, historians recorded a "frost," which was so severe that by New Year's

Illustration entitled "An Exact and Lively Mapp or Representation of
Booths and all the Varieties of Showes and Humours upon the Ice on the
River of Thames by London during the memorable Frost . . ." in 1683.
(Image Courtesy of Pepys Library, Magdalene College, Cambridge.)

Eve of the next year, people were able to cross the Thames on the
ice from London Bridge to Westminster. Indeed, "some played
at the football as boldly there as if it had been on the dry land."
Apparently, even Queen Elizabeth herself crossed the frozen
river during that winter.

But by 1607, the festivities had grown. The science journal
Nature, citing the Watermillock *Register,* recorded "a marvelous
great frost which continued from the first day of December until
the 15th day of February after." It reported that even large companies of men and goods were able to use the river as a giant
highway and, early in the month of January, "the young folk of
Sowlby went unto the midst of the [frozen river] and had a Min-
strel with them and there danced all the afternoon."

The frost fair in 1684 was even more elaborate. The great English
diarist John Evelyn visited the "Thames on the ice," an improvised

city on the frozen river that literally contained many streets of festival booths. The "town" possessed everything from shops selling roasted meat to clothing stores, entertainments from horse and coach races to puppet plays, and even a full printing press, "where the people and ladies took a fancy to have their names printed on the Thames." Purportedly King Charles II himself visited the frozen river festival at the end of January in 1684 and had a card printed by G. Croom on the Ice River Thames.

The last of the great Thames frost fairs occurred in 1814. This fair, according to the London *Morning Post,* included the unusual spectacle of "an elephant on the ice." The paper reported that "a very fine elephant crossed the Thames a little below Backfriars Bridge" to the amusement and delight of thousands. For this final fair, the profiteers were much in evidence. Trinkets of all types—including books and toys—were sold "at double and treble the original cost" as long as they bore the important label "Bought on the Thames." At this fair, there was even an admission price; each person was required to pay a toll of up to three pence before he was admitted to Frost Fair.

(3) Frozen and Boiled People

Throughout history, people have taken unusual measures to experience and survive extreme temperatures. In 1665, in the country of Hungary, early British historian Thomas Short recorded, "When the Frost continued to the End of May; and People, to preserve their Lives, were forced to get into Ovens heated with Wood."

In 1775, a group of European scientists used an ovenlike atmosphere in a weird test of human endurance. As recorded in the journal *Philosophical Transactions,* a researcher named George Fordyce set about to determine how hot of temperatures that a man could survive—Fordyce literally wanted to bake a person! So, he created a suite of rooms "of which the hottest was heated by flues in the floor, and by pouring upon it boiling water; and the second was heated by the same flues, which passed through its floor to the third." The heat eventually became so great that literally every one of the scientists' thermometers broke save one. A fellow scientist named Charles Blagden described one of the strange experiments, "Upon entering the room a third time, between five and six o'clock after dinner, we observed the quicksilver in our only remaining thermometer at 198° (F)." Sometime later, one of the scientists entered the room alone, and recorded on the remaining functioning thermometer a temperature of 210°F. Another of the researchers noted, "Men remained in [Fordyce's heated rooms at 260°F] for fifteen minutes, without any noteworthy rise in body temperature, while a beefsteak was nicely cooked in thirteen minutes."

Other people haven't handled the heat as well. A short note in *Nature* described a heat wave in 1901 New York City that caused hundreds of deaths. The heat in the city became so intense that the street asphalt actually softened, and wheels ploughed deep ruts in the streets. Even the Stock Exchange closed because of the excessive heat. News reports stated that more than a thousand horses died from heatstroke during the massive summer heat wave.

On the other side of the temperature spectrum, people have also experienced incredibly cold temperatures. For instance, Guy Murchie, in his 1954 book *Song of the Sky*, described the fantastic story of "Johnnie" Stevens, a "tough" twenty-three-year-old woman from Chicago's South Side. On a frigid winter night in 1951, a thoroughly intoxicated Johnnie had stumbled into a windy Chicago alley and fell unconscious onto the ice-cold bricks. When a policeman discovered her lying in the alley the next morning, he first thought Johnnie was undoubtedly dead. After all, the Windy City's air temperature had dropped to a bone-chilling -11°F and the woman definitely appeared frozen. The police officer began the normal recording procedures. He determined that Johnnie's jaw was locked tight, her stomach was rigid, and her unseeing eyes looked "like two glass beads." With a sad shake of his head, he was about to call the coroner to pick up the frozen body . . . when Johnnie Stevens abruptly groaned.

The policeman immediately rushed the woman to a local hospital where doctors discovered that they couldn't even register a body temperature for her; their regular medical thermometers simply didn't go that low. Only an hour or so later after additional warming did one of their rectal temperatures produce a frigid reading of 64.4°F. Incredibly, by midafternoon, Johnnie's body temperature had risen to 77°F and by evening it was up to 86°F with almost normal pulse and respiration. Late that evening, she opened her eyes, let out of a sigh and mumbled, "I'm cold." The next morning, the amazingly tough Chicago lady's body temperature was close to normal.

Others haven't been as fortunate. Meteorologist George Hartwig, in his 1887 book *The Aerial World,* described what happens when the desire to partake in history overwhelms common sense. After Napoleon died in December of 1840, his body was carried along the Champs Elysées in Paris. Thousands of spectators and guardsmen gathered along the street in the very early hours of morning in anticipation of the procession but dawn temperatures fell as low as 7°F. Some of the guardsmen tried to warm themselves by drinking brandy, but still fell dead because of "congestion to the brain." Other spectators, who had climbed trees early in the morning to observe the procession, paid the ultimate price for sightseeing. Because of their increasingly frozen arms and legs, many of the climbers couldn't hold onto the hard tree bark and fell to their deaths.

(4) Heat, Cold, and War

Beyond the merriment of the London frost fairs discussed earlier, the intense cold of the Little Ice Age also led to some of the strangest "battles" in human history. In one of the strangest, discussed by Roger Bentley in a 1907 issue of the *Quarterly Journal of the Royal Meteorological Society,* a cavalry regiment managed to capture an entire battle fleet of ships—without a single shot being fired! The tale took place in the Napoleonic Wars of the late eighteenth century. By the start of 1795, the French continental army had gained control of much of Holland but still faced the well-respected sea might of the Dutch navy. At the same time, the bitter cold of the Little Ice Age made any military movements difficult. Indeed, a winter blast had completely entrapped the Dutch navy in confining thick ice around Texel Island near the coast. A total of fifteen ships of the line, two cargo vessels and several smaller cannon boats were all solidly frozen in the ice.

When the French general heard the news, he immediately dispatched his nearest available forces—a small cavalry force under the command of Commandant Louis Joseph Lahure. In order to gain as quick of an advantage as possible Lahure raced his 128-man force across the frozen tidal flats. As the French cavalry rode up to the ice-locked helpless Dutch ships, Lahure demanded the entire fleet's immediate surrender. Realizing the hopelessness of his position, the Dutch admiral calmly proposed, "Why don't we discuss such serious matters over dinner aboard my flagship?" And so it happened that a cavalry regiment captured a battle fleet at sea—admittedly a frozen sea—without any loss of any life.

In a more gruesome story, the Nazi advance into Russia was hounded by appalling cold. Erik Durschmied, in his fascinating 2000 book *The Weather Factor,* discussed the weather misfortunes experienced by the ill-prepared German troops in detail. In early December of 1941, the Thirty-first Nazi Infantry advanced on Moscow as air temperatures plunged to -40°F and below. Adding to their misery, the Germans' thinly woven uniforms were completely unsuited for the brutal Russian weather. The Nazis' final assault began at night to take advantage of a full moon, but that meant temperatures had plunged to life-threatening glacial temperatures. Some of the German survivors reported their fellow soldiers' beards were completely coated with layers of ice. More ominously, the German soldiers were wearing only threadbare regulation overcoats as compared to their Russian counterparts who were dressed in warm sheepskin coats and fur mittens. When the order to advance came, some of the soldiers were so chilled that they almost couldn't grasp their rifles. After the attack, the ground outside the Nazi headquarters was literally covered with soldiers not only suffering from wounds but also severe frostbite. The sheer number of casualties made it impossible to treat them all, and most of the German soldiers were simply left lying outside to die of exposure in the frigid Russian winter.

In stark contrast, sweltering heat in battle can also lead to strange sights. A very odd pause occurred during a late July 1904 battle in Manchuria during the Russo-Japanese War. In the middle of what British military observer Lieutenant-Colonel C. V. Hume termed an "exceedingly hot" and "airless" day, the combatants simply suddenly stopped fighting. Military historians agree that the reason for the halt was the stifling weather; for a time, the sweltering heat (with "no shade on the hills") literally defeated both armies. During this rest break at 10:30 A.M. in the morning, C. V. Hume noticed a curious "shimmer" on the Japanese side of the battlefield, which seemed to vibrate back and forth along its entire firing line. When he peered closer, the British colonel discovered that hundreds of Japanese soldiers had simply pulled out small hand fans and were using them vigorously in a desperate attempt to cool off.

(5) Chinooks and Heatbursts

A *chinook* is an abnormally hot dry wind that is created by compression of air as it is forced down a mountain. The name is linked to an American Indian tribe that formerly lived near the mouth of the Columbia River. Early traders of the Hudson Bay Company at Astoria, Oregon, originally applied the term to a warm southwest wind blowing from the direction of the Chinook Indian villages on the lower Columbia River. Now the term is applied specifically to any warm, dry, local wind that descends the lee side of a mountain. In Europe, chinooks are called *föehns*.

Chinooks can create massive variations in temperature. In 1900, residents of Harve, Montana, experienced a chinook that raised temperatures by 31°F in only three minutes from 11° to 42°F. Undoubtedly one of the strangest U.S. chinooklike phenomena, however, was reported in the journal *Monthly Weather Review* and concerned the weird situation in the Black Hills on January 22, 1943. One of the first indications of the strange weather conditions was when weather observers at Spearfish, South Dakota, saw the temperature abruptly shoot from -4°F to 45°F (a 49° difference!) in a mere two minutes. As the strange day progressed, people across the Black Hills experienced vastly different weather conditions only a scant few feet apart. For example, around noon, the east side of the Alex Johnson Hotel in Rapid City was entombed in bitter subzero temperatures while a mere fifty feet around the corner on the south side of the hotel, a warm blast of springlike air was surging down the street. Many motorists were forced to park because they couldn't remove thick frost that appeared almost instantly on windshields as they turned corners. In the nearby city of Lead, plate glass windows literally shattered due to the rapid rise in temperature.

The strange weather phenomenon called a "heat burst" can also lead to massive warming. But, in contrast to Chinooks, this type of almost instantaneous temperature change is the result of rapidly descending (and warming) air from a huge thunderstorm rather than air being compressed through mountain descent. One of the most famous heat bursts occurred along the coast of

Portugal in 1949. According to a variety of news reports at the time, this heat burst shot thermometers up to an unofficial reading of 158°F in the sun in an astounding two minutes! The burst reportedly left hundreds of persons lying helpless in the streets and thousands of fish and fowl were killed by the scorching wave of hot air.

Heat bursts have also occurred in the United States but have not received as much attention as other weather events. One of the strangest was a heat burst in Kopperl, Texas, near Dallas. That event rightly earned the title "what Hell might be like" yet beyond a short news story by a local television station (with cameraman Floyd Bright and forecaster Harold Taft) in Fort Worth, no official record of this unusual Texas heat burst exists. According to area witnesses, the heat burst's origins were the scattered thunderstorms over the area. As the storms abruptly died out, a suffocating hot blast of air accompanied by the hurricane-force winds swept out of them and into the small Texas town. At midnight, a thermometer outside Kopperl's Bait and Tackle Shop went from 70°F to 100°F within minutes and then, amazingly, continued upward to 140°F! Residents reported that ears of corn were roasted on their stalks, cotton plants wilted or burned, and fields of grass morphed immediately into dry hay ready for baling. Sleeping families awoke gasping in the stifling air. Fire sprinkler systems were set off and car radiators boiled over. The next morning, Kopperl residents found that only their local area had been affected by the heat burst.

(6) Droughts and Cannibalism

In today's world, many places suffer from drought-related famine. Graphic television images of suffering, starving children evoke obvious compassion but also imply that child starvation is one of the worst—if not the worst—possible features of drought.

Unfortunately, that is not the case. Droughts in previous times lead to some of the most horrendous acts that humans can inflect on each other. The eminent Arab scholar Adb al-Latif, during a trip to Cairo, Egypt, at the start of the Middle Ages, penned, in his book *The Eastern Key,* a distinctly explicit account of the drought that afflicted the area. Please be aware that this is an extremely graphic narration.

Adb al-Latif compared the drought in the year AD 1201 (or 597 on the Islamic calendar) to "a monster whose fury caused to be destroyed all the resources of life and all the means of subsistence." The drought was born when the life-giving River Nile had failed to flood for two consecutive years—and so by end of the second year, he wrote that "air was corrupted, the plague and contagion began to make itself felt." Following a meager harvest, the poorest of the people were forced by the crippling famine to eat "carrion, corpses, dogs, and the excrement and the filth of animals."

One could hardly think that conditions could be worse than eating excrement—yet the greatest evil lay ahead. The Arab scholar said that when the poor had exhausted all other food sources, they fell to an utterly loathsome state: ". . . they began to eat little children. It was not rare to surprise people with little children roasted or boiled." As this abominable practice gained popularity, the chief magistrate of Cairo immediately instituted a penalty to fit the crime: any murderer or any person caught eating human flesh was to be immediately burned alive.

Still the vile frenzy continued. Adb al-Latif wrote, "Two days previously I had seen a child almost at the age of puberty, who had been found roasted; they had seized, with the corpse, two youths who confessed that it was they who had killed this child, had roasted him, and had already eaten a part." Indeed, according to the Arab scholar, cannibalism—eating of human flesh—became so common that a substantial number of the population actually died (or were murdered) as food for others. In a most grotesque but graphic manner Abd al-Latif exemplified how the drought literally led to an unimaginably hideous business when he reported, "We found barrels in a grocer's cellars full of human flesh, salted in brine."

Although not quite as pandemic of craze, other famines have also led to cannibalism. The 1877 drought in China, which is labeled by some as the worst famine in history, produced reports of eating human flesh. The *New York Times* in 1878 quoted a letter from a Roman Catholic bishop in China in which he stated, "Until lately the starving people were content to feed on the dead; but now they are slaughtering the living for food. The husband eats his wife; parents are eating their children; and, in their turn, sons and daughters eat their dead parents."

(7) Death and Oddities of Floods

Droughts have led tragedy and oddity and so have their wet counterparts, floods. Given that the vast majority of people live next to water, floods have exerted an incredible influence on our history and society. Indeed, one major flood of the Mississippi in 1927 likely influenced a presidential election. When the mighty river overflowed its banks due to spring massive rains, then Secretary of Commerce Herbert Hoover took direct charge of flood relief operations. That pivotal role in helping millions of people probably contributed to his subsequent election the next year as president.

One problem with floods is that sometimes the rising waters swamp things they shouldn't. For example, magnesium is a substance that is highly volatile and explosive in water. So, on August 19, 1955, when floodwaters in Putnam, Connecticut, poured into a warehouse containing twenty tons of magnesium, the element ignited, causing a huge plume of smoke to rise up from the warehouse. Reports stated that the smoke could be seen twenty miles away. As firefighters worked to put out the strange fire, the area would periodically light up "like a giant flash bulb" as another barrel filled with magnesium blew up.

A heap of cars carried downstream in Rapid City South Dakota by the force of the great flash flood in June 1972. (Photo Courtesy of National Oceanic and Atmospheric Administration/Department of Commerce Photo Library Historic NWS Collection.)

Although not as explosive, the effects of the long heavy rains in 1966 on the River Arno in Florence, Italy, were equally disastrous. Many irreplaceable art treasures stored in the historic Italian city were in grave danger. For instance, the Arno's floodwaters poured into Florence's largest library and threatened more than a million books and manuscripts. Incredibly, three hundred university students quickly formed a human chain extending down into the flooded basement collections and began to transfer the water- and mud-soaked rare books and manuscripts out of danger. Even though the air in some of the basement rooms was so foul as to warrant gas masks, the students were not deterred. Their selfless devotion in saving the books earned them the titles of *angeli del fango* or "angels of the mud."

In another part of the city, at the Institute and Museum of the History of Science, the elderly superintendent of fine art continued to risk his life and retrieve priceless art objects although he had been directly ordered to leave the flooded building. One of his colleagues recalled later that when they had tried to stop the aged professor, he had angrily retorted that they were young and had children while he was old and could take the risk for himself.

The worst floods in history are undoubtedly the floods of the Yellow (or Huang He) River. Just ten years after the terrible drought and sporadic cannibalism in China described in the section above, the Huang He River, swollen by heavy rains, broke through the dikes at a sharp bend in the heavily populated province of Honan. At its crest, the flood covered three hundred miles and flooded fifteen thousand villages. There is no way to determine the actual death toll from this horrible flood but authorities have suggested that it could be as high as six million people who drowned or were lost through later disease. A missionary described the survivors as being stunned, hungry, and dejected, without a rag to wear or a morsel of food to eat.

In the United States, three monster floods have achieved great prominence. First, in 1889, a dam failure upstream of the town of Johnstown, Pennsylvania, caused a mammoth flood that destroyed the entire city and killed over 2,200 people. A number of "freaks" were recorded with this flood. Three of the strangest were a lady who insisted on styling her hair before being rescued from her shattered house, a small menagerie of animals, including a cow, a dog, and five hens, that somehow survived the floodwaters all together under two wrecked freight cars, and, a partially wrecked house that had floated down the river to Pittsburgh over sixty miles away—with a five-month-old baby still alive inside.

In 1972, a summer evening thunderstorm over the Black Hills of South Dakota produced massive rainfall in the highlands and a subsequent flood cascaded through the valleys and into the town of Rapid City. Keystone, a small village of five hundred people, was completely swept away. Literally every one of its buildings was damaged or destroyed by the floodwaters. In Rapid City, people quickly climbed up onto rooftops, onto trees, and onto the tops of floating cars and houses—any place higher than the rising floodwaters. A Rapid City police lieutenant nearly drowned when a floating house crashed into his patrol car. As the waters receded, emergency service personnel were forced to issue messages stating, "If you find a body, do not touch it. Call emergency services. Stay in your homes. Don't drink the water. Boats are needed immediately." Over 230 people were killed and hundreds more were injured.

A third historic flash flood occurred on the eve before Colorado's state centennial in 1976. As thousands of tourists and residents enjoyed the holiday weekend in the state's beautiful mountains, a massive thunderstorm hit. People in the scenic Rocky Mountain National Park were struck by floodwaters traveling at nearly fifty miles per hour. A Colorado State Patrol trooper was in his police car when he was radioed, "I'm stuck. I'm right in the middle of it. I can't get out . . . Tell them cars to get out of that low area down below. As soon as the water starts picking up . . . [static] . . . high ground . . ." Unfortunately, the police officer never made it out of the canyon. His battered body was later found eight miles downstream from the spot where he had made his final desperate warning.

(8) Deadly Fogs

A fog is simply a cloud whose base is either near or touching the ground. As nothing more (or less) than a ground cloud, a fog—like its aerial counterpart—is composed of small water droplets that are suspended in air. Because fogs are easily ripped apart by winds or storms, fogs are generally associated with the calmer conditions of high-pressure systems and inversions (basically cold air trapped under warm air). However, these are exactly the same type of weather features that creates unhealthy pollution conditions in an industrial area. When fog and pollution are combined into a toxic mixture called smog, the results can sometimes be fatal.

In late 1930, the air over Belgium became increasingly stagnant as a high-pressure-created inversion held sway over the small country. At the same time, massive amounts of toxic pollution were being poured into the air by several iron-ore smelters in the town of Liege. Increasing amounts of sulfur dioxide and other gases lay trapped under the inversion and mixed with fogs developing in the Meuse River valley. Within a couple of days, over sixty people had died and the smog had sickened hundreds more. The *London Times* later called the smog over the Meuse valley in Belgium a "poison fog."

A similar event happened in the United States nearly two decades later. In October 1948, a huge inversion capped the air in the Monongahela River Valley in Pennsylvania. As pollution levels over the area grew, people in the area began to sicken and die, particularly near the city of Donora near Pittsburgh. Death and illness were graphic. News reports described the first victim as initially gagging and then a ghastly white froth bubbled up out of his mouth. Within a short time, the man simply gasped for breath, his skin turned blue, and he died. Over the next couple of days, twenty more people had perished in the thickening toxic smog and hundreds more were becoming ill. The industrial factory owners, hearing of the deaths, quickly shut down their plants. Fortunately, a rainstorm soon hit the area and cleansed the atmosphere. Residents who experienced the terrible episode claimed that the smog smelled like a sickening sweet perfume but no single source was ever identified as the cause of the Donoran smog deaths.

(9) Pea-Soupers and their Consequences

Traditionally, London, England, has been linked to some of the thickest fogs (and smogs) of the planet. By the sixteenth century, Queen Elizabeth banned coal burning while Parliament was in session to limit their nuisance (the smog's, not Parliament's).

George Hartwig, in his 1887 book *The Aerial World,* reported that John Evelyn, a prominent London resident, claimed the city fogs were so thick by 1661 "that people lost their way in the streets, it being so intense, that no light of candles or torches yielded any or but very little direction." In an effort to eliminate these more frequent (and occasionally deadly) annoyances, Evelyn published a pamphlet addressed to the King entitled, "Fumifugium, or the Inconvenience of the Air, and Smoke of London Dissipated; together with Some Remedies Humbly Proposed." He noted that most Londoners "breathe nothing but an impure and thick mist, accompanied by a fuliginous and filthy vapor, corrupting the lungs, so that catarrhs, coughs, and consumptions rage more in this one city, than in the whole Earth."

But relief was slow to come. For instance, in 1873, a heavy fog settled over London that totally stopped river traffic and port business. Hartwig reported that the fog was so thick that several people died by unsuspectingly falling into the Thames River and drowning. Cattle at an agricultural show being held at the time reportedly were unable to breathe in the polluted atmosphere and exhibited painful symptoms as if they had been inhaling a noxious gas. Many of the livestock had to be put down.

Yet other areas also have been afflicted with thick fogs. New York City, for example, has experienced a number of dreadful fog and smog events. Free and Hoke, in their 1929 book *Weather,* reported that over a two-day period in 1928, a total of eight ocean liners collided in the fogbound ports of the metropolitan port city. But the area particularly known for dense fogs is the region of the North Atlantic between the coast and the Gulf Stream, an incredibly strong and warm ocean current. One of those fogs led to a very strange and lethal disaster. In the summer of 1956, the *Andrea Doria* sailed from Genoa toward New York City. As it neared the island of Nantucket, the *Andrea Doria* entered into a thick fog bank. Unfortunately, the *Stockholm,* a Swedish passenger ship, had left New York City early that morning with 534 passengers and was traveling on the same course. As the two plowed through the fog-laden sea, without warning the *Stockholm* crashed into *Andrea Doria.* Dozens were immediately killed on both ships.

Undoubtedly, the oddest story of the *Andrea Doria* occurred when a seaman onboard the *Stockholm* went forward to survey damage to his ship. As he made his way through the mass of twisted steel, he was startled to hear a young voice crying in Spanish for her mother. Moments later, he discovered a fourteen-year-old girl lying on a mattress in the midst of the wreckage. The teenager was Linda Morgan and a few moments earlier she had been asleep in her parents' cabin on the *Andrea Doria.* When the *Stockholm* crashed into the ship, its prow went into the Morgans' room, and, as the Swedish ship reared back after the collision, Linda, on her mattress, was whisked away, unaware that she was aboard the *Stockholm's* framework.

(10) Dry Fogs

Normally, fogs are the result of suspended water droplets. Occasionally, suspended dust can accomplish much the same effect. A fog of this type occurred in 1783 and extended across most of the Northern Hemisphere. Scientists and the general public called the event a "dry fog." The 1783 dry fog, according to many observers, had a most "disagreeable smell and was entirely destitute of any moisture, whereas most fogs are moist." In addition, many people commented that the fog was luminous and even at midnight gave off a glow as bright as a full moon. American scholar Benjamin Franklin was one of the early scientists to speculate on the cause of such "dry fogs."

Franklin proposed that the 1783 dry fog was the result of an earlier eruption of a volcano in Iceland. Others weren't so sure. One scientist at the time attributed the strange haze to a supposed accumulation of electricity that he claimed was produced when a very warm summer followed a moist winter while others asserted that the fogs occurred when "metallic emanations united with electricity" as a result of earthquakes. Even fifty years later, meteorologist L. F. Kaemtz suggested that dry fogs in 1834 resulted from the burning of "heaps of bad grass and potato-culms." Others suggested that the Earth periodically passed through the tails of comets and the comet's dust tail created the dry fogs.

Today, scientists tend to agree with Franklin; dry fogs occur when large volcanic eruptions inject massive quantities of sulfur gases and aerosols into the high atmosphere. If aerosols get high enough, say above six miles or so and, therefore, into the stratosphere, an atmospheric haze can last for years. Interestingly, however, one of the densest and most persistent dry fogs that occurred over Europe and the Middle East in AD 536 is also one of the most difficult to explain because no large volcanic eruption has been linked to it. Following the spectacular impact of the Shoemaker-Levy comet into Jupiter in 1994, some researchers have recently theorized that the dry fog of AD 536 may have been caused by the entry of a relatively small (perhaps only a fourth of a mile in diameter) comet into the Earth's atmosphere. Computer modeling of comets indicate that if a small comet disintegrated due to the heat of entry into the upper atmosphere and released sizeable amounts of dust and debris, the result would correspond to a dry fog.

(11) The Fog of War

The shrouding ability of fog had often played a huge role in warfare. For example, a meteorologist might convincingly argue that the United States owes its independence to the formation of a heavy evening fog in August 1776. Following the defeat of American rebels by the British in the Battle of Long Island, the Americans were effectively trapped on the island. The overwhelmed American army lay open to siege and eventual annihilation because a British fleet of naval ships blocked their only potential retreat path across the East River. The night after the defeat, however, a dense fog blinded the British sentries, and under the cover of the enveloping mist, the retreating American army daringly escaped across the river. As C. C. Hazewell noted in an 1862 article in *Atlantic Monthly*, "Americans should ever regard a fog with a certain reverence, for a fog saved their country in 1776."

Many think that with the exception of a few bi- and triplanes, World War I didn't experience a great deal of aerial warfare. But in 1917, London came close to facing destruction from the air—except for a fortunate fog. The journal *Nature* reported in October of 1917 that a fleet of thirteen Zeppelin airships was dispatched to attack the English capital. Unexpectedly, as they traveled across the Channel, however, a thick fog settled over the British Isles and the German dirigibles weren't able to determine even their own locations, let alone find any effective targets. Things quickly went from bad to worst. Cold northerly winds in the upper atmosphere then propelled the Zeppelin fleet southward over France and the intense cold seized up the engines. In their helpless condition, the mighty Zeppelin fleet became an easy target for Allied forces.

Sixty years later, the Siege of Khe Sanh was one of the most famous or infamous battles of the Vietnam War—in part due to incredibly persistent fog. H. A. Winters, in his 1998 book, *Battling the Elements*, gave a fascinating account of the siege that lasted for nearly two and a half months from January to April of 1968. The Siege of Khe Sanh is regarded as one of the most prolonged and intensive battles of the entire war. Over that entire time period, the U.S. Marine camp of six thousand at Khe Sanh was under virtually continuous fire from the North Vietnamese Army. The camp itself was located on a barren plateau surrounded by vegetation-covered hills. That unique landscape allowed for the formation of *crachin*, a wintertime drizzly fog created by continual uplift of moisture from the surrounding warm lowlands.

During the siege, weary American soldiers noted that, during the course of a day, the quasi-clear skies only lasted for a few hours and visibilities were never much better than five miles. This made aerial resupply of the base incredibly difficult. One of the generals commented that February 1968 transformed him into an old man because of the consistent "zero ceiling and zero visibility." Unfortunately for the American troops, the camp's runway often remained shrouded in mist even when the rest of the plateau was clear. In fact, the Marines began to refer to the ravine below the airstrip as the "fog factory." After nearly two months, the weather finally cleared enough to allow a fleet of B-52 bombers to begin a saturation bombardment of the Vietnamese attackers who were slowly digging toward the besieged camp. The bombing was devastating—the siege broke. But the fog battle had cost the lives of 250 Americans and perhaps thousands of Vietnamese.

(12) Pressure

An Italian student of Galileo named Evangelista Torricelli is credited with the invention of the barometer—a device that measures changes in atmospheric pressure—in 1643. The weather instrument is relatively simple in design. One version of it consists of a "J"-shaped tube open at the top end, sealed with a slight vacuum at the other end, and filled between with mercury. The "weight" (or more correctly the force) of air pushes through the open tube down on the mercury. Given the density of mercury, air at sea level pushes mercury down in Torricelli's barometer about thirty inches or so of distance—hence an atmospheric pressure of "thirty inches of mercury."

Barometers based on other less dense liquids would have to be much bigger because the weight of air can push those liquids a much greater distance. In 1650, Blaise Pascal created a barometer using red wine instead of mercury. Since wine is 13.6 times lighter than mercury, Pascal's barometric tube necessarily had to be forty-six feet tall. Similarly, in Magdeburg, Germany, the mayor, Otto van Guericke, erected a huge water barometer on his house. Again, given the lower density of water compared to mercury, van Guericke's barometer was over fifty feet tall and its top actually projected from the roof of his house. To add a bit of fun to the device, van Guericke floated a wooden doll in the barometer's water so that, when the weather was stormy, the doll disappeared out of sight but would pop out again when the weather was fair.

In the past, using a barometer to forecast the weather sometimes

Illustration of a man using an early barometer. (Photo Courtesy of National Oceanic and Atmospheric Administration/Department of Commerce Photo Library Historic NWS Collection.)

led to charges of Devil worship. For instance, the owner of the first barometer in Scotland, David Gregory, nearly was charged with witchcraft. Local people thought because he (with his barometer) excelled at forecasting weather, he must have made a pact with Satan. Only his exceedingly good nature and philanthropy saved him from a potentially fatal religious persecution.

For many superstitious people, the oddities of pressure often appeared magical. During Charles Darwin's travels around South America in the HMS *Beagle,* he found that some of his sailing companions were puzzled by the relationship between lowering pressure and the lowering of water's boiling temperature as they trekked through the Andes Mountains. He recorded in his *Diary* that "our potatoes, after remaining for some hours in the boiling water, were nearly as hard as ever." His two traveling companions discussed the situation and "had come to the simple conclusion, that the potatoes were bewitched, or that the pot, which was a new one, did not choose to boil them." Conversely, nineteenth-century British spies in Tibet even used the pressure/boiling temperature relationship to covertly determine the elevation of high mountain passes.

Many early aeronauts learned the fundamentals of atmospheric pressure the hard way—particularly the basic fact that air pressure is reduced dramatically with increasing elevation. C. M. Botley, in his 1938 book *Air and Its Mysteries,* recorded a couple of interesting episodes. In 1862, two Englishmen, James Glaisher and Henry Coxwell, piloted a balloon to a height of nearly twenty-nine thousand feet. Glaisher fainted and Coxwell, with nearly frozen hands, just barely succeeded in yanking the gas release cord with his teeth before he too collapsed. In a similar but more tragic occurrence, early balloonist and French scientist Gaston Tissandier with two companions in 1875 reached an elevation above twenty-six thousand feet in his balloon. All three fainted. When Tissandier regained consciousness, he discovered that the balloon was descending but his two companions were dead.

(13) Safety from Extreme Heat, Cold, and Humidity

Heat and cold exposure force the human body to its limits and beyond. While the human body does have basic mechanisms that act to regulate temperature, those mechanisms can break down if pushed beyond their capacity. Although the symptoms are different for severe cold and extreme heat exposure, both can be life-threatening.

a. Heat

Normally the body produces sweat and perspiration so that heat from the body is used to evaporate moisture rather than as a basic heat source. If body temperature becomes excessive, that defense mechanism breaks down. Heat cramps—demonstrating strong muscular pains and spasms—can sometimes be the first sign of a body being stressed by heat. A generally effective treatment is moving the victim to a cooler place and in a comfortable position. If possible, you should have the person drink a half glass of cool water every fifteen minutes but avoid giving beverages containing alcohol or caffeine as those substances lead to dehydration, which worsens the situation.

If a person works or exercises too heavily during hot conditions, he or she may suffer heat exhaustion. Such a condition is marked by an increased blood flow to the skin and a resulting loss of blood flow to internal organs. This can sometimes lead to a mild form of shock. As with heat cramps, you should get the victim into a cooler place and start giving them a half glass of cool water every fifteen minutes. Remove or loosen their clothing and apply wet cloths. If heat exhaustion is not treated quickly and effectively, it can occasionally worsen into heat stroke.

Heat stroke occurs when the body temperature is as high as 105°F—often the skin is red and hot to the touch and the person displays changes in consciousness with a rapid pulse and shallow breathing. This condition can be fatal without direct action.

Therefore, immediately call emergency services and move the person to a cooler place. Try to cool the body with a cool (not cold) bath or wet sheets. You should keep the person lying down.

To avoid the greatest risk from extreme heat, one should (a) try to find areas of greatest temperature relief (for example, if your home doesn't have air-conditioning, go to a library, theater, or other community facility that does), (b) plan your activities to avoid working in the hottest time of the days, (c) verify any medications you or family members may be taking to see if they cause poor blood circulation or reduced ability to tolerate heat, (d) check on family, friends, or neighbors who do not have air-conditioning, particularly those who are elderly or who need assistance, and (e) wear light-colored, lightweight clothing.

b. Cold

In a similar fashion, the body handles cold conditions by a unique defense mechanism, shivering. Shivering produces kinetic energy or, in essence, heat for the body. When cold conditions become extreme, the body's natural defense mechanisms against the cold can break down or become ineffective and there is a higher possibility of frostbite or hypothermia.

Frostbite is a severe reaction to cold exposure—skin can't freeze if the temperature is above 32°F. Actually, for frostbite to occur, the temperature must be below 28° F because of the large salt content in body fluids. Parts of the body with a high surface area compared to the thickness of the tissue are the most susceptible. Specifically, the ears, nose, fingers, and toes (a nice little rhyme to use as a means of checking yourself and others) are at risk to frostbite. Technically, frostbite involves destruction of skin layers resulting in blistering and minor tissue loss. Blisters are formed from the cellular fluid released when cells rupture. One should not rub frostbitten skin; rubbing causes cell tearing from the ice crystals.

Hypothermia occurs when the body temperature falls below 95°F. Often, the symptoms of hypothermia may not be apparent, both to the sufferer or any companions. Sometimes, in the primary stages, the victim may even refuse to acknowledge that there may be a problem. Hypothermia progresses with a natural sense of cold accompanied by shivering. Then numbness increases and speech becomes garbled or incoherent, indicating that the thought process has slowed. The victim's body movements become increasingly erratic. Uncovered skin swells and appears blue. Eventually, unconsciousness occurs, followed by a possibly fatal lowering of the body core temperature.

The key treatment for hypothermia is to get the victim in a warm shelter as soon as possible. Patients in severe hypothermia often appear to be dead. You should gently remove wet clothing from them and replace with dry clothing. Above all, try to keep the patient lying down and warm (direct skin-to-skin contact is preferable).

If the sufferer is conscious and able to swallow, give sugar and sweet, warm (not hot) fluids—but not alcohol—by mouth.

c. Fog

A major difficulty with fog is often the quick and marked reduction in visibility. If you are driving and encounter heavy fog, first drive only with your headlights on low beam. High beams reflect off the fog, creating a "white wall" effect that masks objects. Consequently, it is a good idea—even with low beams—to reduce your driving speed. In particular, keep a watch on your speedometer. Fog can sometimes create the optical illusion of slower motion and you may be traveling faster than you realize. Finally, open your driver's window to be able to listen for traffic.

d. Pressure

Reduction in barometric pressure (and the corresponding decrease in the amount of oxygen) as one gains elevation, particularly when the altitude change occurs rapidly to heights above eight thousand feet or so) can cause what is termed *acute mountain sickness*. While individual symptoms vary, some of the most common warning signs are headaches, fatigue, shortness of breath, nausea, poor appetite, and in some cases, an inability to sleep. Acute mountain sickness can occur to anyone. The effects of acute mountain sickness generally can be minimized or even prevented by allowing for acclimatization, the gradual natural adjustment of the body to lower levels of oxygen. Acclimatization, however, is a relatively slow process, often taking place over a period of days.

Before going to higher elevations, there are several suggestions for minimizing acute mountain sickness. These include avoiding excessive exercise, work, last-minute packing, alcohol, sleeping pills, or narcotics, but do drink plenty of fluids and eat high-carbohydrate foods (rice, pasta, cereal) while avoiding fatty foods.

The treatment for someone suffering from acute mountain sickness depends on the severity of the symptoms. If the signs (such as headaches and nausea) are mild, they will generally improve without treatment over several days. However, if the sufferer's symptoms become more acute, recommended treatment is to contact a doctor and then either directly administer oxygen or remove the sufferer to a lower altitude.

Chapter 8
SNOW

A S MENTIONED IN CHAPTER FIVE, MANY RAINSTORMS ACTUALLY begin as snowstorms high in the clouds. Snow must be created in "cold" clouds—those clouds with tops that are below freezing. In a cold cloud, ice crystals, or minute frozen kernels of water, exist in suspension with a multitude of supercooled droplets (microscopic water that remains in a liquid state far below 32°F). As the ice crystals collide with the supercooled water, the water instantly freezes onto the droplet, normally on one of six sides, given the underlying hexagonal structure of the ice crystal. If a sufficiently large number of collisions occur, the crystal aggregate becomes a snowflake and, if the air and the ground remain near freezing temperature or below, the aggregate remains a snowflake as it falls to the ground.

Snow is one of our most basic—and humanly taxing—types of weather and, as such, it is an element of nature that we have recorded for centuries. Indeed, this weather type is a staple in many of the more unbelievable father and grandfather tall tales, such as "walking through snow drifts above my head uphill to and from school." Undoubtedly, some snow stories are exaggerations. But it is equally true that occasionally snow can just be plain weird. This oddness can take the form of such strange snow creations as "natural snowballs," or bug-filled snowfalls, or even the bizarre icy fog known as *pogonip*. In this chapter, I've categorized odd snows into twelve basic categories and added a thirteenth section that discusses general safety recommendations for snow and blizzards.

(1) Red Snow

As mentioned earlier, "blood" or "red" rain is often either due to droppings from butterflies or from Saharan sands blown into Europe. The explanations for red snows, however, must be treated separately. Writers have mentioned red snows for as long a time as they have blood rains, but their explanations have been quite different. As far back as the third century BC, Aristotle reported on the occurrence of red snow but didn't suggest a cause. A few centuries later, the Roman historian Pliny originated the unique idea that the occasional red color in snow is the equivalent of rust! He basically suggested that snow becomes redder in color with increasing age.

Over the next thousand years, English historians recorded many strange blood snows occurring in Europe. For example, the English historian, Reverend Thomas Short, reported that once near Genoa, Italy, a red snow fell that "gave a bloody Liquor" when squeezed. In 1755, a six-foot-deep blood snowfall in the Alps reportedly contained a huge mass of red material while, in 1810, French newspapers reported a shower of red snow (together with a fall of insects) fell over Paris. Even in the United States, the *Monthly Weather Review* has reported occurrences of reddish snow. In 1895, residents of Alma, Colorado, found themselves in the midst of a pink snowstorm. "The voluntary observer,

Mr. W. H. Powless, at Alma reports that on the evening of April 14 . . . the snow that fell was tinged with pink. Those who were out in this snow reported their clothing covered with a deposit resembling mud."

The Colorado account touches upon one explanation for a number of the red snow reports, specifically the occurrence of dust storms. In the case of the 1895 snow event, the observer noted that, coincident with the Colorado pink snow, "showers of mud fell in Oklahoma . . . The number of cattle killed is estimated at five thousand and a score of these were smothered. Drifts of sand six feet deep were reported along the railroad tracks of western Kansas." In a similar situation, national park rangers at the ancient Pueblo ruins in Mesa Verde during the Dust Bowl days of the 1930s reported to *Monthly Weather Review* of an occurrence of red snow following massive dust storms through the Southwest and Central Great Plains.

Blood snows in the polar or alpine regions have a quite different explanation. British Naval Captain John Ross is one of the first recognized explorers who observed polar red snow. In 1818, he discovered and photographed extensive deposits of red snow near Cape York, Greenland, in a region that he gave the apt name Crimson Cliffs. According to his report, these cliffs were several hundred feet high and extended for at least eight miles. Ross described the color of the cliffs as a faint, dirty, dull red. Upon arriving at the area, the Arctic explorer found the snow was speckled with small round red particles. The expedition's botanist concluded that the particles were vegetable in nature but couldn't identify from what plant they originated.

A couple of decades later, the great naturalist Charles Darwin encountered red snow as he hiked the higher reaches of the South American Andes. He wrote in his Diary that he first observed the material described by the Arctic navigators as red snow near the summit of one of the Andean mountains. Actually, concern for his mules initially brought the phenomenon to his notice: "My attention was called to it, by observing the footsteps of the mules stained a pale red, as if their hoofs had been slightly bloody."

In a fashion that Sherlock Holmes would undoubtedly approve, Darwin first eliminated the obvious in his determination of the cause of the reddish color. "I thought at first that [the red snow] was owing to dust blown from the surrounding mountains . . . for the groups of these microscopical plants appeared like coarse particles." He began detailed observations. First, he determined that the snow became red only when it was thawed rapidly or when it been accidentally crushed. Second, after he rubbed a bit of the red material on paper, he saw that the paper was marked a faint rose tinge mingled with a little brick-red. Finally, he scraped some substance off the paper, and found under the microscope that it consisted of "groups of little spheres in colorless cases, each the thousandth part of an inch in diameter." From that point, Darwin soon discovered that the spheres were actually collections of a type of algae.

Actually, the first scientist to publish the algae explanation for the red snow phenomenon was R. J. Shuttleworth, an English naturalist residing in Switzerland. Shuttleworth published in a technical journal regarding his detailed examination of red snow collected near the Hospice du Grimsel in the Swiss Alps. He said that the snow contained a number of minute algae organisms, primarily *Protococcus nivalis*.

(2) Yellow Snow, Black Snow

Besides the many crude jokes associated with yellow snow, actual and reliable observations of such colored snow have been made through history. For example, residents of South Bethlehem, Pennsylvania, reported a fall of yellow snow in March 1879. Using microscopic study of some of the sample, the Surgeon-General of the U.S. Army at that time concluded that the yellow color was "due to the presence of the pollen of pine trees that were then in bloom throughout the States farther south."

A 1902 issue of *Monthly Weather Review* contains a Michigan newspaper's account about a similarly colored snow, "From 3:40 to 5 P.M. occurred the unusual phenomenon of a fall of snow of a dull yellowish tint . . . It is reported that this yellow snowfall extended eastward of the station about twelve miles and northward about the same distance to Muskegon." However, in this case, the Michigan State Geologist determined that the snow contained quantities of the fine clay-based soil found in Wisconsin and Iowa called loess. Consequently, the scientist concluded a Wisconsin windstorm likely picked up the loess, carried it across Lake Michigan before dumping it as a yellow-tinted snowfall in Michigan.

Even in modern times, reports of yellow snow continue to be made. The 1995 fortean book *Encyclopedia of the Unexplained* (by Randles and Hough) recounted that, in March 1991, a large weather system traveling through central Europe and into Scandinavia produced up to a foot-thick cover of yellow snow in parts of northern Finland. Modern chemical analysis of the snow showed that the yellow particles in it were similar to sand found in Africa.

The occurrence of black snow generally suggests the presence of soot or ash from a fire. Black snows have been reported in New York State in 1889, over most of Indiana in 1895, Broughton, Illinois, in 1919, and over Yellville, Arkansas over in 1940. All of these black snows had professional assessments of being either smoky in texture or taste (suggesting that ash or soot from fires was caught up in the snow) or muddy (suggesting that dark soil sediments were picked up in dust storms and then dumped out with snow downwind of the original location).

(3) Snowrollers and Other Natural Snow Formations

On a few very rare occasions, nature creates fantastic works of beauty and strangeness out of snow. Reverend D. A. Clark

observed one of these occasions in January of 1809 when he witnessed the formation of natural snowballs, commonly called
snow rollers. He wrote in the *American Journal of Science* that, after a
snowfall of three-fourths of an inch, the sky abruptly cleared, the
temperature dropped and the wind suddenly picked up speed. At
this point, according to Clark, "Nature now began her sport."
Bits of snow were blown along the icy snow crust a foot or two so
that the core of a snowball was formed, and then continued to be
rolled by the wind, accumulating more snow during the process.
Eventually, some of the natural snowballs reached the edge of
hills whereupon gravity, aided by the wind, allowed the snow
rollers to accumulate even more snow until they reached the
bottom of the hill and were of the size of a barrel and some even
larger. According to Clark, "thus the whole creation as far as the
eye could see, was covered with snow balls differing in size, from
that of a lady's muff, to the diameter of two and half or three feet,
hollow at each end to almost the very center, and all as true as so
many logs shaped in a lathe." He noted, as do people even today,

Nature's natural snowballs: Snow rollers on Fossil Lake near Russell
Kansas taken on December 18, 2000. (Photo Courtesy of John Sten-
nard, County Extension Agent, Russell County Kansas.)

that "the oldest men in the neighborhood had never witnessed the like phenomenon, and all were filled with amazement at the spectacle which the fields exhibited in the morning."

Renowned writer Henry David Thoreau in midnineteenth century wrote a detailed description of snow rollers and even penned a drawing of one of the cylindrical snowballs in his journal. And the phenomenon still occasionally takes place even today. For example, Decatur, Illinois, television station WPVI broadcast a report that residents of that city awoke on February 12, 2003, to find that natural snow rollers had formed in many of the front yards around town.

Another odd snow formation is the so-called snow mushroom. Snow mushrooms are sometimes formed in forested snowy areas after a tree is felled. Basically, snow collects into the shape of a cap on top of the tree stump that forms the stalk of the mushroom. According to some authorities, in order for the snow mushrooms to be of perfect shape, a number of factors need to be present in just the right quantities. First, the felled tree trunks need to be of a certain size, neither too big nor too small. Second, there must be just the right amount of snow (given the size of the tree stump). Finally, the height of the stump must correspond to the size of the stump and the amount of snow. In other words, conditions have to be almost unique. Beautiful snow mushrooms were photographed in the journal *Scientific American* in 1902.

In 1860, the noted physicist John Tyndall, in his book *The Glaciers of the Alps,* first observed another odd snow formation on the summit of Monte Rosa in Europe. He described an odd snow and ice formation that resembled frozen flowers, "All of them were six-leafed; some of the leaves threw out lateral ribs like ferns; some were rounded, others arrowy and serrated; some were close, others reticulated, but there was no deviation from the six-leafed type." Yet Tyndall also had a bit of the poetic in him for he continued his description of the snow flowers as "lovely blossoms of the frost; and had a spirit of the mountain inquired my choice—the view or the frozen flowers—I should have hesitated before giving up that exquisite vegetation. It was wonderful to think as well as beautiful to behold."

(4) Bug Snow

As far back as 1749, occurrences of worm snow have been reported. In one of the first, the King of Sweden's chamberlain received reports from Leufsta, Sweden, of snowfalls with living worms and insects of various kinds. Indeed, supposedly the chamberlain actually was shown several worms that had dropped on people's hats. To ensure that the worms had actually fallen and not crawled out of the ground below the snow, the chamberlain had the snow dug up where these worms had been witnessed and found several that appeared to be only on the surface of the snow. He concluded that it was impossible that they could have come from under the ground, which was then frozen more than three feet deep.

Other bug snows have occurred since then—many in Eastern Europe and Russia—including a few twentieth-century reports. A number of fortean reports detail that during a Swiss snowstorm in March 1922, thousands of insects, including spiders, caterpillars, and huge ants fell on many mountains in the Swiss Alps. According to newspaper accounts of the time, "Local naturalists are unable to explain the phenomenon, but one theory is that the insects were blown in on the wind from a warmer climate."

(5) Blizzards

Blizzards have long been influencing the history of the United States and the world. Indeed, at the same time that the Jamestown colony in Virginia was struggling to survive the terrible winter of 1607 and thirteen years before the foundation of the Plymouth colony, a blizzard played a tragic role in the fate of a British colony at Sagadahoc County, Maine, according to Frazier's 1979 book *The Violent Face of Nature*. The colony's location was at the mouth of the Kennebec River, across the bay from present-day Portland. However, the particularly severe winter of 1607 with blizzard winds and snow led to horrific starvation and suffering in the small colony. Fully half of all the inhabitants of the settlement perished in that bitterly cold season. Finally, when a supply ship eventually arrived in June of 1608, the remaining half elected to return to England and abandon the colony rather than suffer another winter in the Americas.

The origin of the word "blizzard" itself as a reference to a massive wind-driven snow event is somewhat debatable but the best claimant is an Iowa newspaper, the Esterville *Vindicator*. Before the

Frozen livestock after a March 1966 blizzard in Brookings, South Dakota. (Photo Courtesy of National Oceanic and Atmospheric Administration/Department of Commerce Photo Library Historic NWS Collection.)

Vindicator's usage, *blizzard* originally meant "a stunning blow," such as a boxer's knockout punch. Even Davy Crockett used the word to refer to "taking a blizzard" (in this case a rifle shot) at a deer. Then, on March 24, 1870, the Iowa newspaper editor used the word (although with only one *z*) to describe a severe snowstorm that had "K.O.'ed" his city. Within a year, an Iowa baseball team changed its name to the Blizzards. Within ten years, many New York and Canadian newspapers were using the term.

In the 1800s, blizzards were all too familiar occurrences. A summary of blizzards described in a 1948 *Report of the Kansas State Board of Agriculture* contained a graphic account of a Kansas blizzard in 1886. That blizzard froze scores of settlers who were living in makeshift houses, as well as cowboys and travelers who became bewildered and lost when landmarks were obliterated. But worse still was the cattle loss. The Garden City, Kansas, *News* reported that dead frozen cattle were piled up along the railroad tracks in such an extent that they had to be cleared up before trains could pass.

One of the worst (and most recounted) blizzards in American history is the infamous Great Blizzard of 1888. This storm—a nor'easter that pulled massive warm moist air from the Atlantic over cold Arctic air pouring in from Canada—produced seventy-mile-per-hour winds in New York City that piled up continually falling snow into twenty-foot plus drifts. More than four hundred people were killed in the storm and thousands more were marooned in the city.

One of those who died was Senator Roscoe Conkling. He had left his Wall Street office and tried to reach the New York Club by walking through the blizzard. When he reached Union Square, he became stranded in a snowdrift but quickly became buried. After a huge struggle, he did manage to free himself from the drift. Unfortunately, when Conkling did finally arrive at his club and had a drink, he fell in a delirium and eventually died the next day.

Another story of the Blizzard of 1888 is a bit more comic but also points out the incredibly effects of the snowstorm. A businessman by the name of C. H. McDonald was struggling through a snowdrift when he abruptly collided with a hard object, giving himself a nasty gash on his head. Investigating the frozen object, McDonald found it to be the hoof of a dead horse. He later told friends that he was the only man ever to be kicked in the head by a dead horse.

(6) Snow in Odd Places

Normally we think of snow as only occurring in certain places, such as mountains or northern places. Yet, occasionally, nature throws some snow in very odd places. One of my prized possessions is a T-shirt that reads "I Survived the Great Phoenix Blizzard of 1990" that commemorates a light dusting of snow that the desert city received in late December of that year.

Other equally odd—normally warm—places have sporadically received measurable snowfall. On January 20, 1977, coverage of national and international events, even news about the U.S. presidential inauguration, was relegated to inside pages of newspapers around the world to allow coverage of one very strange weather event: It snowed in Miami! Why was this event a major news story? Because it had never happened before in recorded history—at least as far back as our existing weather records go. In 1977, snow fell as far south as the suburb of Homestead (a town made more famous fifteen years later when it was the target of Hurricane Andrew) located about twenty-three miles south of Miami. At the time, a local Miami hardware store even put up a sign stating, "Today's Special: Snow Shovels."

Snow has actually fallen in the Saharan Desert a few times in the last century. In February 1979, enough snow fell in southern Algeria during a rare half-hour winter storm that the accumulated snow briefly stopped traffic in one town. In a similar fashion, while rare, snow can fall in the Middle East and, perhaps not surprisingly, can sometimes lead to religious problems. According to John Kohut and Roland Sweet in their 1993 book *News from the Fringe,* a snowstorm that struck Jerusalem in 1992 led to the accidental cutting of the Eruv, an eighty-mile long rope that completely surrounds the city. For ultraorthodox Jews, the Eruv symbolically morphs the city into a single dwelling, thereby permitting those residents to carry objects outside of their individual homes without violating the strict injunctions of the Sabbath. Following the rare snowstorm, notice had to be given that until the rope was repaired, ultraorthodox Jews in Jerusalem would be forbidden from walking with young children in carriages or even carrying food outside of their houses on the Sabbath.

(7) Snowflake Classification

Many people take the observation that "no two snowflakes are alike" as an article of faith. But has anybody ever looked? Actually, believe it or not, quite a few people—even famous people—have devoted a considerable part of their lives doing exactly that. Famous astronomer Johannes Kepler was one of the first people to describe in detail the six-sided symmetry of a snow crystal. Kepler even wrote a book entitled *Concerning Hexagonal Snow* in 1611. A few years later, the French philosopher and mathematician René Descartes penned one of the first detailed accounts of snow crystal structure in 1637.

However, one person stands far above the rest with regard to snowflake research. That person is Wilson A. Bentley, resident of the small town of Jericho, Vermont. Bentley, who has since become known as the Snowflake Man, dedicated his entire life to the study and photography of snowflakes. In 1884, he constructed a relatively simple but effective camera system for photographing snow crystals and, for the next forty years, he developed nearly six thousand detailed photographs of snow crystals. Toward the end of his life in

The Snowflake Man, Wilson A. Bentley, demonstrating his snowflake photo-
graphic equipment. (Photo Courtesy of National Oceanic and Atmospheric
Administration/Department of Commerce Photo Library Historic NWS
Collection.)

1931, he published a book entitled *Snow Crystals* that contained two
thousand of his best photographs of snow and frost. As he penned
in 1902, "it seems hardly necessary to add that this most charming
and delightful branch of nature study is as yet at its beginning; it
still processes the charm of novelty; many of its problems are
unsolved, and many will find its pursuit a source of great pleasure
and instruction."

Japan's equivalent to Bentley was Ukichiro Nakaya, a professor of
physics at Hokkaido University. He also began a systematic investigation of snow in which he collected over twenty-two hundred photographs. Nakaya took Bentley's work one step further by creating a
detailed classification of snow. In fact, a group called the International Commission on Snow and Ice codified Nakaya's snowflake
work by devising a classification system that recognizes seven basic
forms of snow crystals: plate crystal, stellar crystal, column, needle,
spatial dendrite, capped column, and irregular crystals.

But has any scientist ever found two identical snowflakes? Canadian weather historian David Phillips mentioned that snow researchers from Boulder, Colorado, announced the discovery of two identical snow crystals. The crystals were columnlike with vase-shaped hollow centers. Phillips added, however, after closer inspection, tiny but important variations in structure and form were discovered.

Kenneth Libbrecht, a physics professor and snow expert at the California Institute of Technology, addressed the elusive snowflake question from a more philosophical view. He wrote in his book, *The Snowflake: Winter's Secret Beauty* that the question of identical snowfalls is "almost like a Zen koan." He stated that unless one can check all possible snowflakes, it is really impossible to tell if two identical snowflakes have fallen. That being the case, he nevertheless has begun a scientific search for an eventual answer by studying the multitude of snow-crystal characteristics and their repeatability in nature.

(8) Avalanches

Avalanches have occurred throughout human history, often with devastating results. As early as 1618, one of the earliest recorded avalanches crushed the Swiss town of Plurs. It killed all but four of the fifteen hundred residents (and that was only because the four had been away from town). Even in the United States, avalanches have caused massive death and destruction. The town of Wellington, Washington, was a small railroad maintenance and refueling station located at the west entrance to a tunnel through the Cascade Mountains in the Stevens Pass area. In 1910, two trains—a passenger and a mail train—were stopped at the station due to two earlier avalanches. Then, as a snowstorm brought heavy rain and strong winds during the early morning hours of March 1, a huge mass of snow on the nearby mountain gave way, tumbling down the valley. Within seconds, both trains and several buildings were pushed down into the canyon. Ninety-six people were killed and several of the twenty-two survivors were seriously injured. Miraculously the avalanche missed a small but crowded hotel at the station.

The danger of avalanches has led to the creation of rescue services around the world. One of the earliest was set up over a particularly treacherous but important mountain pass in the European Alps now known as the Pass of the Great St. Bernard. In the Middles Ages, Bernard de Menthon originated the idea of a rescue service and hospice at this pass to aid travelers. History has honored his idea—and him. Bernard was canonized as a saint and, since AD 1050, the Hospice of the Great St. Bernard has

A plate from "Studies among the Snow Crystals . . ." by Wilson Bentley, "The Snowflake Man" taken from the 1902 Annual Summary of the *Monthly Weather Review*. (Photo Courtesy of National Oceanic and Atmospheric Administration/Department of Commerce Photo Library Historic NWS Collection.)

welcomed and aided mountain travelers and hikers. To help them in performing their rescue service, the monks of the hospice bred a particularly useful breed of dog. The massive Saint Bernard dog breed originated from native dogs of the lower valleys that were bred with large mastiff-type dogs brought by Roman armies. The monks brought some of these dogs to the hospice for use as watchdogs and companions, and began a breeding program to help them withstand the harsh mountain winters with thick coats and large feet.

The responsibilities of the St. Bernard monks and their four-legged companions sometimes led them into fatal danger. For example, in the winter of 1825, a party of three monks set out with two dogs to search for travelers in terrible weather. They managed to meet one traveler, whom they were guiding to the hospice, when an avalanche overwhelmed the entire group. All perished except one of the dogs—their bodies were only found after the melting of the snows in the following year. The dogs, however, also proved invaluable rescuers. One dog, for example, was honored specifically with a medal, in commemoration of his having saved the lives of twenty-two people.

However, history is changing. Recently, it has been reported, that due to a lack of monks at the hospice, the St. Bernard dogs might have to be adopted out to locals in the area. The news article noted that the monks simply didn't have the financial resources to maintain their care for the dogs and still continue their own religious duties.

(9) Snow and History

Snow has often played a critical role in history. As far as the Peloponnesian War around 400 BC, snow determined the outcome of battles. As a band of Athenian warriors under the command of General Thrasybulus occupied the mountain fortress of Phyle between Athens and Thebes, a massive snowstorm hit. Most historians agree that if the snowstorm had not happened, the opposing army of the Spartan-controlled Thirty Tyrants would likely have overwhelmed and destroyed the Athenians. As it was, Thrasybulus was in a position later to conduct a bold night march to seize the strategic hill of Munychia and later defeat the Thirty Tyrants.

Francis Bacon is widely recognized as one of the leading scientific figures of the seventeenth century; indeed, some have speculated that he might also have penned some of the plays credited to William Shakespeare. And what is his relationship to snowy weather? According to W. S. Walsh's 1912 book, *A Handy Book of Curious Information,* Bacon's death in 1626 is strangely linked to a very bizarre experiment combining snow and food storage. On a blustery day in March, the illustrious scientist and philosopher had left his horse-drawn coach to collect snow samples in a quest to determine how effective cold and snow were in food preservation. Consequently, he planned to stuff a bird with snow and observe its changes over time. Unfortunately, as Bacon was collecting the snow, he reportedly caught a chill and was forced to retreat to a nearby colleague's house—which he never left. A short few days after arriving at his friend's house, he died of bronchitis. Yet, ever the scientist, even with fingers no longer steady, Bacon still took the time to write in his last letter that his snow preservation experiment had been spectacularly successful.

In one of the more curious links between snow and history, a snowball pelting might have been one of the immediate causes of the American Revolution. History shows that on March 5, 1770, a mob, which John Adams later described as "a motley rabble of saucy boys, negroes and mulattoes, Irish teagues, and outlandish Jack tars," moved into the community square in front of the customhouse in Boston. At that time, the British customhouse was heavily guarded by the Twenty-Ninth Regiment of the British army. After the mob commenced a spirited snowball attack on the Brits, the soldiers eventually returned fire—with their rifles.

So, oddly enough, a snowball fight was transformed into an event now called the Boston Massacre and was one of the critical opening salvos in the American Revolution.

Even avalanches have been used as war weapons. During World War I, Italian and Austrian troops in southern Tyrol used guns to trigger avalanches. Records indicate that during this strange mountain snow war, sudden avalanches killed over ten thousand soldiers of both armies in a single twenty-four-hour period. On one occasion an entire valley in the Dolomites was buried in an avalanche of snow, and the Austrians and Italians were both forced to seek shelter in the one safe spot. The hostility between the two groups was forgotten as both groups set about rescuing their trapped comrades against the common enemy.

In an incredible feat of cold-weather engineering during this odd snow war, the Austrians built a tunnel almost six miles long inside one of the glaciers on Mt. Marmolada, and in the glacier they constructed an actual city in the ice. Even as late as in 2004, parts of the ice city and well-preserved bodies in WWI uniforms were emerging from the area's glaciers. The snow war ended abruptly in the autumn of 1917, when the combatants suddenly shifted their emphasis to the Isonzo River and the alpine war in the snows was abandoned.

Finally, people's attitudes on snow and ice have changed over the years. In 1605, residents of the French alpine town of Chamonix demanded a reduction in taxes due to the damage done by "abnormal advances" of the nearby glaciers. Conversely, exactly four hundred years later, a Swiss ski resort has resorted to wrapping parts of the Gurschen glacier with plastic sheets in order to preserve the ice due to global warming.

(10) Pogonip
When tiny ice crystals are suspended near the ground as a mist or fog, the term sometimes used is *pogonip*. The phenomenon is

attributed to the mixture of warm air from the valley rising up into a cold wind that is generally blowing lengthwise in a valley such that a freezing fog descends and covers everything with minute frost crystals. A five-day pogonip at Winnemucca, Nevada, in January 1892 deposited a coating of ice to a depth of two inches upon trees, bushes, fences, building, men, and cattle. An observer at Virginia City described the ice fog coming to the area for the *Monthly Weather Review,* "It came suddenly . . . filled up the valleys and rolled up the mountain sides, leaving the tops of the largest hills like islands and rocky headlands; its waves tumbled over each other and rolled over its shores."

I personally experienced a pogonip while doing paleoclimatic research at a remote field camp in central Antarctica in 1987. It first appeared as a bright line of frosty white on the horizon and slowly trekked across the flat ice sheet for several hours before finally reaching our camp. At that time, all outside action in our camp shut down. We were encased in a white featureless tomb that lasted throughout the next few hours.

Other pogonips have been recorded in Greenland. As far back

An ice fog, or pogonip, appears on the Antarctic horizon in 1987. (Photo by Author)

as the 1800s, according to D. P. Thomson in his 1849 book *Introduction to Meteorology*, Greenland explorers had observed that the "frost smoke" could cause injuries. One person wrote that it frequently caused blisters on the face and hands, and was "very pernicious to the health." Indeed, the Native Americans of Nevada who first coined the word pogonip greatly feared the phenomenon. They believed that to breathe the pogonip was deadly because it could rupture the lungs and nicknamed it the "white death." My own experiences to the contrary, there are even some accounts of deaths from pogonip. In the late 1800s, a party of five in North Park, Colorado, reportedly became sick with violent coughs and fever after passing through a pogonip. One of the five was reported to have died within twenty-four hours, and the others recovered only after a long sickness.

(11) Artificial Snow

A new era in snow studies opened when a General Electric scientist named Vincent Schaefer, a founder of the science of cloudseeding, created artificial snow from a natural cloud. In November 1946, Schaefer conducted a historic experiment aboard an airplane flown by GE pilot Curtis Talbot over Mt. Greylock, Massachusetts. As Schaefer and Talbot flew at a height of fourteen thousand feet over an existing cloud mass, Schaefer scattered hundreds of small dry-ice pellets. Unfortunately, the scientist only managed to release three of his six pounds of dry ice because his onboard dry-ice emitter jammed. Thinking quickly, Schaefer simply proceeded to dump the remainder of his dry ice directly out the plane's window. General Electric observers stationed around the area subsequently discovered that snow was produced by the dry ice but because of very dry air beneath the cloud, the manufactured snow evaporated before reaching the ground.

Dry-ice pellets (and, in today's cloud-making, the more effective substance silver iodide) act as seeds to which microscopic liquid droplets can collide and freeze. It is an oddity of rain and snow that water doesn't generally condense directly into water droplets or freeze into snow but normally requires a core material. In the case of snow, that core is often a tiny ice crystal (and that is the fact that Schaefer exploited in his famous experiment).

As a sideline to Schaefer's famous experiment, one of the ground observers was meteorologist Bernard Vonnegut, brother of the famous author. As he watched the skies, Vonnegut thought that he had spotted Schaefer's plane. He became more and more excited as a cloud began to form as if by magic behind the plane. Then, with a bit of chagrin, Vonnegut realized he was watching the wrong plane—the "cloud" created by the plane he observed was spelling out the name of a popular soft drink as a skywriting advertisement.

(12) Thundersnow and St. Elmo's Fires

At one time, common thought was that snowstorms should not produce thunder. If snow thunder happened, it portended evil. In medieval days, a British historian recorded, "On S. Lucius's Day [October 26, 1253], there fell a great snow, and with all a winter's thunder, for a token of some evil to follow." Today, we know that, although rare, thundersnow can happen if great enough instability and coincident electric buildup is present in the snowstorm.

St. Elmo's fire—a small static electric discharge that sometimes occurs with thunderstorms—has also been seen with snow. A British surgeon in 1817 observed in an article in *Blackwood's Magazine* that, during a snow shower, his horse's ears suddenly became luminous and the brim of his hat appeared as if on fire. He wrote, "I could observe an immense number of minute sparks darting toward the horse's ears and the margin of my hat, which produced a very beautiful appearance, and I was sorry to be so soon deprived of it."

When Sir Douglas Mawson was researching conditions in an extremely windy part of Antarctica, he noticed that the wind-blown snow created very strong electrical fields. These fields were often seen as St. Elmo's fires around the camp. As a more accurate measure of their frequency, researchers set up equipment with a bell attachment to record the electrical discharges. However, the recorder bell rang so continuously that it had to be dismantled because of its irritation to sleepers.

Arizona meteorologists observed (and reported in the British magazine *Weather*) an odd electrical display during a rare 1964 snowstorm in Tucson, Arizona. Atop an eighty-foot observation tower at the University of Arizona, they could see single, short flashes of light originating at or near the ground all across the city. The flashes were less flickering and intense than normal bolts. There was neither thunder nor radio static. One of the meteorologists speculated that the unusually large, wet snowflakes were able to pull electric charges down from the clouds in the fashion raindrops normally do.

(13) Snow and Blizzard Safety

As with other types of severe weather, the National Weather Service has initiated a watch/warning system for basic snow-related weather. A Winter Storm Watch indicates that conditions are favorable for a winter storm (a storm with heavy snow up to four inches in six hours, cold temperatures and possible strong winds) to occur. Such a watch should be taken as a call for awareness and preparation for safety actions. These include staying informed of latest weather information (by radio and television), avoiding unnecessary travel, being stocked up with food and medicines, and moving animals and pets to sheltered areas that have fresh-water. Most animal deaths in winter storms occur as a result of dehydration.

There are two basic snow-related official weather warnings. The first is a Winter Storm Warning. This indicates that a winter storm is imminent or is occurring. The National Weather Service issues a Blizzard Warning if blizzard conditions, specifically winds averaging thirty-five miles per hour or higher with either falling snow or snow already on the ground, are about to occur or are occurring and are expected to last for at least three hours. The critical characteristic of blizzard conditions is the loss of visibility to a quarter of a mile or less. Consequently, with winter storm and blizzard warnings, immediate steps should be taken to preserve life.

For both types of warning, the fundamental advice is not to expose one's self to the life-threatening conditions. One should stay indoors and dress warmly in layers. Second, listen to the latest news. Often under winter conditions, areas will experience power outages so having battery-powered radios is critical. Third, eat regularly as this enables your body to make its own heat. Finally, drink water and fruit juices regularly. An often-overlooked aspect of cold is the lowered moisture content of the air and increased risks of dehydration.

If you become stranded due to severe winter conditions, first and foremost, stay with your vehicle! It is extremely easy to become disoriented and lost in blizzard conditions. You are much more likely to be rescued if you stay with your vehicle. Second, display some kind of signal from your vehicle—like a red cloth—preferably from a radio antenna or from the top of your vehicle. Third, run the engine occasionally (about ten minutes per hour) to keep the car warm but make sure that your exhaust pipe is clear of snow to avoid carbon monoxide poisoning. Fourth, use newspapers, maps, and even car mats as extra insulation in your clothing. Layering of materials helps to trap more body heat. Fifth, keep a window slightly cracked open on the side of the car away from the window to allow fresh air in. Lastly, try to keep hydrated by drinking water but don't directly eat snow—melt it first! Eating snow lowers your body temperature and thereby increases the risk of hypothermia.

Chapter 9
WIND

I ONCE WROTE AN ENCYCLOPEDIA ENTRY ON THE TOPIC OF WIND that began, "Wind is simply the movement of air." While that statement is true enough, it doesn't really tell us what causes wind. Wind is fundamentally created by the differences in air pressure (and associated temperatures). A basic physics principle is that air tends to flow from high pressure toward low pressure. Consequently, air wants to flow into low-pressure systems (storms) and out of high-pressure systems. It gets more complex, of course, when one has to consider the spiraling effects induced on wind by the rotation of the Earth (termed the "Coriolis Effect") and the slowing influence of friction. But wind, in general, is something that we understand in scientific terms.

That hasn't always been the case. Stories of wind magic, of deadly wind shears, and even of strange upper atmospheric rivers of wind abound in literature. I have collected here a set of anecdotes involving wind, categorized into twelve classes; plus, that ever-present lucky thirteenth category concerning wind safety.

(1) Wind Magic

Throughout history, the control of wind has been considered one of the preeminent divine or infernal powers (depending on who wielded it). In Marco Polo's travels across Asia and the Middle East, the renowned traveler described the island of Socotra as a land filled with sorcery and witchcraft. In particular, he claimed that the inhabitants of Socotra (which is a real island located in the Gulf of Aden) had the ability to control the winds. According to Polo, if a pirate ship raided any of their ports or sank their ships, Socotran sorcerers would cast a spell. This spell was so powerful that even if a wind might be blowing favorably for the pirates, the spell would change it and cause the pirates, in spite of themselves, to be returned to the island. Polo wrote (in Book Two of his travels as translated in a 1903 edition) that the sorcerers could "in fact make the wind blow as they wish, and produce great tempests and disasters; and other such sorceries they perform, which it will be better to say nothing about in our Book."

Sometimes weather magic occurred because of the supposed good or evil nature of the individual. Oliver Cromwell was one of the most controversial figures in British history. In his brief overthrow of the monarchy, he became the only nonroyal to be declared the Lord Protector of the British Isles and was a central figure in the trial and execution of King Charles I. People at the time either loved him or hated him. That dichotomy of opinion is quite evident in the legend that grew from the horrible weather on the night of Cromwell's death in 1658. Laughton and Heddon, in their 1931 book *Great Storms,* suggest that many British Royalists at the time believed that the severe windstorm that struck the British Isles on the very night of his death was none other than Satan himself coming for Cromwell's soul.

The famous writer Voltaire even suggested that the death of Cromwell's chief rival, Charles I, might have been indirectly related to the wind. Voltaire wrote that the east wind was responsible for "numerous cases of suicide" and noted that, when he expressed his surprise at learning of this suicide/wind relationship, a famous court doctor responded, "This wind is the ruin of our island." The doctor told Voltaire that when the east wind blows, everyone "wears a grim expression and is inclined to make desperate decisions. It was literally in an east wind that Charles I was beheaded."

Wind control has sometimes proven to be a fatal occupation. According to nineteenth-century meteorologist David Purdie Thomson, a man named Sopater of Apamen was convicted and put to death during the days of Constantine the Great (~AD 800), because he supposedly claimed the ability to "still" the winds. The stagnation of the winds led, it was charged, to the delay of ships carrying food supplies from Egypt and Syria and subsequently to a great plague that raged throughout Constantinople. Consequently, the would-be wind wizard was put to death.

Even kings can be linked to wind magic. Eighteenth-century writer Sir Walter Scott in his novel *The Pirate*, reiterated the opinion first opined by Olaus Magnus, a noted writer of Scandinavian history, that a semilegendary King of Sweden, Eric Väderhatt, was a weather wizard. According to Scott and Magnus, the king was so linked to the spirit world that the wind would blow in response to whatever direction Eric turned his cap. For this, the Swedish king was sometimes referred to as Eric Väderhatt, which translates as "Weather-cap" or "Windy-cap."

Scott also mentioned in a footnote of his novel that he knew of situations where winds were even "sold" in Britain. He related the mysterious story of an aged British wind peddler named Bessie Millie (whom Scott described as "nearly one hundred years old, withered and dried up like a mummy . . . [with] two light-blue eyes that gleamed with a lustre like that of insanity"). According to Scott, Bessie lived in a small village in the Orkney Islands during the early 1800s, and made a living by selling favorable winds to mariners. Apparently, her fee for providing auspicious winds to the

sailors was extremely moderate, only a single sixpence. Sir Walter
Scott wrote that agreeable winds always arose from her prayers and
magic—but, he added tongue-in-cheek, sometimes the sailors did
have to wait a spell for them.

(2) Sandstorms

Descriptions of sandstorms date almost back to the limits of
human history. In his *Histories,* the famous Greek historian
Herodotus related the strange story (told to him by a Libyan) of
the Psylli—a North African people who had been afflicted with a
protracted and terrible drought, which had been characterized by
a prevalent south wind. Herodotus said (noting that "I do but
repeat their words") that, as the profound aridity continued, the
Psylli decided to take matters into their own hands—their leaders
literally declared war on the south wind. Consequently, the Psylli
sent out their warriors into the southern deserts to fight the wind
(Herodotus didn't detail exactly how such a fight was to be

A massive dust storm enters Tempe, Arizona. (Photo Courtesy of Dr. Malcolm Comeaux,
Arizona State University.)

waged). Sadly, the wind apparently won the war; a massive sand-storm (raised by a fierce south wind) completely buried the entire army. Thereafter, the Greek historian philosophically wrote, with the Psylli army annihilated, their lands "passed to the Nasamonians."

In the Southern Hemisphere, the hot winds come from the north. David Livingstone, the famous humanitarian doctor, vividly described the seasonal occurrence of the Kalahari sand-storms in his 1912 book *Missionary Travels and Researches in South Africa*. He stated that during the South African dry season, a hot northerly wind occasionally blew over the desert. The wind felt, he wrote, "as if it came from an oven" and that, since the time the English missionaries first arrived in Africa in the 1880s, "it came loaded with fine reddish-colored sand." The great humanitarian noted that the sandstorm winds were "so devoid of moisture as to cause the wood of the best of seasoned English boxes and furni-ture to shrink."

When strong winds consistently blow sand over an area, things can become buried. In 1775, near the village of Skagen in Den-mark, a coastal sandstorm literally submerged an entire church under an enormous mound of sand. The white steeple tower was the only part of the structure left above the sand. Indeed, that very steeple—called *Den Tilsandede Kirke* (the "church buried in sand")—still exists at the site of the storm.

(3) Wind Trains

David Ludlum, the founder of the entertaining weather magazine *Weatherwise*, was apparently an avid railroad enthusiast. He delighted in his collection of odd anecdotes involving trains and the weather, particularly the wind. For instance, he discovered that, in 1884, residents of Nebraska were treated to the weird sight of a strong Great Plains' windstorm pushing a train of six fully loaded coal cars unattended down the rails. In fact, the wind managed to propel the Burlington and Missouri train a remarkable distance of a hundred miles in just three hours. A manned locomotive finally managed to catch up and couple with the wayward wind-jammer train and stop the runaway.

Even as late as 1965, the wind was acting as a natural locomotive for train cars. Ludlum recorded that a winter windstorm pushed five railroad cars over a distance of ninety miles across the prairies of North Dakota. The five stock cars of the Minneapolis, St. Paul and Sault Ste. Marie Railroad made the unscheduled road trip from Portal to Minot in North Dakota.

In the 1956 movie version of *Around the World in 80 Days,* Phileas Fogg and his companions improvised their travel across Nebraska by fabricating a wind-powered railroad hand trolley (conversely, in Verne's original book, they constructed a wind-powered snow sled). In reality, the movie type of railed wind vehicle was truly designed and used. According to Ludlum, Mr. C. J. Bascom of the Kansas Pacific Railroad constructed in the 1880s a wind-powered rail trolley using an eleven-foot high mast with a huge triangular sail. The railroader managed to get his wind trolley up to speeds of forty miles an hour even over a section of track full of curves and with a hampering crosswind.

(4) The Prairie-nauts

Others also had thoughts of harnessing the power of the Great Plains' winds for transportation. As Kansas and Nebraska began to be exploited and settled in the mid-1800s, a number of inventors began construction of "wind wagons"—wheeled carts with full sails that would take advantage of the prevailing prairie winds. Few, however, actually even reached the stage of testing their vehicles.

Samuel Peppard of Oskaloosa, Kansas, was cut from a different cloth. His story, told in detail by David Dary in his engaging 1979 book *True Tales of Old-Time Kansas,* aptly demonstrates the innovative spirit of this early "prairie-naut." Peppard, with the help of friends, first began construction of his prairie sailing ship early in 1860. The wheeled windjammer he designed was shaped much like a boat on wheels, with a total length of eight feet, a width of three feet and a two-foot draw. Peppard placed his boat hull construction onto a set of twin axles with wooden wheels about as large as those used for buggies. A ten-foot mast projected up through the bottom of the wind wagon's hull from the front axle. Peppard designed his wind wagon so that two different sails could be rigged to this tall mast. One measured eleven feet by eight; the other was seven by five. The dual sail arrangement was an ingenious attempt to allow the wind wagon to operate under either strong or weak winds. If the winds were strong, the small sail was unfurled, and if they were relatively slow, the greater surface area of the large sail was selected. The ship's prairie-nauts could adjust either set of sails using ropes run through a pulley at the top of the mast.

Two imitators (George Bull and Clint McIntosh) of the great Samuel Peppard pose on their wind wagon in Logon County Kansas in the 1880s. (Photo Courtesy of Kansas State Historical Society.)

Additionally, the wind wagon was equipped with a handbrake and a steering rudder. Surprisingly with all this equipment, the craft weighed a trim 350 pounds and yet reportedly could still carry a full crew of four and a cargo up to five hundred pounds. In fact, the inventor claimed that the more the ship weighed, the better it was ballasted, thereby preventing it from becoming airborne.

After conducting a short distance field test that revealed potentially dangerous design flaws, Peppard made the necessary modifications to his wind wagon and set sail with two companions across the Great Plains on May 11, 1860. His goal was to reach the gold fields near Denver some six hundred miles away. He and his crew first traveled northward to follow the Oregon Trail through Nebraska along the Platte River. At a brief stop at Fort Kearney, a reporter from one of the country's major newspapers, *Leslie's Illustrated,* interviewed them. They then continued to travel past present-day North Platte, Nebraska, and finally turned southwest following the south fork of the Platte River.

Amazingly, Peppard's wind wagon rolled over five hundred miles of the Great Plains, eventually succeeded in making it to about fifty miles north of Denver. Then disaster struck. As the wind wagon rumbled through the eastern Colorado prairie, a large dust devil approached the wind wagon, lifted the contraption twenty feet in the air, and slammed it down on the hard ground. As Peppard recalled, it was a miracle that he and his crew survived the whirlwind encounter without injuries. Unfortunately, the wind wagon was less lucky—the rear wheels snapped under the weight of the impact. So the ever-pragmatic Sam Peppard and his companions fashioned a handcart from the windjammer's remains and journeyed on to Cripple Creek to work at a silver mine. Thus ended, unfortunately, without much fanfare, one of the world's greatest early wind engineering adventures.

(5) Wind Electricity

Snowden Flora was one of the greatest of Kansas's meteorologists. He also was a weather enthusiast of the first degree who ensured that his state's bizarre weather in the first half of this past century was duly recorded. In particular, he was intrigued with the electrical peculiarities of the Great Plains' huge sand- and dust storms. He wrote in *Monthly Weather Review* that during a series of dust storms in 1912, Kansans discovered all types of metallic objects throughout their farms had become highly electrified. In essence, the friction of trillions of dust particles colliding with each other generated an incredible amount of static electricity, often commonly called St. Elmo's fire. Flora interviewed people who touched prairie windmills and unexpectedly experienced huge electric shock—sometimes enough to knock a person down! He wrote that, during these storms, it was not uncommon for a housewife to have to cover the handle of cooking utensils with dishcloths to avoid being shocked by the electric discharges.

Again in *Monthly Weather Review,* a Wyoming weather observer corroborated those Kansan observations when he reported that, during a dust storm in his state in 1894, a strong healthy cow, which had been enclosed in a corral of wire fence, had been forced against the fence and held there. The next morning after the windstorm, the farmer discovered the cow was dead—as there were no visible marks on her, the farmer thought that long contact with the heavily charged wires must have electrocuted her. Another Wyoming man reported that two of his employees were severely shocked when they attempted to cross a wire fence. One of the men received such a shock that he "was unable to take it from the wire but had to release it with his other hand. The injured hand and arm remained nearly helpless for several moments."

Most oddly, some residents of the Great Plains saw entire

herds of cattle manifesting St. Elmo "balls of fire as large as marbles" on their horns during these dust storms. Indeed, Flora reported that in one instance a ranchman in northwestern Kansas actually drove his cattle home using the continuous electrical display from their horns as a source of light.

Other people also used the dust storm's static electricity for more comical purposes. A noted British explorer P. F. H. Baddeley wrote in his book *Whirlwinds and Duststorms of India,* that, while passing through the desert city of Lahore, Pakistan, in 1860, he observed the American missionaries amused their students by jolting the boys with electric shocks from a Leyden jar, which was charged with electricity accumulated during the frequent dust storms. Fortunately for today's students, the practice hasn't seemed to catch hold with modern desert-area teachers.

Yet the electrical charge from these dust storms can also have a detrimental effect. During the Dust Bowl sandstorms, many weather observers reported that the sandstorms effectively stalled out the electrical systems of cars, trucks, and tractors. Consequently, many motorists were temporarily stranded "in-the-middle-of-nowhere" on the Great Plains. In a bizarre reversal, the *Monthly Weather Review* reported that the city engineer of Cheyenne discovered that the static electricity generated by these storms could in some cases actually start small motors.

(6) Dust Bowl Storms

In the 1930s, a combination of an extended severe drought and maintenance of impractical agricultural practices for those conditions led to a creation of massive sand- and dust storms called "black rollers" or "black blizzards." Some of the worst of these were the massive dust storms that hit in April and May of 1935. Indeed, in early April of that year, senators gathered on the steps of the U.S. Capitol Building in the afternoon to watch huge dust clouds roll over Washington. While these dust storms were dangerous and caused immense hardship on the local residents, they weren't without their odd redeeming qualities.

Edward Teele, a writer for *Popular Science Monthly* in 1935 wrote that, prior to the black blizzards of that year, a county road project near Hutchinson, Kansas, had been tasked with the removal of ten thousand cubic yards of dirt. Before the project could begin in earnest, one of the black rollers had hit and, when the workers returned to their job, they found that all the dirt they were to remove was already gone. The incredible windstorm had simply carried the dirt completely away! In a similarly productive manner, those 1935 storms—and their parent, the seemingly endless drought—provided the inspiration for Oklahoma-born folk balladeer Woody Guthrie's song "So Long, It's Been Good to Know You" as well as many of his folk ballads such as "I Ain't Got No Home," "Goin' Down the Road Feelin' Bad," and "Talking Dust Bowl Blues."

Other places of the world have experienced true "black blizzards." In Russia in 1892, a scientist wrote that a winter storm not only removed the fine snow cover over the area but also dry

A black blizzard hits the Great Plains during the Dust Bowl days of the 1930s. (Photo Courtesy of National Oceanic and Atmospheric Administration/Department of Commerce Photo Library Historic NWS Collection.)

loose soil, all while blanketing the area in temperatures of a bone-chilling frigid temperature of -18°C (0°F). The Russian researcher reported that clouds of dark dust and snow filled the frozen air and made communication between the villages extremely difficult. The dirty snow dunes (or snowy sand dunes) apparently also badly affected railroad traffic.

Arminius Vambéry, a Hungarian professor and explorer, experienced many dust storms in his journeys through the Middle East. According to George Hartwig's 1887 book *The Aerial World,* when Vambéry and his party reached the aptly named desert *Adamkrylgan* (or "the place where men perish"), the Hungarian experienced the passage of a severe dust storm. "Our poor camels, more experienced than ourselves, had already recognized the approach of the Tebbad (as this wind is called), and, after raising terrible clamor, they fell down upon their knees, stretching out their necks upon the ground, and trying to hide their heads in the sand." The travelers had just enough time to crouch behind the camels "when the wind passed over us with a hollow murmur, and covered us with a thick coat of sand. The contact of its first grains seemed like a rain of fire. If we had been exposed to the shock of the Tebbad some twenty miles farther on in the depth of the desert, we should undoubtedly have perished."

Many survivors of dust storms have commented on the prevalence of dust on everything—even in supposedly sealed rooms. One sufferer of the Oklahoma Dust Bowl declared that while shopping at a country store, the candies in the showcase initially appeared to be consistently of the same kind—all displaying an unappealing brown color. Only after blowing on the treats, could a person see any differences in them.

A few people didn't survive these dust storms. The Kansas State Board of Health officially reported that seventeen deaths in Kansas by April 1935 were directly linked to complications caused by the dust. Of these, fourteen were from pneumonia while suffocation was blamed for fatalities of three persons caught out in the open. Animals also suffered. A cooperative weather observer's report noted that dust even drifted into feed-lots and covered pastures so that thousands of head of cattle experienced great distress in the Dust Bowl. Dead livestock lying along roads in the Great Plains unfortunately became a common sight in the 1930s.

(7) Wind Shear

Wind shear is simply the change in wind speed and direction with height. Normally, winds do indeed increase with height through our lower atmosphere but when this change occurs abruptly—as under a thunderstorm—wind shear can be catastrophic. Such an event, when it occurs in a small area, is called a "microburst."

The discovery of a microburst as a scientific phenomenon belongs to the brilliant atmospheric scientist Dr. Ted Fujita, who first deduced its existence in 1975 after investigating the crash of Eastern Airlines Flight 66. As the Boeing 727 aircraft made its final approach to Kennedy International Airport in New York City and penetrated a severe thunderstorm near the runway, Flight 66 was hit by a strong downdraft of air. When the pilots couldn't compensate for the changes in lift of the wings as a result of that downdraft, the plane crashed. One hundred and thirteen people onboard Flight 66 were killed.

In contrast to the spiraled damage patterns common to tornadoes, microbursts—because at their strongest they can be one hundred-mile-per-hour downward winds blasting outward of a central point—create a radial damage pattern. When I had the opportunity to meet Fujita, I was intrigued to hear him explain his discovery. He said that he first identified the type of damage that a microburst could create in part by comparing damage patterns created by the atomic-generated air blasts of Hiroshima and Nagasaki to the radial destruction patterns found after severe thunderstorms in the American Great Plains.

Much damage initially attributed to tornadoes has now been linked to the occurrence of microbursts. Microbursts can be "wet," thereby associated with massive amounts of rainfall in a localized area or "dry," virtually invisible in many areas except for radar or, sometimes, seen as an expanding circle or wave of dust blown out of the storm.

Although we have only identified the microburst as a meteorological phenomenon in the last fifty years, the phenomenon itself has occurred throughout the history of mankind. Are there any references to microbursts in literature? A few years ago, I undertook a study of the Greek poet Homer's epic *The Odyssey*, for the *Bulletin of the American Meteorological Society* and demonstrated that the weather descriptions in it were very reasonable, given our present knowledge of weather. One passage I found particularly intriguing reading with regard to microbursts. Briefly, it stated that the great sea god Poseidon attacked the hero Odysseus by massing the clouds, whipping the waves and urging all the winds—the specific winds of the North, South, East, and West—to blow simultaneously such that they all attacked the wandering mariner together. The result, Odysseus distressingly lamented, was that "the force of all winds crushes me." Those lines appear to be a very good early description of the kind of event that we now call a microburst. Indeed, modern researchers have discovered that the mountains around the northern Mediterranean often create downdrafts dangerous to the sailors of square-sailed vessels.

(8) Injuries and Death

As mentioned above, by whipping up dust and sand, windstorms can sometimes cause death and injury through suffocation and pneumonia. Yet, even without dust, winds can also lead to oddity and to tragedy. In 1866, *Harper's Weekly* wrote that a young St.

Louis, Missouri, boy "made an unexpected and somewhat appalling voyage through the air." According to the story, he was playing baseball with other boys, when a thunderstorm broke over the city. As the children raced for shelter under some trees, the ten-year-old boy was suddenly picked up by the winds, and carried over a fence some twenty or thirty yards distant. He landed abruptly upon the top of a shanty building but apparently without injury.

An English girl was less fortunate in 1910. British meteorologist G. L. Symons personally investigated an account of a young schoolgirl who was carried to a height of twenty feet or so by a mere "gust of wind." During the subsequent inquest, one witness testified that the girl had entered the playground from the school at 8:40 A.M., and he saw the girl in the air three minutes later. Another witness said the girl appeared in the air parallel with the balcony of the school some twenty feet above the ground, her arms extended, and her skirts blown out like a balloon. Then, after the gust had lifted her, the wind abruptly dropped the girl back to the ground with fatal results. According to Symons, the jury reached a judgment that her death resulted from "a fall caused by a sudden gust of wind."

A related danger is the peril of windblown debris. Samuel Pepys wrote that a January windstorm in 1666 made it difficult even to walk down the London streets. According to the writer, flying bricks and tiles—even whole chimneys—crashed down from the neighboring houses and onto the streets. The wind was so intense that people were forced to stoop—almost crawl in some places—to cross London Bridge "for fear of blowing off the bridge." After the windstorm, Pepys wrote that whole streets were literally covered with the storm's rubble.

Similar accounts of disastrous windstorms have been reported in the United States. In 1869, Colorado was visited by a mammoth windstorm. A small town west of Colorado, Georgetown, was demolished by the storm and many people injured by the storm's shrapnel. One young girl, only seven years old, was killed instantly by wind-flung debris and her father was also fatally injured. Even the town sheriff was injured as he drove his horse and buggy into town as the windstorm picked up his carriage and dashed it to pieces.

(9) Winds of War

Wind has played a key role in Japanese history. In 1273, the Mongol leader and would-be world emperor Kublai Kahn ordered the construction of a thousand ships to attack Japan. It took some time to mass the immense fleet but, finally in November of 1274, Kublai Khan began his assault on Kyushu, the most southerly of the main Japanese islands. His forces created a beachhead on the island of Tsushima. However, as darkness fell, the Mongols made the mistake of retreating from their forward positions back to their ships. That night, a violent windstorm blew in from the north, which was the only direction to which the bay was exposed. The invasion fleet and its army were completely decimated under the force of the storm. Only three hundred ships successfully reached their homeports in Korea.

But Kubla Khan wasn't deterred by the failure. Six years after his first defeat, the Mongol leader created another massive fleet of ships, which far exceeded the number from the original invasion particularly when the supportive Chinese junks were also counted. After sailing across the Sea of Japan, the Kahn's fleet split into smaller units and began a hard-fought assault on the southern islands of Japan. However, unexpected heavy resistance forced the Mongols to reevaluate their tactics so, after six weeks of heavy fighting, Kubla Khan decided to reunite his fleet. Unfortunately, as soon as they begun to reorganize as a single fleet, a massive typhoon struck Japan and completely destroyed the Mongol fleet.

According to Japanese records, due to the typhoon, the loss of the Khan's ships was so great that a person could walk across one side of the bay to the other without getting wet—just by walking across the mass of wreckage. An estimated four thousand ships and one hundred thousand Mongol lives were lost. A sonar survey in 1980 located seventy-two wreck clusters on the bottom, and an archaeological expedition during the last few summers has begun to recover the vast hoard that includes anchors, iron ballast, vases, gunpowder jars, and catapult balls.

After the wind disasters of 1274 and 1281, the Mongols left Japan alone. Over time, the legend of the shimpu was born. *Shimpu* means "divine wind" and refers to supernatural salvation of Japan by these two storms. In 1944, Japan resurrected the legend of the *shimpu* and formed the *kamikaze* corps, the company of the spirit winds. Kamikaze is a Japanese word fundamentally linked to shimpu. This idealistic corps of the human-flown flying bombs in WWII, according to a Japanese tally, accounted for up to 80 percent of American losses in the final phase of the war in the Pacific. But even so, the military effect of kamikaze tactics is generally considered to be significant but not overwhelming. The divine winds that destroyed the Mongol invasion 650 years earlier failed to save the Japanese nation from attack in World War II.

(10) Lack of Wind

Certain areas of the Earth are noted for their widespread absence of winds rather than their presence. One region, located between 30 degree and 35 degree latitude in the North Atlantic, is notorious throughout sailing history for its frequent calms. The common lulls of this area have led to the name "the horse latitudes." According to one legend, that name resulted from sailing ships carrying horses in colonial times being forced, when becalmed in this area, to throw the horses overboard for lack of feed or to lighten the ship. A similar windless zone occurs near the equator and is called the equatorial doldrums.

Commodore Sinclair, onboard the United States frigate *Congress* in 1818, called the horse latitudes, "one of the most unpleasant regions on our globe." According to William Ferrel in his 1904 book *A Popular Treatise on the Winds,* Sinclair labeled the horse latitudes' prevalent still air as "almost insufferable." He claimed the region was so intensely unpleasant that it was extremely difficult to adequately explain the sensations to a person who hadn't experienced it first-hand. Sinclair complained the horse latitudes induced "a degree of lassitude" that was so overwhelming that "not even sea-bathing, which everywhere else proves so salutary and renovating, can dispel. Except when in actual danger of shipwreck, I never spent twelve more disagreeable days in the professional part of my life than in these calm latitudes."

Suffering such doldrums can even lead to revolt. According to Bentley's 1907 article on war weather, when Sir Walter Raleigh's small fleet endured a mind-numbing forty-day stretch in the equatorial doldrums in 1617, the starving and diseased sailors threatened mutiny—a crime almost unheard of at that time in the British navy because of its draconian penalty, immediate execution. Reportedly, the crew even refused to post lookouts for possible Spanish gold vessels known to be in the area.

(11) Wind Madness

Many people have noted on the depressing effects of continuous rain and clouds. Few people, however, realize the apparent psychological affects of constant wind. According to Sutton and Sutton in their 1962 book *Nature on the Rampage,* some of the members of Sir Ernest Shackleton's heroic expedition to Antarctica wrote of suffering from "amenomania," or wind madness. One of the participants said that the effects of the blasting Antarctic winds could cause two different reactions in people. One was that a person could become morbidly anxious about the strength and direction of the wind, constantly wanting to discuss it. The second reaction was that a person could "go insane" from listening to the first sufferer's continual rants. Having been snowbound myself in Antarctica with a few sometime-obsessive scientific colleagues for an all-too-long couple of days, I can attest that nerves in such a situation can easily become frayed. Morale can indisputably become a function of the wind.

Snowden Flora, in his compilation of reports for *Monthly Weather Review* involving the savage sand- and dust storms in Kansas during the Dust Bowl days, also noted that the consistent windstorms produced continual depressing effect on the psyche and a pronounced tendency for headaches. Studies from throughout the last century have suggested that the hot föehn winds of Europe are to blame for increased depression and general ill heath. Indeed, De La Rue, in his 1955 book *Man and the Winds,* wrote that some scientists even suggested that the suicide rate might be unusually higher during föehn winds. More modern studies of chinook winds in Canada lend support to some of these contentions. For example, in 2000, Dr. L. J. Cooke and his colleagues conducted a study of migraine sufferers in Calgary and found a relationship between strong winds and the occurrence of migraines.

People in other places around the world have also tied illness to wind. A relatively common sickness in Southeast Asia goes by the name of *khyol,* which literally means "wind." It appears, however, that this wind illness isn't necessarily linked to the wind although the symptoms match many of those given above. Patients who have experienced this Asian wind illness describe it primarily as when the body is out of balance from overwork, lack of food and sleep, and exposure to diverse weather from hot to cold to rain.

A predecessor to Charles Fort—that is, someone opposed to the traditional aspects of science—proposed a bizarre new kind of "wind" in 1871. A man by the name of Ruskin gave a lecture at the London Institution in that year on what he termed a "Plague Wind." As the editor of the journal *Knowledge* recounted, Ruskin said, "We would describe it accurately, not like 'the scientific people.' It always blew tremendously, giving the quivering leaves an expression of anger as well as distress!" Ruskin declared that this plague wind "polluted the character as well as enhanced the violence of the storm! The gloom was Manchester devil's darkness, sulphurous chimney-pot vomit (let scientific people note this) and blanched the sun instead of reddening it after the manner of healthy clouds." Perhaps not surprisingly given Mr. Ruskin's apparent opinion of scientists, to my knowledge, no work was ever undertaken on his Plague Wind.

(12) The Secret of the Jet Stream

In the upper regions of our atmosphere at around thirty thousand to thirty-six thousand feet, a strange narrow, fast-moving "river" of air blows around the world with a speed that at times can be over two hundred miles per hour. That river of wind, called the jet stream, is the fundamental result of the marked temperature difference between the cold polar regions and the warm subtropical regions. It normally wanders between 30° and 60° latitude in both the Northern and Southern Hemispheres. Even today, eastward traveling commercial airliners often hitch a ride in it to arrive at their destinations faster and use less fuel. But until World War II, very few people knew about it—the jet stream was actually a state secret.

Meteorologist Theo Loebsack, in his 1959 book *Our Atmosphere,* revealed that the Germans had actually first discovered the jet stream in 1930s. The weather officer who first observed and undertook the study of the upper winds, H. Seilkopf, apparently coined the phrase "high jet currents" for the phenomenon that has since become known as the jet stream. Because he was also in charge of navigation of the zeppelin fleet, however, Seilkopf also took great pains not to reveal his weather knowledge to foreigners.

Consequently, people across the world were constantly amazed and puzzled throughout the 1930s at how the mammoth German zeppelins, huge gas dirigibles that were equipped with only relatively weak steering motors, were able complete their flights in record time. Britons and Americans, in particular, realized that the flights were taking much less time than even the added speed of the small motors should have permitted but aviation experts of those two countries attributed the fast flights to the Germans' justifiably renown flying skill.

Of course, most of the praise actually belongs to the Germans' meteorological, rather than flying, expertise but Seilkopf kept his knowledge of the jet stream a state secret. He ordered the zeppelin pilots to lift their dirigibles up to the extremely high altitudes of the jet streams and then the blimps would basically fly with the force of the winds at unparalleled speeds until they neared their destination. At that time, the Germans would release gas, lower their zeppelins to the calmer regions near the ground, and land well ahead of their schedule.

The secret of the jet stream was not revealed to the rest of the world until 1940, when the United States was fighting in the Pacific. At that time, the U.S. military had ordered over a hundred B-29 bombers to fly from the island of Saipan to bomb industrial sites near Tokyo. One new aspect of this mission was that the bomber armada was to travel at high altitudes—nearly thirty-three thousand feet. As the planes approached Japan from the south, they were suddenly caught up in an incredible westerly wind of nearly 150 miles per hour and were shot to the east, bypassing Japan. Almost all of the planes were forced to dump their deadly load of bombs harmlessly at sea. On other subsequent bombing missions, pilots reported that as they were flying due west toward Japan, they encountered such powerful winds that they made no progress at all. Indeed, sometimes planes were forced to turn back without completing their missions before their fuel was exhausted. Eventually, American meteorologists realized that something odd was happening in the upper atmosphere and subsequently reconstructed the work that the great zeppelin meteorologist Seilkopf had accomplished a decade earlier.

(13) Wind Safety

For high wind events that are not related to tornadoes, hurricanes, or other types of severe weather, the fundamental advice is basic protection. If you are driving a high-profile vehicle (such as a RV or van), slow down, particularly on overpasses, bridges, or through mountain valleys and passes, as sudden gusts can easily cause you to lose control of your vehicle. People engaged in activities in wind-sensitive areas, such as construction sites, rooftops, or on scaffolding, should use extreme care or postpone such activities until the strong winds subside. Finally, people should secure any outdoor items, such as lawn furniture and trash cans that can become airborne shrapnel.

Dust storm events are very common in the desert Southwest, particularly in the summertime. If you are driving when you hit a dust storm, the primary difficulty is the abrupt and sometimes almost total loss of visibility. Consequently, the basic advice is to pull off the road and wait until the dust storm passes. Normally this delay is not long. Dust storms are generally short-lived and last only fifteen minutes or so for a given location. When you pull your car off the road, however, turn off all of your lights! If you leave your car's head- and park lights on, drivers in cars that are behind you may believe that you are still driving and could therefore collide with your vehicle.

Chapter 10
DUST DEVILS AND WATERSPOUTS

DUST DEVILS AND WATERSPOUTS HAVE SOMETIMES BEEN CALLED "tornado wannabees." These vortices are relatively weak spinning columns of air (and, in the case of waterspouts, water and water vapor) that normally don't have the terrible wind speeds associated with tornadoes. Waterspouts are the watery equivalent of tornadoes and can occur over ocean areas, lakes, and, in some cases, rivers. When such whirlwinds move over land, they can morph into true—and more deadly—tornadoes.

Dust devils, on the other hand, are not formed in the same manner as tornadoes. They are created by intense surface heating that causes the air above it to rise. If local wind shear (a vertical change in wind speed and direction) can cause that rising air to spin, a dust devil will sometimes form.

The oddities of waterspouts and dust devils generally involve such strange events as "how to cut a waterspout" and the terrible dust-devil-like vortices known as "fire-nadoes." As always, the last category of this chapter involves general safety concerns from these types of weather.

A scientist and his son examining an Arizona dust devil up close. (Photo Courtesy of Dr. Sherwood Idso.)

(1) Franklin's Dust Devil

According to weather historian David Ludlum, Benjamin Franklin became the country's first scientific storm chaser while on a visit to Maryland in 1755. As he and his companions rode horseback through the countryside and reached a small hilltop, they saw a dust devil forming a bit down the road. They stopped and observed the funnel as the whirlwind moved toward them, growing larger and taller until it was perhaps fifty feet high and thirty feet wide. A moment later it had passed them and the party prepared to ride on when Franklin abruptly decided to make a closer inspection. He spurred his horse to a gallop and caught up with the devil.

Immediately, the great scientist's mind turned to experimentation. Common opinion at that time held that firing a cannon through a waterspout would disrupt the disturbance's central vortex and cause it to die. Franklin, as a good scientist, decided to subject the theory to an immediate field test so he pulled out his riding whip and began vigorously to beat the whirlwind.

His whipping had no effect on the vortex but he continued to gallop alongside as the dust devil exited the road and moved into the surrounding woods. It continued to grow by introducing old dry leaves into its core rather than dirt from the road. Franklin noted that the noise was increasing as the whirlwind twisted and pulled at tree branches in the woodlands. The famous scientist continued to follow the whirlwind for another three quarters of a mile until he began to be concerned that the size and speed of the debris—tree limbs and such—could cause injury to his horse or himself so he pulled up and returned to his party.

When Franklin finally arrived back to his group, one of the group was asking their host, Colonel Tasker, if such whirlwinds were common in Maryland. Tasker smiled in response, "No, not at all common, but we got this one on purpose to treat Mr. Franklin."

(2) Cutting the Waterspout

A characteristic that dust devils and waterspouts have in common is their religious connotation. With few exceptions (discussed below), both are regarded as incarnations of evil. For example, the movements of dust whirlwinds (or *zawabi* in Arabic) were taken to be the visible signs of a battle between two clans of demons. Waterspouts, in a similar fashion, have been linked to satanic powers. Often in past times, sailors would carry a black-handled knife, called *La cultellë di sandë Libborië* as a means of exorcising a waterspout's demon.

Meteorologist C. F. Talman, in his 1931 book *The Realm of the Air,* wrote that the exorcism ritual generally had one of the ship's officers first kneeling down by the mainmast with the black-handled knife in his hands. Then the sailor would begin reading from the Gospel of John, and when he came to the words *Et verbum caro factum est et habitavit in nobis,* he would turn toward the waterspout and make a cutting motion with the knife. Supposedly at that instance, the actual waterspout would be severed and it would collapse. Slight variations in the ritual had the sailor drawing the sign of Solomon with the knife and throwing the weapon at the waterspout or simply tracing the sign of a cross in the air with the knife.

During his fourth voyage to the New World in 1502, Columbus encountered a waterspout that passed dangerously close to his ships. According to Talman, Columbus followed the established tradition of reading from the Gospel of John but then ended the ritual by tracing a circle in the air around his feet with his sword. The waterspout did no damage to the Admiral's ships.

The English explorer Samuel Purchas witnessed a slightly modified waterspout exorcism in the seventeenth century. He observed that when sailors saw waterspouts, they would draw new swords and beat one against the other in the form of a cross upon the prow of the ship to prevent the waterspout from attacking the ship.

In the days of gunpowder, cannons became the chosen instruments of exorcism. According to Brown's 1961 book *World of the Wind,* even as late as in 1889, the captain of the steamship *Pensacola* attempted to disrupt a group of waterspouts spinning off the coast of Africa. He shot a six-pounder cannon into them, causing one of them to collapse, the captain claimed, after a few seconds. The other "sea tornadoes," however, continued to circulate.

(3) Birds and Devils

Because we now know that dust devils are associated with strong surface heating and rising air, some whirlwind observations made in the past now are more understandable. English scientist P. F. H. Baddeley in Pakistan witnessed an odd relationship between dust devils and birds in 1847. He stated, "Frequently, birds, such as kites and vultures, soar about these heights, and evidently follow the direction of the column, as though it gave them pleasure."

A modern meteorologist, Edwin Kessler, wrote in the *Wilson Bulletin* that he also had observed a strange behavior of birds around dust devils. He was driving north of Oklahoma City in 1965 photographing dust devils for study, when he spotted a whirlwind forming near a woodlot. At the same instance, he spied six vultures flying "with rapid strong flapping of winds" toward the devil. Within an instance, they shot upward on the power of the rising hot air of the dust column until they were out of sight. Kessler concluded that the "vultures rose from the ground because they saw a dusty column and recognized it as the strong updraft they required for low-energy ascent to a great altitude."

Sometimes, though, such bird knowledge can go horribly wrong. David A. J. Seargent, in his entertaining 1991 book *Willy Willies and Cockeyed Bobs, Tornadoes in Australia,* related the story of a tornado—as opposed to a much weaker dust devil, or "willy willy" as they are called in Australia—that hit Binnaway, New South Wales, in February of 1990. A man, Seargent said, watched the tornado from just few hundred meters away and then witnessed a flock of birds (possibly galahs, the man thought) just fly right into the tornado, where they were flung away and slammed into the ground, probably on the birds' mistaken impression that the tornado was a simple dust devil.

(4) Waterspout Damage

Wind speeds in a waterspout are much less than those associated with its land-based counterpart, a tornado. Consequently, waterspouts don't generally create much damage in comparison to tornadoes. Yet, occasionally, water whirlwinds will strike ships and inflict serious destruction and injury. Back in 1875, the *London Times* reported that a waterspout flung a fishing vessel to such a height that, when the boat dropped, it crashed into the water and sank. Fortunately, nearby boats were able to rescue the crew.

Respected meteorologist W. E. Hurd in 1948 reported the

A 1969 waterspout off the Florida Keys photographed by Dr. Joseph Golden from an aircraft. (Photo Courtesy of National Oceanic and Atmospheric Administration/Department of Commerce Photo Library Historic NWS Collection.)

story of how the much larger White Star liner *Pittsburgh* encountered a seventy-foot high, fifty-foot wide waterspout in the mid-Atlantic in 1923. According to official reports, the waterspout dumped so many tons of water on the *Pittsburgh*'s decks that her bridge was wrecked, the chart room damaged, electrical connections destroyed, and the officers' cabins flooded. Indeed, even the crow's nest was filled with water. According to reports, the liner was forced to anchor for an hour while the crew attempted to repair the worst damage.

In another instance reported by waterspout specialist Joseph Golden in a 1973 issue of *Weatherwise,* one day in Boca Grande, Florida, a couple were enjoying themselves on their twenty-seven-foot trimaran. Abruptly, a waterspout approached the seaside shelter to which they were tied. Seeing the water funnel heading toward them, the couple quickly disembarked from their boat and climbed into the shelter. Seconds later, the sea tornado entirely ripped the shelter, complete with its concrete foundations, out of the water and carried it fifty to sixty feet. Inside, the couple were also tossed about and flung out into a thick patch of mangrove trees. Amazingly, the couple and their trimaran escaped serious damage, but some heavy items onboard, including a stove, a large ice chest, and diving equipment, were destroyed.

A waterspout was also responsible for Britain's worst bridge collapse, the infamous Tay Bridge Disaster in 1879. The huge waterspout formed as part of a severe thunderstorm and witnesses claimed that it was more than three hundred feet high. According to W. B. Thomson, an engineer who experienced the event, the watery whirlwind hit the north end of the bridge first just as an Edinburgh mail train was crossing. The mail train plunged into the River Tay, killing seventy-five people onboard. An official Court of Inquiry found that Thomas Bouch, the designer, had failed to take the winds of the Tay Valley into consideration in his bridge design and had failed to supervise the work of his contractors. One of the contractors' foreman testified, "I wouldn't like to say that [the iron] was the best, but . . . it was not what you would call terribly bad iron." Others, however, used the words "appalling" to describe the quality of the iron. Bouch, the bridge designer, died a short six months after the disaster.

(5) Waterspout Death

As with damage, death by waterspout is a rare, but not impossible, occurrence. For example, when a 1980 waterspout sank a shrimp boat in San Antonio Bay, Texas, two people were injured but a third crew member was tossed overboard and never found. A more directly waterspout-caused death is that of a windsurfer in Chicago. He had been surfing along Lake Michigan waterfront in 1993 when he encountered the waterspout and drowned.

Canadian weather historian David Phillips recorded the case of a young man in Alberta who was killed when a vortex hit his parasail as he was sailing over a lake. The man had been wearing the parachutelike apparatus while being pulled behind a boat. He was parasailing perhaps two hundred feet in the air when a small whirlwind hit him, snapped his nylon tow rope, and then dropped him a quarter mile from the lake onto a barbed-wire fence. He died on impact.

More frequently, death and injury can occur when a waterspout moves over land and becomes a tornado. R. N. Hardy reported in *Meteorological Magazine* that in 1969 a group of waterspouts were observed off the southern coast of Cyprus. Two of the spouts moved onto Cyprus, causing a tree to fall and kill one person and several buildings to collapse, killing three more.

The reverse can also occur: a tornado can move water and become a waterspout. W. A. Macky related in *Weatherwise* that a tornado crossing the island of Bermuda in 1953 killed a girl when she was hit by a flying door. Afterward, the tornado moved over the ocean and became a waterspout but still managed to throw two cars into the water.

(6) Dust Devil Damage

In much the same fashion, dust devils seldom cause damage because they are created by surface heating and have maximum winds of only fifty miles per hour with an average speed of thirty to thirty-five miles per hour. Yet, even so, damage from dust devils can occur. In Arizona, a 1902 whirlwind demolished a livery stable in downtown Phoenix. The local newspaper reported, when the dust devil hit the western town in the early afternoon, its primary focus was the horse stable. There, according to the paper, "more than half the building was unroofed and half the north wall was blown into the alley on the north . . . [roofing] sheets ten feet square were carried into the sky so high that they looked like small shingles."

In 2001, the Associated Press reported that a Texas skydiving plane was hit by a dust devil moments after its takeoff. The encounter caused the plane to injure seven people but killed no one. Twenty-one skydivers were onboard at the time of the crash. According to the pilot, the dust devil hit the aircraft when the plane was at an altitude of three hundred feet. The devil got under the left wing of the single-engine plane and rolled it abruptly to the right. The aircraft crashed into a grove of trees near the airstrip and had its left wing snapped off.

(7) Dust Devil Injury and Death

The winds of a dust devil are seldom strong enough to cause injury but if somebody is in exactly the wrong place at exactly the wrong time, injury can occur. I was once asked to investigate a weather-related accident that occurred in the Phoenix, Arizona, metropolitan area a few years ago. A giant inflatable bounce-hut had been blown up for a child's party in a city park. As a number of children were inside playing, a dust devil moved over the park, lifted up the inflatable structure with the kids inside and tumbled it end over end several times. A couple of the children inside suffered broken bones from the incident.

In another instance, also in Arizona, the Associated Press reported that a massive dust devil hit a renewable energy expo (including, ironically, wind power) that was being held a local county fairground in 2000. The dust devil hit several of the large commercial tents with winds up to sixty miles per hour and, in the ensuing wreckage, three people in the tents at the time were hurt and needed to be hospitalized. One of the dealers at the expo observed that the lightweight pipe frameworks of the tents snapped like twigs as the dust devil passed over. Nearby, a tin roof was blown three hundred feet into the air.

Finally, a lethal dust devil apparently hit Lebanon, Maine, in 2003 when it lifted off the roof of the body shop and caused the two-story building to collapse. According to the Associated Press, the owner of the shop was killed in the collapse. The collapse was initially thought to be caused by an explosion but a witness report linked it to a dust devil.

(8) Fire-nadoes and Other Whirls

Whirlwinds composed of an incredible variety of materials have been observed. For example, in 1854, Dr. D. P. Thomson observed a "pollen devil" in England—a whirlwind composed of pollen. He wrote, "The wooded part of Morayshire appeared to smoke, and, for a time, fears were entertained that the fir plantations were on fire." He reported that a northerly wind had suddenly blown up, "and above the wood there appeared to rise about fifty columns of something resembling smoke, which was wreathed about like waterspouts." After the winds subsided, he found that "the mystery was solved, for what seemed smoke was in reality the pollen of the woods."

In massive fires, relatively common but dangerous sights are "fire-nadoes"—whirlwinds created by the intense heat and winds of a large fire. According to J. Brocklesby in his 1851 book *Elements of Meteorology,* one of the first fire-nado reports in the United States was made in 1784. A man named Mr. T. Dwight who was watching a brush fire near his house in Massachusetts suddenly noted an oddity in the flames. He observed that abruptly flames from the fire were drawn from all sides into a single fiery column that was broad at the base and tapered upward. The total fire column extended to a height of perhaps two hundred feet. He wrote, "This pillar of fire revolved with an amazing velocity, while from its top proceeded a spire of black smoke, to a height beyond the reach of the eye, and whirling with the same velocity as the fiery column." But, Dwight wrote, even this "majestic column of flame" could cause sufficient damage as it moved around the field. He reported that the fire-nado's winds were "so great, that trees six or eight inches in diameter, which had been cut, and were lying on the ground, were whirled aloft to the height of forty or fifty feet."

In 1923, a disastrous 8.3 magnitude earthquake shook Tokyo, broke gas lines, and started thousands of fires across the damaged city. In these fires, the victims reported seeing huge fire-sheathed vortices called *tatsumaki* or "dragon whirls." One of the tatsumaki whirled along the Sumida River overturning the small boats laden with fire-singed survivors. Some of its flames ignited the enormous flammable stores in the heavily stocked Military Clothing Depot and even more tatsumaki were created in its incineration.

Climatologist C. F. Brooks, in his 1935 book *Why the Weather*, tells the story of the terrible Tillamook, Oregon, fire in 1933, which created fire-nadoes that literally pulled great trees right out of the ground. One of those trees, a gigantic fir, killed one of the fire crew when it fell and crushed him after being uprooted by a fire-nado. Canadian weather historian David Phillips wrote that a 1958 whirlwind created from a forest fire in the Douglas Lake rangelands of British Columbia moved over two firefighters. The fire-nado burned over 75 percent of their bodies and, unfortunately, both men later died from their injuries.

Volcanoes can also produce fiery whirlwinds. In 1964, S. Thorarinsoon and Bernard Vonnegut observed an active volcano near the south coast of Iceland create a series of volcanic fire whirls. Similarly, an immense "steam screw" rose to a height of nineteen thousand feet when the volcano on Santorini erupted in 1866 (according to H. D. Northrop in an old 1887 book entitled *Earth, Sea, and Sky, or Marvels of the Universe*). One of the largest volcanic eruptions in recorded history, Tambora in 1815, produced "columns of flame" that whirled throughout the night. One of the violent whirlwinds generated from the volcano blew down nearly every house of the village of Sangir, carrying the roofs and light parts away with it. It reportedly sucked up houses, cattle, horses, even people, and carried them to their death in the air.

Some of these fiery vortices have occasionally been man-made. According to a report in *Monthly Weather Review* at the time, when lightning in April 1926 ignited three million barrels of oil in San Luis Obispo, California, literally hundreds of fiery whirlwinds were observed over or near the massive oil fire. Analysis has suggested that one of the fire-nadoes may have even reached a significant F2 status on the Fujita scale of damage. It purportedly lifted a small house several feet into the air, carried it about fifty yards and then dropped it, killing the two people inside. Debris carried by the fire-nadoes was found as far as three miles away. Fruit trees were uprooted and some were twisted so that their boles cracked.

(9) Religious Dust Devils

Although dust devils have often been linked to evil and demons, as with the Arabic jinn mentioned above, they have sometimes been associated with divine miracles as well. The great Israeli prophet Elijah was lifted up bodily by a whirlwind to heaven at the Jordan River. In 2 Kings 2:11, it is written, "And Elijah went up by a whirlwind into Heaven." David Wagler, in his 1966 book *The Mighty Whirlwind,* argued from a meteorological standpoint that Elijah's translation might actually be one of the first reported whirlwind or tornado causalities.

The prophet Mohammed employed a dust devil in an even more direct divine intervention. Many centuries before Mohammed, the prophet Hosea proclaimed, in Hosea 8:7, "For they have sown the wind, and they shall reap the whirlwind." Several thousand years later, according to Islamic legend, the prophet Mohammed transformed that prophecy into reality in his first battle in the valley of Bahr near Medina. The founder of Islam supposedly created a monster dust devil by merely picking up a handful of sand and flinging it toward his enemies with a curse.

The Prophet then immediately mounted his horse and sprinted with his followers toward his enemies. Meanwhile, the tiny whirlwind that he had created grew in size and tore across the desert until it drew abreast of the Prophet and then passed him. The dust devil swept with full fury into the masses of Koreishite swordsmen opposing the great Islamic Prophet. In a few minutes the enemy was so blinded and confused by the unexpected dust that most of them turned around in frustrated retreat. Mohammed's first major victory was assured.

A Greek myth detailed how unparalleled love could vanquish whirlwinds and other severe winds—at least for a short period of time each year. As related by G. W. Stimpson in *A Book About a Thousand Things*, a severe thunderstorm unexpectedly struck the ship of the Greek hero Ceyx as he was journeying to the Oracle of Delphi. Ceyx drowned in the maelstrom and his body eventually washed up on the coast to be discovered by his wife Halcyone, daughter of Aeolus, who was the God of the winds. In unrestrained sorrow, Halcyone threw herself into the sea, whereupon the great god Zeus, out of sympathy, transformed both Halcyone and Ceyx into birds known as halcyons, a species of kingfisher. Love and weather plays a role here in that the halcyon bird's nesting habits are linked to calm conditions.

The halcyon bird, it was believed in ancient times, spends seven days in winter in building a floating nest of fish bones and laying its eggs. Then it needs seven more days for the eggs to incubate and hatch. Under natural winter stormy conditions in the Aegean Sea, such a nest could not survive the storms of wind and waves for so long a period. Therefore, according to the myth, the gods saw to it that the fourteen days when the halcyon was building its nest and birthing its young were calm and storm-free. Subsequently, the period of seven days before and after the winter solstice, the shortest day of the year, is called the "halcyon days."

(10) Waterspouts and Slave Ships

Slave ships plying the waters between Africa and the rest of the world were unfortunately all too common a practice in the sixteenth and seventeenth centuries. The great pirate and learned scholar William Dampier recounted in his *Voyages* an exciting story told by a slave ship's quartermaster of its disastrous encounter with a waterspout in 1674.

According to Dampier, the slave ship ironically called the *Blessing* was off the coast of Guinea, when several waterspouts were spotted nearby. One of them moved directly toward the *Blessing,* which unfortunately for the crew lay becalmed in the waters. The ship's captain ordered the sails furled and waited for the inevitable.

The waterspout hit the right side of the *Blessing* with a great noise and caused the sea around the ship to surge. The sea tornado then proceeded to snap off the boltspit and the foremast of the *Blessing* and almost succeeded in tipping the ship completely over. But the ship managed to right itself just as the waterspout hit the ship on its left side. This time, the waterspout took its fury out on the mizzenmast, which broke under the strain of the impact. Three sailors had been in the foretop when the foremast broke, and one on the boltsprit. All three were tossed into the sea but eventually saved. With the injured aboard, the wrecked *Blessing* slowly limped back to port.

William Lackland's 1886 translation of Zürcher and Margollé's *Meteors, Aerolites, Storms, and Atmospheric Phenomena* retells the amazing story of a waterspout's interference in the chase of a slave ship. The French cutter *Le Vautour* in 1804 was, according to French meteorologist Peltier, chasing a British slaver along the coast of Africa. Again, the weather prior to the waterspout's formation had been a dead calm. As the cutter pursued the British slaver, a huge three-hundred-foot column of water rose from the sea to meet another column of air descending from the cloud deck overhead. At this instant, the calm broke and a storm struck the two ships, causing tremendous damage to both. According to Peltier, even after the waterspout disappeared, the rough seas lasted for fourteen hours, and caused many maritime disasters throughout the area.

(11) Mischievous Waterspouts and Dust Devils

In 1869, *Harper's Weekly* recounted the rather juvenile antics of a waterspout that formed on the Cumberland River near Nashville, Tennessee. According to the magazine, one hot summer day, a group of a dozen men and boys, who had wanted to cool off, had hung their clothes on trees and then began swimming in the river. Abruptly a waterspout that eventually reached a height of seven feet tall formed on the river.

As the waterspout neared the swimmers, it shifted course, and moved on land and unceremoniously whisked away not only their clothes but also even the trees on which they hung! Fortunately, for the embarrassed swimmers, rescuers came in response to the loud calls of the men and boys and finally "a sufficient number of articles of apparel were secured."

Other whirlwinds have been picky about clothing but not quite so risqué. In 1842, according to the *London Times,* servant girls who were washing clothes outside of Cupar Scotland experienced a "gust of wind of most extraordinary vehemence, and only of a few moments duration." The wind carried all of the clothes that had been laying around the green upward to an immense height—most to be never seen again. The strength of the whirlwind was such that a woman who had been folding a blanket was forced to release it, for fear of being carried away with the clothing.

Willard Hurd in a 1920 issue of *Monthly Weather Review* recounted that the crew of the British steamship *Hestia* was off Cape Hatteras in 1902 when they sighted a large waterspout bearing down on the ship. Quickly, the captain ordered all hands belowdecks. The waterspout then thundered over the ship. Afterward, they discovered that the waterspout had torn the tarpaulins right off the hatches, carried away everything movable off the deck, and indeed had somehow lifted the heavily weighted distance-measuring log line "right up in the air."

(12) Multivortex Dust Devils

One unusual aspect of dust devils and, to some extent, tornadoes, is that larger whirlwinds often have smaller whirls within them. The Englishman P. F. H. Baddeley while in Pakistan first noticed these smaller whirlwinds in 1851. He observed that some dust devils, instead of appearing as a simple column, often are composed of several distinct vortices, each one rotating on its axis as it revolves round and round the whirling circle. The English scientist remarked, "This remarkable sight gives the idea of a fairy dance round a ring;—and the motions are, from all accounts, exactly imitated by the dancing Dervishes of Turkey; one of their holy exercises being to whirl round and round like a top; singly, or in company with several others, performing at the same time a gyration round in a circle, as if their dance originated in the very phenomenon now described."

Multivortex dust devils have also been observed in the United States. As early as 1902, a weather observer in North Carolina described for *Monthly Weather Review* such a group of whirlwinds south of his home in Statesville. He wrote that the dust devil consisted of four separate whirlwinds, which followed each other around a circle about twelve feet in diameter, "like horses going around a horsepower thrashing machine." The whole dust devil, he said, also seemed to be moving to the left and around the center of an enlarging coil. He watched "this beautiful and curious motion" for five minutes before it abruptly vanished.

(13) Waterspout and Dust Devil Safety

In general, whirlwinds, like waterspouts or dust devils, are not lethally dangerous, at least in comparison to tornadoes and hurricanes. Although this chapter has detailed a few examples of noteworthy deaths, injuries, and property damage associated with waterspouts and dust devils, the National Weather Service does not specifically issue watches or warning for these phenomena, except as they are linked to other severe weather. Occasionally, in places such as Arizona, "special weather statements" involving the dangers of dust storms will be issued when conditions warrant.

However, waterspouts can become tornadoes—and, consequently, cause great injury and damage—if they move onto land. As mentioned in this chapter, dust devils can cause injury and damage if their winds lift lightweight or extended structures such as roofs or tents. Therefore, I would suggest that interested people consider some basic precautions. If waterspouts have been sighted in the area during the day, stay off the water. This is because if the conditions are favorable to create one waterspout, they are conducive to forming more than one. In a similar fashion, as dust devils are normally created on hot clear afternoons, some care can be taken on such days to make sure that lightweight structures, such as tents and canopies are carefully staked down.

Chapter 11

THE ODDEST WEATHER EXTREMES

W E ALWAYS LOVE TO HEAR ABOUT THE EXTREMES OF WEATHER. Many places take great pride (and commercial success) by being one of the hottest or coldest or wettest or driest places in the country. In order to preserve integrity (and prevent disputes), an official government group called the National Climate Extremes Committee evaluates all extreme weather records for the United States. This committee was established in 1997 to assess the merit of any claim for a record weather event. It consists of a representative from the United States' premier climate archive, the National Climatic Data Center, a person from the National Weather Service's Office of Climate, Water, and Weather, and a representative from the American Association of State Climatologists. At this time, there is no equivalent committee for the world as a whole other than the World Meteorological Organization, which is tasked with such duties as creating the name lists of tropical cyclones around the world. A number of the records given in this chapter were compiled by P. F. Krause and K. L. Flood for their 1997 U.S. Army Corps of Engineers report *Weather and Climate Extremes*.

(1) World's Highest Temperature

The hottest place on the Earth in recorded weather records is generally accepted to be El Azizia, Libya, a desert location about twenty miles south of the coastal capital of Tarabulus (Tripoli). On September 13, 1922, the weather instrument shelter there recorded a staggeringly high temperature of 136°F (57.8°C). Subsequent study of the site and equipment by a meteorologist named Fántoli, however, suggested the maximum temperature at this site on that day may have "only" been 132.8°F (56°C).

The next hottest "official" temperature recorded in the world was measured in Death Valley, California, at the Greenland Ranch (now called Furnace Creek Ranch) on July 10, 1913. The high temperature measured in the shaded instrument shelter on that day reached a sweltering 134°F (56.7°C). Climatologist Arnold Court conducted an analysis of that Death Valley measurement and determined that such a high temperature has a probability of occurring only once in 650 years. Therefore, he concluded, "no future official observation will exceed the present high temperature record for North America now held by Death Valley."

(2) World's Coldest Temperature

The Russian research facility in central Antarctica named Vostok Station holds the record for the world's lowest temperature. On July 21, 1983, during the height of the Southern Hemispheric winter, the temperature at the Soviet research station reached a bone-chilling reading of -129°F (-89.4°C). Part of the explanation for the record low temperatures recorded at this location is its extreme elevation. Vostok Station is located near the middle of the ice sheet comprising the eastern Antarctica Plateau and is at an elevation of 11,220 feet (3,420 meters).

One of the hottest places on Earth: the current Furnace Creek "beehive" temperature sensor in Death Valley California. Near this site, an official thermometer measured a temperature of 134°F (56.7°C) on July 10, 1913. (Photo by author.)

The coldest temperatures in the Northern Hemisphere are also recorded at Russian weather stations. In the Siberian cities of Verkhonyansk and Oimekon, a record low temperature of -90°F (-67°C) was achieved on February 5 and 7 in 1892 (at Verkhonyansk) and on February 6, 1933, (at Oimekon). North America's lowest temperature of -81.4 °F (-63°C) occurred at the Snag Aerodome in the Yukon Territory of Canada on February 3, 1947. The United States' coldest temperature was -79.8°F (-62.1°C) recorded at Prospect Creek, Alaska, a camp along the Alaska pipeline in the Endicott Mountains, on January 23, 1971.

(3) The Biggest Tornado

"Biggest" in reference to tornadoes has many potential meanings. However, one tornado, now tagged "The Tri-State Tornado," holds title to many variations of twister "bigness." On

March 18, 1925, at I P.M. that tornado first touched down in Missouri—and entered the history books. The Tri-State Tornado was on the ground, doing damage, for a mind-boggling three and a half hours. It traveled on the ground an amazing distance of 219 miles, eventually ending in Indiana after crossing the entire southern portion of Illinois. Although an exact death toll is extremely difficult to determine, tornado historian Thomas Grazulis cited a probable fatality tally of 710, of which seventy-two were children who were killed in or on their way from school.

However, the world's deadliest single tornado was not in the United States, but in the heavily populated Asian country of Bangladesh. On April 26, 1989, an estimated thirteen hundred people were killed and an additional twelve thousand were injured as a tornado cut a long track, up to a mile wide, through about fifty miles of the poor country. The Bangladeshi towns of Salturia and Manikganj were leveled and about eighty thousand people were left homeless.

A word of caution should be given about tornado reports—especially given in North American Plains newspapers—for the subcontinent of India, however. *Cyclone* is the general term used in the Indian Ocean to refer to tropical storms of hurricane strength; it is *not* used for tornadoes. The term *cyclone* is, however, sometimes used in the Midwest United States to refer to tornadoes. I have seen headlines in Midwest newspapers (particularly in Iowa, home of the Iowa State University Cyclones football team) that have mistakenly referred to Indian or Bangladeshi tropical cyclones deaths as being caused by tornadoes (because international news wires apparently used the term *cyclone*).

While single tornadoes can be incredibly destructive, some of the world's worst tornado episodes are related to "tornado outbreaks"—the occurrences of multiple tornadoes over an area. The "biggest" outbreak (by all measures except total deaths) in recorded history occurred on April 3–4, 1974, over the Midwest

United States, including the states of Kentucky, Illinois, Indiana, Ohio, and Pennsylvania. Pouring over the witness accounts and photographs, noted tornado researcher Ted Fujita eventually determined that 148 tornadoes, including thirty F4–F5 tornadoes and forty-eight killer tornadoes, hit the region.

The most deadly tornado outbreak in U.S. history is apparently the thirty-six tornadoes that hit the southern United States on March 21, 1932. Tornado historian Tom Grazulis tallied 330 deaths in this outbreak. Sheriff Gore of Chilton County in Alabama described three of those deaths when he and his son ventured out after the storm to see how their neighbors had survived. First, they regrettably discovered one neighbor, a man named Battle Hamilton, down the road a ways from where his house once stood, "cut to pieces by barbed wire, hanging on a fence." A bit further on, they found Hamilton's wife lying critically injured in a cornfield—and, although they tried to save her, the woman's injuries were simply too grave and she died. Finally, the Gores found the Hamiltons' six-month-old son's body in a nearby creek. The sheriff said that the baby had likely "been drowned, if he hadn't been killed before reaching the creek."

(4) The Biggest Tropical Cyclone

For the Atlantic, the "biggest" hurricane isn't ranked in geographic size but rather by the lowest sea level atmospheric pressure, which generally corresponds to the fastest core wind speeds of the hurricane. By that measure, Hurricane Gilbert, a terrible hurricane that made landfall in Mexico south of Brownsville, Texas, in September 1988, achieved a low pressure of 26.13 inches of mercury or 888 millibars. Cancun, Mexico, was particularly hard hit by Gilbert: seventeen people were killed; three hundred thousand left homeless and ninety percent of the corn and fruit crop destroyed. The total death toll for Gilbert was more than 350 people.

One particularly tragic story involving Gilbert involved four buses, loaded with perhaps two hundred passengers. The buses stalled in water near the overflowing Santa Catarina River near Monterey, Mexico. Panicked passengers climbed onto the roofs of the buses and waited nearly six hours for rescue. Unfortunately, the rescue proved deadly for all concerned—even the rescuers. Four police officers drowned when the tractor they were using as a rescue vehicle overturned in the water and even two civilian rescue workers in a boat drowned in the floodwaters. As the rescuers frantically attempted to reach the buses, all four buses toppled over and the passengers were thrown into the floodwaters. Only thirteen of the two hundred passengers were saved. Bodies of the drowned were later recovered fully thirty-five miles away at Cadereyta, Mexico.

But in terms of Atlantic death tolls, Hurricane Mitch in 1998 must be considered one of the deadliest. This Category Five hurricane killed more than eleven thousand lives, most by flooding, making it the most deadly hurricane to hit the Caribbean since

Damage in Tegucigalpa, Honduras, following the passage of Hurricane Mitch in 1998. (Photo taken by Debbie Larson, NWS, International Activities and courtesy of National Oceanic and Atmospheric Administration/Department of Commerce Photo Library Historic NWS Collection.)

the Great Hurricane of 1780 that killed six thousand people on the island of Antigua alone. For the United States, the most deadly hurricane to ever hit the country is the great Galveston Hurricane of 1900 that flooded the island of Galveston, Texas. Estimates placed the Galveston death toll at over six thousand people, making this hurricane the most deadly natural disaster ever to hit the United States.

One problem involved with determining death tolls is the imprecision of tally. A number of my students and I recently completed a study published in the *Bulletin of the American Meteorological Society* that demonstrated some federal datasets of weather-related causalities are markedly inconsistent with one another. These inconsistencies are due in part to different recording procedures. For instance, following the deadly 2004 hurricane season in which Florida was struck by four strong hurricanes, the Federal Emergency Management Agency reportedly paid for 315 funerals in the area even though medical examiners only registered 123 hurricane-related deaths.

Many people might be surprised to learn that the Pacific Ocean on average has far more tropical cyclones than the Atlantic. The western Pacific equivalents to Atlantic hurricanes are called "typhoons"—and many typhoons have been stronger than their Atlantic hurricane counterparts. The most intense tropical cyclone on record is Typhoon Tip, which spun in the North Pacific in mid-October 1979. This "supertyphoon" had a measured central sea level pressure of 870 millibars and corresponding sustained surface winds of 165 knots or 190 miles per hour.

The most deadly tropical cyclone is undoubtedly the terrible cyclone that struck the Ganges Delta in what was then called East Pakistan on November 12, 1970. One of the tragedies of that storm was recounted in Chapter Five. The storm hit the coast with winds up to 150 miles per hour and a sea wave estimated to be fifty feet high. The death toll ranged from between three hundred thousand to five hundred thousand with most either killed by debris or carried out to sea when the water retreated back to the Bay of Bengal. The central government of Pakistan seemed indifferent to the plight of their eastern province. Although some forty Pakistani army helicopters were available to send aid, the machines sat idle on their airfields. Finally, the resentment and social disorder turned to rebellion and after a short but bloody civil war, the East Pakistani created the new state of Bangladesh.

(5) Rain Extremes

The official world's record for a one-minute rainfall is an astounding 1.23 inches of rain in a single minute on July 4, 1956. This incredible rainfall occurred at a U.S. Geological Survey stream gauging station—a weather station primarily designed to measure river levels—located in Avondale, about ten miles northwest of Unionville, Maryland. According to local weather observers in the area, the streets of small cities north of Unionville resembled rivers, and many basements were flooded with several inches of water. The heavy rains knocked out telephone lines, and fields were badly eroded. The wife of the local weather observer reported rainfall so heavy that "new gutters and downspouts installed on a warehouse were almost useless as water poured off the roof like the Niagara Falls." An unofficial report of 1.5 inches in one minute is said to have occurred in Guadeloupe in the West Indies on November 26, 1970.

The world's record one-hour rainfall took place in two places— Holt, Missouri, and on the Kilauea Sugar Plantation on Kauai in the state of Hawaii. Both locations recorded an extraordinary rainfall total of twelve inches in one hour. The Holt, Missouri, storm took place on June 22, 1957, and was reported by seven volunteer observers, two of whom noted the twelve-inch occurrence in forty-two minutes. Many roads and bridges were washed out in the area surrounding this small Missouri town located near Kansas City.

The Hawaiian rainfall occurred during a massive thunderstorm occurring during the evening of January 24, 1956. Measurements indicate that while over thirty-six inches fell within a twenty-four-hour period, about twelve inches fell within one hour. However, the twelve-inch rainfall in one hour is an estimate only because the rain gauge was already overflowing when it was emptied for the first time. A near world's record one-hour rainfall of 11.5 inches is reported to have occurred at Campo San Diego in California on August 12, 1891.

An Indian Ocean tropical cyclone named Hyacinthe, which developed during the last part of January in 1980, was the source of intense rainfall that produced the world's greatest twelve-hour and five-day rainfalls. These two records were witnessed on Reunion Island, located in the Indian Ocean, east of Madagascar and Africa. The village of Grand Ilet on Reunion recorded forty-six inches of rain within a twelve-hour period while the town of Commerson received 169.3 inches of rain over a five-day period. The twelve-hour rainfall amount actually approaches the theoretical estimate for the greatest amount of rain that could potentially fall in such a time.

Reunion Island in the Indian Ocean was also the location for the world's record twenty-four-hour rainfall. The town of Foc-Foc on Reunion recorded an astounding seventy-four inches on January 7–8, 1966. This rainfall, as with the twelve-hour and five-day rainfall mentioned above, was linked to the passage of a tropical cyclone over the island. In this case, the tropical cyclone was named Denise. The record United States' twenty-four-hour rainfall is forty-three inches at Alvin, Texas, on July 25–26, 1979, associated with Hurricane Claudette.

The world's greatest measured twelve-month rainfall took place between August 1860 and August 1861 with the almost unbelievable amount of 1,042 inches—over eighty-eight feet—of rain falling. During that year, rainfall in one single month, July

1861, was measured at 366 inches—over thirty feet. This rainfall occurred in the mountainous city of Cherrapunji, India, located in the eastern Himalayan foothills. A part of the explanation for such tremendous rainfall is the funneling character of the topography around Cherrapunji, which forces monsoonal moisture up steep cliffs, thereby creating massive rainstorms.

For the United States, the record twelve-month rainfall took place between December 1981 and December 1982 at the town of Kukui on Maui in Hawaii. During that one-year period, Kukui received a total rainfall accumulation of 739 inches. Kukui is located on windward mountains of Maui and so receives the abundant moisture coming from southeast trade winds.

Although the actual location is subject to some debate, few experts argue that one of the world's driest places is the Atacama Desert in southern Peru and northern Chile. Arica, Chile, averaged a yearly precipitation of only 0.03 inches (0.08 cm) during a fifty-nine-year period. Apparently, no measurable rain fell in Arica from October 1903 to January 1918 (more than fourteen years). Many dry areas around the world such as in the Sudan, however, do not have instrumentation to record the long-term drought. In the United States, the record for the longest dry spell is held by the city of Bagdad, California. The desert city went without precipitation for a total of 767 days from October 3, 1912 to November 8, 1914.

(5) The Biggest Hailstones

The "biggest" hailstone is again a term that has many possible nuances. When hail scientists refer to the "largest" hailstone, they usually are referring to the "heaviest" one since the weight of a hailstone corresponds very well to its volume. Contrary to most public weather reports (e.g., "softball" size or "grapefruit" size), measurements of a hailstone's size (such as its circumference or to its diameter) are problematic in that large hail is virtually never perfectly spherical. Additionally, such measurements are fairly subjective, anyway. A hailstone usually has lost some of its mass, and maybe length and circumference as well, due to its passage through the last layers of air, through collision with the ground, and through exposure to warm air between when it falls and when it is measured.

Yet, with that cautionary note, meteorology textbooks have noted three remarkable hailstones in the United States over the past century. First, Potter, Nebraska, located in the western panhandle of the state, experienced a thunderstorm that contained hailstones "as large as grapefruit" in July 1928. One of those icy masses reportedly measured seventeen inches in circumference, weighed one and half pounds and was certified with those measurements by a local notary public. Second, forty-two years later, on September 3, 1970, three children in Coffeyville, Kansas, found a hailstone that was determined to be 17.25 inches in circumference and 5.6 inches in diameter and weighed an incredible 1.67 pounds (0.77 kilograms) (its image appeared as a cover shot for an issue of *Weatherwise*). When a model, based on the dimensions of the Coffeyville hailstone, was made and dropped from a helicopter, it achieved an amazing speed of 105 miles per hour when it hit! The third of the "biggest" U.S. hailstones of the last hundred years fell recently in Aurora, Nebraska, in June 2003. Gene Orth, a supervisor at a local pet food manufacturer, picked up a hailstone that measured 6.5 inches in diameter and 17.37 inches in circumference.

This type of large hailstone is not limited to the United States. For example, in July 1984, Munich, Germany, was pummeled in Europe's worst modern hailstorm with ice bombs that measured 3.7 inches (9.5 centimeters) in diameter, 10.6 ounces (300 grams) in weight, and may have reached 93 miles per hour (150 kilometers per hour) in speed as they fell. The roofs of over seventy thousand buildings were torn off or damaged over a quarter million cars were damaged, twenty-four major airliners were damaged, and four hundred people injured. Damage totals exceeded one billion dollars.

But, by far, the world's worst modern hailstorm took place in April 1986. During that incredible hailstorm, an astounding ninety-two people and thousands of animals were killed in Gopalganj, India. The world's largest hailstone fell during this storm. Officials recorded one hailstone in the Gopalganj hailstorm that weighed 2.25 pounds (1.02 kilograms).

(6) Lightning and Thunder

a. Lightning

One of the world's foremost lightning detection companies, Vaisala, detected an enormous 118-mile-long (190 kilometers) lightning flash over Texas using a new lightning detection network. This incredible hundred-plus-mile lightning flash occurred on October 13, 2001, and only lasted a couple of seconds. The flash originated near Waco, Texas, moved north to near Dallas, then turned east. This lightning flash reportedly had no breaks at all along its entire length and had two cloud-to-ground positive (as opposed to the more common negative) connections along its path.

When a lightning channel is established, there are additional flows of electrons surging through the channel every few tens of milliseconds. These so-called return strokes give the lightning flash its characteristic flickering or strobelike nature. A normal stroke of lightning may contain from as few as a couple to as many as twelve return strokes. According to lightning expert Ron Holle and authorities at Vaisala, the greatest number of return strokes in a single lightning flash was a relatively undocumented account of fifty-five return strokes in Austria some years ago.

The one place in the world that experiences the most frequent lightning and thunderstorms is Kampala, Uganda, in Africa. This village reported daily thunder (and associated lightning) two out of every three days during the course of a year with an average of 242 thunderstorm days. Another claimant to thunderstorm king is Bogor, Indonesia, on Java where old records indicated that the village averaged 322 thunderstorm days per year between 1916 and 1920. This account is questionable, however, due to the definitions that may have been used there to define a "thunderstorm" day. In the United States, the location that experiences the most frequent lightning is Tampa International Airport in Florida. The airport records an average of one hundred days on which thunder is heard throughout the year.

Although in modern times lightning deaths have dropped dramatically to about a hundred people a year in the United States, such deaths were much more common in past times. The reason for the decrease is that we now have much better knowledge of treatment (for example, as heart attack is the most common result of a lightning strike, CPR should be applied if necessary to a lightning victim), better knowledge of the victims (including the fact that lightning victims are not "electrified" and so treatment can begin immediately), and different lifestyles (more people nowadays live and work most of their lives indoors as opposed to past times). Nevertheless, people do die of lightning strikes and, unfortunately, if people are bunched together, groups of people can be injured and even die from a single lightning strike.

Such a "group strike" happened near Umtali, Rhodesia, in Africa. A single lightning strike electrified a hut in which twenty-one people were crowded to escape the thunderstorm. Regrettably, that single strike reportedly killed all twenty-one people. Soccer games are particularly vulnerable to multiple deaths and injuries from a single lightning strike. When lightning struck a crowd watching a soccer game in Puerto Lempira, Honduras, in

1995, the strike killed seventeen and injured another thirty-five. Other authorities cite the September 1995 lightning strike on a group of children playing football in England as the largest documented group of people hit by a single strike. That single lightning bolt hit and injured seventeen people.

However, a scientific lightning "experiment" in 1760 almost had similar results. In a display to demonstrate electricity to French King Louis XV and his court, the Abbé Nollet arranged seven hundred monks in line, each holding an iron wire to connect him to the adjoining monk. The ends of the line were joined to the prime conductor and the capacitor. At the moment of electric discharge, to the great amusement of the king and his court, all seven hundred monks leapt in shock into the air.

b. Thunder

The speed of light—at which the lightning flash travels—is approximately 186,000 miles per second. The speed of sound—at which the thunder travels—is roughly 770 miles per hour. Consequently, there is an increasingly longer difference in time between seeing the flash and hearing the thunder as the lightning is more distant from the observer. The relationship between "flash" and "bang" is very straightforward. For every five seconds between seeing the flash and hearing the thunder, the distance increases by a mile. For example, if fifteen seconds elapse between seeing the flash and hearing the thunder then the lightning strike occurred about three miles away from the observer.

The apparent world's record for longest separation distance between flash and bang, according to a published scientific study by meteorologist L. C. Veenema, were two separate occasions in which there was an astounding difference of more than one hundred seconds between seeing the lightning flash and hearing the thunder. Such a difference between flash and thunder would indicate that the actual lightning strike was more than twenty miles away from the observer. No other reports suggest such a long audibility. The next contender for most distant observable lightning/thunder pair was recorded at Paris in 1712. An astronomer in the city noted a difference of seventy-two seconds between seeing the lightning flash and hearing the thunder. A seventy-two-second difference would correspond to a distance of more than fourteen miles away from the astronomer.

(7) Snow Extremes

While precipitation is, in general, difficult to measure accurately, snowfall in particular can be extremely challenging to measure accurately because it can settle, melt quickly, and, with strong winds, pile into drifts. Consequently, accurate determination of snow records can be very difficult. Nevertheless, the U.S. National Climate Extremes Committee takes on the task of evaluating snowfall records by whether a given station's snow measurements meets the observation standards and practices of the National Weather Service. For instance, normal snow measurements must be taken once a day over a flat surface and a snow stake for snow depth measurement must also be in place. Interestingly, a claim of a record twenty-four-hour snowfall for Montague Township, New York, was rejected in part because snowfall measurements were "too frequent." Because of the difficulties in obtaining such measurements and the lack of regularity in taking measurements around the world, extreme snowfall records are generally only available for European and American locations.

Outside of the United States, Bessans, France, is recognized as having a record snowfall on April 5–6, 1959, when sixty-eight inches (over five and half feet) of snow fell during a nineteen-hour period. This region of France is noted for very intense snowstorms that are pushed into area by *la lombarde,* a very strong southeast wind.

With regard to snowfall in the United States, Silver Lake, Colorado, a U.S. Bureau of Reclamation hydrology station, is located in northern Colorado. Over a twenty-four-hour period from April 14–15, 1921, that station recorded a total snowfall accumulation of 75.8 inches (over six feet). Actually, the record is more substantial than even that. Over an eighty-five-hour period, the station recorded a total snowfall of one hundred inches. A National Weather Service official who examined the record noted, "There is no evidence to indicate that the measurement was any less reliable than that of other heavy snowfalls, and it appears that a snowfall of this magnitude is meteorologically possible." For the longer time frame of five days, during a massive snowstorm, Thompson Pass in extreme southern Alaska received 175.4 inches (14.6 feet) of snow from December 26 to December 31 in 1955.

From the one-year period of July 1, 1998 to June 30, 1999, the recording station at Mount Baker, Washington, received a total of 1,140 inches (ninety-five feet) total snowfall, which set the single season world snowfall record. Mount Baker is located approximately sixty miles east of the Pacific Ocean at an elevation of 4,200 feet, nine miles northeast of the summit of the Mt. Baker volcano in the Northern Cascades of Washington State about twenty miles from the U.S./Canadian border.

Tamarack, California, located between Lake Tahoe and Yosemite recorded the greatest depth of snow on the ground with a depth of 454 inches (37.8 feet) on March 11, 1911. For a contender as the world's biggest snowdrift, Frank Lane put forth a British blizzard in 1891 that filled a ravine on Dartmoor known as Tavy Cleave to a depth of three hundred feet.

Although death records on blizzards are a bit more fragmentary than other natural disasters, it appears that the famous Great Blizzard of 1888 that hit New York City and the eastern seaboard is one of the most deadly as it purportedly killed more than four hundred people during its three-day stay over that area of the country.

The world's worst avalanche occurred in Peru near the mountain of Huascarán in Peru. In May of 1970, an earthquake created a snow and rock avalanche that buried the towns of Yungay and Ranrahirca in Peru. The death toll from the avalanche is put at an appalling eighteen thousand. When it began, the avalanche was three thousand feet wide and a mile long but moved at more than one hundred miles per hour. At the time, it passed through Yungay, Peru, eleven miles from its origin, and was estimated to contain eighty million cubic yards of water, mud, and rocks.

(8) Strongest Winds

The claimant for the record of world's fastest sustained surface winds (excluding tornadoes) is the Mount Washington Observatory in New Hampshire. On April 12, 1934, the peak gust recorded by a rotation anemometer was 231 miles per hour (372 kilometers per hour). The wind occurred during a major storm

A portion of the meteorological observatory at the summit of Mount Washington. (Photo taken by Captain Albert E. Theberge, NOAA Corps [ret.] of National Oceanic and Atmospheric Administration/Department of Commerce Photo Library Historic NWS Collection.)

on the mountain and observers were hard-tasked to keep the instruments working properly. As one of the staff at the observatory recorded in the observatory's logbook when the instrument peaked at 231 miles per hour, " 'Will they believe it?' was our first thought . . . Was my timing correct? Was the method OK? Was the calibration curve right?" The fundamental cause of the persistent incredible winds on Mt. Washington is the unique topography of the area that literally funnels air over the peak.

Mount Washington also holds several other wind records. The highest mean wind speed maintained over a twenty-four-hour period was recorded on the mountain on April 11–12 of 1934 when winds over the course of the day averaged 128 mph (206 kilometers per hour). In addition, the observatory holds the record for a highest mean wind speeds over the course of a month. Throughout the month of February in 1939, the observatory on the mountain maintained an average wind speed of 70 miles per hour (112 kilometers per hour). At a much lower location (and consequently more likely to produce a greater force wind) on the coast of Antarctica, Port Martin in Adelie Land also is known for its consistently windy conditions. On March 21–22, 1951, a French polar expedition measured mean wind speed over a twenty-four-hour period of 108 miles per hour (174 kilometers per hour). Throughout the month of March in 1951, they recorded a mean wind speed of 65 miles per hour (105 kilometers per hour). However, the Port Martin wind-measuring installations did not fully comply with international standards.

(9) Highest and Lowest Air Pressures

The world's highest atmospheric pressure (adjusted to sea level to allow comparison with other locations) was recorded in central Siberia where frequent huge high-pressure air masses develop over the wintertime. In December of 1968, the atmospheric pressure of one such air mass at Agata, Russia, reached an amazing 32.01 inches of mercury (1083.3 millibars). The temperatures in this air mass measured at this time were on the order of −45°F. North America's record high atmospheric pressure was recorded at Northway, Alaska, in January of 1989 when the sea-level pressure reached 31.85 inches (1078.6 millibars).

The lowest sea level pressure (again adjusted to sea level to allow comparison with other locations) was recorded by a "dropsonde," an instrument dropped from one of the hurricane hunter aircraft into the center of Typhoon Tip in 1979. This typhoon, as noted above in the hurricane section, is regarded as the most intense tropical cyclone on record. In North America, the lowest sea-level pressure ever recorded was at Matecumbe Key, Florida, in September 2, 1935, with the infamous "Labor Day Hurricane." As the hurricane passed, the weather station on Matecumbe Key recorded a pressure of 26.35 inches of mercury (892.3 millibars).

(10) Humidity and Fog

a. Humidity

The amount of water vapor in the air is one of the more difficult atmospheric quantities to measure. This is because water vapor is a gas and, moreover, a gas that is mixed with all the other gases in our atmosphere. In addition, as still another complicating factor, the amount of water vapor that the air can hold is a function of temperature. This means that the hotter the temperature, the more water vapor the air can hold. Consequently, expressing the amount of water vapor is often accomplished by more indirect measures. Relative humidity, for example, is simply the actual amount of water vapor in the air compared to the amount that the air could hold given its temperature. A relative humidity of fifty percent means that the air is holding half of the water vapor that it could conceivably hold at that temperature. Of course, this means that in order for relative humidity to have meaning, you need to know the temperature. A relative humidity of 50 percent under hot conditions means the air is holding much more water vapor than a relative humidity of 50 percent under cold conditions.

Many meteorologists therefore prefer another measure of humidity, one that does not depend on air temperature. That measure is called the *dew point,* the temperature to which air must be cooled so that it becomes saturated (its relative humidity is 100 percent). So, if the dew point is 60°F, the air temperature must be cooled to 60°F for condensation (in this case, dew) to occur. An air sample that has a higher dew point subsequently has a higher moisture content regardless of the air temperature than a sample of air at a lower dew point.

That being said, the highest dew points in the world have been recorded on the western shore of the Persian Gulf at the town of Sharjah in Saudi Arabia. The dew point recorded at that location reached an astounding 93.2°F. The highest average dew points have been measured along the Red Sea in Africa, specifically the coastal areas of Ethopia. Records suggest that the average June afternoon dew point along this coast reaches 84°F. For the United States, NASA's Global Hydrology and Climate Center noted that during the regional heat wave of 1995, Appleton, Wisconsin, recorded a dew point of 90°F.

b. Fog

Fog is created when the air is cooled to saturation and water droplets begin to condense into it. Basically, it is a cloud that forms at ground level. Generally, mountain locations often experience fog as clouds form around the mountain during the day. Not surprisingly, a place like Mount Washington Observatory in New Hampshire records an average 308 days of fog during the course of a year.

For nonmountainous locations, Cape Disappointment in

Washington averages 2,552 hours (over 106 days) of fog per year while on the other side of North America, Cape Race in the southeast corner of Newfoundland has fog an average of 158 days each year.

(11) Drought and Flood

a. Drought

The world's worst drought disaster—and, indeed, the world's worst natural disaster—is likely to be the one that created a massive famine in northern and central China from 1876 to 1878. Some sources cited a death toll of as many as thirteen million people. The situation actually degraded into starvation, murder, slavery, and cannibalism. A Baptist missionary reported that people were reduced to eating tree bark, buckwheat stalks, turnip leaves, and grass seeds. Many were even forced to eat rotten sorghum stalks used to roof houses. In one area in China the dead were buried in huge pits, which are still today called "ten-thousand-men holes."

Deaths from drought are rarer in the United States and, on death certificates, are seldom directly linked to the large-scale phenomenon of drought. However, it is likely the "worst" drought in the United States is the one that occurred in the 1930s in the south and central United States. Indeed, during those Dust Bowl days, a story even spread around the world concerning starvation riots in the United States. The truth is less dramatic. In 1931, five hundred farmers and their wives marched into the office of the local American Red Cross chairman of England, Arkansas (a small town southeast of Little Rock), and asked for food. When the chairman replied that he didn't have any, the farmers responded that they were not beggars and willing to work but they were not going to let their children starve. When they were again refused aid, the farmers proceeded to go to the town's stores and take food and lard from the shelves. Neither the farmers nor sheriffs, however, fired any shots during the incident.

b. *Floods*

As to the world's worst flood, the great flood of the Huang He River in 1887 is the most likely aspirant to the title. In that year, the river, swollen by heavy rains, broke through the dikes at a sharp bend in the heavily populated province of Honan. When the river finally crested, the flood covered three hundred miles and flooded fifteen thousand villages. The extent of damage was such that there is no way to determine the actual death toll from this horrible flood. Authorities, however, have suggested that it could be as high as six million people who drowned or were lost through later disease. Yet even in 1931, a flood of the Hwang Ho River is reputed to have been responsible for 3.7 million deaths.

In the United States, many of the greatest floods are associated with the Mississippi River. For instance, in 1993, due to rainfall exceeding three times the normal amount, the Mississippi River flooded over 13.9 million acres of land, destroyed 35,500 homes, and killed up to fifty people. At places where normally the Mississippi River was one mile in width, the 1993 flood pushed the mighty river to over seven miles in width.

(12) Dust Devils and Waterspouts

a. *Waterspout Extremes*

The scientific literature lists a waterspout that occurred off the coast of Eden, New South Wales, in Australia on May 16, 1898, as the tallest. Using a portable surveying device called a theodolite, observers measured the waterspout to be an amazing 5,014 feet (1,528 meters) high and ten feet wide. Most of the waterspout tube (forty-five hundred feet) was estimated to have a relatively uniform width of ten feet, with greater widths occurring only along about 250 feet of base and summit.

One of the world's authorities on waterspouts, J. H. Golden, has documented an incredibly wide waterspout that occurred on Lake Tahoe, California, in the early morning of September 26, 1998. His analysis of this waterspout indicated that at its largest the Lake Tahoe waterspout funnel was 250 to 275 feet in diameter and its spray sheath reached over five hundred feet across the lake surface. This is the largest scientifically documented waterspout on record. However, Captain Cleary of the British steamship *River Avon* on January 28, 1888, sighted a waterspout that was visually estimated to be over a mile in diameter.

The greatest reported number of waterspouts occurring within a single day appears to be thirty. In February of 1888, the British steamship *Earnmoor* reported passing thirty separate waterspouts in one day over the coast of Cape Hatteras, North Carolina.

b. Dust Devil Extremes

The biggest dust devils that we have observed actually haven't been on the planet Earth. A researcher on both terrestrial and Martian dust devils, Dr. Peter Smith of the University of Arizona, has commented that Martian dust devils can grow to sizes exceeding a third of a mile in diameter and perhaps as six miles high. Normally terrestrial dust devils average only ten to fifty feet in diameter and less a few hundred feet in height.

In 1947, atmospheric researcher R. L. Ives witnessed a dust devil on the Bonneville Salt Flats in western Utah that lasted for seven hours. During that time, the whirlwind grew to a maximum height of twenty-five hundred feet and traveled a distance of forty miles.

Chapter 12
ODDEST FORECASTS

A MERICAN HUMORIST MARK TWAIN WAS A MASTER AT SPECIFYING the troubles with weather . . . and with forecasting. His sharp wit and pithy writing style were tailor-made for lampooning our most-talked-about subject. For example, Twain once described the "typical weather forecast" for New England as "Probably no'east to sou'west winds, varing to the southard and westard and eastard, and points between; high and low barometer, sweeping round from place to place, probable areas of rain, snow and hail and drought, succeeded or proceeded by earthquakes with thunder and lightning." And even if, by luck or skill, a meteorologist was somehow able to produce a good forecast, Twain wasn't even certain that he or she should put that forecast to print. After all, the American master of humor observed, "Weather is a literary specialty and no untrained hand can turn out a good article on it." However, even with that warning, I will turn my hand to illustrating some of the all-time best—and the worst—examples of weather forecasting and the many ideas about this toughest of professions.

(1) Biblical Meteorologists

In the biblical book of Genesis, the Israeli patriarch Joseph's meteoric rise from slave to imperial advisor is a story of the incredible power of superb weather forecasting. In fact, renowned climatologist Stephen Schneider coined the phrase "Genesis Strategy" to illustrate dramatically the vulnerability of the ancient world to weather and climate vagaries. At the core of the biblical narrative recounted in the Book of Genesis is Joseph's masterful interpretation of the Egyptian Pharaoh's troubling dream as a weather forecast. Joseph contended that the dream involving seven fat, and seven thin, cows could be construed to mean that seven years of "feast"—years of plentiful rains and good harvest—would be followed by seven years of drought and famine. To avert such a climatic catastrophe, Joseph counseled that a fifth of each year's harvest for the next seven years be placed in storage, to provide for the drought years to follow. Pharaoh believed Joseph's interpretation and ordered him to implement the revolutionary agricultural strategy. Seven years later, when a great drought did indeed strike the Middle East, the Pharaoh bestowed great rewards and honors on his advisor. Obviously, Joseph's forecast was, as Schneider said, "one of the best" long-range forecasts ever made.

In a similar fashion to that of Genesis's Joseph, the great biblical figure Elijah also first divulged his prophetic powers in the arena of weather forecasting. As famous science writer Isaac Asimov related in his 1981 book *Asimov's Guide to the Bible,* Elijah was initially acclaimed throughout Israel "as the forecaster of a drought that was to take place as punishment for the policies of Jezebel." Indeed, in 1 King 17:1, it is stated that "Elijah the Tishbite, who was of the inhabitants of Gilead, said to Abah, 'As the Lord the God of Israel lives, before whom I stand, there shall be neither dew nor rain these years, except by my word.' "

After this drought forecast was "verified," Elijah extended his abilities into rain forecasting. In 1 Kings 18:43–16: "And Elijah went up to the top of Carmel . . . said to his servant, 'Go up now, look toward the sea.' And he went up and looked and said, 'There is nothing.' And [Elijah] said 'Go again seven times.' And at the seventh time he said, 'Behold, a little cloud like a man's hand is rising out of the sea.' And [Elijah] said, 'Go up, say to Ahab, 'Prepare your chariot and do down, lest the rain stop you.' And in a little while the heaven grew black with clouds and wind, and there was a great rain." Given Elijah's intimacy with the weather, it is probably not a coincidence that the venerable prophet ascended to Heaven in what some researchers have speculated might have been a tornado or whirlwind.

(2) The Personal Cost of Weather Forecasting?

Before meteorologists start patting themselves on the back (being in the esteemed company of biblical prophets after all), it would be best, however, to remember the words of one of our great weather archivists, François Arago: "Whatever may be the progress of the sciences, never will observers who are trustworthy and careful of their reputation, venture to foretell the state of the weather." Indeed, even if a meteorologist is willing to sacrifice his or her reputation for the sake of weather forecasting, the personal risks of meteorological prognostication can be great indeed. Renowned Dutch meteorologist, C. H. D. Buys-Ballot, pointed some of the occupational problems of being a meteorologist when he said, "He who shall predict the weather, if he does it conscientiously and with inclination, will have no quiet life any more, and runs great risk of becoming crazy from nervousness."

Throughout history, major figures in meteorology have proven Buys-Ballot correct regarding the traumas of being a weather forecaster. Most notably, Admiral Robert FitzRoy, the sailing captain of Charles Darwin's HMS *Beagle* and, later, the founder of the first British weather forecasting service, committed suicide in

1865 by cutting his throat with a razor. According to meteorologist C. F. Talman, Admiral FitzRoy's suicide "was attributed to the criticisms aroused by this work [weather forecasting]."

Even if one is successful in weather prediction, a good forecaster may find life difficult. As a classic case in point, Charles Tomlinson in 1860 recounted the tale told to him by British Major Jonathan Forbes of an old "rain-doctor" in Ceylon, now called Sri Lanka. The rain-doctor had apparently achieved a long and profitable trade in rainmaking and at long last decided to retire from his "business." The locals, however, weren't happy about losing this vital service to their community, especially as an awful drought was plaguing the island nation at the time of the rain-doctor's retirement. First they simply tried persuading the man—even offering him vast amounts of goods and money to shape the needed rains but, when those incentives failed to change the rain-doctor's mind, the villagers decided that more direct inducements should be brought to bear on him. They proceeded to beat the old magician and then whip him with thorns. The old man even tried to admit that he had no power over the rains—but the villagers didn't believe him. They dragged the feeble rain-doctor from village to village, all the time demanding him to perform his magic and tormenting him when he didn't. Finally, the enraged vigilante villagers encountered Major Forbes, who stopped the torture and took the elderly rain-doctor under his protection. According to Tomlinson, the Englishman's deed probably saved the old man's life but the man's weather problems still remained. Immediately after Forbes saved the rain-doctor, a few slight showers fell near the man's own village, while the rest of the neighboring villages stayed in the midst of the drought.

(3) Who Takes the Blame for Forecasting Errors?

One characteristic of a few incompetent weather forecasters is the ability to shift the blame for a wrong forecast. One of our nation's founding fathers, and noted meteorological prognosticator, Benjamin Franklin, even gave sage advice to such inept forecasters on how to transfer the culpability of a bad forecast. He relayed his recommendations in *Poor Richard's Almanack* for 1737 (and these are retold in D. W. Hering's 1924 book *Foibles and Fallacies of Science*). First, Franklin claimed that his *Almanack*'s daily forecasts were always fashioned for *precisely* the reader's weather—no matter the actual geographic location of the reader at the time! However, "Poor Richard" did "modestly" desire a bit of a forecasting window "of a day or two before, and a day or two after the precise day" to match his weather prediction.

If the reader still didn't get his perfect weather forecast, then the colonial prognosticator suggested that "the fault be laid upon the printer, who, 'tis very like, may have transpos'd or misplac'd it, perhaps for the conveniency of putting in his holidays." Franklin argued that because people continued to give the printer "the great part of the credit of making my *Almanack*s," it was only reasonable that the printer should have "some share of the blame."

If the typesetter is error-free, a weather forecaster will often cast around for other scapegoats to share the blame of a bad prediction. In 1860, Charles Tomlinson communicated the interesting story of the South African rainmaker as told him by an Englishman named Shaw. According to Tomlinson, in the middle of the nineteenth century, the Kaffirs of Southern Africa were starting to have doubts about the abilities of their local rainmaker and so visited a resident Englishman for his insights. They asked Shaw if he could establish the actual expertise of the rainmaker. Shaw agreed and asked the chief of the Kaffirs to summon the rainmaker for a public demonstration.

Accordingly, at the appointed time and place, thousands of Kaffirs assembled in their finest wardress. Standing before the rainmaker and his huge audience, Shaw began the confrontation

by publicly declaring that God alone gave rain. At the indignant
retort from the rainmaker, Shaw then offered a deal. He proposed to give the rainmaker a very valuable team of fine oxen if the
witch doctor should succeed in making it rain within a certain
specified time. The rainmaker agreed and set about performing
his elaborate ceremonies but to no avail; the rain didn't fall.

After the contest's time limit finally expired without any signs
of rain, the leader of the Kaffirs called the rainmaker to him and
asked why he hadn't made the skies release their waters? The local
witch doctor began a litany of complaints, chief among them that
he hadn't been paid well enough in the past for his rain. The
Englishman, Mr. Shaw, listened with a smile and then pointed
out that some of the cattle suffering from the drought actually
belonged to the rainmaker himself. Shaw asked, "If you really
possessed the ability to make rain, surely you wouldn't neglect
your own property. Would you?"

For a moment the rainmaker was dumbstruck, but then
offered a clever retort. "I never found a difficulty in making rain
until *he*," the rainmaker pointed to Shaw, "came among us; but
now, no sooner do I collect the clouds, and the rain is about to
fall, than immediately there begins a sound of *ting, ting, ting,*"
pointing to the church bell, "which puts the clouds to flight, and
prevents the rain from descending on your land." According to
Tomlinson and Shaw, even with this ingenious shift in blame for
his poor rainmaking, the Kaffir chief apparently never bought
any more rain from the tribal witch doctor.

(4) Forecasting's Ups

Sometimes meteorologists can get it right—even if unintentionally. For example, the winter of 1837 to 1838 was one of the
coldest on record in England—and it was correctly forecast well in
advance. Even with today's modern equipment, computers, and

methods, a prediction of temperatures for a particular day a season or more in advance is beyond our forecasting abilities. Yet, in the year before that cold winter of 1837 to 1838, Patrick Murphy wrote in his *Weather Almanac* for 1838 that January 20 would be "Fair. Probable lowest degree of winter temperature." Indeed, that winter day in January turned out to be, as the science journal *Nature* later determined, "the coldest day of the century in London."

The amazing accuracy of Murphy's forecast caused a rush upon the publishers of the *Almanack* to supply more copies. The first edition was quickly exhausted and the work actually underwent more than fifty reprintings. Murphy, on the strength of that cold January forecast, made, for that time, the unbelievable profit of more than three thousand pounds. In fitting tribute, for many years afterward, the cold winter of 1837 to 1838 was known in England as Murphy's Winter.

Another unintentionally good forecast was made by English almanac publisher Francis Moore. According to historian William Walsh, Moore would quickly and methodically dictate his weather predictions simply off the top of his head—snow, sleet, rain, dry, cloudy, cold, and so on—as fast as his secretary could write them down. One unusually accurate "spur-of-the-moment" weather prediction secured Moore's place in forecasting's hall of fame. Apparently, he had been sleeping one afternoon when his secretary roused him to ask, "Sir, what weather do you forecast for Derby Day [June 3]?" Disgruntled at having been awoken from a nice nap, Moore is said to have replied irritably, "Cold and snow, damn it!" And so that was the official forecast put into his *Almanack*. Of course, as it turned out, it did indeed snow on June 3, 1867, in England. From then on, no matter how many times Moore was subsequently wrong, people would forgive him by saying, "Ah, but remember Derby Day!"

(5) Forecasting's Downs

Bad or missing forecasts can sometimes change the course of history. A case in point occurred during the Crimean War in 1854. An extremely violent—and unexpected—thunderstorm caused French and English warships to flounder off the coast of Balaklava. The loss of their vital supplies resulted in intense suffering among the troops during the ensuing bitter winter. Investigation later proved that the disaster might have been avoided if news of the coming storm had been transmitted by telegraph to the Black Sea port. Consequently, France is generally credited as the first country to establish a national storm-warning service in reaction to the disaster. Emperor Napoleon III ordered French astronomer Urbain Leverrier (the student of early meteorologist archivist François Arago) to make a thorough study of weather with the ultimate goal of forecasting it.

Even modern weather prognosticators have a point in sometimes fearing the public's reaction to their forecasts. An extreme example of this is seen in a New Delhi, India, story recounted in the *Fortean Times*. In 1994, a local weatherman in New Delhi forecasted clear skies—and it snowed. Later in the year, his forecast of frost was followed by a heat wave. Finally, the television station fired him when he actually began to cry on the air following another blown forecast. According to local reports, after receiving death threats, he then went into hiding.

The BBC reported in 1996 that an Israeli woman sued a television forecaster for allegedly causing her to catch the flu. She charged that because the forecaster had assured his audience during his program that temperatures would increase, she had consequently dressed too lightly and caught the flu. In another case, the cable news organization CNN reported in 2005 that, in Russia, the Moscow city mayor even threatened to fine the weather forecasters if they mispredicted the weather.

There may be ways to avoid such a morbid prognostic fate. Perhaps meteorologists should follow the somewhat flexible forecasting scheme given in Josh Billings' *Almanac* for January 5, 1870: "Perhaps rain, perhaps not."

(6) The Government and Weather

The U.S. government's reactions to weather throughout the history of the republic might be best referred to as extreme. For example, ex-president and congressman John Quincy Adams in 1842 summarized the progress in weather forecasting as "crackbrained discoveries in meteorology" and termed a proposed weather-study office under the War Department as "interloping."

Conversely, the government can also occasionally see when a weather forecast can be an extremely powerful tool—such as in the case of war. Willis L. Moore of the U.S. Weather Bureau proved this to President McKinley at the beginning of the Spanish-American War when he stated that more ships had been sunk by weather than by war, and that a weather warning service should be immediately put into force. Moore wrote in *American Mercury* for September 1927 that the tropical weather prediction service's origins lie in a meeting he had with his boss, Secretary of Agriculture James Wilson. Following that meeting, Wilson took Moore directly to see President McKinley. There, according to Moore, McKinley carefully studied the various weather maps that the meteorologist had brought to the meeting. Then the president suddenly turned to the agriculture secretary and said, "Wilson, I am more afraid of a West Indian hurricane then I am of the entire Spanish navy." Afterward he turned back to Moore and ordered, "Get this service inaugurated at the earliest possible moment." And so, the start of American hurricane forecasting was begun as a war necessity against an enemy potentially more dangerous than any human foe at the time.

(7) Forecasts and Warnings

For some time, the Weather Service and its forbearers had difficulty in stating their fundamental goal. Although the Signal Corps' forecasting began on November 8, 1870, when it posted a storm warming for the Great Lakes, the Corps' weather predictions were only referred to as "probabilities" until the end of 1876. After that, weather "indications" became the accepted expression. Only after 1889 did the Signal Corps switch the term used for their weather predictions to "forecasts."

While such weather forecasts can be of incredible value, it was thought at one time that some of them could also lead to widespread panic. In the Weather Bureau regulations for the year 1905, governmental weather officials decreed that "forecasts of tornadoes [are] prohibited." This brusque clause was repeated verbatim in the revised regulations published in 1915 and again in 1934. The reason that forecasters were given for this rather draconian instruction was that "it would cause public alarm and panic." As such, meteorologists were instructed to forecast local thunderstorms but specifically not to mention the word "tornado." That policy was finally dropped in 1938.

This early concern for avoiding panic and misinformation—and the independence of weather staff—sometime forced the Weather Bureau publicly to rebut the claims of its own employees. After the terrible St. Louis tornado of 1896, Professor H. A. Hazen of the Weather Bureau apparently advocated in public interviews "the planting of forests on the southwestern edge of cities and the discharge of dynamite bombs" as means for protection against tornadoes. The Chief of the Weather Bureau at that time wrote in *Monthly Weather Review* that "it should be clearly understood that the Weather Bureau . . . does not endorse the theories set forth in the interviews above referred to . . . From personal observation of the havoc wrought by several tornadoes, I am fully convinced that any attempt to destroy them by the means suggested will be a failure."

(8) The Spider Forecaster

Those who are close to nature, such as farmers, have often employed plants, animals, and insects as fairly reliable forecasters. But, during the Napoleonic Wars, there is an interesting case of where spider forecasting may have won a battle. Frank Cowan, in his 1865 book *Curious Facts in the History of Insects,* recounted the bizarre story of a Frenchman named Quatremer Disjonval who was an officer in the Holland army and a supporter of the Dutch resistance. During a battle with the Prussians, Disjoval was captured and imprisoned in a dusty, spider-infested prison cell. During his long confinement, the Frenchman used his time to watch his cellmates, the spiders, and discovered that their habits and web design could be used to forecast changes in the weather. Reportedly, over time, he became so adept at reading spider movements and webs to the point that he could foretell the approach of severe weather an astounding ten to fourteen days in advance.

While Disjonval still languished in a Prussian spider-filled prison cell, French troops invaded Holland in the winter of 1794. They moved quickly over the ice-covered seas and rivers but the French army was in grave danger of being stranded in Holland if there was a sudden and unexpected thaw. The situation was so grave that the French generals were seriously considering a Dutch offer of a large bribe to withdraw their armies.

From his jail cell, Disjonval saw a chance at gaining his freedom and wrote a long letter to one of the French generals in 1795 in which he assured the general that, based on his observations with spiders, within fourteen days there would be a hard and severe frost. Such a frost would ensure that the French would be able to cross the frozen rivers and canals, thereby allowing them to continue their military advance. Disjonval's spider forecast convinced the French general and he ordered that the French troops continue their advance through Holland.

Twelve days after that order, a frost hit the area with such intensity that the ice over the rivers and canals was capable of supporting even the heaviest French artillery. Consequently, on the twenty-eighth of January 1795, the French army was able to enter the city of Utrecht in triumph; and Quatremer Disjonval, as a reward for his incredible weather forecast, was released from prison.

(9) The Rewards of Forecasting

Today, one of the most lucrative, but also one of most difficult, types of weather forecasting is that associated with commodities futures trading. For example, such forecasters are asked to stake their reputations (and their clients' monies) on questions such as, "How much will it snow or rain next season?" and "How will that weather influence the price of orange juice, hogs' bellies, or wheat?" Many today would probably think that such commodities forecasting is a relatively new type of meteorology, but that is not so. According to Aristotle, the Greek philosopher Thales of Miletus may be the first successful weather commodities forecaster and, as such, a forecaster who, at least for a short time, greatly profited from his forecast.

Thales's success story begins with taunting by his friends about the lack of financial rewards that his undoubted wisdom had brought him. The great philosopher decided to give a very practical demonstration of its usefulness. Consequently, he tracked weather trends for the region and concluded from his observations that the next olive crop around Miletus (on the eastern shore of the Aegean Sea) would be a very good one. So, armed with that forecast, he proceeded to buy every olive press in the vicinity. When the next crop, as he had forecasted, resulted in an enormous harvest, Thales became rich overnight. But, having made the point and being unimpressed with wealth, the ancient Greek scholar abandoned his commodities forecasting enterprise and returned to his former life as a philosopher.

Others have also benefited from weather forecasting although they did so in less honest (or skillful) means. W. A. Kals, in his 1977 book *The Riddle of the Winds,* told the story of Captain Henry W. Howgate, one of the most unscrupulous government weathermen of all time. After gaining a relatively high position in the Signal Corps (which housed the government's weather activities at the time), Howgate became a specialist in generating bogus equipment receipts. When he was finally arrested and brought up on charges, Howgate had embezzled more than $237,000 from the government—an incredible sum for the late nineteenth century. As the federal investigators began to prepare their case, the judge released Howgate upon payment of a $30,000 bail bond— and the pseudometeorologist made a run for it. Within a short time, Howgate was recaptured and jailed. But a few months later, the judge allowed the crooked weatherman to return to his home—in the company of a guard—in order for Howgate to visit his daughter. Once again the dishonest forecaster escaped—and this time he succeeded. Unfortunately, Howgate's illicit activities had a profound financial effect on the infant Weather Service. Acting in response to the disgraceful affair, Congress slashed the Signal Corps' annual budget from $375,000 to $312,000. As a direct result, the Corps was forced to close eighteen of its weather stations.

(10) Do We Change the Weather?

Today, many scientists, politicians, the public, and the media hotly debate the magnitude and effects of human-generated global warming. What many people don't realize is that the concept of weather changing as a result of people and their activities is not a new idea. In the 1800s, many people thought that cutting down the extensive forests of the eastern United States was creating a marked change in climate. Dr. Noah Webster, creator of the first American dictionary, made a pronouncement in 1844 following a "most thorough review" of the climate records of both America and Europe. He concluded that any claim of climate change for either continent was at that time unsupported.

A Canadian journalist in 1853 wrote that frost had become less severe and frequent, snows fell in smaller quantities, and both ended sooner because Canada had cleared many of its forests and drained many of its swamps. Coupled to that idea, a letter by John Whitford in 1869 to the magazine *Scientific American* suggested that the opening of the prairie created more rain in the Great Plains. Whitford wrote that all the scouts, guides, and hunters in the Great Plains were in agreement that there were less summer rains in the area prior to the great expansion westward. He raised the question, "Has the iron of the [train] rails or the upturned ground the credit of the change?"

As far back as the seventeenth century, some suggested that even the world's biggest storms, hurricanes, were being influenced by people. M. S. Douglas, in her 1958 book *Hurricane,* discovered an interesting old climate proclamation by Father du Tertre. The Catholic priest declared in 1680 that, although hurricanes used to only hit the Antilles once every seven years, "they have become much more frequent since the Antilles have been inhabited."

In 1929, Sir R. A. Watson Watt delivered a lecture to the Royal Meteorological Society. In that lecture, he contested the popular notion at the time that the creation of radio led to a marked change in the weather. He theorized that, since rainfall is produced by evaporation, the only way in which radio could affect weather is by creating more evaporation. He pointed out that in comparison to the energy required for normal evaporation, the amount produced by broadcasting stations was insignificant. Hence, he concluded, radio didn't affect weather.

In the early 1950, many people believed that the atomic bomb testing in Nevada was influencing the weather. In early 1953, Harry Wexler of the U.S. Weather Bureau, stated, "The A-bomb's effect [from testing in Nevada] on weather is only local in character." Then, on June 5, 1953, the military exploded an atomic bomb high above Nevada and on June 8, a huge outbreak of tornadoes struck the upper Midwest, and particularly demolished Flint, Michigan. The events seemed to be connected. In the *New York Times,* science writer Waldemar Kaempffert reported, "As might be expected, the recent explosions of atomic bombs in Nevada are held by many to be the cause of the tornadoes that have swept from the Midwest to Massachusetts. The Weather Bureau and the Air Force have tried to dispel this notion."

Of course, in these modern times, we wouldn't fall victim to jumping to human-weather connections, right? In 1995, an ultranationalist politician in Russia, Vladimir Zhirinovsky, blamed a spell of extremely hot weather on the capitalistic West. He called on all true Russian patriots to resist this blatant meteorological aggression.

Perhaps when we hear talk of whether climate and weather are changing, we should remember the comment made by the father of modern computer science and great meteorology enthusiast, John von Neuman. He said that the intricacies of meteorology offer "without a doubt the most complicated series of interrelated problems not only that we know of, but that we can imagine."

(11) Knowing Your Environment

A critical aspect of any good forecast is an underlying knowledge of the area for which it is made. The story of an amazing escape attempt by twenty-five German prisoners from a Phoenix, Arizona, prison camp during World War II is a classic example of that point. An excellent retelling of the story is given by Moore in his 1978 book *Faustball Tunnel*. Two days before Christmas 1944, twenty-five German U-boat officers finished digging a two-hundred-foot tunnel through hard desert soil from their prison to a nearby canal. As the men exited their tunnel and readied their handmade canvas boat, a light rain began to fall. Ordinarily, this would be a detriment to an escape. However, rain is an abnormal—and generally avoided—phenomenon for people in the desert areas of the Southwest United States, at least more so than in other parts of the country. So the prisoners found the surrounding area generally peaceful and uninhabited.

The would-be escapers, however, faced a really insurmountable problem as they headed south toward Mexico. The problem was directly related to both the unusual rain during their escape and the general climatic conditions of Arizona. Although the boaters had been able to travel for several days down the canal and into the Gila River—swollen with the recent

The dry Gila River—the unfortunate sight seen by the twenty-five German escapees from a Phoenix, Arizona, World War II prison camp. (Photo by author.)

rains—by December 29 there simply was not enough water in the Gila River to float their tiny raft. One of the escapers recalled, "It was one of those frustrating moments in life when you don't know whether to laugh, cry, swear, or kick the ground in disgust. We should have known that the Gila wasn't much of a river. Of course everybody who lives in Arizona knows that. We didn't." Another German escaper expressed his frustration this way, "In Germany, if we mark a river on a map, it has water in it. Why in Arizona do you draw rivers on your maps that don't have water in them?" Moral of the story: Good forecasters should always know their environment!

(12) Elements of a Good Forecast

Many people regard weather forecasting as a science, involving computers and high-tech equipment, or an art, using inborn talents to see weather patterns. Actually, most meteorologists would probably suggest that there are elements of both in a good forecast. For instance, William Lackland's 1886 translation of Zürcher and Margollé's *Meteors, Aerolites, Storms, and Atmospheric Phenomena,* contains an interesting description of how a "scientific" weather forecast was made in those times. Lackland translated the meteorological rationale of French scientist Hubert-Burnaud's successful forecast of the severe winter of 1830. Hubert-Burnaud said it was "no prophecy but a very simple calculation." First, he concluded that, since south and southwest winds had dominated the area for six months, the north winds "would have their turn." Second, he claimed that, because of the number of cloudy days in July and October, "it was natural to think that the earth would be cooled, at its surface, more than usual." Finally, Hubert-Burnaud stated, "The autumn having been very rainy, the winter, according to all appearances, would be dry." In true forecasting fashion, the scientist then said that these three factors are only partially responsible for a season's weather and so "no conclusion can be drawn; but their general prevalence, throughout Europe, would be likely to produce simple effects."

Sometimes the elements of a good forecast can't be precisely detailed; they are more intuitive than explicit. For instance, Grady Norton, the chief hurricane forecaster of the United States Weather Bureau from 1935 to 1954, is still regarded by many in the profession as one of the nation's best weather prognosticators. One of his more famous predictions was made in 1944 with regard to a hurricane that had been heading past Florida into the Gulf of Mexico. Meteorologist Robert Simpson (of "Saffir-Simpson Hurricane" category ranking fame) recalled that Norton had abruptly changed the forecast to say that the storm would make a sudden turn northward and hit Tampa Bay forty-eight hours later. To Simpson's amazement, the storm did just that. When he later asked Norton for an explanation, Norton first turned toward a set of glass doors that led onto a nineteenth-floor deck outside his office. He then responded, "When I am not sure about

The legendary hurricane forecaster Grady Norton.
(Photo Courtesy of National Hurricane Center.)

the way things are going, I go out there, sit down and put my feet on the parapet and look out over the everglades. I watch the clouds and ask my question. Usually the answer comes to me."

(13) The Ultimate Sacrifice

For many forecasters throughout the ages, forecasting has been often more than a simple duty or job; it is also their avocation. In particular, Grady Norton, mentioned above as the chief of the National Hurricane Center, was known for going the extra mile to make sure the public was informed of weather dangers and took appropriate actions. For instance, when a relatively small hurricane struck Florida in 1950, Director Norton was on the radio even before the hurricane crashed into the coast and continued his warning throughout the hurricane's demolition of the coast. One elderly Miami lady reportedly said afterward, "There I was all through it, along with Grady Norton."

The sad but heroic finale of the great forecaster Grady Norton is a fitting way to end this set of anecdotes of the trials and tribulations in weather forecasting. In October of 1954, as Hurricane Hazel, a lumbering hurricane that would eventually catastrophically flood North Carolina and even Toronto, Canada, plodded its way northward, the diligent chief of hurricane forecasting continued to put in long hours plotting its wandering course. Unfortunately, while doing that vital work, Norton suffered what proved to be a fatal stroke. Although the dedicated hurricane expert had been repeatedly warned by his doctor to avoid long hours of work and stress, the diligent forecaster had already put in a twelve-hour shift on that fateful last day of work. Grady Norton had been more concerned with accurately projecting the hurricane's movement—and thereby potentially saving the lives of thousands of people—than with his own health.

Chapter 13
STATE WEATHER ODDITIES

WEATHER HAPPENS TO ALL OF US. AS THIS BOOK HAS SHOWN, A great amount of that weather can be quite strange. Most importantly, weird weather is not limited to one part of the world, or to just one area of the country, but is experienced by all of us. To demonstrate that key point, I have selected to end this book with a bizarre weather story for every state in the country, plus the District of Columbia and Puerto Rico. These stories are not only meant to entertain you but also to make you ponder weather's impact on virtually every part of our lives. Weather is a fascinating subject and, undoubtedly, the future holds even more fascinating discoveries—and assuredly more weirdness—in this constantly changing area of study.

Alabama, *The Turtle Hurricane* (July 27, 1819): The oddest feature associated with this 1819 hurricane is that many of its casualties were caused not by the storm itself but rather by hordes of snapping turtles and alligators washed into the city of Mobile at the

Raining rats during a thunderstorm as depicted in *Der Wunder-reiche Uberzug* [sic] *unserer Nider-Welt....* by Erasmus Francisci, 1680. (Photo Courtesy of National Oceanic and Atmospheric Administration/Department of Commerce Photo Library Historic NWS Collection.)

height of the storm. When the eye passed over Mobile around midnight, many residents thought the worst was over but then the sudden rush of wind and water from the opposite direction caused many buildings to collapse and brought hordes of snapping turtles and alligators. Some sources suggest that fully half of the two hundred casualties were the result of alligator and turtle bites. In a similar fashion, a contingent of U.S. soldiers who had encamped for the night in a shallow valley were forced to flee to higher ground where "trees were falling like nine-pins." At least one man was killed and twenty others were seriously wounded by the falling trees.

Alaska, *A Shower of Lemmings?* (April, 1952): Noted explorer and naturalist, Sally Carrighar, observed evidence of what she deemed might have been a "lemming fall" in Nome, Alaska. In April 1952, an Eskimo postmaster at Unalakeet told her that a few lemmings—small mouselike rodents—had fallen from the sky that day at the end of the town's airstrip. She expressed great skepticism about the story and headed out to personally investigate it. Her fascinating book *Wild Voice of the North*, tells what happened when she reached the airstrip. She discovered the runway had been covered with less than an inch of new powdery snow—unmarked by any tunnels that a lemming might have made. But there, on top of that new snow, were a number of mysterious little trails. Those trails, according to Carrighar, "began rather faintly for a couple of inches, as if an animal had come down and gently coasted onto the snow. The tracks then continued more deeply, the individual footprints where the hairs on the lemming's feet dragged." She was left with the bewildering question: "How could those tracks just begin suddenly, out there on the smooth white surface? I have no idea." We are left with the unanswered question: Did the lemmings really fall from the sky?

Arizona, *The Night the Temperature Rose* (July 28, 1995): Residents of Phoenix, Arizona, sweltered through the hottest July day on record and the second hottest day of all time in Phoenix as the temperature peaked at 121°F but, believe it or not, that wasn't the strangest weather event of the day! As evening descended on the arid city, people were praying for the start of the desert's typical night cooling. By 9 P.M., the temperature had dropped to 105°F and the whine of overworked air-conditioners had begun slowly to diminish. Then something strange happened. Outflow from a huge complex of thunderstorms far to the south at the Arizona/Mexico border was pushing northward toward Phoenix. High-and-middle level clouds moved over the sweltering city and fiery cloud-to-cloud lightning filled the sky. At 10 P.M., the National Weather Service reported Phoenix's temperature had climbed back to 109°F. And by 11 P.M., the heat was surging upward to 114°F! Evening TV weathercasters were shaking their heads in bewilderment as they reported the bizarre heating known as a "heat burst."

Arkansas, *Lightning and the Preacher* (August 2, 1894): As H. F. Kretzer recounted in his privately published 1895 book *Lightning Record,* the small town of Walnut Ridge experienced "excitement today over the terrible answer that was made to a prayer at a camp meeting near the town last night. Reverend Robinson, a local preacher of strong lungs, was praying. He asked the Lord to bless them now with rain, saying: 'Lord, come down now and pour out a blessing of some nature upon us; one of such a nature as we can remember; one that we can feel certain that it is from you, and come now.' Here the prayer stopped, not because the 'Amen' was reached, but because a flash of lightning came down with a roar of ten or more cannons, shattering a huge tree near by, scattering its branches over the entire audience, knocking some senseless, wounding others and frightening all, most of the audience believing that the end of the world had come. They had scarcely recovered from the shock when such a volume of water came down as to almost drown them . . . It was a remarkable occurrence, and, it broke up the meeting, and but a few of those present can be induced to go near the ground again."

California, *Calling Mr. Niño 'Bout that Rain* (December, 1997): Buck Wolf of ABC News reported on the trials and tribulations of a retired seventy-four-year-old Navy seaman with the unfortunate name Al Nino. During the 1997 wet El Niño winter, many people called Nino's home, apparently holding him personally responsible for the rainy weather. Nino said that he tried to be polite to the callers but that he didn't really understand why people would think the much maligned weather phenomenon would have its own telephone number. Nino's strangest phone call was from a man who held Nino responsible for his daughter's loss of virginity because she was unable to get home one night after a major rainstorm. "I said I was sorry, although I assured him I didn't have anything to do with it."

Colorado, *The Golden Cloudburst* (summer, 1929): As mentioned earlier in this book, cloudbursts have been linked to great human tragedy and suffering, but as with all natural events, determination of "good" and "bad" is sometimes a matter of perspective. In the summer of 1929 near Lake City in southwest Colorado, the *Literary Digest* reported on a massive downpour of rain so intense that it scoured the surrounding hillsides down to the bare rock. But what some might consider a potential disaster turned out to be a blessing. The rainstorm's scouring revealed valuable deposits of gold ore in those denuded hills and, soon after the storm, the area experienced a brief but profitable gold rush. Interestingly, locals reported that a similar downpour many years previous in the same region also exposed several million dollars' worth of gold and silver.

Connecticut, *The Dancing Tamarack Tree* (June 19, 1794): When a large tornado hit New Milford, newspapers at the time said that one of the more bizarre sights was a large tamarack tree that the tornado had pulled up by its roots and, incredibly, carried upright along the road. Witnesses claimed that sometimes the tree would settle down almost to the ground, and then rapidly rise more than three hundred feet in the air. And, to add to the spectacle, a few other large objects, likely someone's barn doors, played attendants to the dancing tree, moving around it until the whirling foliage eventually was carried out of sight. Indeed, tornado historian Thomas Grazulis reported that a barn door was discovered ten miles from its original building.

Delaware, *First-Hand Encounter with a Waterspout* (April 27, 1860): Mr. McMurray, an agent of the British and Foreign Bible Society reported (as recounted by P. F. H. Baddeley in his 1860 book *Whirlwinds and Duststorms of India),* that, as McMurray's ship was becalmed just off the coast near Delaware, "our attention was called to two large waterspouts, which were approaching us with a speed of from fifteen to twenty miles an hour . . . With feelings of delight, we gazed upon them, as they crossed our bows within pistol shot, making the surface of the water . . . boil and stream like an immense furnace." But then things turned more threatening, according to McMurray, when a bit later, "the attention of all on board was called to five or six waterspouts, on our starboard quarter." One particularly big waterspout approached the becalmed ship in a menacing fashion. The captain yelled out, "Let go the Halliards! Haul down the jib!" but, before the orders could be obeyed, "the waterspout was upon us; it struck us midships and gave us such a lift, we thought we were gone. What an anxious moment! The past, the present, and the future crowded on the mind with a force, that to be comprehended must be experienced . . ."

District of Colombia, *Lincoln's Response to the Forecaster* (April 25, 1863): According to weather historian David Ludlum, when Francis L. Capen had applied for a forecasting job by making a rather long-term weather forecast of clear weather starting on April 22, President Abraham Lincoln made the following observation on April 25, 1863: "He told me three days ago that it would not rain again till the thirtieth of April or the first of May. It is raining now and has been for ten hours. I cannot spare any more time to Mr. Capen."

Florida, *Golf Ball Rain?* (September 3, 1969): As recounted by a number of fortean authors, hundreds of golf balls apparently fell during a thunderstorm that produced five inches of rain in Punta Gorda Isles suburb on the west coast of Florida. A police investigation led by a lieutenant in the Punta Gorda Police Department failed to explain the hundreds of golf balls that had fallen into gutters, on the streets and sidewalks. Two patrolmen from the department picked up a huge number of golf balls while a security patrolman collected enough golf balls to fill a satchel case and complained that he was tired of picking them up. A check of local golf courses and country clubs failed to find any missing golf balls.

Georgia, *Rebel Snowball Fight* (March 1864): A 1963 trivia book *Strange but True,* reported that, after a freak southern snowstorm in Dalton, a small town northwest of Atlanta, many young soldiers of the Confederate Army, many of whom had never seen snow before, began a vigorous snowball fight in late March. Eventually, even the colonels and generals joined in to organize the fun and official positions were assigned. General Cheatham's Tennessee division fought General Walker's Georgia soldiers over a battle line that stretched for more than a mile, reportedly containing five thousand men. When it was over after several hours, both sides loudly claimed victory.

Hawaii, *"Safety" in Iniki* (September 11, 1992): According to Kathleen Duey and Mary Barnes's juvenile-oriented but entertaining weather book *Freaky Facts about Natural Disasters,* the antics of a couple of thieves caused a bit of humor amidst the destruction of massive Hurricane Iniki in Kawai. Two men reportedly took advantage of the hurricane's confusion to break into a grocery store, and steal a safe. However, once outside and subject to Iniki's hurricane winds, they were unable to move the heavy safe. The would-be robbers finally were forced to abandon the lockbox in the middle of the street. Locals joked that the two "didn't know another way to keep 'safe' in a storm."

Idaho, *Pulaski of the Big Blowup* (August 20, 1910): Ranger E.C.
Pulaski led one hundred and fifty men fighting a mammoth fire,
which would become known as the Big Blowup, on a high divide
between the St. Joe and Coeur d'Alene Rivers in Idaho. Flames
cut off Pulaski from part of his team and so he led his remaining
men to a nearby mine to escape the fire. At first, Pulaski tried to
wet down blankets at the mine entrance to stop the smoke but the
sheeting dried up and burned away, leaving the ranger's hands
badly burned. Later, one of Pulaski's men attempted to leave but
was stopped by the ranger who drew a pistol and ordered the man
back into the mine. As the massive fire passed over the area, all
the men—including Pulaski—passed out from the heat and
smoke. Afterward, amazed rescuers found that of the forty people
in the mine, only five were dead. One of the rescuers, seeing the
apparently lifeless body of Pulaski, called to his companions,
"Come on outside, boys, the Boss is dead." "Like hell he is,"
snarled the indomitable ranger.

Illinois, *The Ninth Body* (March 28, 1920): The official count for
the death in Elgin, northwest of Chicago, following the passage
of a F3 tornado was eight. However, according to the *Literary Digest,*
a news photographer at the scene, spying what he thought was a
body, suddenly threw down his camera and began to dig wildly,
shouting to a reporter, "Call my paper and tell them there are
nine dead in Elgin!" The reporter raced off and word was flashed
to Chicago but to the photographer's chagrin, the ninth "body"
proved to be a wax mannequin.

Indiana, *Oddities of the Great Tri-State Tornado* (March 25, 1925): *The*
Literary Digest recounted (citing newspaper reports) several oddities
associated with the longest-lasting and longest-traveling tornado
in U.S. history. Many strange spectacles were found near the end
of the 219-mile tornado path at Princeton, Indiana, including

an upright barber's chair that was found in an open field nearly two miles from the shop where it had once been bolted to the floor. In another field nearby, searchers found an intact Victrola phonograph. In an innovative response to the disaster, one business clerk actually saved himself by crawling into the office safe as the tornado ripped off the walls and roof of the building around him. The tornado also tore open the doors of a car containing four people, sucked them out of the car, and then dropped them uninjured to the ground. It did, however, proceed to tear the car into a multitude of metal fragments scattered along the road.

Iowa, *Paying for the Sandwich* (September 16, 1978): J. L. Stanford, in his 1987 book *Tornado (Accounts of Tornadoes in Iowa),* recounted the story of the truck-stop restaurant in Grinnell, Iowa, as a destructive F3 tornado slammed into it. According to the restaurant owner, when the tornado touched down, the hundred or so customers "hit the deck like tenpins." That is, all the customers except for one man in his early twenties who had ridden up in a motorcycle. His prime-rib sandwich had just been served and he wasn't going to be bothered by Mother Nature to stop eating it. Then, the tornado slammed a board through the café's window and knocked the man to the floor. After a few minutes of lying dazed on the floor, the man looked up at the owner who had come to help him, "Mister," the man said, "I just can't eat that sandwich now. Do I have to pay for it?" The owner shook his head with a smile as he helped dress the man's wounds.

Kansas, *The Charred Roof Beam Through a Building* (June 3, 1927): The great Kansas climatologist Snowden Flora reported in his classic 1954 book *Tornadoes of the United States,* that a tornado's winds ripped a badly weathered and charred roof beam from a Topeka, Kansas, barn and then jammed it into the siding and two-inch sill of a nearby new house. The long wooden beam was jammed pointed end first into the new house, and was found still sticking through the hole it had punched. Flora commented after personally visiting the site, "The most incredible part was that the charred, tapered end of the old rafter showed no battering effect whatever. The speed of its impact must have been tremendous."

Kentucky, *Shower of Beetles* (September 1880): The journal *Scientific American* reported that residents of Owensville and nearby towns in Kentucky had been bombarded by a "veritable shower of large brown, oval-shaped beetles." The water beetles measured about one and a half inches in length by half or three-quarters of an inch in breadth. The journal suggested for explanation that perhaps the beetle had been either migrating or had been swept into the air by some nearby tornado.

Louisiana, *The Ultimate Hurricane Party* (August 10, 1856): Four hundred inhabitants had gathered for a grand ball at the fashionable Trade Wind Hotel on Isle Derniäre (Last Island). Even as the hurricane struck, partiers danced on. Indeed, according to Lafcadio Hearn, in his 1889 book *Chita, a Memory of Lost Island,* one of the girls at the party shrieked when she found her dancing slippers becoming wet due to the driving rains seeping through the building. Then, around midnight, the grand ballroom collapsed and the entire hotel was washed away carrying two to three hundred of the revelers. Only forty people managed to reach the steamer *Star,* under the capable command of Captain Abraham Smith, and survived the ordeal. Following the hurricane, Isle Dernière was discovered to have been completely cut into two parts. A deep channel where the grand hotel had once stood separated the two parts of the island. The only survivor on the island was a cow that was found in its meadow trying to eat the salt-encrusted grass. How it survived the great storm remains a mystery.

Maine, *Saxby's Gale* (October 4, 1869): According to meteorologist C. F. Talman, in his 1931 book *The Realm of the Air*, a violent storm, accompanied by a tide of extraordinary height, came up from the West Indies and struck New Brunswick, Maine. The storm became known as Saxby's Gale, after a British lieutenant named Saxby, who had predicted a full year earlier that a great storm and high tide would occur on October 5. However, Saxby's prediction apparently was only based on lunar considerations and did not actually specify New Brunswick as the storm's target. Nevertheless, this storm was popularly hailed across America and England as a verification of the lieutenant's forecast and is therefore remembered as "Saxby's Gale."

Maryland, *The Susquehanna Ice Bridge* (January 15, 1852): David Ludlum, the esteemed weather historian, recounted the odd story of how, on one very cold winter, the local railroad came up with a very unique way to speed mail, freight, and passenger traffic between Havre de Grace and Perryville, Maryland. A former army engineer created an enormous ice bridge with iron rails across the frozen Susquehanna River. Baggage and freight cars, one at a time, were let down to the frozen river by gravity, using their brakes for control. Once upon the ice, the railcars were hauled across the river by ropes attached to horse-drawn sleighs. At the opposite bank, each car was hauled up the inclined plane by means of a rope attached to a waiting locomotive. According to Ludlum, up to forty cars were moved across the river by this method. The ice bridge was completed on January 15 and served for over a month until a general thaw set in.

Massachusetts, *Too Embarrassed to Be Rescued* (June 9, 1953): According to John O'Toole, in his 1993 book *Tornado! 84 Minutes, 94 Lives,* when the massive F4 tornado struck the Massachusetts

city of Worcester in 1953, one unfortunate woman was in the
bathroom using the toilet. Before she had time to finish, the tornado demolished the house around her. Afterward, although
safe, the woman was pinned in the wreckage and unable to move.
A few minutes later she heard her husband frantically calling her.
But the woman didn't respond. After a few hours, she was rescued—her cheeks flaming red in embarrassment—from her con-
fines. After her husband's initial relief had subsided, he asked in
puzzlement why she hadn't answered his initial yells. She told him
that she had been too mortified at her undignified predicament
to risk being rescued by strange men.

Michigan, *Dark Day in Detroit* (October 19, 1762): N. F. Morrison
retold the story of a very strange day in Detroit in a 1963 issue of
the *Anthropological Journal of Canada* (and later recounted by William
Corliss). A Detroit merchant back in 1762 spent—as did all of his
neighbors—most of the day in nearly total darkness. Indeed,
many people were forced to eat their noon meal by candlelight.
According to the entrepreneur, the stygian darkness deepened
throughout the afternoon until the wind shifted to the southwest
and "brought on some drops of rain, or rather sulfur and dirt,
for it appeared more like latter than former, both in smell and
quality." Speculation for the odd "dark day" abounded in the
city. The man said that some of the lower classes—specifically
"Indians and uneducated among the French"—thought that
Englishmen had brought the dark-day elements with them when
the English arrived in Michigan while others theorized that the
darkness was the result of forest fires. The businessman himself,
however, speculated that the dark day "might have been occa-
sioned by the eruption of some volcano, or subterraneous fire."
With due respect to the businessman, the greatest likelihood—
particularly given the mention of dirt rain—is that massive dust

storms and/or prairie fires from the Great Plains drifted over the city, thereby producing the darkness.

Minnesota, *The Gentle Kitchen Mover* (June 6, 1906): Mr. T. S. Outram of the Weather Bureau reported in *Monthly Weather Review* on the strong F3 tornado that hit North Branch, Minnesota, "The characteristic freaks or strange happenings so common in tornadoes were present in these storms also, and a few may be mentioned. A kitchen cupboard, filled with china, standing in a house which was completely torn to pieces, was carried four rods and set down so gently that not a piece of china was broken. When the storm struck the Inglett place, Mr. Inglett, Sr., was sitting in the kitchen with a child on his lap; the house was completely demolished, even to the carrying away of nearly all the floor but that on which the man was still sitting uninjured after the storm past. Articles of furniture were carried four and a half miles from their starting point. The rung of a chair was driven thru a large tree, so that its ends projects from each side."

Mississippi, *The Natchez Twister's Towel* (May 7, 1840): One of the major oddities found in the destruction of Natchez, Mississippi, left by a massive F5 tornado, according to A. H. Godbey's 1890 book *Great Disasters and Horrors in the World's History,* was the position of a bath towel hanging on the wall. Residents found that the towel had been blown nearly through the wall behind it. Apparently, the expanding air of the building (caused by interior air rushing out toward the low pressure of the tornado) had opened a large crevice in the wall and then caused the towel to be blown into it. Then, when the storm passed on and the pressure once again was equalized, the crevice closed as the building's air no longer expanded outward. The result: a towel embedded in the wall to puzzle residents long afterward.

Missouri, *The Luckiest Man in the St. Louis Tornado* (May 27, 1896): Julian Curzon, in his 1896 book *The Great Cyclone at St. Louis,* recounted how A. M. Meintz became, quite possibly, the luckiest man in the ruined town following the terrible F5 tornado of 1896. Meintz, a wealthy and shrewd man, owned a two-story office building at the corner of Third Street and Missouri Avenue in East St. Louis. Prior to the tornado, he had decided to add an extra story to his building and was preparing to remove the roof so that the addition could be built. Then the great tornado hit, devastating the city and, for the most part, causing tremendous misery and destruction. For A. M. Meintz, however, the tornado was a blessing—it ripped off his building's roof but left the rest of the building untouched. And, equally fortunate, Meintz was one of the few men in East St. Louis who—prior to the twister—actually had purchased tornado insurance. So his "losses" on the roof were entirely covered and he saved the expense of roof demolition for his third-story addition.

Montana, *The Shocking Death of Old Pitt* (August 6, 1943): According the fine people at the Dillon (Montana) *Tribune* and other sources, Old Pitt started out as one of the "world-famous" elephants of Robinson's Great Combination Show in the late 1800s and early 1900s. When that show closed, the elephant went into a well-deserved retirement until 1942, when she was sold to the Cole Brothers circus. Unfortunately, for Old Pitt, the circus encountered a violent thunderstorm as they began a Friday matinee for the small town of Dillon, Montana. As the elephants were being led to the Big Top, a violent blast of lightning struck and killed their leader, the venerable Old Pitt. Three nearby elephants were also hit and badly stunned but they recovered. The circus owner, Zack Terrell, asked to have "Old Pitt" buried at the Country Fairgrounds and left funds in have a marker erected over her burial site (and that marker is still there). The elephant burial occurred the next day with county road equipment being used to dig Pitt's grave. A large crowd of local residents and circus performers attended the rather unusual funeral.

Nebraska, *The Suction Tornado* (June 3, 1890): A critical debate in the late nineteenth century revolved around whether a tornado's major destructive effect was from suction (due to intense low pressure at the core) or from rotating winds (associated with the spiraling vortex). A massive F4 tornado, which passed over the town of Bradshaw in York County, Nebraska, played a role in that discussion. According to early tornado researcher H. A. Hazen, the Nebraska tornado passed over a full water storage tank measuring ten feet long, three feet wide, and twenty inches deep. The tank was airtight with only a small opening in the top measuring one-foot square. Yet, a weather observer reported in the aftermath of the tornado that the twister had completely sucked all the water out of this tank. According to Hazen, "A moment's

The moment at the Dillon Montana fairgrounds commemorating the passing of Old Pitt the circus elephant in 1943. (Photo Courtesy of Elaine Spicer.)

reflection will show that this could have been done only by the [direct] insertion of the [tornado] funnel into the opening one foot square. Of course this is absurd, and we must resort to some other explanations of the phenomenon." Hazen, in attempt to see if this tornado had some unusual suction ability even had another observer make "a most diligent search for evidence of corks being blown from bottles, but did not find a single case, although there were several apothecary-shops and bottling-establishments in the centre of the tracks."

Nevada, *Snowbound in Nevada* (January, 1890): According to B. Mergen's 1997 book *Snow in America,* a massive blizzard created a formidable ice prison for passengers on a Southern Pacific train in 1890, while traveling west near Reno Nevada, the S.P. train became snowbound in the Sierra Nevada following the immense blizzard. For the unfortunate crew and over seven hundred passengers, the train was stopped there in the wilderness for more than two weeks. For that time, the passengers onboard were forced to remain—and attempt to survive—in their Pullman cars until the tracks could be cleared. In fact, one of the passengers, George T. McCully, used the enforced idleness to publish a twenty-five-cent, four-page newspaper, that he called the *Snowbound.* The masthead of the *Snowbound* informed the reader that the ad hoc paper was published "every week-day afternoon by S. P. Prisoner."

New Hampshire, *Blue Snow* (March 1, 1934): An excerpt from an article in the Manchester *Union* (cited in a 1934 issue of the *Bulletin of the American Meteorological Society*) declared that "a singular phenomenon" occurred at the famous Mount Washington observatory on the first of March. According to the report, one of the observatory scientists had decided to haul a few bags of coal that were located a couple hundred yards from the main building up to the observatory. When he began to dig out the area in front of the doors of the garage to gain entry, he was shocked to see that the holes he had dug "were promptly filled with deep blue light." Apparently, the observer was able to exclude the possibilities of the blue-lighted snow resulting from "reflection from the sky or of bacteria collecting on the snow." No explanation for the weird blue light snow was ever given.

New Jersey, *The Fake Forecast* (1901): Dr. Cleveland Abbe, respected meteorologist and editor of the weather science journal *Monthly Weather Review,* was outraged about a forecast put out in New Jersey. So angry was he that he wrote an editorial in *Monthly Weather Review* that demanded to know "who was it that in 1901 started a newspaper paragraph purporting to come from some responsible person, predicting a hurricane for the coast of New Jersey on a certain date? So great was the anxiety that it was necessary for the secretary of agriculture to issue a counteracting telegram showing that the original was certainly a fake."

New Mexico, *Las Cruces Tornado, Waterspout, or Downburst?* (September 10, 1875): A weather observer in Las Cruces, New Mexico, reported in *Monthly Weather Review,* "On the 10th at 5:30 p.m. at Las Cruces, New Mexico, a waterspout suddenly appeared in the hills one mile back of the town, toward the north, and passed over the town as a tall, dark column of water and dust, destroying, building, &c., in less than ten minutes. The water in the streets was from four to five feet deep, and two hours later rain commenced and fell in torrents for several hours." Another report of this disaster stated, "It was midnight before the flood abated; and this morning our town, which was yesterday one of the most flourishing in the Southwest, stands a mass of ruins sad to contemplate. It is impossible to estimate the value of property destroyed."

New York, *The Buffalo Blizzard of 1977 and the Zoo* (January 28, 1977):
According to Carole Garbuny Vogel, in her 2000 book *Nature's Fury: Eyewitness Reports of Natural Disasters,* the general curator of the Buffalo Zoo was forced into some odd situations during this terrible blizzard. Since many of the zoo employees couldn't get to the zoo because of the snowstorm, four zookeepers took over the work of fifteen—and to speed things up, they even improvised sleds to haul food over the eight-foot high snowdrifts. The biggest problem, however, was preventing the animals from escaping over the drifting snow. In fact, three reindeer did indeed jump their barricades and had to be rounded up. One of the interesting—but false—rumors involving the zoo, according to the curator, was that the news media reported that some of the polar bears had gotten loose during the blizzard. He recalled, "We got calls from a lot of nervous residents, but there never was any danger of the bears going free."

North Carolina, *Fran and Petey* (September 5, 1996): In J. Barnes's fascinating 2001 book *North Carolina's Hurricane History,* we learn the amazing story of a plucky dog named Petey. When Hurricane Fran hit North Carolina, an auto-salvage-yard owner in New Bern, North Carolina, was forced to leave his guard dog Petey at his shop. Petey was only a small ten-inch-tall mutt and, as the storm surge flooded the area, and particularly the auto salvage shop in which he was locked, floodwaters rose to a level sixteen inches above the floor. The spunky little dog was up to the task. Apparently Petey swam continually throughout the night to keep his head above the water—a mind-boggling seven hours. Finally, by early the next morning, the owner was able to return to his shop and rescue the aquatic canine. According to reports, Petey subsequently slept for the next two days after his long-duration swim.

North Dakota, *Imitating Mr. Franklin* (August 28, 1919): Simple weather observation can sometimes be a fatal occupation, according to 1919 issue of *Monthly Weather Review*. In the days before weather balloons became the primary means for recording upper air information, lightning killed a volunteer weather observer, Charles H. Heckelsmiller, at Ellendale, North Dakota. On a fateful August afternoon, Mr. Heckelsmiller was assisting in a series of data-gathering kite flights for the National Weather Bureau. Apparently, he was standing close to the main kite wire when the lightning strike occurred. At the time of the flash, two other weather observers were in the reel shed (which contained the kite's tow wire) and they said the shed immediately filled with flame. According to the incident report, prompt "first aid" was attempted (although at the time the modern procedure of using CPR for lightning victims was unknown so we don't know what they actually did as "first aid") but to no avail. Doctors reported severe burns across Mr. Heckelsmiller's chest and on the inner side of his right wrist. When the strike occurred, a line of sparks

Kite operations at an aerological station such as described for North Dakota. (Photo Courtesy of National Oceanic and Atmospheric Administration/Department of Commerce Photo Library Historic NWS Collection.)

resembling a huge skyrocket was seen to follow the wire and these set the grass beneath on fire. This was the first—and perhaps only (at least to my knowledge)—accident of its kind that occurred to a Weather Bureau employee.

Ohio, *"The Battle of the Fallen Timbers"* (August 27, 1794): The Battle of Fallen Timbers was the climax of a western military campaign that pitted the U.S. Army, under the leadership of Major General "Mad" Anthony Wayne, against one of the largest assemblages of Native American tribes to ever stand in opposition to the new United States, all led by Miami Indian Chief Little Turtle. For our purposes, it is the scene of the battle that has meteorological significance. Over a thousand Native American warriors and a hundred British volunteers had exploited a large forested area near modern-day Toledo in which a huge number of trees had been torn about and blown down by the passage of a recent tornado. The broken and tangled trees provided excellent cover for ambush and effectively denied easy mobility by the U.S. cavalry. When battle was engaged, a small force of Indian warriors was quickly drawn out of the forest's protected setting by the lure of apparently easy prey, a small cluster of Kentucky skirmishers. But the warriors were driven back in disarray by the concentrated gunfire of the main army that had come up behind the skirmishers. Caught away from the cover of their fallen trees, the Indian warriors were overwhelmed by the U.S. infantry and cavalry. Casualties were fairly light on both sides. The major consequence of the battle, however, was that the Native Americans were forced to sign the Treaty of Greenville in 1795 and the British to sign the Jay Treaty in 1796 that, first, allowed for continued U.S. expansion into Ohio, Indiana, Illinois, Wisconsin, and Michigan and, second, forced a final British troop withdrawal into Canada.

Oklahoma, *Sooner Waterball* (November 6, 1904): The Feltons, in their 1976 trivia-filled book *More of the Best, Worst and Most Unusual*, address a strange weather oddity concerning football at the start of the twentieth century. The rules of college football were a bit different in those early days of the sport. Back then, a loose punt was "free" to whomever fell on it regardless of whether the ball fell inside the playing field or not. This rule was put to the ultimate test during a very windy autumn day in 1904 when the University of Oklahoma Sooners played the Oklahoma State Aggies. The Aggies were down quickly—indeed, they needed to punt within their own one-yard line only minutes into the game. The punter's hurried kick was caught by the strong wind, drifted backward beyond the Aggies' endzone and landed into the cold Cottonwood Creek, a stream that ran about twenty yards from the field. Following the abovementioned rule, since the backward punt was a free ball, both teams immediately splashed into the creek to recover the football. A cold wet melee broke out until Sooners' left halfback Ed Cook finally gained possession. After swimming furiously upstream for ten yards, the halfback splashed onto the bank and carried the ball up to the endzone for a touchdown. Cook's wet play set the tone for the remainder of the game as Oklahoma won the game with a score of seventy-five to zero.

Oregon, *The Weather Goats of Mt. Nebo* (1965): TV weatherman Spencer Christian and his coauthor, in their 1997 book *Can It Really Rain Frogs?*, discussed some rather unusual forecasters who "worked" in the late sixties. A herd of goats grazing on Mt. Nebo in southwest Oregon near Roseburg actually gained international fame as master weather predictors. Residents began to note that when the goats foraged on the higher part of the mountain, the weather tended to be fair and dry while, when the goats were grazing on the lower slopes, the weather inevitably turned overcast or rainy. Finally, the local radio station KRSB (still in existence) took official notice and began to issue the daily "Goat Weather Forecast." A comparison by the radio station indicated that the goats were right nearly ninety percent of the time while the National Weather Service forecast were correct only sixty-five percent of the time.

Pennsylvania, *Franklin's Mattress Rule of Lightning Safety* (1770): Richard Proctor in 1888 article in the magazine *Knowledge* related a set of household safety rules for lightning that he claimed were espoused by the renowned Benjamin Franklin. First, one should "avoid the neighbourhood of the fireplace; for the soot within the chimneys forms a good conductor of electricity, and lightning has frequently been known to enter a house by the chimney." Second, it is best to also "avoid metals, gildings, and mirrors." On the positive side according to Proctor, Franklin proposed that the safest place "is in the middle of a room, unless a chandelier be suspended there" but that one should "avoid contact with the walls or the floor." Consequently, Franklin gave those who might be inordinately scared of lightning a relatively bizarre safety suggestion that we should lie "in a hammock suspended by silken cords; or, in the not unlikely absence of such a hammock, we should place ourselves on glass, or pitch. Failing this, we may adopt the plan of placing ourselves on several mattresses heaped up in the centre of the room."

Puerto Rico, *San Ciriaco's Razor Blades* (August 8, 1899): J. R. Nash, in his 1976 fascinating disaster book *Darkest Hours,* recounts the horrific hurricane that hit the island in 1899. In those days before the modern naming system, a hurricane was often named by the saint's day of the year on which it hit. An incredibly destructive hurricane now called the "San Ciriaco" hurricane moved across the entire length of Puerto Rico on August 8, 1899. In particular, the small village of Aguadilla was hit by winds gusting to 125 miles per hour. One witness claimed that roofs were being ripped tile-by-tile and plank-by-plank by the terrific winds—and the pieces proceeded to go whipping through the air. The witness observed, "Plates and metal strips soared through the streets like giant razor blades, cutting and slicing, decapitating, amputating, maiming, killing." Estimates placed the death toll by this hurricane at more than three thousand people.

Rhode Island, *The Hessian Gale* (December 17, 1778): According to Edward Rowe Snow, in his engrossing 1946 book *Great Storms and Famous Shipwrecks of the New England Coast,* this December blizzard is often referred to as the "Hessian Gale." The reason involves the incredible dedication of the Hessian sentries who guarded the British army in Newport, Rhode Island. As the wind chill plummeted and snow swirled about them, these resolute sentries remained at their posts throughout the blizzard. As the storm mounted, British officers noticed that some of the guards failed to return from their posts and first assumed that these soldiers had used the cover of the storm to desert the army. However, because of the storm's fury, no immediate hunt could be made. Indeed, the terrible wind and snow even made changing the sentries impossible. Finally, after the blizzard finally retreated, the next shift of guards found the missing Hessians—they were still heroically manning their posts, completely frozen to death.

South Carolina, *A Shower of Alligators?* (December 26, 1877): The *New York Times* in 1877 related a story they received from the Aiken South Carolina, *Journal.* They reported that, while surveying his new turpentine farm, Dr. J. L. Smith of Silverton Township, South Carolina, noticed a large "something" fall hard to the ground. He took even greater interest when that "something" began to crawl toward the tent in which he was sitting. Staring at it closely, Dr. Smith discovered the creature to be a small twelve-inch alligator. Moments later, a second reptile made its appearance at his tent flap. The doctor quickly realized something strange was happening and he searched the immediate area to see if any more alligators had suddenly materialized. Within the small space of a couple hundred yards, Smith tallied six more alligators. He stated that all of the alligators were "quite lively, and about twelve inches in length." Smith's turpentine farm was situated on high sandy ground—apparently not the normal habitat of alligators—about six miles north of the Savannah River. The *Times* article concluded, "the animals were supposed to have been taken up in a waterspout at some distant locality, and dropped in the region where they were found."

South Dakota, *Humphrey's Dust Economics* (1931): According to H. E. Smith's 1982 book *Killer Weather (Stories of Great Disasters)*, Vice-President Hubert H. Humphrey lived as a child in Huron, South Dakota, with an eventual dream of taking over the family drugstore. Then came the terrible Dust Bowl days of the 1930s. In South Dakota some of the dust storms were particularly devastating. Humphrey wrote, "God, it was terrible . . . so hot, so terribly hot . . . the dust, it was everywhere . . . You felt trapped." Indeed, according to Smith, it eventually became too much for the future vice president as apparently one day during a dust storm, Humphrey went berserk, smashing dirt-covered windows throughout his family's house. The dust storms even affected Humphrey's health—along with many others, he actually became ill from inhaled dust. Finally, the drought won and Humphrey surrendered to the prevalent dust, gave up thoughts of entering the family business and left Huron for good. Later the future vicepresident recalled, "I learned more about economics from one South Dakota dust storm than all my years in college."

Tennessee, *Wind, Gnats, and Mules* (1901): Willard Hurd reported in a study on insect migrations for *Monthly Weather Review* of the bizarre relationship between wind, gnats, and mules in Memphis, Tennessee. In those days, any sudden infestations of buffalo gnats from the southern swamps and bayous were cause for general alarm throughout the city. During the "season of development" in the St. Francis bottoms on the opposite bank of the Mississippi River, Hurd reported, a strong west wind would literally bring vast clouds of the dangerous insects across the river and into Memphis. One of the biggest concerns was for urban transportation; at that time, sturdy work mules pulled the streetcars in Memphis. Hurd recalled that the gnats' "numbers and voracity would be so great that they were known to stop the street cars by killing the mules in their tracks."

Texas, *Transforming Peaches to Pecans* (May 4, 1922): Howard C. Key, in a book called *Madstones and Twisters,* edited by Mody Boatright and others, told the story of a tornado that uprooted and removed a peach tree in the backyard of a farmer who lived near Austin,

A 1935 ranch house in South Dakota saved from burial from heavy clay soil by a wooden fence taken from *Soil Blowing and Dust Storms* by Charles E. Kellogg, Miscellaneous Publication No. 221, U.S. Department of Agriculture. (Photo Courtesy of National Oceanic and Atmospheric Administration/Department of Commerce Photo Library Historic NWS Collection.)

Texas. However, before it dissipated, the tornado then dropped a young pecan tree in the hole left by the uprooted peach tree. According to Key, the farmer tapped the new tree into an upright position and filled the rest of the hole with earth. Some thirty-six years, the transplanted pecan tree still grew and, indeed, one of the editors of the book, Mody Boatright, actually ate some of the peach-flavored nuts from the hands of the farmer himself.

Utah, *Salt Water Dust* (April 4, 1919): Utah's *Deseret News* reported an odd weather story (later recounted in *Monthly Weather Review*) that a huge salty dust storm fell over a large part of Utah in 1919. Even in Salt Lake City itself, the salty rain fell as the dust hung over the city, resulting in considerable inconvenience from bespattered windows, automobiles, etc. According to witnesses (who apparently went to the trouble of sampling the dust), the mud had a distinctly salty taste. The *Deseret News* reported that many people speculated that the salty dust had come come from the Great Salt Lake "but it was simply desert mud containing a high percentage of salts."

Virginia, *Lightning Dating* (1887): As described in P. E. Viemeister's *The Lightning Book,* a very "fortuitous" lightning strike helped to reveal the age—and the resulting historical promi-nence—of Old St. Luke's Church. The historic Gothic church, located near Smithfield, Virginia, had been in a state of disrepair since about 1852 with weeds enveloping the building and many of its buttresses crumbling. However, when the church was struck by a lightning strike during a summer thunderstorm in 1887, a few of its handmade bricks became dislodged and fell to the ground. Inspection of the bricks revealed that one of them had the date "1632" chiseled on it. The event (and subsequent historical inquiry) therefore established Old St. Luke's as the oldest existing Protestant church in this country.

Vermont, *The Electroplated Cat* (1891): Probably one of the most bizarre (and frankly least believable) of all weather oddity stories has to be the electroplated cat of New Salem, Vermont. In his rare 1895 book *Lightning Record,* Henry Kretzer retold the story of Arent S. Vandyck's cat. According to Kretzer, the cat was in Vandyck's parlor in which hung a collection of revolutionary swords, one of which was heavily plated with silver. During a terrific night thunderstorm, lightning hit the house. The next morning, Vandyck came into the parlor and found what appeared to be a pure silver statue of his cat lying on the sofa. Then Vandyck noticed that one of his revolutionary swords that had hung just above the sofa had been stripped of all its silver. The hilt of the sword was gone and the scabbard was but a strip of blackened steel. Apparently, the lightning had somehow transferred the silver from the sword and onto the cat; in other words, lightning had electroplated the family cat. Unfortunately, no independent confirmation of this story exists.

West Virginia, *On the Road to Hell* (January 1, 1862): In Major Henry Kyd Douglas's civil war book *I Rode With Stonewall,* Douglas noted that one of General Stonewall Jackson's greatest traits was his incredible tenacity—there was no place that he wouldn't go to purse the enemy—or so his troops believed. Just before a New Year's raid into the Union in 1862, the Confederate troops were camped in a cold and damp field. Many of Stonewall's troops huddled shivering around a large fire as they tried to keep warm in their thin and patched blankets. When sparks from the fire ignited one Confederate's blanket on fire, the soldier jumped up and stamped out the flames cursing, "I wish the Yankees were in Hell." Another soldier nearby shivered grimly in the cold and responded, "I don't, because Old Jack would follow them there with our brigade in front!" Major Douglas wrote that when he retold the story to Stonewall Jackson, the general actually laughed aloud—a reaction that the stern warrior seldom permitted himself.

Washington, *The Great Olympic Blowdown* (January 29, 1921): E. L. Phillips in a 1962 issue of *Weatherwise* told the amazing survival story of Washington State Weather Bureau chief Perry Hill. The weatherman was traveling to North Head with his wife through a forest of spruce and hemlock when the massive windstorm struck. According to Hill, "We saw the top of a rotted tree break off and fall out of sight in the brush." The couple slowly drove on, trying to avoid sizeable tree branches that had fallen on the road. Visibility, however, became difficult as literally "showers" of tree twigs and small limbs filled the air. Hill continued, "We soon came to a telephone pole across the roadway and brought our car to a stop, for a short distance beyond the pole an immense spruce tree laid across the road." The two left the car and started to run down the road to get out of the storm. Hill then recalled, "Just after leaving the car, I chanced to look up and saw a limb sailing through the air toward us; I caught Mrs. Hill by the hand and we ran; an instant later the limb, which was about twelve inches in diameter, crashed where we had stood." Hill said that the deafening southeast wind literally brought down trees as big as four feet wide.

Wisconsin, *Frozen Alive* (January 19, 1985): Fortean sources, including Charles Berlitz's 1988 book *World of Strange Phenomena,* restated the amazing story of a Wisconsin two-year-old. During a major polar outbreak with temperatures plummeting to -60°F below, little Michael Troche of Milwaukee apparently decided to go for a walk wearing only his light pajamas. His father found the baby collapsed in the snow literally frozen stiff. Michael wasn't breathing, his arms and legs were frozen hard and ice crystals had even formed on and beneath his skin. His parents immediately rushed him to Milwaukee Children's Hospital where they determined that his body temperature had dropped to -16°C. Still, doctors immediately attempted to revive the young boy. One news report even stated that the doctors actually heard ice crystals in his body cracking as they lifted him onto the operating table. They warmed his blood through a heart-lung machine, and slowly began to thaw his body using drugs to prevent brain swelling. Young Michael remained semiconscious for a period of three days and then began to make rapid recovery. Although there had been minor muscle damage to his left hand, he avoided critical brain damage. Doctors attributed the lack of injury to the incredible wind-chill that froze him so rapidly that his metabolism apparently had little need for oxygen.

Wyoming, *The Caboose and the Wind* (October 20, 1908): Western newspapers reported, "One of the most horrible and unusual catastrophes which has ever occurred in the history of American railroading took place near Cheyenne today." Reports from Wyoming stated that a "heavy gust of wind" caused a train caboose to be blown off the track and into a huge thirty-foot "fill-in." A total of six laborers were dead, several others were believed dead and twenty-five or thirty more were reported injured. Apparently, the wind pushed the caboose, which was being used to house the rail workers, over the edge of the gully and the laborers inside were tossed from one end of the car to the other before being crushed when the caboose hit the bottom. Newspapers reported that the rail workers were piled in helpless confusion among the wreckage of the caboose.

SELECTED BIBLIOGRAPHY

Works of Major Weather Archivists:
These are works of many of the archivists mentioned in Chapter One.

Arago, D. F. J., 1855: *Meteorological Essays with an Introduction by Baron Alexander von Humboldt*, Longman, Brown, Green and Longmans, London, p. 500.

Flammarion, C. 1906: *The Atmosphere* (translated and abridged from M. Flammarion's *L'Atmosphère*, Paris, 1872), Drallop Publishing, New York, p. 453.

——, 1901: *The Unknown (L'inconnu)*, Harper and Brothers, New York, p.487.

——, 1905: *Thunder and Lightning*, Chatto and Windus, London, p. 281.

Tomlinson, Charles, c1860: *The Dew-Drop and the Mist: An Account of the Phenomena and Properties of Atmospheric Vapour*, Society for Promoting Christian Knowledge, London, p. 346.

——, c1860: *The Rain-Cloud and the Snow-Storm: An Account of the Nature, Formation, Properties, Dangers, and Uses of Rain and Snow*, Society for Promoting Christian Knowledge, London, p. 402.

——, c1860: *The Thunder-Storm: An Account of the Properties of Lightning and of Atmospheric Electricity in Various Parts of the World*, Society for Promoting Christian Knowledge, London, p. 348.

Fort, C., 1974: *The Complete Books of Charles Fort*, Dover Publications, New York, p. 1125.

——, 1982: *Lightning, Auroras, Nocturnal Lights, and Related Luminous Phenomena: A Catalog of Geophysical Anomalies*, Sourcebook Project, Glen Arm, Maryland, p. 242.

——, 1983: *Tornados, Dark Days, Anomalous Precipitation, and Related Weather Phenomena: A Catalog of Geophysical Anomalies*, Sourcebook Project, Glen Arm, Maryland, p. 173.

Corliss, W. R., 1977: *Handbook of Unusual Natural Phenomena*, Sourcebook Project, Glen Arm, Maryland, p. 542.

Douglas, Marjory Stoneman, 1958: *Hurricane,* Rinehart and Company, New York, p. 393.

———, 1954: *Tornadoes of the United States,* University of Oklahoma Press, Norman, Oklahoma, p. 221.

Flora, S. D., 1956: *Hailstorms of the United States,* University of Oklahoma Press, Norman, Oklahoma, p. 201.

Grazulis, T.P., 1993: *Significant Tornadoes,* The Tornado Project of Environmental Films, St. Johnsbury, Vermont, p. 1326.

———, 1997: *Significant Tornadoes Update 1992–1995,* The Tornado Project of Environmental Films, St. Johnsbury, Vermont, p. 113. (Page numbering continues from *Significant Tornadoes.*)

———, 2001: *The Tornado: Nature's Ultimate Windstorm,* University of Oklahoma Press, Norman, Oklahoma, p. 324.

Lane, F. W., 1965: *The Elements Rage,* Chilton, Philadelphia, Pennsylvania, p. 346.

———, 1986: *The Violent Earth,* Salem House, Topsfield, Massachusetts, p. 224.

Longshore, D., 1998: *Encyclopedia of Hurricanes, Typhoons, and Cyclones,* Facts on File, Inc, New York, p. 372.

Michell, J. and R. J. M. Rickard, 1977: *Phenomena: A Book of Wonders,* Pantheon Books, New York, p. 128.

Nalivkin, D.V., 1982: *Hurricanes, Storms, and Tornadoes: Geographic Characteristics and Geological Activity (Uragany, Buri i Smerchi . . .),* (translated from Russian and published by National Oceanic and Atmospheric Administration), Nauka Publishers, Leningrad, p. 597.

———, 1993: *The Day Niagara Falls Ran Dry: Canadian Weather Facts and Trivia,* Key Porter Books, Toronto, p. 226.

Phillips, David, 1998: *Blame It on the Weather,* Key Porter Books, Toronto, p. 240.

Simons, P., 1996: *Weird Weather,* Little, Brown and Company, Boston, p. 307.

Tannehill, Ivan R., 1944: *Hurricanes: Their Nature and History, Particularly those of the West Indies and the Southern Coasts of the United States,* Princeton University Press, Princeton, p. 269.

Classical Weather Sources (pre-1920): These are the relatively rare pre-1920 volumes involving weather and meteorology events cited throughout the text.

Abercromby, Ralph, 1892: *Weather: A Popular Exposition of the Nature of Weather Changes from Day to Day,* Kegan, Paul, Trench, Trübner & Co., London, p. 472.

Alexander, W.H., 1902: *Hurricanes: Especially those of Porto Rico and St. Kitts* (U.S. Depart. of Agriculture, Weather Bureau, Bulletin No. 32, Government Printing Office, Washington, p. 79.

Andrews, William, 1882: *The Book of Oddities,* Simpkin, Marschall and Company, London, p. 85.

Belden, C., 1883: *Belden's Guide to the Natural Sciences, History, Biography, and General Literature,* C.B. Beach & Company, Chicago, p. 828.

Blodget, Lorin, 1857: *Climatology of the United States,* J.B. Lippincott, Philadelphia, Pennsylvania, p. 536.

Brocklesby, J., 1851: *Elements of Meteorology,* Pratt, Woodford & Co., New York, p. 240.

Buchan, Alexander, 1871: *Introductory Text-Book of Meteorology,* Blackwood and Sons, Edinburgh, p. 218.

Cowan, Frank, 1865: *Curious Facts in the History of Insects (Including Spiders and Scorpions),* J.P. Lippincott & Co., Philadelphia, Pennsylvania, p. 396.

Curzon, Julian, 1896: *The Great Cyclone at St. Louis and East St. Louis, May 27, 1896: Being a Full History of the Most Terrifying and Destructive Tornado in the History of the World,* Cyclone Publishing Co., St. Louis, Missouri, p. 416.

Darwin, Charles, 1897: *Journal of Researches into the Natural History and Geology of the Countries Visited During the Voyage of* HMS Beagle Round the World, Under the Command of Capt. FitzRoy, R.N., Appleton and Company, New York, p. 519.

De Fonvielle, W., and T. L. Phipson (trans) 1867: *Thunder and Lightning* (translated by T. L. Phipson), Charles Scribner & Co., New York, p. 216.

Espy, J. P., 1841: *The Philosophy of Storms,* Little and Brown, Boston, Massachusetts, p. 552.

Ferrel, William, 1904: *A Popular Treatise on the Winds: Comprising the General Motions of the Atmosphere, Monsoons, Cyclones, Tornadoes, Waterspouts, Hail-Storms, Etc. (Second Edition),* John Wiley & Sons, New York, p. 505.

Finley, Sergeant J.P., 1881: *Report of the Tornadoes of May 29 and 30, 1879,* (U.S. Department of War, Professional Papers of the Signal Service No. 4), Government Printing Office, Washington, D.C., p. 166.

Forbes, Jonathan, 1840: *Eleven Years in Ceylon, Comprising Sketches of the Field Sports and Natural History,* R. Bentley London (vol. 2), p. 356.

Fulke, William, and Theodore Horberger (ed), 1979: *A Goodly Gallerye: Book of Meteors,* (reprinted from 1563), The American Philosophical Society, Philadelphia, p. 121.

General Staff, 1907: *The Russo-Japanese War (Reports from British Officers Attached to the Japanese Forces in the Field* (Volume One), Whitehall, p. 682.

Giberne, Agnes, 1894: *The Ocean of Air: Meteorology for Beginners,* New York Tract Society, New York, p. 398.

Godbey, A. H., 1890: *Great Disasters and Horrors in the World's History,* Royal Publishing, St. Louis, Missouri, p. 612.

Greely, A. W. 1888: *American Weather,* Dodd, Meade and Co., New York, p. 286.

Hartwig, G., 1887: *The Aerial World*, Longmans, Green, and Co., London, p. 556.

Hazen, H. A., 1890: *The Tornado*, N. D. C. Hodges, New York.

Hearn, Lafcadio, 1917: *Chita: A Memory of Last Island* (reprinted from 1889), Harper and Brothers, New York, p. 204.

Herodotus, 1910: *The History of Herodotus :* Volume two, (translated by George Rawlinson, edited by E. H. Blakeney), E. P. Dutton, New York, p. 353.

Holder, Charles Frederick, 1892: *Living Lights: A Phosphorescent Animals and Vegetables*, Charles Scribner's Sons, New York, p. 187.

Holinshed, Raphael, 1578: *Holinshed's Chronicles of London, Scotland, and Ireland . . .* , J. Johnson, London.

Hone, William, 1827: *Every-Day Book:* Vol.ume two, Hunt and Clarke, London, p. 1711.

Horner, Donald W., 1919: *Meteorology For All*, Witherby & Co, London, p. 184.

Jackson, Colonel Julian R., 1845: *What to Observe; or, The Traveller's Remembrance*, Madden & Malcolm, London, p. 570.

Kaemtz, L. F., and C. V. Walker (trans) 1845: *A Complete Course of Meteorology* (translated by C. V. Walker), Hippolyte Bailliére, London, p. 598.

Kretzer, H. F., 1895: *Lightning Record: A Book of Reference and Information*, Henry F. Kretzer, St. Louis, Missouri.

Lackland, William, 1886: *Meteors, Aerolites, Storms, and Atmospheric Phenomena* (from the French of Zürcher and Margollé), Charles Scribner's Sons, New York, p. 324.

Langtry, Lillie, 1925: *The Days I Knew*, George H. Doran Company, New York, p. 300.

Loomis, Elias, 1879: *A Treatise on Meteorology with a Collection of Meteorological Tables*, Harper and Brothers, New York, p. 305.

Martin, Edwin C., 1913: *Our Own Weather*, Harper and Brothers, New York, 281 p.

Northrop, Henry Davenport, 1887: *Earth, Sea, and Sky, or Marvels of the Universe*, National Publishing Company, Philadelphia, Pennsylvania, p. 864.

Piddington, H., 1852: *Conversations About Hurricanes: For the Use of Plain Sailors*, Smith, Elder, London, p. 317.

Plutarch, 1864: *Lives* (translated by John Dryden), Random House, New York, p. 1309.

Russell, Rolo, 1893: *On Hail*, Edward Stanford, London, p. 224.

Short, Thomas, 1749: *A General Chronological History of the Air, Weather, Seasons, Meteors, etc. in Sundry Places and Different Times:* Volume one, T. Longman and A. Millar, London, p. 494.

——, 1749: *A General Chronological History of the Air, Weather, Seasons, Meteors, etc. in Sundry Places and Different Times:* Volume two, T. Longman and A. Millar, London, p. 536.

Steinmetz, A., 1867: *Sunshine and Showers: Their Influences Throughout Creation*, Reeve & Co., London, p. 432.

Swan, John, 1643: *Specvivm mundi, or A Glasse Representing the Face of the World, printed by Roger Daniel for Troylus Adkinson, Cambridge, Massachusetts*, p. 504.

Thomson, David Purdie, 1849: *Introduction to Meteorology*, W. Blackwood and Sons, Edinburgh and London, p. 487.

Waldo, Frank, 1894: *Modern Meteorology: An Outline of the Growth and Present Condition of Some of its Phases*, Scribner's Sons, London, p. 460.

Werner, E. T. C., 1825: *Myths and Legends of China*, Tun huang shu chü, Taipei, p. 454.

Post-1920 Book Sources: These include many of the more modern fortean and meteorology sources of information cited and used in this book.

Ackermann, A. S. E., 1970: *Popular Fallacies (Fourth Edition)* (Reprint of the 1950 edition published by Old Westminster Press, London), Gale Research Company, Detroit, Michigan, p. 843.

Adams, R. B. (ed), 1990: *Forces of Nature*, Library of Curious and Unusual Facts, Time-Life Books, Alexandria, Virginia, p. 144.

Allen, O. E., 1983: *Atmosphere* (Plant Earth series), Time-Life Books, Alexandria, Virginia, p. 176.

Allen, Troy, 1974: *Disaster*, Castle Books, New Jersey, p. 176.

Asimov, I., 1979: *A Choice of Catastrophes: The Disasters that Threaten Our World*, Simon & Schuster, New York, p. 377.

——, 1979: *Book of Facts*, Gosset & Dunlap, New York, 1979, p. 466.

——, 1981: *Asimov's Guide to the Bible*, Random House, New York, p. 1295.

Barnes, J., 2001: *North Carolina's Hurricane History* (Third Edition), The University of North Carolina Press, Chapel Hill, North Carolina, p. 319.

Barry, James Dale, 1980: *Ball Lightning and Bead Lightning*, Plenum Press, New York, p. 298.

Bell, C., 1957: *The Wonder of Snow*, Hill and Wang, New York, p. 269.

Benstead, C. R., 1940: *The Weather Eye*, Robert Hale Limited, London, p. 287.

Berlitz, C., 1988: *Charles Berlitz's World of Strange Phenomena*, (1991 reprint), Fawcett Crest, New York, p. 331.

——, 1991: *Charles Berlitz's World of the Incredible but True*, Fawcett Crest, New York, p. 265.

——, 1991: *Charles Berlitz's World of the Odd and the Awesome*, Fawcett Crest, New York, p. 272.

Bixby, W., 1961: *Havoc: The Story of Natural Disasters*, David McKay Company, New York, p. 181.

Blair, Thomas A. and Robert C. Fite, 1965: *Weather Elements* °Fifth Edition), Prentice-Hall, Inc., Englewood Cliffs, New Jersey, p. 364.

Blumenstock, D. I., 1959: *The Ocean of Air,* Rutgers University Press, New Brunswick, New Jersey, p. 457.

Bord, Janet and Colin Bord, 1989: *Unexplained Mysteries of the Twentieth Century,* Contemporary Books, Chicago, p. 432.

Boschke, F. L., 1975: *The Unexplained, the Unknown World in which We Live,* (translated from the German *Das Unerforschte: Die Unbekannte Welt in der Wir Leben*), Simon & Schuster, New York, p. 273.

Botley, C.M., 1938: *The Air and Its Mysteries,* G. Bell and Sons, Ltd., London, p. 296.

Brandon, J., 1978: *Weird America: A Guide to Places of Mystery in the United States,* Dutton, New York, p. 257.

Briggs, Peter, 1969: *Mysteries of Our World,* David McKay Company, Inc., New York, p. 240.

Brooks, Charles F., 1935: *Why the Weather?* Harcourt, Brace and Company, New York, p. 295.

Brown, Billye Walker and Walter R. Brown, 1972: *Historical Catastrophes: Hurricanes and Tornadoes,* Addison-Wesley Publishing, Reading, Massachusetts, p. 223.

Brown, S., 1961: *World of the Wind,* Bobbs-Merrill Company, Indianapolis, Indiana, p. 224.

Brown, Walter R. and Norman D. Anderson, 1976: *Famines: Historical Catastrophes,* Addison-Wesley Publishing, Reading, Massachusetts, p. 191.

Cade, C. M. and D. Davis, 1969: *The Taming of the Thunderbolts: The Science and Superstition of Ball Lightning,* Abelard-Schuman, New York, p. 176.

Calkins, C. C., 1982: *Mysteries of the Unexplained,* The Reader's Digest Association, Inc. Pleasantville, New York, p. 320.

Carrighar, Sally, 1959: *Wild Voice of the North,* Doubleday & Company, Garden City, New York, p. 191.

Christian, S. and A. Felix, 1997: *Can It Really Rain Frogs?* Wiley and Sons, New York, p. 121.

Clark, C., 1982: *Flood,* Time-Life Books, Inc., Alexandria, Virginia, p. 176.

Clark, J., 1993: *Encyclopedia of Strange and Unexplained Physical Phenomena,* Gale Research, Inc., Detroit, Michigan, p. 395.

——, 1993: *Unexplained!* Visible Ink Press, Detroit, p. 443.

Clark, Jerome and Pear, Nancy, 1997: *Strange and Unexplained Phenomena,* Visible Ink Press, Detroit, Michigan, p. 476.

Clowes, Ernest S., 1939: *The Hurricane of 1938 on Eastern Long Island,* Hampton Press, Bridgehampton, New York, p. 67.

Cohen, Daniel, 1985: *The Encyclopedia of the Strange,* Dorset Press, New York, p. 291

Cohen, I. B., 1941: *Benjamin Franklin's Experiments, Part B,* Harvard University Press, Boston, p. 453.

Colby, C. B., 1963: *Strangely Enough!* (Abridged Edition), Scholastic Book Services, New York, p. 184.

Colligan, Douglas, 1980: *Amazing Real Life Coincidences,* Scholastic Books, New York, p. 134.

Constance, Arthur, 1956: *The Inexplicable Sky,* The Citadel Press, New York, p. 288.

Cornell, J., 1982: *The Great International Disaster Book* (Third Edition), Charles Scribner's Sons, New York, p. 472.

Crean, Patrick G (ed), 1982: *Ripley's Believe It or Not! Book of Chance,* Coward, McCann & Geoghegan, Inc., New York, p. 333.

Darling, David, 2003: *The Universal Book of Astronomy,* John Wiley & Sons, Inc., Hoboken, New Jersey, p. 570.

Dary, David, 1984: *True Tales of Old-Time Kansas* (Revised Edition), University Press of Kansas, Lawrence, Kansas, p. 322.

Davidson, K., 1996: *Twister: The Science of Tornadoes and Making of an Adventure Movie,* Pocket Books, New York, p. 202.

Davies, A. F., 1999: *Biblical Weather,* Essence Publishing, Belleville, Ontario, Canada, p. 388.

Davies, Pete, 2000: *Inside the Hurricane: Face to Face with Nature's Deadliest Storms,* Holt, New York, p. 266.

Davis, L., 1992: *Natural Disasters: From the Black Plague to the Eruption of Mt. Pinatubo,* Facts On File, New York, p. 321.

De La Rue, E. Aubert, 1955: *Man and the Winds,* Hutchinson, London, p. 206.

Dennis, Jerry, 1992: *It's Raining Frogs and Fishes: Four Seasons of Natural Phenomena and Oddities of the Sky,* Harper Perennial, New York, p. 323.

Dick, Everett, 1963: *Tales of the Frontier: From Lewis and Clark to the Last Roundup,* University of Nebraska Press, Lincoln, Nebraska, p. 390.

Donnan, Jack and Marcia Donnan, 1977: *Rain Dance to Research,* David McKay Company, New York, p. 148.

Douglas, Henry Kyd, 1940: *I Rode With Stonewall,* The University of North Carolina Press, Chapel Hill, North Carolina, p. 401.

Duey, Kathleen and Mary Barnes, 2000: *Freaky Facts About Natural Disasters,* Aladdin Paperbacks, New York, p. 184.

Duff, D. V., 1936: *Palestine Picture,* Hodder & Stoughton, London, p. 318.

Dunn, G. E. and Miller, B. I., 1960: *Atlantic Hurricanes,* Louisiana State University Press, Baton Rouge, Louisiana, p. 326.

Dwyer, Jim (project ed), 1989: *Reader's Digest Strange Stories: Amazing Facts of America's Past,* The Reader's Digest Association, Pleasantville, New York, p. 416.

Dyson, James L., 1962: *The World of Ice,* Alfred A. Knop, New York, p. 292.

Eagleman, J. R., 1983: *Severe and Unusual Weather,* Van Nostrand Reinhold, New York, p. 372.

Editors of *Fortean Times,* 1995: *Strange Days #1: The Year in Weirdness,* Cader Books (Andrews and McMeel), Kansas City, Kansas, p. 141.

Edwards, F., 1959: *Stranger than Science,* Citadel Press, Secaucus, New Jersey, p. 303.

———, 1961: *Strange People,* Lyle Stuart, New York, p. 287.

———, 1962: *Strangest of All,* Ace Books, New York, p. 189.

———, 1964: *Strange World,* Ace Star Books, New York, p. 251.

Evans, Bergen, 1946: *The Natural History of Nonsense,* Alfred A. Knopf, New York, p. 275.

Felton, B. and Fowler, M., 1976: *Felton and Fowler's More of the Best, Worst and Most Unusual,* Fawcett Crest, New York, p. 316.

Ferrara, G. M., 1979: *The Disaster File: The 1970s,* Facts on File, Inc., New York, 173 p.

Floyd, E. Randall, 1989/1990: *Great Southern Mysteries* (Two Volumes in One), Barnes & Noble, New York, p. 177 and 190.

Foggitt, B., 1992: *Weatherwise: Facts, Fictions, and Predictions,* Running Press, Philadelphia, Pennsylvania, p. 88.

Forbes-Robertson, Sir Johnston, 1925 (1971 reprint): *A Player Under Three Reigns,* Benjamin Blom, Inc., New York, p. 292.

Frazier, K, 1979: *The Violent Face of Nature: Severe Phenomena and Natural Disasters,* William Morrow and Company, Inc., New York, p. 386.

Free, E. E. and T. Hoke, 1929: *Weather,* Constable & Company, London, p. 337.

Freier, G. D., 1992: *The Wonder of Weather,* Gramercy Books, New York, p. 214.

Gadd, L. D., 1981: *The Second Book of the Strange,* World Almanac Publications, New York, p. 333.

——— , 1965: *Invisible Horizons: True Mysteries of the Sea,* Ace, New York, p. 256.

———, 1968: *Mysterious Fires and Lights,* Dell Publishing Company, New York, p. 236.

Geddes, A. E. M., 1930: *Meteorology: An Introductory Treatise,* Blackie & Son Limited, London, p. 392.

Gokhale, N.R., 1975: *Hailstorms and Hailstone Growth,* State University of New York Press, Albany, New York, p. 465.

Goldman, Jane, 1996: *The X-Files Book of the Unexplained,* (Vol. two), Simon & Schuster, London, p. 339.

Gould, R. T., 1965 *Oddities: A Book of Unexplained Facts,* Bell Publishing, New York, p. 228.

Gribbin, J., 1979: *Weather Force: Climate and Its Impact on Our World,* G.P. Putnam's Sons, New York, p. 191.

Halacy, Daniel, Stephen, Jr., 1968: *The Weather Changers,* Harper & Row, New York, p. 246.

Hellman, H., 1967: *Light and Electricity in the Atmosphere,* Holiday House, New York, p. 223.

Hering, D. W., 1924: *Foibles and Fallacies of Science,* Van Nostrand, New York, p. 294.

Hewitt, R., 1957: *From Earthquake, Fire, and Flood,* Scribner's Sons, New York, p. 215.

Hitching, Francis, 1978: *The Mysterious World: An Atlas of the Unexplained,* Holt, Rinehart & Winston, New York, p. 256.

Hix, Elsie, 1953: *Strange As It Seems,* Hanover House, Garden City, New York, p. 256.

Holford, Ingrid, 1976: *British Weather Disasters,* David Charles, London, p. 128.

——, 1977: *The Guinness Book of Weather Facts and Feats,* Guinness Superlatives Limited, Enfield, England, p. 240.

Holland, G. J., 1993: *Global Guide to Tropical Cyclone Forecasting* WMO/TC-No. 560, Report No. TCp-31, World Meteorological Organization, Geneva.

Humphreys, W. J., 1926: *Rain Making and Other Weather Vagaries,* Williams & Wilkins Company, Baltimore, Maryland, p. 157.

——, 1940: *Physics of the Air,* McGraw-Hill Book Company, New York, p. 676.

——, 1947: *Ways of the Weather,* Jaques Cattell Press, Lancaster, Pennsylvania, p. 400.

Hunt, Gerry, 1988: *Beyond Belief: Bizarre America,* Berkley, New York, p. 152.

Huschke, R. E., 1959: *Glossary of Meteorology,* American Meteorological Society, Boston, Massachusetts, p. 638.

Irving, R., 1955: *Hurricanes and Twisters,* Alfred A. Knopf, New York, p. 144.

Jakes, John, 1966: *TIROS: Weather Eye in Space,* Julian Messner, New York, p. 191

Jeffries, W., 1980: *That's Incredible,* Jove Publications, New York, p. 190.

Jennings, Gary, 1970: *The Killer Storms: Hurricanes, Typhoons, and Tornadoes,* J.B. Lippincott Company, Philadelphia, Pennsylvania, p. 207.

Kals, W. A., 1977: *The Riddle of the Winds,* Doubleday, New York, p. 201

Kane, J. N., 1950: *Famous First Facts,* H.W. Wilson Company, New York, p. 888.

Keel, John A., 1971: *Our Haunted Planet,* Fawcell Gold Medal, Greenwich, Connecticut, p. 222.

Keller, David, 1990: *Great Disasters,* Avon Books, New York, p. 132.

Kimble, G. H. T., 1955: *Our American Weather,* McGraw-Hill, New York, p. 322.

King, E. F. (ed), 1970: *Ten Thousand Wonderful Things,* (original 1860 published in London, Rutledge and Sons), Gale Research Company, Detroit, Michigan, p. 684.

Kingston, J., 1991: *Mysterious Happenings,* Bloomsbury Books, London, p. 256.

Kingston, Jeremy and David Lambert, 1979: *Catastrophe and Crisis,* Facts on File, New York, p. 336.

Kohut, John J. and Roland Sweet, 1993: *News From the Fringe,* Plume Books, New York, p. 204.

Krause, P. F. and Flood, K. L., 1997: *Weather and Climate Extremes,* TEC-0099 (September, 1997), U.S. Army Corps of Engineers Topographic Engineering Center, 7701 Telegraph Road, Alexandra Virginia 22315-3864, p. 89.

Lamb, H. H, 1984: *Climatic History and Future,* Princeton University Press, Princeton, New Jersey, p. 835.

Landsea, C. W., 1999: FAQ Hurricanes, Typhoons, and Tropical Cyclones (Ver. 2.7), www.aoml.noaa.gov/hrd/tcfaq/tcfaqE.

Latham, J. and Fuchs, V. (ed) 1977: *Forces of Nature*, Holt, Rinehart and Winston, New York, p. 303.

Laughton, L. G. Carr and V. Heddon, 1931: *Great Storms*, William Farquhar Payson, New York, p. 254.

Leokum, A., 1976: *The Curious Book*, Sterling Publishing Co., New York, p. 256.

Lilenthal, M. S., 1947: *Dear Remembered World: Childhood Memories of an Old New Yorker*, Richard Smith, New York, p. 226.

Loebsack, Theo, 1959: *Our Atmosphere* (translated by E. L. and D. Rewald), Pantheon, New York, p. 256.

Louis, D., 1983: *2,201 Fascinating Facts*, Greenwich House, New York, p. 377.

——, 1979: *More Fascinating Facts*, Crown Publishers, Inc., New York, p. 191.

McCarthy, Joe, 1969: *Hurricane!* American Heritage Press, New York, p. 168.

McCrown, L. J., 1974: *The Indianola Scrap Book*, Calhoun County Historical Survey Committee, Port Lavaca, Texas, p. 235.

McEwan, Graham, 1991: *Freak Weather*, Robert Hale Limited, London, p. 192.

McWhirter, N. and R. McWhirter, 1970: *Dunlop Illustrated Encyclopedia of Facts*, (Revised Edition) Doubleday & Company, Garden City, New York, p. 864.

Mergen, B., 1997: *Snow in America*, Smithsonian Institution Press, Washington, p. 321.

Meyer, Jerome, S., 1961: *The Book of Amazing Facts*, Lancer Books, New York, p. 159.

Meyers, J., 1979: *Mammoth Book of Trivia*, Hart Publishing, New York, p. 512.

Miller, R. DeWitt, 1956: *Forgotten Mysteries*, The Citadel Press, New York, p. 202.

Mooney, Julie and Editors, 2002: *Ripley's Believe It or Not! Encyclopedia of the Bizarre, Amazing, Strange, Inexplicable, Weird, and All True*, Black Dog & Leventhal Publishers, New York, p. 318.

Morgan, E. S., 1956: *The Birth of the Republic, 1763–1789*, University of Chicago Press, Chicago.

Morris Scott, *The Book of Strange Facts and Useless Information*, 1979: Doubleday & Company: Garden City, New York, p. 143.

Murchie, Guy, 1954: *Song of the Sky*, Houghton Mifflin, Boston, Massachusetts, p. 438.

Nash, J. R., 1976: *Darkest Hours*, Nelson Hall, Chicago, Illinios, p. 812.

Norman, J. R., 1963: *A History of Fishes* (second edition), Hill & Wang, New York, p. 398.

Persinger, Michael A. and Gyslaine F. Lafreniére, 1977: *Space-Time Transients and Unusual Events*, Nelson-Hall, Chicago, Illinois, p. 267.

Pliny, and P. Turner (ed) 1962: *Natural History* (Book two), Southern Illinois University Press, Carbondale, Illinois, p. 496.

Pope, Dan and Clayton Brough (ed), 1996: *Utah's Weather and Climate*, Publishers Press, Salt Lake City, Utah, p. 245.

Priestley, Harold E., 1979: *Truly Bizarre,* Sterling Publishing Co., Inc., New York, p. 224.

Ramsay, Helena and Sandy Ransford, 1996: *501 Horrible but True Things You'd Rather Not Know!* Barnes & Noble, New York, p. 46.

Randles Jenny and Peter Hough, 1995: *Encyclopedia of the Unexplained,* Barnes & Noble Books, New York, p. 240.

Reader's Digest (Kaari Ward, ed), 1989: *Great Disasters,* Reader's Digest Association, Pleasantville, New York, p. 320.

Reader's Digest (Richard Williams, ed), 1992: *Bizarre Phenomena: Quest for the Unknown,* Reader's Digest Association, Pleasantville, New York, p. 144.

Reader's Digest Editors, 1978 (third printing), *Reader's Digest Strange Stories, Amazing Facts,* The Reader's Digest Association, Inc., Pleasantville, New York, p. 608

Reader's Digest, 1997: *Natural Disasters: The Earth, Its Wonders, Its Secrets,* Reader's Digest Association, Pleasantville, New York, p. 160.

Rickard, Bob and John Michell, 2000: *Unexplained Phenomena* A Rough Guide Special), Rough Guide Ltd., London, p. 390.

Ripley, R. L., 1933: *The Omnibus Believe It or Not,* Stanley Paul, Great Britain, p. 384

Ripley's Editors, 1978: *Ripley's Believe it or Not! Stars, Space, UFOs,* Pocket Books, New York, p. 194.

Ripley's Editors, 1979: *Ripley's Believe It or Not! Great Disasters,* Pocket Books, New York, p. 176.

Robins, J., 1990: *The World's Greatest Disasters,* Hamlyn, London, p. 192.

Robinson, A., 1993: *Earth Shock,* Thames and Hudson, London, p. 304.

Rogers, Stanley, 1932: *Twelve on the Beaufort Scale,* Melrose, London, p. 284.

Rosenfeld, J., 1999: *Eye of the Storm: Inside the World's Deadliest Hurricanes, Tornadoes, and Blizzards,* Plenum, New York, p. 308.

Sanderson, I. T., 1972: *Investigating the Unexplained,* Prentice-Hall, Englewood Cliffs, New Jersey, p. 339.

Schonland, B. F. J., 1950: *The Flight of the Thunderbolts,* Clarendon Press, Oxford, p. 152.

Seargent, David A. J., 1991: *Willy Willies & Cockeyed Bobs: Tornadoes in Australia,* Karagi Publications, Australia, p. 115.

Seff John, and Nancy R. Seff, 1990: *Our Fascinating Earth: Strange, True Stories of Nature's Oddities, Bizarre Phenomena, and Scientific Curiosities,* Contemporary Books, Chicago, Illinois, p. 291.

Seneca, Lucius Annaeus (with English translation by Thomas H. Corcoran), 1971: *Naturales quaestiones* (Vol. two), Harvard University Press, Cambridge, Massachusetts, p. 312.

Simpson, G., 1948: *Information Roundup,* Harper & Brothers Publishing, New York, p. 587.

Sisman, A., 1998: *The World's Most Incredible Stories: The Best of Fortean Times,* Barnes & Noble Books, New York, p. 192.

Sloane, Eric, 1956: *The Book of Storms,* Duell, Sloan & Pearce, New York, p. 109.

Smith, Anthony, 2000: *The Weather: The Truth about the Health of our Planet,* Hutchinson, London, p. 285.

Smith, H.E., Jr., 1982: *Killer Weather: Stories of Great Disasters,* Dodd, Mead & Company, New York, p. 224.

Smith, Roger, 1992: *Catastrophes and Disasters,* W & R Chambers, Edinburgh, p. 246.

Snow, Edward Rowe, 1946: *Great Disasters: Marine Mysteries and Dramatic Disasters of New England* (three vol. in one), Avenel Books, New York, p. 672.

——, 1946: *Great Storms and Famous Shipwrecks of the New England Coast,* The Yankee Publishing Company, Boston, Massachusetts, p. 376.

——, 1978: *Adventures, Blizzards, and Coastal Calamities,* Dodd, Mead & Company, New York, p. 275.

Special Publications Division, 1978: *Powers of Nature,* National Geographic Society, Washington, D.C., p. 199.

Special Publications Division, 1986: *Nature on the Rampage: Our Violent Earth,* National Geographic Society, Washington, D.C., p. 199.

Spence, Clark C., 1980: *The Rainmakers: American "Pluviculture" to World War II,* University of Nebraska Press, Lincoln, Nebraska, p. 181.

Spignesi, Stephen J., 1994: *The Odd Index: The Ultimate Compendium of Bizarre and Unusual Facts,* Plume Books, New York, p. 399.

Stanford, J.L., 1987: *Tornado: Accounts of Tornadoes in Iowa,* (Second Edition), Iowa State University Press, Ames, Iowa, p. 143.

Steiger, Brad, 1974: *Mysteries of Time and Space,* Prentice-Hall, Inc., Englewood Cliffs, New Jersey, p. 232.

Stewart, George R., 1941: *Storm,* Random House, New York, p. 349.

Stimpson, G., 1946: *A Book About a Thousand Things,* Harper & Brothers Publishers, New York, p. 552.

——., 1970: *Popular Questions Answered,* Gale Research Company, Detroit, Michigan, p. 426.

Sutton, A. and M. Sutton, 1962: *Nature on the Rampage,* Philadelphia, Lippincott, Pennsylvania, p. 328.

Talman, C. F., 1931: *The Realm of the Air,* Bolls-Merrill, Indianapolis Indiana, p. 318.

Trobec, Jay, 1995: *State of Extremes: Guide to the Wild Weather of South Dakota,* Where's?ware Publishing, Sioux Falls, South Dakota, p. 166.

Thompson, P. D., R. O'Brien, and Editors of *Life,* 1965: *Weather,* Time Incorporated, New York, p. 200.

True Magazine, 1963: *Strange but True,* Fawcett Publications, Greenwich, Connecticut, p. 144.

Uman, Martin A., 1969: *Lightning,* McGraw-Hill Book Company, New York, p. 264.

Urton, Andrea, 1992: *Superweird,* Lowell House Juvenile, Los Angeles, California, p. 95.

Viemeister, P. E., 1961: *The Lightning Book*, Doubleday & Company, Garden City, New York, p. 316.

Vogel, Carole Garbuny, 2000: *Nature's Fury: Eyewitness Reports of Natural Disasters*, Scholastic Reference, New York, p. 115.

Wagler, D., 1966: *The Mighty Whirlwind*, Pathway Publishing, Aylmer, Ontario, Canada, p. 266.

Walsh, W. S., 1970: *Handy Book of Curious Information*, Gale Research Company (a reprint of the 1912 edition), Detroit, Michigan, p. 942.

Watson, Benjamin A., 1993: *Acts of God: The Old Farmer's Almanac Unpredictable Guide to Weather and Natural Disasters*, Random House, New York, p. 246.

Watson, L., 1984: *Heaven's Breath: A Natural History of the Wind*, William Morrow and Company, Inc., New York, p. 384.

Weems, J. E., 1977: *The Tornado*, Doubleday & Company, Garden City, New York, p. 180.

——, 1986: *"If You Don't Like The Weather,"* Texas Monthly Press, Austin, Texas, p. 121.

Welfare, S. and Fairley, J., 1980: *Arthur C. Clarke's Mysterious World*, A & W Publishers, Inc., New York, p. 217.

Wenstrom, William Holmes, 1942: *Weather and the Ocean of Air*, Houghton Mifflin Company, Boston, Massachusetts, p. 484.

Whittow, J., 1979: *Disasters: The Anatomy of Environmental Hazards*, University of Georgia Press, Athens, Georgia, p. 411.

Winchester, J. H., 1968: *Hurricanes, Storms, Tornadoes*, Putman, New York, p. 128

Winship, George Parker (ed), 1990: *The Journey of Coronado, 1540–1542*, Fulcrum Publishing, Golden, Colorado, p. 233.

Journals and Newspapers: These include many older journals and newspapers and other sources as well as the scientific journals cited and used throughout the book.

ABCnews.com

All the Year Round

Ambio

American Journal of Science and Arts

American Mercury

American Naturalist

Annals and Magazine of Natural History

Annual Register

Athenaeum

Anthropological Journal of Canada

Appleton's Journal

Arizona Republic

Associated Press

Atlantic Advocate

BBC News

Billings (Montana) *Gazette*

Blackwood's Magazine

Boston *Transcript*

Bulletin of the American Meteorological Society

Catholic World

Chamber's Journal

China Daily

Doubt

Eclectic Magazine

Edinburgh New Philosophical Journal

English Mechanic

FATE

Fortean Times

Gentleman's Magazine

Geographical Magazine

Geographical Review

Geotimes

Graham's Magazine

Harper's Weekly

INFO Journal

Journal of Applied Meteorology

Journal of Meteorology

Journal of the Asiastic Society of Bengal

Journal of the Atmospheric Sciences

Journal of the Franklin Institute

Knowledge

Leisure Hour

Leslie's Illustrated Weekly

Literary Digest

Living Age

London Evening Post

London Times

Los Angeles *Examiner*

Manchester Union Leader

Meteorological Magazine

Monthly Weather Review

National Geographic Magazine

Natural History

Natural History (New York)

Nature

Nature Magazine

New Scientist

New York Telegram

New York Times

Norton (Kansas) *Daily Telegram*

Notes and Queries

Nubila

Penny Magazine of the Society for the Diffusion of Useful Knowledge

Philosophical Transactions

Popular Mechanics

Popular Science Monthly

Public Safety, National Safety Council

Railroad Magazine

Report of British Association for the Advancement of Science

Report of the Kansas State Board of Agriculture

Reuters News Agency

Saline County Journal

Science

Science News

Scientific American

Scientific American Supplement

Sea Frontiers

Strand Magazine

Survey of Ophthalmology

The Cosmopolitan

Weather

Weatherwise

INDEX